THE NUN

Simonetta Agnello Hornby

THE NUN

Translated from the Italian
by Antony Shugaar

Europa
editions

Europa Editions
214 West 29th Street
New York, N.Y. 10001
www.europaeditions.com
info@europaeditions.com

Copyright © Giangiacomo Feltrinelli Editore Milano
First publication 2012 by Europa Editions

Translation by Antony Shugaar
Original title: *La monaca*
Translation copyright © 2012 by Europa Editions

Library of Congress Cataloging in Publication Data is available
ISBN 978-1-60945-062-5

Agnello Hornby, Simonetta
The Nun

Book design by Emanuele Ragnisco
www.mekkanografici.com

Cover illustration: *Reflection* by John Francis (1808-1886)
Copyright © by Getty Images

Prepress by Grafica Punto Print – Rome

Printed in the USA

But, as I've read love's missal through to-day,
He'll let me sleep, seeing I fast and pray.
—John Keats

CHARACTERS OF THE NOVEL

The Padellani di Opiri Family

Don Peppino Padellani, younger son of the Prince of Opiri, gentleman of the chamber of King Ferdinand I, field marshal in the royal army in Messina;

Donna Gesuela Aspidi, daughter of Baron Aspidi di Solacio of Palermo, wife of Don Peppino Padellani.

Anna Lucia, born in Naples, married in Catanzaro, died in childbirth at age fifteen;

Amalia, born in Naples, married in Messina to Domenico Craxi, a citrus fruit merchant;

Alessandra, born in Naples, married in Naples to Tommaso Aviello, a lawyer and Carbonaro;

Giulia, born in Naples, married in Messina to Salvatore Bonajuto, owner of a maritime shipping firm;

Anna Carolina, born in Naples, engaged to Fidenzio Carnevale, a landowner and wealthy manufacturer of essential oils;

Agata, later Donna Maria Ninfa in the convent of San Giorgio Stilita, born in Messina;

Carmela, born in Messina, where she marries the Cavaliere d'Anna.

The Relatives

Cousin Michele Padellani, Prince of Opiri, and his wife Ortensia;

Aunt Orsola, *née* Pietraperciata, Michele's stepmother and widow of Prince Antonio Padellani di Opiri, older brother of Don Peppino;

Admiral Pietraperciata, brother of Princess Orsola Padellani;

Aunt Clementina Padellani, married to the Marchese Tozzi; the cousins Eleonora and Severina Tozzi;

General Cecconi, Donna Gesuela's second husband.

The Household Servants

Annuzza, housekeeper;

Totò, footman;

Nora, personal maid of Donna Gesuela in Messina;

Rosalia, personal maid of Donna Gesuela in Palermo.

Others

Giacomo Lepre, Agata's first inamorato;

James Garson, captain in the British navy, Agata's last inamorato;

The Cavaliere d'Anna, Agata's first suitor, later the husband of Carmela;

Dr. Minutolo, physician of the Benedictine convent of San Giorgio Stilita.

The Religious

The clergy

Cardinal Vincenzo Padellani, first cousin of Don Peppino Padellani;

Father Cuoco, Agata's father confessor;

Father Cutolo, father confessor at San Giorgio Stilita.

At the Benedictine convent of San Giorgio Stilita
Donna Maria Crocifissa, sister of Don Peppino Padellani
and mother superior and abbess;
Donna Maria Brigida, sister of Don Peppino Padellani;
Donna Maria Clotilde, prioress;
Donna Maria Giovanna della Croce, teacher of the novices;
Donna Maria Immacolata, sister infirmarian;
Donna Maria Celeste;
Angiola Maria, lay sister of Donna Maria Crocifissa; Sarina,
lay sister of Donna Maria Crocifissa; Checchina, lay sister of
Donna Maria Brigida;
Nina, servant of Donna Maria Brigida;
Brida, servant and cook.

At the Benedictine convent of Donnalbina
Sister Maria Giulia, sister of Don Peppino Padellani.

THE NUN

1.

Messina, August 15, 1839.
The reception at the Padellani home for the
Feast of the Assumption of the Blessed Virgin Mary

The tender morning sunshine sifted down through the skylight, filling the room below and highlighting the pink marble of the Baroque staircase. "Make haste, Don Totò!" Annuzza cried urgently. Standing on tiptoe, she leaned over the balustrade and emphasized her words with broad gestures: "Make haste, His Excellency is waiting!" The footman's arms were wrapped around a huge, broad-bottomed hamper covered with a heavy cloth. He panted at each step, but he climbed steadily all the same, the mingled aromas of warm bread, olive oil, salty sardines, and toasted oregano infusing his creaky old knees with renewed vigor.

Another footman hurried down the last flight of stairs to meet him. Don Totò refused to be lightened of his load and so, preceded by the two other servants, he made his entrance into the yellow bedroom. They were breaking down the furnishings. The wrought-iron bedsteads—footboards, headboards, and crossbars adorned now with painted roses—lay stacked on mattresses whose midpoint was stained with faded menstrual blood. An armoire door, swinging half open, revealed the desolate cavity from which Annuzza and the two governesses had extracted the gauzy summer dresses belonging to the Padellani girls. In the middle of the bedroom stood an improvised table: the footmen had tossed a tablecloth over a pile of cardboard boxes and now they stood waiting, with their master, for the arrival of the *sfincione*.

"Excellent, Totò!" Without even waiting for his wife, Don Peppino Padellani whisked the cloth off the hamper, unveiling carefully arranged, overlapping squares of the Sicilian-style pizza, each layer protected by lengths of oiled paper. The aroma of *sfincione* wafted impetuously through the air. The old field marshal eagerly wolfed down a bite, and as he ate he pointed a finger at the hamper, encouraging the footmen to take some for themselves. They ventured forward with a restraint that proved short-lived: they were soon tearing off mouthfuls of *sfincione* with their teeth and gulping them down; their mouths still full, they made a beeline for the hamper, fingers straining for another piece.

Don Peppino Padellani di Opiri, the cadet son of a venerable Neapolitan aristocratic family and a Gentleman of the Order of the Golden Key of the late King Ferdinand I, had been transferred to Messina in 1825, with the rank of field marshal in the army of the Kingdom of the Two Sicilies. He had seen the town before, on military duty in 1808, when he was sent to observe the trial of the pro-French conspirators, and again in 1810, on the glorious occasion of the English army's success in repelling King Murat's attempted invasion. He had also spent several months there in 1820, with his spouse, the Marescialla—as the wife of a field marshal is known in Italy—at the time of the Sicilian uprisings, when the prince and heir apparent, who was also the king's lieutenant general in Sicily, moved the seat of government from the rebellious capital of Palermo to the steadfast, loyal city of Messina.

A general shortage of funds, the enormous expense of life in the capital city of Naples, the cost and burden of educating and marrying off his five daughters—in the meantime, two more daughters had swelled the family's number—and the desire to live in a city that was in easy contact with Naples and the rest of the world had convinced the field marshal to ask the king to transfer him to Messina, and he hadn't regretted it for a single day ever since. Despite their difference in age, the field marshal in his mid-seventies and his thirty-seven-year-old wife were determined to enjoy their lives there and make the most of Messina's high society, where they were treated with all the deference due to his rank and Padellani lineage.

The Marescialla was renowned for the elegance and refinement of her balls and soirées, but the *ferragosto* reception was unrivaled. Every August 15, the Padellanis began celebrating the Feast of the Assumption of the Blessed Virgin Mary first thing in the morning, offering piping hot *sfincione* to the entire household—coachmen, stable boys, and house servants alike. On that day, and that day alone, Don Peppino, Donna Gesuela, and their numerous daughters mingled with the help and treated them as equals—though the reverse did not apply. It was their way of winning forgiveness for their occasional failure to pay salaries and encouraging the servants to take on cheerfully the task of breaking down the household furnishings in the early morning and then reassembling the whole place that evening—at midday the great reception was scheduled to begin, and the Marescialla would entertain the most prominent townspeople and the most influential visitors for the entire duration of the religious procession, and even afterward. All of the drawing rooms, two of which were normally used as bedchambers, would have to be brought back into ceremonial use. The three daughters who still lived at home slept in fact in the yellow drawing room, where the reception for the household servants was now taking place.

The servants and the footmen "on loan" from relatives and friends for the occasion considered it a signal honor to be offered *sfincione*—a magnificent dish—with the masters of the house. Every year the baker added a new variety of *sfincione*, on the specific instructions of Donna Gesuela, who always ordered enough to ensure that no one was left wanting more.

The leftovers were then bestowed upon the footmen and maid-servants of the woman who owned the palazzo. She was a distant relative of the Aspidi, Donna Gesuela's family, and she offered her distinguished tenants the use of her own staff and a room, on the other half of the residential floor, in which to stack the furnishings that were being cleared away from the drawing rooms. Before long, the two coachmen and the stable boy also trooped upstairs, followed in turn by the kitchen staff. Don Peppino, who had preserved his captivating Neapolitan sense of humor, unfailingly amusing and never mean-spirited, kept them entertained with his renowned witticisms. The unmarried chambermaids came upstairs two-by-two and stood at a respectful distance: they listened raptly, eyes sparkling, speaking only when addressed by their master. The two governesses, on the other hand, joined freely in the general conversation, even when Don Peppino spiced up the talk with a bit of bawdiness.

The Marescialla was running late, and neither she nor the girls had yet arrived for their taste of *sfincione*. "Girls" is how Annuzza—who had been in Donna Gesuela's service since the day she came into the world, and who was now a nanny in what spare time she had—still described Anna Carolina, sixteen and on the verge of being engaged to be married, Agata, thirteen, and Carmela, the youngest, who was seven. Despite the field marshal's urging, the respectful servant refused to sample the *sfincione* before her mistress had a taste. As soon as she saw her opportunity, she darted out of the room to go in search of Donna Gesuela. She knocked at the door of the master bedroom—the last of the drawing rooms, the blue room. There was no answer. She put her ear to the door. Donna Gesuela was loudly scolding one of her daughters, but Annuzza, who was hard of hearing, couldn't tell which of the three it was. She knocked again and waited. Then she made up her mind to go in—she alone, of the household staff, could occasionally venture to cross that boundary. Without furniture, the field marshal's bedroom seemed enormous. Along the walls, unmatched chairs stood in a row, provided for the occasion by the neighbor; in one corner, the men had piled up headboards and bed slats to be used in setting up the *tablattè*, or buffet. Beneath the Murano chandelier, and arranged in a circle, facing outward, were four armchairs, over which were draped—like so many ghosts in search of a body—the clothing and accessories that the women of the family would wear at the reception: dresses and gowns were draped over the backs, arms, and seats of the armchairs. Gloves and hats were laid on the skirt, without wrinkling it. Arrayed in front of each armchair was a pair of pastel-colored silk slippers.

Still wearing her dressing gown and nightcap, Donna Gesuela had shoved Agata against the wall and was speaking to her urgently, gesticulating as her voice rose and fell. Her daughter wasn't answering. Annuzza tried to catch a glimpse of Agata's face, but the mother's body blocked her view.

"Enough! I told you: enough!" At that, Donna Gesuela dropped her arms and stepped away; ashen-faced, Agata stared at her and said nothing. Her mother resumed her assault: "I'm telling you for the last time: they won't have you, and it's because you're not rich! Do you understand? Keep your hands off that one! He'll play with you as long you amuse him! But after he drops you, who'll ever want you again? No one! No one! You understand? Answer me!" The disheveled sleeves of the blue brocade dressing gown concealed the girl, who had slid back against the wall, from Annuzza's gaze.

"Answer me!" she said again, in a voice dripping with menace.

Annuzza was afraid that Agata had fainted; then she heard a faint murmur: "But I already told you, Madame Mother, his grandfather approves." A brief pause. Then, with furious conviction: "He wrote that to me in a letter!"

"Wrote to you? In a letter? What! Who gave him permission to write to you? And I suppose you've written back to him, too, you hussy!" she yelled, slipping into dialect; she paused, and then continued in Italian: "Are you trying to ruin your prospects? Are you trying to make sure your sisters can never be married?"

"I haven't done anything wrong! He's the one who writes to me. I never write to him—well, almost never."

Her mother threw her arms out in a melodramatic gesture, then stood arms akimbo, fists on her hips, and inhaled, puffing out her chest. "*Almost* never! *Almost* never!" she said, over and over, her large black eyes glittering like smoldering embers.

"Begging Your Excellency's pardon, but they've brought the *sfincione*," Annuzza broke in, and then added, lying: "His Excellency the field marshal asked me to come find Your Excellency." Gesuela turned to look at the servant. She hadn't heard Annuzza come in. Gesuela's lovely face was drenched with sweat and twisted with emotion. Her black ringlets, painstakingly pinned back and now damp, were poking out from under her lace nightcap. Annuzza felt a surge of pity for her, but she didn't know what else she could do. She was released from her predicament by little Carmela, who had taken refuge on the balcony. When she heard the word *sfincione*, she cried: "Let's go!" and held out her hand to her mother. After a moment's hesitation Donna Gesuela took her daughter's hand and, without even bothering to fix her hair, headed for the door, muttering under her breath: "I swear I'll kill her!"

Annuzza trailed along behind her, scuffing her feet, and clutching with one hand in her pocket the latest letter that Giacomo Lepre had given her to deliver to Agata.

The crowd of servants parted to make way for the arrival of the Marescialla and her two youngest daughters; they greeted them with a chorus of *Voscenza benadica*—bless Your

Excellency! Leaning over the hamper and revealing to the household help more of her generous bosom than was entirely necessary, Donna Gesuela checked to be sure that the baker had followed her orders to the letter. With her languid Palermo accent she reeled off a string of questions without waiting for answers: "Ciccio, how was the *sfincione* with cheese?" "Filomena, the black olives were pitted, weren't they?" and last of all, addressing everyone: "Did you like the soft-bread crust?" Then she handed Carmela, who was glued to her hip, a slice of *sfincione alla palermitana*—a bed of boiled and sliced onions, with bits of anchovy and strong cheese mixed into the dough, barely visible, and covered with a crunchy layer of breadcrumbs sprinkled with olive oil—and then sank her teeth into her own piece, dressed with finely sliced potatoes and eggplant. As she chewed, she glared at her other daughter. Don Peppino watched them and then wrapped one arm around Agata's waist and offered her a bite of his *sfincione*—"*Mangia, mangia,* daughter of mine"—whispering in her ear: "Don't worry, deep down, your mamma is a good mother!"

The food was simple but tasty. The lemonade and the water with anise seed were both refreshingly cool—the Marescialla had told her cook to add crushed ice—and the house servants, who remained behind while the other servants went back to their respective stables and kitchens, were still laughing at Don Peppino's witticisms. Donna Gesuela listened, lips twisted in a smile, an absent gaze in her eyes. Suddenly she exclaimed: "Who brushed the formal uniforms? Have the white gloves been washed?" This time she wanted an answer, and so she broke up the party. Then, having received no reply whatsoever, she retraced her steps in furious haste, followed by Anna Carolina and Carmela. Before crossing the threshold, she shot one last parting glare of reproof at Agata, but Agata was looking at her father, who had bent down to pick up the fan her mother had dropped and was now extending it to her. Donna

Gesuela arched her handsome eyebrows and did nothing to retrieve the fan. Then she strode off, entering the room, swinging her hips.

"Where's Anna Carolina?" her father asked.

"She's fixing her hair. A curl from her hairpiece fell into her cup of chamomile tea!" Agata giggled.

"Hair is a very important matter for a young woman who is going to be engaged today," her father reproached her. "I can just imagine the state you would be in, if the same thing happened to you." The field marshal ran his wrinkled fingers through his daughter's chestnut ringlets. "You're thirteen years old. Your mother was already my wife, and if I'm not mistaken, a mother as well, at that age." He paused. Agata, shorter than Gesuela, resembled her closely. She was likely to be even prettier than her mother, because she had the grey Padellani eyes—sloe-eyed, with the oriental eyelids introduced into the family by a Mongol princess who had captured the heart of one of their forefathers. The field marshal wanted his little Agatina to be happy and loved. "Start casting your gaze around you, and tell me who it is that pleases you . . . " Then he withdrew his hand, and his voice grew serious: "But remember, it's my decision. You must have a husband who is wealthy and worthy of you and of our family." Agata blushed. "Ah, so there's already a sweetheart? Well, we'll talk it over, after Anna Carolina's engagement . . . one daughter at a time, otherwise you'll wear me out. I really am becoming an old man." And Don Peppino fixed his eyes on the green-and-white herringbone majolica tile. He was sweating: his chest was heaving faster than it had been, while the hand that was fluttering the fan was slowing down. But Agata noticed nothing. She'd been thinking of Giacomo.

It had all begun in February. She regularly woke up before

her sisters and went out to sit on the balcony and read; spring was already in the air and a light shawl over her shoulders was enough to keep her warm. The street was deserted. He was sitting on the balcony across the way. They hardly knew one another: they certainly frequented the same drawing rooms, but Giacomo was twenty, and for months he'd paid no attention to her. They fell in love on the basis of stealthy glances, followed by bold direct gazes, then by holding up the title pages of the books they were reading and communicating by hand signals. Giacomo had sent her a note and she had replied. During the Carnival season, her mother threw open their house every night, for a succession of balls, and he hadn't missed a single one. But the two of them had never been alone together. Their true moments of intimacy came during the long early morning gazes from one balcony to the other.

Giacomo Lepre, the only son of a dynasty of notaries and the heir to three bachelor uncles, was an excellent catch. Agata's mother had warned her that the Lepres were looking for a bride with a substantial dowry for their son. Now, even though the Padellanis had no such dowry to offer, if Agata used her charms and wiles to make the young man fall in love with her, and if he stood up to his parents, the Lepres were likely to be won over by the honor of becoming relatives by marriage to one of the first families of the kingdom. The previous year, when His Majesty paid a royal visit to Messina—one of three Sicilian cities that had just adopted a new administrative system—he not only treated the Padellanis publicly as something very close to blood relations, but he'd even asked the field marshal for his advice on the best candidates to appoint as chief police magistrate and to the senate; it was at the field marshal's advice that the king had appointed senator the notary Lepre, the young man's grandfather. That morning, Donna Gesuela was brutally frank with her daughter: the Lepres had already identified a very wealthy young woman and it was only a matter of time before Giacomo announced his engagement; she accused her daughter of bungling everything and letting an excellent catch slip through her fingers. Agata turned her sorrowful gaze to her father but he just went on fanning himself and listening with renewed interest to another conversation in the room.

The clock on the wall struck ten. In the Padellani home, there was a feverish hustle and bustle of preparation. The reception was scheduled to begin at noon, at the exact moment that the cart bearing the statue of Our Lady of the Assumption would be passing down the street beneath their balconies, on its way back to the cathedral. Before dressing for the party, Donna Gesuela stopped by the pantry to sample the sherbets and check on the jelly *trionfi*, trembling multicolored mountains cast in molds of varying sizes, shaped like castles, towers, and crowns, either to be stacked or else displayed on the table in simple geometric compositions. She spent a great deal of time nibbling tiny spoonfuls of sweets and ices; they struck her as lacking in sugar—they smacked of bitterness, like her thoughts.

During the first few years of marriage in Naples, she and her husband had merrily run through her dowry with lavish spending, spectacular entertaining, and gambling debts: she'd never regretted it for a moment. A deeply spoiled daughter, born to the second wife of a coarse and ambitious baron of the Nebrodi Mountains, Gesuela had been given an excellent education, imparted by the Collegio di Maria boarding school and an English governess. Her education was later completed, after she was married, by observing the Padellanis. It was from them that she learned the art of entertaining and seducing the high nobility of Naples. Inferior to the women of the house of Padellani by birth and inheritance, but not by education and beauty, the youthful bride decided that she would outshine the rest as mistress of her household: in terms of food, presentation of the table, and entertaining. When her husband's uncle, a duke and the ambassador to the court in Vienna, died, he inherited a number of handsome porcelain dinner sets, although not particularly expensive ones; she then dared to ask her aunt the dowager duchess to let her have the extra livery that she no longer needed. She could count on the fact that she had helped her aunt to gain access to the circle of the Duchess of Floridia, the morganatic wife of King Ferdinand and the godmother of her eldest daughter Anna Lucia. The generosity of her aunt the duchess proved to be fruitful, and even providential once money problems forced the family to opt for a move to Messina. There, the family received a warm welcome, and the Padellani name counted for more than any dowry, especially when it was judiciously served with a little extra something; a mediocre cup of coffee—reheated but presented on a tray by a page boy in white gloves and a white periwig, silk stockings and a uniform in English broadcloth complete with silver buttons—smacked of paradise, and had proven invaluable in arranging marriages for the four eldest daughters.

Times were changing rapidly; the scent of revolution was in the air throughout Europe. Ferdinand II was an isolationist king, completely green in terms of diplomatic experience. The whole matter of sulfur mining, an export of paramount importance both for the economy of the kingdom at large and especially in Sicily, had become a nightmare for the government and a tragedy for the Sicilians. Ever since St. Stephen's Day in 1798, when the English navy landed the fugitive king Ferdinand I and his royal family on the docks of Palermo, England had gradually consolidated its economic and political dominion over the island. The English army, deployed in Sicily, had twice prevented the island being taken by French forces. They had been rewarded for the efforts, establishing a tidy monopoly on sulfur exports. Two years earlier, a French consortium had made a very attractive offer for control of the sulfur trade and the king had recklessly insisted on accepting that offer. But the Englishmen who lived in the kingdom had substantial business concerns and represented a sizable market for Bourbon exports. To lose that market would spell considerable economic damage to the kingdom. The king turned a deaf ear to the protests lodged by the British government, and as a result sulfur sales plunged. The field marshal—who had maintained his friendships with Freemasons and a wide-ranging network of contacts throughout the many nations involved in the kingdom's affairs dating back to his earliest days as a gentleman at court—feared the worst imaginable: a general collapse of exports to England. It would have dealt a crushing blow to the thriving seaport of Messina and the business concerns of both his sons-in-law: Domenico Craxi, husband of Amalia and a trader in citrus fruit and silk, and Salvatore Bonajuto, husband of Giulia and the owner of a shipping agency. Both men depended on trade with the English.

Moreover, the Masonic uprisings in Spain had undermined the Bourbon monarchy; Freemasonry was powerful in Messina as well. In that city the age-old power of the aristocracy, long since stripped of their feudal rights and now shuttered into life at court, had weakened and waned. The newly rich bourgeoisie now placed greater value on money than lineage. The actions of the Lepre family made that perfectly clear, to the discomfort of Donna Gesuela. Now she was even starting to worry about Anna Carolina's engagement—even though it had been worked out to the last detail, dowry included, and was to be announced that very afternoon.

Even as the Marescialla was in the kitchen sampling desserts, a message was brought to her—Anna Carolina's future father-in-law, Cavaliere Amilcare Carnevale, had requested a meeting at eleven o'clock, to discuss a matter of some delicacy. Donna Gesuela flushed beet-red and hurried to her dressing room. Her daughter, certain that her betrothal was about to vanish into thin air, flew into a hysterical fit. That fit was followed by a series of tantrums over her hairpiece, and in the end two hairdressers had to be summoned to appease her.

At last, mother and daughter, dressed, brushed, and lustrous, left the bedroom to the footservants who were impatiently waiting to set up the *tablattè*.

Now there was a problem, however: while everyone else was busy gobbling down the *sfincione*, Anna Carolina, unsure which outfit would look best at the reception and then afterward, at the procession, had transported to her parents' bedroom, one item at a time, her entire formal wardrobe—dresses, slippers, hats, shawls: entirely too many items of apparel to be easily concealed under the tablecloths of the *tablattè*. It was now necessary to carry that vast array of clothing back from the bedroom of the mistress of the house, and in so doing, necessarily pass before the eyes of Cavaliere Carnevale.

It was just five minutes to eleven now. Footservants and mistress stared into one another's eyes in utter horror.

"The bathtub!" cried Donna Gesuela.

As Cavaliere Carnevale, with a hint of unease, was informing the field marshal and the Marescialla that, due to the sudden demise of a relative who had appointed him sole heir and executor, he was obliged to postpone the wedding day, a creaking noise reached their ears. With synchronized movements, four liveried footmen threw open the two doors at the far end of the drawing room and ushered in two young pages, also garbed in the sky-blue livery of the Padellani family. The pages were pushing before them an extraordinary dining table on wheels, low, narrow, and rectangular, covered with a tablecloth made of Brussels lace that hung down to the floor. The table was lavishly set for one, complete with crystal glassware, silverware, and candelabra: this was in fact the bathtub, crammed to the brim with Anna Carolina's clothing.

"It's for an invalid relative of mine. That poor woman never leaves the house and it seems a shame to have a banquet table groaning with such delicacies knowing that, prisoner of ill health that she is, she can't enjoy it. We're going to serve her every dish we enjoy out here, in her bedroom," explained Donna Gesuela; then, in a sudden burst of modesty, she lowered her lovely lashes.

That very afternoon, yet another story of the Marescialla's exquisite kindness was making the rounds of Messina.

2.

During the procession Agata Padellani
has a secret meeting with her inamorato,
Giacomo Lepre

Perched at the foot of the Nebrodi Mountains, whence it looks across the water to the mountainous region of Calabria, Messina the Noble, loyal to the Bourbon king, the second capital of Sicily and a border town, had long controlled the shipping traffic on the strait that shared the city's name. Constantly feuding with its rival Palermo and tormented by a series of natural disasters, Messina recovered from the plague of 1742, the earthquake of 1783, and the cloudburst and flooding of 1824. It was now once again one of the great cities of the kingdom. Messina was enclosed by a ring of walls with seven gates, and it boasted a three-century-old university, numerous convents and monasteries, two theaters and four libraries, five piazzas, six fountains, and twenty-eight aristocratic *palazzi*; its thriving port had attracted a sizable contingent of foreign residents, many of whom owned manufacturing plants and ran businesses.

The populace of Messina expressed its unity and civic pride every year in its celebration of the Feast of the Assumption of the Blessed Virgin Mary, a grab bag of the sacred and the profane that began on the twelfth of August and had its crescendo in the procession on the fifteenth, a procession that was renowned throughout the kingdom for its extraordinary "machines." Enjoying pride of place in the Piazza dell'Arcivescovado, outside the archbishop's palace, were two enormous horses ridden by a pair of giants, all made of papier-mâché. In the days leading up to the procession of *ferragosto*, on August 15, two men covered with a camel skin trotted through the city, accompanied by bands, troops of the faithful and the common folk, singling out peddlers and shopkeepers to ask for alms; it was considered an act of devotion to slip a sample of one's merchandise into the gaping mouth of the alms-seeking camel. These goods were collected in sacks to offset the expenses of the festivities. In the past, there had been many other papier-mâché figures and animals with human beings concealed inside them, but in the wake of the devastation caused by the latest earthquake, the tone of the celebrations had become considerably more subdued.

The intensity of surging popular sentiment was palpable. On August 15 all the streets of Messina, not just those along the route of the procession, were overflowing with people: the deeply loyal Messinese expatriates who returned to their birthplace for the feast day, numerous contingents from neighboring towns and villages, and hundreds of Calabrians who made their way across the Strait of Messina for the day. Then there were the worshipful crowds who had made the pilgrimage to fulfill a vow, to ask for a holy grace, or simply as an act of devotion—it was a dazzling spectacle.

Agata had sought a moment of seclusion on the balcony. Her puffy muslin petticoat with pink and sky-blue polka dots filled the rounded protruding balcony railing; her sky-blue silk slipper tapped in time to the band. She was restless and excited. Her sharp eyes wandered from the crowd filling the street up to Palazzo Lepre; she knew that Giacomo was somewhere inside. From concealment in the folds of the curtains, Annuzza was watching her; every so often Agata looked down and studied the crowd. The faithful, gathered in separate groups, uttered the repetitive short prayers and aspirations specific to the occasion; their voices wafted upward in unison like the murmuring of the sea, pierced now and again by the harsh cries of those who were trying to find companions from whom they had been separated in the milling morass, or of others who had already secured excellent spots and were defending them with shouts and shoves. Others, visibly overwrought, were standing expectantly, their gazes fixed on the corner around which the cart bearing the statue of Our Lady of the Assumption would appear any minute. Everywhere, children were dressed up as little angels.

Agata was spying on the balcony across the way out of the corner of her eye. From time to time, she fought back tiny tears of sorrow and wounded pride. At last, she managed to glimpse him: from the shadows of the front carriage door of his palazzo, Giacomo was staring up at her; he conveyed with hand gestures that he was still waiting for a reply to his note. Agata, suddenly afraid that her mother had intercepted the message and taken it from Annuzza and had assigned a chambermaid to spy on her, wasn't even sure that she should run the risk of answering him. She had a moment's hesitation. Just then, Annuzza, who had refrained from delivering the note in an attempt to comply with her mistress's orders, drew it out of her pocket and stepped out onto the balcony. Agata eagerly scanned the note and then remained, with her head lowered. She was thinking. Suddenly she held her head high and blinked her eyes, just once, then stood there, straight as a rod, chin pointing slightly upward, neck taut, lips twitching. Her muslin shawl had loosened around her neckline, revealing her shapely bosom. The greedy eyes of the girl who was becoming a young woman were fixed on the figure in the shadows. Giacomo stepped forward; he leaned languidly on the heavy wooden street door, and from there he met her gaze unwaveringly. Agata ripped the note up and lifted the handful of shredded paper to her mouth. Slowly. She chewed the pieces up and swallowed them, one by one, until none were left. Then she dried her eyes with the back of her hand and went back inside.

Wrapped in the coolness of the silk damask, Annuzza stood there, psalmodizing a litany to St. Joseph, invoking the saint's protection on that young girl who was the spitting image of her own mother and, like her mother had been when she was a girl, trapped in the coils of a hopeless love.

Cavaliere Carnevale had taken his leave of the Padellanis just as the first few guests were coming upstairs. The reception would last exactly as long as the procession. The guests came and went, leaving to follow the Vara and then returning for refreshments whenever they chose: this was a new style of entertaining introduced in Messina by Donna Gesuela, the novel notion of an "open house," a foreign custom taught her by her English governess.

Elderly and plagued by aches and pains though the field marshal was, he still greeted his guests, standing erect, at the threshold of the second good drawing room; he then circulated among the guests, with a word for everyone, recounting the amusing jokes and stories for which he was renowned. The guest list included not only the chief police magistrate and the member of the city senate, but also the crème de la crème of the local aristocracy, the highest officers of the Messina garrison, and many of the foreigners who lived in town. There was also an abundance of other people, lacking aristocratic rank but who could still prove useful, or else people whom the Padellanis either owed a favor or planned to ask one: credentialed professionals, businessmen, shopkeepers, and even craftsmen. No one ever turned down the invitation. Don Peppino, who was said by many to be saddled with debts, each year seemed to refute that rumor by hosting another party: from the beginning of the reception until the last guest left in the evening, the *tablattè* stood groaning under the renowned array of refreshments prepared under the careful eyes of Donna Gesuela. Pastries, ice creams, and shaved ice syrups made according to Padellani family recipes as well as delicacies cooked as prescribed by the chef that Donna Gesuela's father, God rest his soul, had poached from an Austrian prince with the offer of a fabulous salary—people whispered that the chef made as much money, if not more, than the salary that Don Peppino was paid by His Majesty's army. The guests little suspected that many of the waiters and footmen were on loan or hired for the occasion. Nor could they guess that Donna Gesuela's older brother, Francesco Aspidi, Baron of Solacio, who had been more than a brother to her and who still had a weakness for his sister, every year for the occasion sent carts overbrimming and mules overburdened with all sorts of delicacies and delights. Donna Gesuela presided over the reception, assisted by her two married daughters who lived in Messina, Amalia and Giulia. At the age of thirty-seven, with her large dark eyes, her lips as red as ripe cherries, and her lovely neckline, Donna Gesuela was still far more alluring than her daughters, respectively twenty-two and twenty years old. Anna Carolina, sixteen years old, smiled in straight-backed pride next to her fiancé: the other Carnevales had already left before the doors to the *tablattè* were thrown open, in a show of respect for the death in their family, and they had seemed contented. Gesuela took comfort: even Agata, the last daughter left to marry off, would surely find a husband, however difficult it might prove—to all appearances she was as tractable as the other girls, though in fact this daughter was obstinate.

The footmen moved among the guests carrying trayfuls of lemonade and *acqua e zammù*—water with a few drops of anise seed. It wouldn't be long now before the procession of the Vara went past the palazzo. The approach of the procession was preannounced by a buzz of voices, at first far off in the distance and then gradually closer and higher-pitched: a blend of music, the shouts of the faithful—"Long live the Virgin Mary!"—and a psalmody that, murmured by hundreds of mouths, turned into a roar. Leading the procession was a line of twelve altar boys carrying the insignia of the Virgin Mary, followed by the confraternities and religious orders, both male and female, in two lines on either side of the street, as if they were flanking an invisible simulacrum. Between them walked the nuns and the female orphans of the Collegio di Maria, the boarding school that Agata and Carmela had been attending since the year before, when they were obliged to make do without the services of the English governess, Miss Wainwright. The din was something terrible. The faithful were crammed together on the sidewalks, in the front halls, in the doors of the shops, and in the narrow alleys. Two lines of altar boys, caparisoned in brocade vestments, marching shoulder to shoulder in compact rows, filled the street: the vanguard of Our Lady of the Assumption.

At the shout of *"La Vara!"* the guests poured out onto the balconies. Then silence fell. The tension was unmistakable. The façades of the aristocratic houses seemed to have been garlanded with the colorful dresses of the women on the balconies. The grated windows of the monasteries were all aglitter with dream-glazed eyes. The Vara would appear at the crossroads where it would make the only deviation from a straight line in the course of the entire procession: a ninety-degree turn. A thousand eyes were fixed on the intersection. Music, chants, and shouts of invocation grew to a deafening roar.

The first ones to appear around the corner were the men carrying bucketfuls of water: the "machine," which had no wheels, rode, as if on a sledge, on a smooth wooden log, and it was their job to wet the pavement in order to make it slippery. They cast the water in all directions, as if sowing seed in an open field. Then silence fell. No music, no litanies, only the humming voices of the faithful. At the intersections, the haulers appeared, barefoot, pulling the cart by sheer force of forearms and faith. This was the moment of the procession's greatest intensity. It was also the most dangerous moment. Rapidly the haulers took their places along the two ropes in accordance with an order that had been clearly established for centuries. Some of them went on pulling to keep the Vara from slowing to a halt. Others, clustering along their ropes, waited for the right moment to exert their strength. Others still waited in line, hands on the rope, ready to haul. Precise. Attentive. Synchronized. At that moment, even the buzzing died away: like a single body, the faithful held their breath. You could hear, faintly, the wailing of the little angels on the Vara. Rhythmic tugs, then one decisive yank from the cluster of haulers: the turn had been completed. As tall as a two-story building, shaped like a narrow pyramid, and immensely heavy, the Vara appeared at the corner. It was vibrating and tottering. For a second it seemed as if it was tipping over. Another yank and it went back to sliding along the wet pavement, solid, erect, accompanied by a gust of applause for the haulers, heroes of the day.

Ever since the late Middle Ages, the Messinese had been the uncontested masters of the whole island in the creation of those ephemeral constructions, unrivaled not only in terms of sheer beauty, but also in terms of mechanical technique: inside the "machine" there were manually operated gears that allowed a variety of movements. When the Vara moved forward, it was unstoppable. Every year, the decoration changed, but the structure and the chief elements remained the same: large circles at the base that grew progressively smaller, narrowing toward the top, upon which celestial bodies were poised, each with its own rotating movement. From each of the circles, wheels projected, also in movement. There was a time when all the characters were live people, and there were more than a hundred of them, but with the passing of the centuries, the adult figures—the

Apostles that surrounded the coffin of the Virgin Mary at the base, the angels of the three circles, and Jesus Himself—had been replaced by brightly painted papier-mâché statues. The only remaining humans were the Virgin Mary, at the summit of the pyramid, and dozens of tiny angels, tied to the rays of the Sun and the Moon and to the wheels that spun at the side of each of the circles: these were infants or small children volunteered for the occasion by their families. The circles, wheels, and all the other contrivances would spin in alternating directions for the entire seven hours of the procession.

Because the cart was so dizzyingly high, the Padellanis' guests who hadn't been able to find a place to stand on the balconies still had a full view of the upper circles and of the Virgin Mary. Therefore everyone, including the footmen and chambermaids, was looking outside. Agata had hung back. As soon as she heard the sound of footsteps on the wet pavement and the creaking of the machine sliding along, she ran downstairs at top speed to the stables, which were empty at that time of day. That was where Giacomo was waiting for her. Declarations of undying love, tears, and the good news: Senator Lepre, moved by the sincerity of the two young people's love, had offered to request Agata's hand in marriage to his grandson, in his son's stead. There was no more time to talk; when the coachman gave the agreed-upon signal, the two lovers were forced to take their leave.

Agata raced upstairs four steps at a time and elbowed her way silently back among her sisters at the very moment that the Vara passed in front of the balcony. The third circle, the one with the constellations, was barely a yard away, and it was revolving like the stars and the constellations. The Sun, as large as a dinner table, had eyes, a nose, a large smiling mouth, and twelve rays. At the tip of each of those rays, a baby no more than six months old, with gilded wings fastened to its shoulders, was confined in a cage that enclosed its body while leaving arms, legs, and head free. Each baby's head was covered by a bonnet with curls that were also gilded. The rays spun in alternating directions: at that very moment, they changed direction and stopped right in front of the balcony. Less than a yard away, Agata found herself face to face with an array of screaming little angels, their faces deformed by terror; then the wheel began turning again and the noise of the procession drowned out the wails of the babies.

"Blessed angels of Our Lady of the Assumption!" "Little beauties!" "Holy souls!" commented the women.

"May the Lord bless them every one," whispered Annuzza as she crossed herself. And then, speaking to Carmela: "See how pretty they are!" The heat of the afternoon sun had become an intolerable flame. Agata could feel herself going into a swoon; she shut her eyes and gripped the railing with all her might. Even the railing was hot; she clamped her fingers down hard, then harder, until she'd hurt herself. When she opened her eyes again, the Vara and the ravaged children were no longer there. Like a torrent in spring spate, the crowd thronging the street had closed ranks behind the sacred cart. The shouts of "Long live the Virgin Mary!" were deafening—to the faithful, that was the moment of utmost pride and religious exaltation.

Meanwhile, the Padellanis' guests already were buzzing around the sherbets.

After the procession with the Vara had passed by the house, it was customary for the field marshal, with the Marescialla on his arm, to lead all his guests to witness the end of the procession in the cathedral square. Followed by the officers from the garrison and the other guests, they created a smaller private procession within the larger one. Donna Gesuela slowed her pace to make it easier on her husband, who suffered from gout; she also took advantage of this opportunity to sashay and pivot volup-tuously, scattering smiles in all directions. This gave the footser-vants a chance to straighten up back at the house, in preparation for the final refreshments. Moreover, it was the Marescialla's opinion that their guests, with the flavor of the sweets still in their mouths, would be less spiteful in the comments they might offer on the party to the people they chanced to meet on the street than they were likely to be the following day. After a good night's sleep, their guests were likely to make a special effort to come up with some detail to complain about. She knew her guests were always afraid that they'd be taken for unsophisti-cated bumpkins if they couldn't find some detail to criticize.

Agata did her best to break away from the festive group without arousing suspicion. She pushed upstream through the crowd and turned into a narrow alley where cobblers and knife sharpeners plied their trade. Not a living soul was around. The fourth door on the right had been left ajar.

They didn't exchange a word of greeting. Keenly aware that they were alone, they were afraid of themselves and each other. A feeble checkered light filtered down through the grated transom over the door; aside from that glimmering light, the little shop was shrouded in darkness. Agata looked around. The filthy walls were studded with hooks, from which hung pieces of leather of every imaginable shape, goat hides, tattered rags stained variously with wax and pitch, lasts for boots and shoes, and all of the cobbler's tools and equipment.

Giacomo reached out and placed a hand on her shoulder. They had danced together once before, and she remembered the way she'd shivered when their bodies—arms and hands—had touched, as well as the exquisite trembling of their alter-nating breaths. It was a game they played: she inhaled the air that he had exhaled, and he did the same in reverse, until they felt as if they had become one. This time, though, when he touched her through the layers of her muslin dress and undergarment, it was different. She felt naked. And that's how she felt to him. He fiddled with her lace shawl. She blushed hotly. He delicately tickled her neck, touching her with his thumb and index finger. Her skin grew moist.

"I want you to be my bride." Giacomo broke the silence. "My grandfather will do as he's promised and my parents, once our engagement is official, will give in. But before anything else I want you to make me a promise: I'm a jealous man, I want you to swear that you'll always be faithful to me." Agata nodded, and placed her hand on his. He took her finger and brought it up to his throat, laying it across his jugular. Together, they felt the heartbeat. Their bodies thrilled. Giacomo was pulling her toward him with imperceptible movements, without haste. In a swelling crescendo of pleasure. His panting breath and his handsome mouth were on her together. Giacomo unsealed his lips as she opened hers. Suddenly, Agata pulled away. "Remember that a woman who takes certain things in her mouth or other places is fallen." Annuzza had said those words to her older sisters when she was just little, but she still remembered it clearly because Amalia, her favorite sister, had burst into tears. "No, no, that isn't right . . . " Agata protested, and looked at him with fright, worried that she'd offended him.

"Let's embrace once, tightly, and then you can go." As he spoke these words, Giacomo slid his fingers down from her neck to her shoulders, running them under the muslin of her dress and her undergarment, where he brushed the bare flesh of her back. Quickly, Giacomo then wrapped his other arm around her waist and tugged her close to him. Agata threw back her head to avoid his mouth, but she allowed him to shower her throat and shoulders with a rain of tiny, delicious kisses. Giacomo's hand began sliding down her back. Agata didn't struggle. Suddenly, he shoved her forward, powerfully, and pressed himself hard against her lower belly.

The aroma of the cobbler's glue—dense, pungent, inebriating—stunned them both.

Agata wandered through the crowd in a daze. She felt a piercing gaze upon her: the Cavaliere d'Anna, one of the guests and a well known libertine, was following close behind her, hobbling along on his rickety legs. When he managed to draw even with her, he flashed her a drooling smile with his pendulous lips. Agata pretended not to have seen him. She despised him, because at her parents' parties he always managed to rub up against her when it was impossible for her to put him in his place; she heard the shouts of the crowd surging around the cart of Our Lady of the Assumption and turned her steps in that direction. The Cavaliere smirked and veered over toward a knot of women who were bending over to help an old woman who had slipped and fallen on the pavement. As they struggled to help the woman up, he circled around them, his gaze fixed on their bosoms, then he rubbed up against the vast and impressive derriere of one of them, and scurried off before the unfortunate woman could straighten up and turn around.

The shouts intensified: the men were dismantling the Vara. It was time to take down the little angels, and their mothers—the poorest of a generally poor populace—came rushing to crowd around. After seven hours of constant twirling motion, devoured by the harsh sunlight, starving and parched, the poor little things were half-dead. Some of them wailed bitterly, others whimpered like stray mutts, a few seemed to be lost in a trance. Two were motionless, their heads lolling to one side. The men on the cart were pulling them out of their cages and passing them down in buckets to other men atop tall ladders who called out from on high: "Who's the owner of this one?" And then they'd hand them down the line, until they were turned over to the mothers. The mothers, cursing and shoving themselves forward, were wrestling to lay their hands on their own child or, more simply, to lay hands on any live child—the ravaged faces were in some cases quite unrecognizable. The laments of the most sorrowful mothers mingled with the crowing shouts of the victorious ones, the deafening jeers of the spectators, and the shrill whistles of the rabble. One mother clutched her comatose child and consoled herself by crooning that the Virgin Mary had decided to take her boy with Her to heaven.

A pair of clergymen watched over the proceedings benevolently. The girl who was playing the part of Our Lady of the Assumption had left the cart. The glittering golden pedestal had reverted to painted papier-mâché and Agata prayed to the Virgin Mary to ask forgiveness for them, but not for herself.

3

The earthquake and the illness of Field Marshal Padellani

It was a cool morning in early September. The two youngest Padellani daughters, accompanied by Annuzza and Nora—the Marescialla's personal maid—were traveling by carriage to their sister Amalia's country home, built high atop a hill not far from their brother-in-law Domenico Craxi's silk mill: the road that ran out from Messina had been widened into a fine thoroughfare lined by mulberry trees, prickly pears, and pomegranates. Their parents and Anna Carolina would join them for lunch and they'd all spend a few days in the country visiting with Francesco Gallida, the nine-year-old son of Anna Lucia—eldest of the Padellani sisters, who had died tragically young in childbirth. Francesco was with his father and the family from his second marriage.

Once they'd passed through the villa's ornate front gate, Don Totò reined in the team of horses. Here the road steepened and the carriage was bouncing and swaying around the hairpin curves. Carmela, already a spiteful harridan at the age of seven, was gossiping about the outfits she'd seen other little girls wearing at the feast of the Assumption of the Blessed Virgin Mary. Agata let her talk; she was looking out the window of the carriage, lost in thought. As the carriage climbed higher and higher, the landscape stretched out before their eyes. The Ionian Sea, beyond Messina, glittered with silver and lay flat as a table; under the lighthouse and off into the distance of Reggio Calabria, the surface of the Tyrrhenian Sea was dark blue and choppy. Beyond the lighthouse were the particolored villages and the steep mountains of the mainland—the "continent." It was the season for catching swordfish—their migration brought them through the Sicilian seas just twice every year. The Strait of Messina was thronged with small vessels that had been jury-rigged and equipped for deep-sea fishing.

At the foot of the hill, monitoring the mouth of the bay, small formations of fishing dinghies rode at anchor, lashed together at the bow, empty of crew, oars, or yards. From them rose straight up a single exceedingly tall mainmast, and at its summit was a man, lashed to the mast, his feet perched on a wooden crossbeam. Motionless, his eyes swept the water: it was his task to spot the first swordfish and point the sailors in that direction. Other formations, each with its own lofty mainmast and lookout, roughly equidistant one from the next, spangled the seawaters from the Sicilian to the Calabrian coast. Each formation had a squadron of fisherman in highly maneuverable watercraft, each manned by four oarsmen, a harpooner, and a man astride a smaller yardarm. The instant the lookout spotted the prey, he signaled as much with a rapid movement of arms and torso, accompanied by high-pitched cries directed toward the lookout of the nearest boat. That lookout, equally noisy and just as prompt, issued orders to the crew, and the fishing boat shot out over the waves to the sound of the seamen's chanteys. Standing erect in the bow of the boat, the man holding the harpoon scanned the surface of the sea—muscles taut, ears alert, eyes peeled. The fishing boats bounced along from crest to trough at furious speeds, forming curves and curlicues, halting and then coming about, slowing, crowding one another, and finally hurtling forward across the water until the harpoonist launched his harpoon. The hissing rush of the hull over the waves was drowned out by the rhythmic shouts of the oarsmen—slow, relentless, warlike—and by the cries of the lookouts—the one high atop the mainmast at the center of the dinghies fastened together in a platform shaped like the petals of a flower and the other lookout on the boat that was trailing after the faster launches of the fishermen—calling out to one another, and once they were out of earshot, gesticulating like madmen to communicate. Once the prey was within range, silence fell as everyone waited for the signal from the man with the harpoon, erect in the bow—half-naked, muscles swollen, stiff-armed, wide-legged—as if he'd been bolted to the wood.

Like a wasp in flight, the fishing boat shot off over the water, zigzagging across the oil-smooth surface. The man shouted and hurled the harpoon with all his might; the harpoon whistled into the sea and vanished under the surface. The harpoonist stood wobbling in the bow of the boat, moving not a muscle, like the rest of the crew. The harpoon's line, coiled in a wide-mouthed half-keg fastened to the bottom of the boat, paid out rapidly until it jerked the keg into the sea. A shout from the boat's lookout and the oarsmen began rowing again, pulling desperately after the keg that was skipping rapidly over the waves, marking the route of the harpooned fish. Then the keg started wobbling and jerking around as if it were possessed. In its death throes, the swordfish was twisting and turning, creating whirlpools and geysers of water, and then it started to slow down; it broke the surface, then plunged back under, emerging again, while its silvery belly glittered in the sunlight, reflecting the light like a mirror held underwater. At last, the fish plunged shuddering into the depths. At a signal from the harpooner, the boat inched forward to haul its prey gently up from below.

The carriage climbed up onto the hilltop. The air was cooler up here. From this distance, the swordfish hunts—hundreds of them at any one time, spread out over the Strait of Messina—sketched arabesques in white foam over the surface of the sea, lingering only for instants, then vanishing; the tiny fishing boats seemed like so many swallows soaring over the water which was dotted with long-pistilled flowers bobbing in place. "Ah, how I love swordfish," Annuzza murmured, licking her wrinkled lips, certain she could already taste it. At the Craxi house meals were lavish affairs, and Amalia would make sure she was given a generous serving of swordfish.

"Mmm," Agata echoed her. She too loved to eat. She flashed a melancholy smile, then shivered.

After the Feast of the Assumption, Giacomo had vanished and she hadn't heard from him since. Every morning, she rose at dawn, tormented by her yearning to see him, thirsting for a sign from him, any sign. But in vain. The shutters of Giacomo's bedroom remained resolutely fastened shut. There was not the slightest sign of life, even from the line of balconies with their jutting "goose-breast" railings, crowded with flower pots and covered with thirsty ivy plants, dangling and tossing in the wind. And each morning, Agata relived the anguish of hope and disappointment that she'd felt on that melancholy August 16, when the city, exhausted from the celebrations of the previous day, still slept, and in the streets below there was not a living soul around, not even one of the nanny-goats with swollen udders that goatherds drove from house to house every morning, milking them at each stop. She'd considered everything imaginable: perhaps his father or his cruel mother had forbidden him ever to see her again, perhaps her beloved had fallen ill or even died, perhaps he was angry at her for her refusal to kiss him, maybe he'd fallen out of love with her, or even decided to go ahead and marry that other girl. Agata wasn't jealous by nature, and she'd come to accept the fact that her mother preferred her other daughters—in fact, she often felt pity for her sisters, forced as they were to suffer the attentions of Donna Gesuela, while Agata remained free to read and spend time on her own pursuits. But now she felt the pangs of jealousy: just the thought that Giacomo might have agreed to marry the other girl was pure torture. She'd rather see him dead than happy with that one. She went so far as to dream of her own death, but only after she'd successfully murdered the two lovers. Jealousy not only clouded her mind, it was driving her into the throes of delirium. That morning in the city, she'd peered into every carriage that they passed, searching for his face: she could have sworn that she spotted him at least twice, sitting between a pair of glowering thugs. The blood of the swordfish hunt, the harsh beauty of the hillside and the bracing scents of the countryside sharpened both her yearning and her despair. She felt a chill. Without a word, Annuzza threw a cotton quilt around her shoulders and tucked it snugly around her.

At the age of twenty-two, Amalia was a happy bride and a contented mother. She lavished the same loving care on her own children and those from her husband's first marriage, and her husband, in his gratitude, never thought of trying to restrain his wife's extravagance toward the Padellanis. Amalia had inherited her father's cheerful good nature and her mother's love of good food; the Craxis' guests invariably enjoyed their stay. Agata and Carmela enjoyed playing with their nieces and nephews. After a quick snack and refreshments, the English governess who was in charge of their Calabrian nephew Francesco took them all out into the garden. They wandered, singing, down the shady garden paths while the youngest children skipped and jumped in time with the melodies. Once they reached the overlook, they threw themselves down to rest on the blankets arrayed beneath the pine trees, all but Agata. She looked out over the panorama and felt cut off from the world and hopelessly unhappy. The pine needles rustled in the gentle autumn breeze. The tall lighthouse loomed up over the deep blue waters. Messina stretched out at their feet, with Reggio facing it, directly across the strait. The fishermen had suspended their swordfish hunt to allow ships to pass back and forth through the strait. The vessels that shuttled back and forth between the two cities left foamy wakes on the dark blue sea, an evanescent spider web linking island and mainland. All it took was two sailing ships flying French colors plying the waters of the Strait of Messina to disturb that illusion of fine, taut threads, making it clear just how distinctly separate the two shores really were.

That afternoon, Agata welcomed her parents with a dazzling smile. She'd persuaded herself that, after *ferragosto*, Giacomo must have gone to his grandfather's villa, there to discuss the best way to win over his parents and that he had succeeded in having his way—that that very morning the Lepres had come calling on her parents; which must be why at the last minute she had been told to ride out to Amalia's house in the first carriage, instead of riding in the carriage with her parents. The more she thought about it, the more sure Agata felt that this was exactly what had happened. She expected her father to give her the good news immediately after lunch. At the table, she kept her eyes glued on her parents' faces, in hope of detecting a look, a signal of some kind, but they were busy talking with their hosts and no one gave her so much as a glance.

She had guessed right—but only in part. That morning, Senator Lepre had, in fact, asked to meet with the field marshal. He'd climbed the stairs alone, leaving Giacomo nervously waiting in the carriage, eager to be summoned inside once the details had been thrashed out. As soon as he was ushered into the apartment, he was informed that Don Peppino was indisposed and that the Marescialla alone would receive him. Caught off-balance, Senator Lepre decided it would be a good idea to reveal to her what he intended to tell her husband: he had come to ask Agata's hand in marriage for his grandson, having chosen to stand in for his own son, as a gesture of respect toward the field marshal, an old friend and contemporary. But then, under a relentless hail of questions from Donna Gesuela, he'd been forced to confess that his daughter-in-law remained implacably determined when it came to the matter of the dowry and that he, moved by the purity of the two young people's feelings, had decided to take action on his own, confident that his son and daughter-in-law would come to accept the fait accompli. Moreover, he would make a sizable gift to Giacomo on his wedding day.

"And if the field marshal bestows our daughter on you, what kind of treatment can I expect my baby to receive from this mother-in-law who doesn't want her?" asked the Marescialla, in a sugary sweet voice.

The kind old man's answer—that he fervently hoped, indeed, he had no doubt whatsoever, that once his daughter-in-law glimpsed Agata's qualities, she would change her mind—only landed him in the trap Donna Gesuela had laid for him. She asked him to reassure her by recounting in detail all the other occasions in which his daughter-in-law had revised her opinion of someone after acknowledging that she'd misjudged them. Senator Lepre was forced to admit that he couldn't recall a single instance and he foolishly confided that, precisely because of his daughter-in-law's prickly personality, once he'd become a widower he had chosen to give his eldest son the main, aristocratic floor of the family palazzo and had himself gone, in open violation of tradition, to live in the apartment of his bachelor sons. He even added that he rarely visited his son's house, so disagreeable did he find his daughter-in-law.

"I've heard enough," Donna Gesuela broke in. "Your family has offended the house of Padellani by turning up its nose at a daughter-in-law of such nobility!" Then she added, imitating her husband's Neapolitan accent: "'O megli'e Napule!'— The finest in Naples!"

She'd made up her mind: in the unlikely case that the field

marshal gave the hand of Agatuzza in marriage, her blessed daughter would be an unwelcome addition to her husband's household, subjected to who could imagine what humiliations at the hands of that mother-in-law, as the notary himself had described her! As for her, she would never consent to such a marriage. Still, the final word remained with the field marshal. From her tone of voice, it was unmistakable that a "yes" was at best a remote possibility.

After lunch, the extended family went downstairs for a walk in the garden. Agata's father leaned on his daughter's arm: that morning, he'd been indisposed with an acid stomach, but glutton that he was, he'd eaten heavily and drunk liberally when Amalia presented him with the usual lavish spread. Agata didn't dare to ask a thing, but even if she had, she'd have been disappointed: the field marshal knew nothing of Senator Lepre's visit; his wife had decided that there was no reason to poison the perfectly nice day that her husband hoped to spend with his Calabrian grandson.

Night had fallen. Agata tossed and turned in her bed. She couldn't sleep a wink. What had become of Giacomo? The day's anxiety had been transformed into a serpent fastened to her breast, eating her alive, as in the image of King Palermo that was so dear to her mother. She heard a noise outside, somewhere deep underground. She lifted her head: Carmela was sleeping peacefully in the next bed, her nightcap askew across her forehead. The dogs were howling, and one in particular was emitting cries that were almost human. Agata tried to sit up, but the room jerked, knocking her back onto the pillows. In the silvery moonlight, the central chandelier was swaying: an earthquake. Doors and windows were creaking, servant bells were chiming. The first person to enter their bedroom was their mother: she ordered them to throw on some clothes and hurry out to safety in the garden, around the fountain.

Then came a second shock, stronger than the first. It was followed by a third, a deep roar. They accompanied by rushed outside, young and old, men and women, masters and servants, some in nightshirts, others half dressed. The birds, abandoning nests, branches, and roofs, were soaring in vast looping circles, never daring to set down.

The villa was shaking. One tremor came hard on the heels of the last; they waited for them, speechless and shivering in the biting damp of the starry night. Suddenly, Agata's jealousy dwindled and vanished. Swept away by the love she felt for her Giacomo, she only wanted him to be safe and happy, whoever that might be with, even if it was the other woman. She prayed to God on his behalf, with all her heart. Her prayer drained her of anxiety; it gave her strength and peace of mind. Agata stared up, as if in a state of ecstasy, at the dark sky crisscrossed by the flight of frenzied birds. The shocks become less frequent.

The earthquake was stronger in Messina. A number of houses that were already crumbling had collapsed entirely, while many others had been damaged, but not severely—nothing comparable to the terrible earthquake of 1783, the memory of which had been impressed in the minds of the people of Messina by the stories of the survivors and the buildings that were leveled. The Padellanis yielded to Amalia's pleas: they would stay a few more days at the villa. Annuzza had been sent down into the city with a carriage to fetch clean linen and medicine for the field marshal's catarrh: he'd caught cold during the night they'd spent outdoors, and he now had a fever. She came back with a note for Agata: Giacomo informed her that his father, having learned of their meeting in the cobbler's shop, had threatened to send Giacomo away to Naples until he got over her. He hadn't written her before this because he was convinced that they were being spied upon; he begged her forgiveness for the brevity and the terseness of that note—when they were able to see one another again, he'd explain the rest to her. Giacomo made no reference to the meeting between his grandfather and the Marescialla. He concluded by pledging his undying love and urging her to await his return from Naples and to remain faithful to him.

Aghast, Agata took comfort in caring for her suffering father. At the first signs of improvement, the field marshal had stubbornly insisted on returning to Messina, despite the doctor's opinion and the wishes of his family. It wasn't often that the field marshal dug in his heels, but when he did there was no dissuading him.

Agata went into her father's bedroom. She perched on a stool next to the night table and poured him a glass of sweet lemonade: then she sat waiting, without a word. He began reminiscing. It was as if he were recalling his life and giving it to her as a gift. She devoured his words.

He told her about the glittering magnificence of his family and the happy years of his childhood with his beloved younger sisters, a childhood idyll that was cut rudely short: "I know that I haven't been a good father to you, or perhaps to your sisters, but I've done my best," he told her. "There's just one thing I'm happy about: I never forced you into a convent." He told her that one day his mother took the three littlest girls—Violante, Antonina, and Teresa—had them dressed in their finest, and left the house with them. He remembered it clearly because after his mother left, the wet nurses seemed heartbroken and he couldn't understand why. "I never saw them again," he said, sorrowfully, and then went on: "She left one at the convent of Santa Patrizia and the other two at the convent of San Giorgio Stilita. Just like that, she left them . . . I complained about it to my father and he told me to shut up and try to understand. King Louis XV, thirty years before that, had sent four of his daughters—the princesses Victoire, Sophie, Marie-Thérèse-Félicité, and Louise Marie—to the Royal Abbey of

Fontevraud, and he left them there for ten years. Then he took them back home—or perhaps I should say, he took the ones that were still alive back home—and everything was all right. 'He was the king and he could provide them with dowries. We are princes but we have to count our pennies, and a monastic dowry is much smaller than a matrimonial dowry. Your sisters will be very well off,' he told me." Then her father's gaze sought out her almond-shaped eyes. "I'm not sure that's how it went." A pause. "But for you girls, I've managed to find good husbands, even with a tiny dowry." He snickered wickedly: "But my daughters have their mother's sharp, clinical eye, and men seem to like that. When I was a boy, the women of the house of Padellani were fine and expensive, but they were dull-eyed."

Frequently he struggled to tell her the story of the Kingdom of Two Sicilies, of the fragile successes of the French revolutionary cause, of how that cause had attempted to sink roots in Naples, likewise without success. Agata did her best to take it all in, but when her father drew political links between the recent past and the present day, she struggled. He could tell. He gazed at her keenly. He took her hands in his. He relied upon her intelligence. And Agata returned his confidence with a sort of hope that took the form of inquisitive glances. One day he sent her to retrieve from a shelf hidden in his secrétaire a copy of the *Historical Essay on the Neapolitan Revolution of 1799*. He hefted the volume as if it were a fine wheel of tuma cheese, and waited until the maidservant had left the room; then he whispered to his daughter, without taking his eyes off the door for a second: "Read it carefully, and don't forget what it says. Remember not to speak about it, even in the family." Lowering his voice still more, he went on: "Cuoco was right. Now it's forbidden even to own this book, or to own any of the others on that shelf. This too is a mistake on our government's part."

He was worried about the state of the kingdom and the state of Europe at large. "There's always something lurking behind the friendship and benevolence of foreigners. Nelson, the friend and protector of the kingdom, persuaded King Ferdinand to burn the fleet stationed in Naples, to keep it from falling into the hands of the French. I was there, on that 9th of January, 1799, and I saw our glorious fleet go up in flames! That's how our English friend cut our legs off at the knee, and ever since we've been at the mercy of the English shipbuilders! King Ferdinand II, many years later, rebuilt our navy, but only at the cost of great sacrifices."

Other times he talked to her about the independence movement. "There are times when I can't understand what 'nation' means. You, for instance, daughter of a Neapolitan father and a Sicilian mother, what nation do you belong to, my Agatina?" He gave her a loving pinch on the cheek and snickered. "Let me tell you, and I want you to remember this, whoever you happen to marry, you belong to the house of Padellani, a house that has survived and will continue to survive all the foreign dynasties that have set up as rulers in Naples." Then he grew serious again. He foresaw other uprisings and revolutions. "There's not a single European state that will emerge intact. We must establish a standing army to protect us against domestic rebellions. Our army isn't effective," he commented dolefully, and that is why he accepted the need to pay mercenary troops, though he detested them roundly.

Her father remembered the days of his youth, before the French Revolution, when King Ferdinand and Queen Carolina sympathized with Freemasonry; he remembered his friendships with people of all stripes. "I was a Freemason, when I was a young man, and I was a sympathizer with the Carbonari, but I never joined their ranks. Their initiation rites put me off: it culminated with Pontius Pilate's trial of Our Lord and a scene of the crucifixion! A national ideology should have noth-

ing to do with political religion; they're two different things."
He absentmindedly murmured to himself in a low voice: "The
Neapolitan Carbonari won our constitution in 1820," and
then, in a louder voice, exhorted her to trust the husband of his
third daughter, Sandra: "Tommaso Aviello, he's a Master
Carbonaro, he's a good young man!"

Agata's father encouraged her to approach all new ideas
cautiously and to be a friend to everyone and an enemy to no
one: "Taking positions is a dangerous hobby for the wealthy
and the utter ruin of the poor, which is what we are." Then he
veered back to politics. "Keep an eye on Mazzini—he's a cunning thinker, now in exile. They tell me that he's opened a
school in London for our youngsters, there are so many
Italians there now. He's doing the right thing. It's necessary to
educate people, but it will take generations before they understand and accept what he dreams of, a unified Italian republic,
God and people. As for me, I'm too old to change."

Agata liked nursing her father. She'd moisten his lips with
rose water and rub his head. The doctor had taught her how to
dose his medicines to alleviate the pain, and she was the
scrupulous and careful executor of all his orders. But above all,
she loved to sing to him. Her father loved bel canto and he
asked her to sing him songs by Giordanello. The Padellani
house echoed with singing at all hours; in the morning the
songs of servant women scrubbing the floors, and in the afternoon arias from the most popular and fashionable operas,
which mother and daughters sang alone, a cappella, or else all
together, providing themselves with piano accompaniment.
Agata, who had a fine mezzo-soprano voice, stood off by herself near the balcony. From there, she could glimpse the shutters of Giacomo's bedroom, invariably shut, and she sang with
all her passion, tears brimming in her eyes, as her father smiled.
Caro mio ben, credimi almen, senza di te languisce il cor. She had

been taught arias from operas by Vincenzo Bellini, one of the most fashionable musicians—the Marescialla had attended a performance of his *Norma* in Palermo and had been dazzled—and she sang them over again a cappella. One day, Agata was humming *Qual Cor Tradisti, Qual Cor Perdesti*, the field marshal's favorite aria; he opened his eyes and called her over to him. "I wouldn't mind dying so much, if it weren't that I'll have to leave you," he told her, and looked at her lovingly. "*Nennella mia*, what will become of you?"

4.

September 17, 1839.
Birth of an infant prince
and death of the field marshal Padellani.
During the crossing to Naples, Agata confides
in Captain James Garson

T he court, controlled by the king and a few powerful
families with close ties to the king, such as the
Padellanis—who had been rehabilitated after serving
under Murat during French rule—was the driving force
behind a system of patronage that helped to strengthen the
iron grip of the large landholding class and increased the pressure that the capital exerted over the provinces.

Over the nine years of Ferdinand II's rule (he had
ascended to the throne at the youthful age of just twenty),
the ranks of the aristocracy had been encouraged, pomp and
ceremony were looked on favorably, as were choreographed
displays of power. In those years, the Spanish aspects of
court life that were first set in place by the king's great-
grandfather, Charles III of Spain, were preserved and even
exacerbated. Pensions, lifetime offices, special endowments,
straightforward gifts of cash, and the responses to the thousand daily supplications that southern society laid at its
monarch's feet were filtered through the office of the Chief
Majordomo, head butler of the royal house. Even the most
minute details of the everyday lives of the king and his family were tangled up with the administration of matters of
public interest. The royal festivities and days of mourning
had to be observed not only by the nobility, but by com-
moners as well. The mood of the people was expected to
match that of the reigning family. The aristocracy, in particular, was expected to be especially loyal: failing to attend a

party or observe mourning could result in falling out of royal favor.

On September 17, 1839, shortly before the death of Field Marshal Padellani, Queen Maria Theresa gave birth to a son, Prince Alberto Maria. The blessed event was commemorated throughout the kingdom with three days of gala celebrations, and the funeral and period of mourning for the field marshal could not be conducted with the solemnity due to the elevated rank and office of the deceased.

Donna Gesuela understood that, with the death of her husband, not only had she lost her family's one means of sustenance, but she herself had now been deposed from the pedestal upon which the Padellani name and her and her husband's assiduous presence in social, political, and civic life had once placed her. The reports of his death, the night previous, were immediately on the lips of all Messina. First thing in the morning, mourners filled the house—there are no established schedules for visits of mourning. Among the first to arrive were the creditors, who kissed the Marescialla's hand and in the same breath delicately alluded to the sum due, "whenever Your Excellency likes, there's no hurry," followed by the elderly female relative who owned the house, and who reassured the Marescialla, between one tearful embrace and the next, that she could certainly continue to live in the apartment, making vague references to the payment of back rent. Even relatives and friends seemed eager for the family to leave Messina, where the field marshal had first been sent in 1825 by express command of the newly crowned King Francis I. The Baron of Solacio encouraged his sister to leave for Naples at the earliest opportunity in order to ask the king for the special bestowal of a pension. Without the slightest hesitation, the general commanding the garrison, a Sicilian officer in his forties, far inferior by birth to the Padellanis—who had long been hoping for

Don Peppino to make up his mind to retire from the army, with a view to his own promotion—immediately informed the Marescialla that she would receive no support from him: that same day he summoned back to the barracks the orderly, the coachman, and the carriage that had been assigned to the field marshal. He did offer for the funeral the finest mourning gear the army could make available.

Whereupon Donna Gesuela understood. She decided to go on the offensive immediately, carrying the attack to the kingdom's capital, Naples. She would depart immediately, and take the field marshal's mortal remains with her. She dispatched a message to his Neapolitan relatives. She would arrive at the end of the period of celebration, and a solemn funeral would be memorialized in the capital city, providing the honor and attention due to a Padellani and, more to the point, making the king or his counselors more likely to come to her assistance. Obtaining the health permits required was quite easy: the previous year, when the king reformed the administration of Messina, the candidate her husband had named and supported was in fact appointed chairman of the senate; she also managed to find a Basilian monk from Alexandria who was able to embalm the corpse. Then, with the dispatch for which she was so well known, and with the assistance of her married daughters, she arranged the prompt sale of all excess property as well as her husband's personal effects and issued orders to dismantle the house; she dismissed all the household staff with the exception of Annuzza and Nora, her personal chambermaid. She then decided that Carmela and Annuzza would stay with Amalia as guests, while Anna Carolina, Agata, and Nora were to accompany her to Naples.

The departure was scheduled for the 20th of September.

Misfortune would have it that on that date the Tyrrhenian Sea was tossed by a furious gale driven by a force 9 or 10 mistral wind, which the Messinese interpreted as an omen of imminent aftershocks. The sea was a mass of crashing waves that broke with brutal might over the few vessels still seeking shelter in the nearest port. Don Totò came back from the harbor with the disheartening news that that afternoon only one steamship was expected to sail, flying the British flag, and the only reason it was setting out was that Captain James Garson, son of the ship owner, wanted at all costs to see his fiancée, who was awaiting him in Naples. "A grand vessel," he said. "The late Field Marshal would have appreciated it." The in-laws inquired and discovered that the Garsons were friends of the Padellani princes. At that point, Donna Gesuela had no more doubts: that was the ship for them.

Agata hadn't stepped away from her father's catafalque for all the long hours during which it had been on display in the largest drawing room of the house. Shabbily dressed in dark clothing and brokenhearted, she sat next to the coffin, taking the place of her mother, who was busy with other obligations. People commented on her pallor and her puffy eyes in a tone that verged on derision. Agata was afraid for the future—her father's last words echoed dully in her head. For her, the departure for Naples was a sign that her love with Giacomo was doomed not to survive.

It was raining and the wind was gusting powerfully. Soldiers, relatives, and household staff had accompanied the Padellani women to the Messina harbor. Salvo Bonajuto, husband of the fourth daughter, Giulia, was the director of a shipping agency and he had reassured them: they would be sailing in an extraordinary and very modern steamboat—the finest ship in the Garsons' Mediterranean fleet. Aside from the two powerful sidewheels driven by the steam engine, the ship was brigantine-rigged with two masts flying square sails and a third mast rigged with a spanker. It carried passengers and it made unthinkable time. If the weather had been good, it would have reached Naples in just thirty-six hours.

Salvo Bonajuto had taken care of the bureaucratic formalities for the Marescialla's embarkation. The luggage and the coffin were already on board; James Garson had come to express his condolences to the Marescialla and had given her the use of his private cabin. It was an act of respect, of piety, and also a highly practical solution: it was the only room on the ship with enough room for the important passengers and the coffin.

The exhausted group of mourners were awaiting the boarding call in a waiting room crowded with harbor workers. With no ships sailing, the longshoremen had no work to do, and so they had sought shelter from the storm. Their sweat, strengthened and made more pungent by the humidity of the enclosed room, prickled Giacomo's sensitive nostrils, as he stood pressed against a window. The bold air and confident words with which he usually concealed his own insecurity had abandoned him. He peeked at the Padellani women for a long time, before he made his way through the dock workers and their stench. Giacomo extended his condolences to Donna Gesuela; then he asked her permission to speak with Agata, who was sitting separately with the married sisters. Caught off guard, and perhaps moved by the young man's solicitude, the Marescialla agreed.

They stood together, apart from the others, next to the large French doors. In the dim light that filtered through the glass splashed by gusts of foaming salt water, in the midst of the crowd of steaming dockworkers, the two lovers said not a word: they communicated through the mute language of emotions. Agata stood in profile against the window, leaning against it with her left shoulder, and pressed her open hand against the glass, as if she were trying to push it away from her, or perhaps rest her weight on it. The trembling of her palm and fingers with every flicker of the lashes on Giacomo's glistening eyes betrayed her deep emotions. He whispered to her about the unfortunate outcome of the meeting between his grandfather and her mother, and as he spoke to her, Agata laid her head against the glass, lowered her eyes, and didn't look up again. Giacomo began to muddle his words, in fear that she might be about to faint. Then he saw Agata's hand emerge from beneath her short cape and he reached out and seized it. The Marescialla was watching them, hard-eyed. "Agata! The son of the steam boat's owner is here! We need to board, come along!" A squeeze of the fingers, a last gaze, and the two lovers took their leave, promising they'd see one another again in Naples.

In the sky, a whirling multitude of gales, lightning bolts, and lashing rain. The steamboat, after emerging from the Strait of Messina, proceeded at low speed, pitching, rolling, and yawing violently. Visibility was minimal and all that could be seen of the island was the dull glare of the lighthouse—nothing more.

The women were in the cabin. Anna Carolina and her mother, both terrified and suffering from seasickness, had curled up in the far corner of the captain's bunk. Wrapped in one another's arms, they were murmuring incantations and prayers to St. Christopher, when they weren't moaning or retching.

Nora, who had never left solid land before, stoically performed her duty as if it were the most natural thing on earth. Kneeling before the coffin, she prayed to St. Nicholas of Bari and Our Lady of the Assumption, providing them with a list of all the cataclysms that had befallen Messina and to which she could personally testify—the devastating cloudburst of 1824, the invasion of the grasshoppers in 1831, the outbreak of cholera of 1836 and the even worse outbreak of 1837, and the more recent, quite modest earthquake—in order to persuade them to intercede with the Lord Almighty to give the late field marshal a tranquil crossing to his native city. But the saint and the Virgin Mary didn't lift a finger, and Nora resigned herself to reciting funereal aspirations and to continuing to watch over the corpse by herself. She only stopped when the rollers tossed the ship so violently that the coffin went sliding across the floor, just like the Vara of Our Lady of the Assumption; at that point, in high dudgeon, she wedged the field marshal into place with all available luggage and then resumed her funeral vigil. She held out until lunchtime, when another duty supervened: feeding her mistresses. A steamer trunk was packed with provisions. Aside from the mourning pastries and black *pignoccata*, curled shortbreads, marzipan "olives"—and the food for the crossing—cutlets, fried rice balls, bread, fruit, and vegetables—there were huge tins of Cappuccinelle pastries and wheels of pungent romano cheese to give as gifts to their relatives. The mistresses, however, refused even to consider taking a bite of food. Indignant, Nora ate something herself and went back to her prayers and aspirations.

Ever since they'd left port, Agata, standing leaning against the door, had looked through the porthole, watching the fury of the gale, without feeling weariness, hunger, or sleepiness. The steamboat was tacking, following a zigzagging course with reduced sails, in order to beat against the wind. It had passed close to the Aeolian Islands; Agata knew only Lipari and with a bit of imagination she was able to make out the castle. Off Stromboli, the ship turned again; in the dark of night, whipped by gusts of wind and buckets of rain, the eruptions of the volcano seemed like menacing firework displays. The steamboat slowed and then suddenly came about, setting a course for the Calabrian coast; the closer they got to Italy, the more the gale seemed to quiet down.

After the encounter with Giacomo, her mother had been unusually solicitous and loving with Anna Carolina and even with Nora, but not with Agata—she hadn't said a word to her.

Agata deeply missed her father. From regret she progressed to a lament over the misfortune that had befallen her, and then to a desire to be with her father again; from there, it was only a short step to a yearning for death. With every ounce of her being, she wished she were dead. Just as a snake sheds its skin, she felt as if she were wriggling out of her own body and, transformed into a light breeze, wafting heavenward to rejoin her father. Her eyes glued to the stern of the ship no longer saw a thing. Not a tear, not a thought of God in Agata, at that moment. She was all spirit.

The blackness of night was torn asunder by bolts of lightning. The mistral wind blew viciously. Once again, the steamer was tossed to port and starboard by angry rollers. Asleep in a deck chair next to the coffin, her head lolling from side to side, Nora was snoring; the two other women catnapped between moaning wails, Anna Carolina curled up against her mother's side.

To the east a pale dawn appeared. The storm was beginning to abate. Agata hadn't moved away from her porthole. She distractedly noticed the work of the sailors out of the corner of her eye and she could hear the orders that the captain was issuing from the bridge behind her. The sea was covered with grayish foam. The cabin reeked of pungent cheese and fresh vomit, and she opened the door. The rain pelted lightly onto the wooden beams, bouncing up again as if in a dance. And, light as the raindrops, the tears she'd held back streamed down from Agata's eyes. The harder she cried, the brighter grew the flaming sky, and the better she felt. Without realizing it, Agata was murmuring the verses of the song that she had sung in Amalia's garden:

Oranges and lemons, say the bells of St. Clement's.
You owe me five farthings, say the bells of St. Martin's.

The clouds were thinning out; those that remained were hurrying westward to recompose themselves. The air was tepid. Agata was outside, flattened against the cabin door, twisting and turning the fringe of her shawl. Her mourning black and the deep bluish rings under her eyes offset the raw beauty of her face. The halo of chestnut ringlets wafting around her forehead in sharp contrast with the heavy tresses that lay gleaming on her shoulders recalled her mother's sensuality as a young woman. The sailors cast sidelong glances at her—the lingering glances of young men. James Garson was watching her too. He was interested in her small, blue-veined hands. He'd noticed them when the steamer was still in port; he'd been waiting for the captain of the brigantine so that he could be introduced to the Padellani women, and he'd been looking into the waiting room from the dock. He could only make out shadows, except for that quivering hand pressed against the mist-pearled plate glass. It had communicated a sense of unease to him, a malaise that was confirmed shortly thereafter when the young woman had pressed her shoulders and head against the window, revealing through the glass wiped clean by her hand a minute, unsmiling profile. He only recognized her by her hands. The breeze was lashing; Agata, like everyone else, was staring eastward, holding her shawl tight around her shoulders with both arms crossed over her bosom. Her tapered fingers were stroking as if she wished to embrace herself.

A gleam of light shot across the sea, heralding the arrival of the sun. All eyes were leveled on the horizon line.

Then, came a voice:

When will you pay me? say the bells of Old Bailey.
When I grow rich, say the bells of Shoreditch.

Agata's voice had grown imperceptibly louder, and now she was singing outright. No one seemed to notice.

"This is the most beautiful time of the day," he said, addressing her in English, and then turned to face her. Agata seemed determined to watch the rising sun and paid him no mind. James Garson scolded himself for his bad manners and remembered that, when he was introduced to the group of female passengers, he had expressed his condolences to the Marescialla but not to Agata—he'd been struck dumb by the unmistakable sorrow of those oriental eyes. He hurried to offer his condolences now, adding that when he was a boy he'd met the field marshal's older brother. Agata politely accepted his condolences and thanked him for his hospitality. Then, she paused. "You gave us your cabin and you haven't slept all night, have you?" she asked him, and uncrossed her arms.

"I wouldn't have been able to sleep in any case, with that storm. I'm sorry only that my cabin lacks the comforts befitting your family and the luxury to which you are no doubt accustomed." The Englishman had made an effort to bring a note of lighthearted frivolity into the conversation, but Agata chose to ignore it. In fact, she corrected him: "We aren't wealthy." He looked at her, baffled, uncomprehending. "Not at all. In fact, we're poor," she reiterated, and stared at him—a doleful, challenging stare. Unsure what to say, he murmured: "The Padellanis are a great Neapolitan family," and kept his eyes focused on her. He was waiting for a reply, and it came. Agata believed that she had detected genuine compassion in this foreigner and, dismissing her natural reserve, she spoke to him about her beloved father, cadet son of his family, the economic hardships her family had suffered in order to scrape together her sisters' dowries, the opposition of the Lepres to her love for Giacomo, and the desperate attempts the elderly notary had made to obtain her hand in marriage for his grandson, and even her mother's scornful rejection of those overtures. "We really are poor women," she said, with simplicity, and added: "Poverty itself wouldn't frighten me if I only had some books:

I could read and educate myself, and then seek employment as a governess; that would be nice work."

"Books?"

"My mother put up for sale those of my father's books that could hope to find a buyer. There were many other books, but he hadn't reported owning them, in violation with King Francis' law, so those books will have to be destroyed. Otherwise we'll have to pay large fines. I hid a few of them in my trunk, but only a very few. I wish I'd taken more of them with me." She looked around her disconsolately, and added: "All of the English books were left at home, to be sold." She fell silent, suddenly aware of how impudent she'd been, and did her best to steer the conversation back to a proper drawing room tone: "You must be very contented; before long now you'll see the love of your life again!"

"It's true, my fiancée is waiting for me in Naples . . . " Leaning against the railing he looked out over the sea:

If ever any beauty I did see,
Which I desir'd and got, 'twas but a dreame of thee.
And now good morrow to our waking soules,
Which watch not one another out of feare;
For love, all love of other sights controules,
And makes one little roome, an every where . . .

Agata had a very acute sense of hearing. Love. That was exactly what she had been thinking about all night long. She thought she'd figured out what it was, love: to feel one with one's beloved and to want only their happiness, even more than your own happiness. She looked out at the sea, one vast glittering field of waves caressed by the glancing rays; then her wandering gaze fell on the Englishman's blond hair and muscular silhouette: he too was looking out at the dawning of the day.

An orange ball was hanging just over the line of the horizon: the sun, whole and round, was gleaming gloriously over a sea that was finally bright blue. Agata relaxed into a long, closed-mouthed smile, and their eyes met. Then came a guttural clamor from inside the cabin: "Why is that door hanging open? Shut it now!" Nora had just awakened, and she wanted an explanation and an apology from Agata for the cold air pouring in through the open door.

5.

Autumn in Naples.
The scathing humiliations of poor relations.
Agata can't understand what her mother wants from her

On a sun-drenched day, the steamer chugged slowly into Naples harbor, steering for the Molo Angioino, and moored at the foot of the looming mass of the castle that was built at the behest of Charles of Anjou. It had docked at Sorrento where Donna Gesuela, as previously agreed, had sent word to the Padellanis of their impending arrival. Anna Carolina was weeping bitterly in the cabin; she had never wanted to leave Messina and she abhorred Naples. Agata, in contrast, had only the finest memories of the place. The first time she'd been there she was four; it was in 1830, after the death of Francis I, whom her father called the "gentleman king." She remembered the enchanted atmosphere of the Gulf of Naples, the roofs, the domes, and the bell towers that loomed taller and bigger before her eyes as the ship drew closer to the kingdom's capital, sails bellying in the wind. "This great-hearted king had the courage to send away the Austrian army, which was here at a steep price to 'protect' the kingdom, though in reality all it had ever done was alienate the kingdom's people. Since that day, the Neapolitan army," and here her father thumped his chest in pride, "has protected the state better than they ever did." Then, with a mischievous glance, he added, in a low voice: "And with the help of a few thousand Swiss! Let's see what this boy king winds up doing!"

The welcome given them by their Padellani relations deeply moved Donna Gesuela and left her daughters open-mouthed in astonishment. A sumptuous funeral carriage was awaiting the coffin on the dock, with a military honor guard in full regalia. Everyone was there: Sandra, Agata's third-eldest sister, with her husband Tommaso Aviello, their three married aunts with children and husbands and their cousin Michele, Prince Padellani, with his wife Ortensia; on his arm was Aunt Orsola, the dowager princess, Agata's godmother. Aunt Orsola embraced mother and daughters and announced that they would be her guests and would stay in her apartment in Palazzo Padellani. After the religious function, with the cardinal of Naples, Vincenzo Padellani, the field marshal's first cousin, officiating, the funeral procession made a slight detour in order to pass beneath the high walls of the convent of San Giorgio Stilita, where two of the aunts who had taken the habit now lived, born Antonina and Violante, now respectively Donna Maria Brigida and Donna Maria Crocifissa, the abbess. Agata had seen again—or met for the first time—other Padellani uncles and aunts and cousins, and she had exchanged a few shy words with His Eminence the Cardinal, who had expressly asked to have a conversation with her. He was a handsome middle-aged man with raven-black hair, imposing in his scarlet cassock; he had looked her up and down and, after questioning her, promised to find her a worthy confessor.

Donna Gesuela, caught up in the condolence visits and other duties, saw very little of her daughters. Tense and drained of all verve though she might be, she never let her appearance slip: she wore the widow's weeds with something bordering on flirtatious elegance and went out now accompanied by one relative, now by another, to discuss business or petition for an audience with the new king. Agata was beginning to understand that the king on whom so many were counting, and who was described as a benevolent and modernizing ruler, was actually a sanctimonious shut-in, remote from the populace and from the aristocracy. In order to approach him, it was necessary to penetrate an odious filter of chamberlains, courtiers, and majordomos. Her mother always returned home empty-handed, with neither a royal grace nor a pension. The sisters were often left alone in their aunt's apartment. Anna Carolina actually preferred things that way, since she was reluctant to socialize with her female cousins and almost never spoke, remembering as she did that they had made fun of her, the last time, for her Sicilian accent. Agata, on the other hand, had established a warm and intimate bond with her aunt Orsola and enjoyed the company of her peers, but she was reluctant to leave her sister alone. She had no inhibitions about her Neapolitan; she spoke the dialect well, albeit with a Messina accent: she was the daughter who had spent the most time chattering away with her father, who had refused to learn to speak Sicilian.

At the end of the second week, Aunt Orsola made it clear to her sister-in-law that she and her family couldn't stay any longer as her guests in the *palazzo*. The *piano nobile*, or master floor, where she had always lived, was now occupied by her stepson's family and she already felt like she'd been exiled to the third-floor apartment, where she claimed that she lacked enough room for them to stay on permanently. Actually, though, there was plenty of room, in Agata's opinion—it was just that her aunt didn't want them in her house: they were poor relations, and therefore a source of embarrassment.

In mid-October 1839, the Padellani women went to live in an apartment on the top floor of Palazzo Tozzi. The apartment was above the building's cornice and directly beneath the roof. It was rented to them by their aunt, Clementina Padellani, and her husband, the Marchese Tozzi. They lived on the main floor—the *piano nobile*—with their daughters, Eleonora and Severina, who were the same age as Anna Carolina and Agata.

It was a small, shabby apartment, but the rent was low and Donna Gesuela was happy to take it.

Palazzo Tozzi was enormous. The front hallway was as large as a cathedral and required two doormen, so many people came and went. It lacked the lovely terraces of Messina, with a view of the Strait and Calabria in the distance; still, the terrace on the *piano nobile*, which overlooked the vast inner courtyard, was luminous and covered with climbing vines and plants. From the courtyard a great many staircases ran up. At the far end of the courtyard was the master staircase, scissors-shaped, made of spectacular white marble. Then there were two others, broad and with marble handrails, and they looked like a master staircase you might see in Messina, and there were others still, modest and almost concealed, for the servants or for apartments like the one they were living in. Right at the foot of the staircase leading up to their apartment was a camellia plant shaped like an elongated egg, with fleshy glistening leaves, concealing the entrance from all eyes. The chief doorman had taken a liking to Nora and he explained to her that the old Marchese Tozzi had built that apartment in empty roof space and by borrowing a room from his own living quarters for a *femmena*—a woman—who had cast a spell on him; once he was a widower he brought her to live in the *palazzo*, up where they were living now. She had borne him two daughters. He went up to eat with her every day at noon, and that's why there was a fine kitchen and a handsome drawing room—the bedrooms that the women slept in, in contrast, were what you'd expect to find in the worst parts of Naples. That *femmena* kept him tied to her by the magic of food. Her minestrone was better than any other soups in Naples. When she died, the apartment was given to obnoxious widows and old maids: it was so high up that it was difficult to go there to visit, and they invariably died alone and forgotten.

All the rooms, except for the kitchen, overlooked a

cramped inner courtyard and were lacking light. Nora slept in the kitchen, and the dining room did double duty as Agata's bedroom. In the large, beautifully furnished parlor, there was an interior window overlooking a narrow airshaft, which was connected via mysterious passageways to the choir of the convent of the Poor Clares, adjoining the *palazzo*. The melodious chants of the nuns wafted up the airshaft.

All things considered, the three women were satisfied with their independent living quarters. At first, the hospitality of their Padellani relations had been warm if overwhelming. The family had behaved impeccably at the funeral and during the brief period of mourning visits at the *palazzo*. After that, however, their relations had vanished from view one by one, offering Donna Gesuela neither consolation nor assistance. In fact, she had been forced to struggle along on her own in her quest for a gracious royal pension bestowed by the king. Visits from their female cousins grew less and less frequent and invitations downstairs to the *piano nobile* of Palazzo Tozzi were now a rarity; Agata had the unmistakable impression that even there, they were treated as inconvenient relations. No one had offered any real help. Their aunts the nuns, her father's younger sisters, had been especially affectionate but they too, however lavish their monastic dowry might have been, still offered only pastries and prayers.

Aunt Orsola's brother, the Admiral Pietraperciata, began to pay visits to the house. He came dressed to the nines to play cards with Donna Gesuela in the late afternoon. Even though she invited him to stay for dinner, the admiral always declined, knowing full well that the invitation was extended merely out of politesse. Before he was due to arrive, Donna Gesuela lightened her face with rice powder and touched up her ringlets under her widow's bonnet; she did her very best to entertain and please him, offering him hot chocolate and the biscottini made of semolina and almond flour that Nora baked in an iron box, which she called her oven, set to cook on the embers. The admiral couldn't resist those delicacies. Every so often Agata was given permission to remain in the drawing room, but she knew that her presence there wasn't welcome and so she left; all the same, the admiral took an interest in her and brought her books to read; once he brought her a book that James Garson had sent her: *Pride and Prejudice*. Agata, caught off guard, didn't know what she should do. Her mother explained that the Garsons were old family friends of Aunt Orsola's and urged her daughter to accept the gift.

The daughters were accustomed to their mother's sudden mood swings; but after the funeral she truly became erratic. Donna Gesuela was afflicted with melancholy and at times she made irrational and contradictory decisions. She'd go out mornings and afternoons, without telling anyone where she was going. She'd come home exhausted and every evening, after dinner, she'd sip *amaro* to assist her digestion. While waiting for the relief of the belch, she repeated the same litany over and over: "No pension and no assistance from all these people that your father entertained as if they were royalty, when we were still rich. What ingrates they are, these Neapolitans!" There was little they could say to comfort her. Anna Carolina didn't even try: she was always on the verge of tears and she spent her days embroidering the linen of her trousseau and sighing. Agata wanted to wrap her arms around her mother, she wanted to offer to help, even go out and find a job, but she was afraid that she would meet with rejection. And so, like her sister, she listened and said nothing. Agata read a great deal and she studied the schoolbooks that she'd brought with her. She hadn't read many novels, because most of the books in their house belonged to their father, who didn't like to read novels. She was enchanted by the Bennet family.

The two girls spent most of their time alone. When their Tozzi female cousins invited Agata down to the *piano nobile*, she was only too happy to go. They had fun playing together, even though, on her mother's orders, Agata—still in mourning—was to be excluded not only from all receptions and festivities but even from visits of her cousins' girlfriends. Agata therefore had to observe the comings and goings of the *palazzo* from behind the scenes.

When Anna Carolina wasn't doing her embroidery, she spent time with a cousin her age who, like her, was engaged to be married. All they did together was dream listlessly about their respective fiancés. Agata thought about Giacomo, too, though she'd had no word from him, but she never talked about him. The only person she would have liked to talk about Giacomo with was her sister Sandra, of whom she was very fond. But she saw very little of Sandra, because Tommaso Aviello—a successful lawyer who was disliked by his Padellani relations because he was a commoner and a Carbonaro—did not meet with her mother's approval. In that period Donna Gesuela forbade Agata to spend time with Sandra, because of a disagreement with her son-in-law. When Agata was finished with her own chores, she would go and help Nora—and Nora needed the help, overburdened with work as she was. Her mother let her do as she liked, but she had made it very clear that Agata was not to let anyone see or know that a Padellani was doing a servant's housework.

When she could wangle her mother into giving her permission, Agata would go out to do a little shopping, without ever venturing far from the *palazzo*. The streets of Naples were crowded, and the traffic was chaotic: she would have been all too happy to go home to live in her own beloved city.

One day her mother received a letter from Cavaliere Carnevale. She had written to him, explaining their financial hardships and suggesting that Anna Carolina's dowry might perhaps be paid out in annual installments. The reply came promptly and unequivocally: the dowry was to be paid in a lump sum, prior to the wedding, as had been agreed with the field marshal. That was a grim day. Anna Carolina went into one of her nervous fits; then, tearful and overheated, she collapsed on her bed and had to be fanned at length by Nora. Her mother stayed to watch her for a while, thoughtfully. Then Donna Gesuela put on her finest clothing and went out.

In the days that followed, she continued to behave the same way: every morning she left their apartment and frequently didn't even come home for lunch. When she returned, she was exhausted, sinking into an easy chair and loosening her sash, complaining that she couldn't stand all those meals that were making her fat, even though she felt as if she were starving inside. She was seeking help in putting together a dowry for her daughter, and everyone she turned to acted as if they were touched, deeply touched, and then gave her nothing but lunch! Agata was heartbroken for her, but her mother steered clear of her. In the meanwhile, Eleonora and Severina, having learned about the problems with the dowry, tormented Anna Carolina by asking her if she'd set a date for her wedding yet. Anna Carolina became increasingly hysterical, and refused to leave the apartment or see her cousins. And so they began inviting Agata downstairs instead.

Suddenly, and without any explanations, Donna Gesuela gave her daughters permission to frequent the Aviellos. Twenty years old, and married for six years now, Sandra was the sister who most closely resembled Agata; she was childless and she helped Tommaso in his work as a lawyer. They were a very close couple. They lived in a spacious apartment, where Tommaso had his law office, in a *palazzo* in the San Lorenzo neighborhood, inhabited by professionals. Every room was lined with bookshelves or built-in shelves covered with books; Sandra let Agata borrow modern novels, ghost stories, stories of cruel and romantic hatreds and love affairs that made her shiver; her brother-in-law encouraged her to complete her education and explained his vision of the future to her. She was thrilled by Carboneria, at least the way that Tommaso presented it to her. The movement originated among the officers and soldiers of the Neapolitan army during the last years of Murat's regime, in reaction to the scorn of their fellow French soldiers who mocked the Neapolitans calling them *Italiani* and *codardi* (cowards). It was a secret society and had as its first objective the creation of an Italian nation with an independent government under a constitutional monarchy.

Many members of the social classes that Murat had marginalized from the kingdom's political, social, and commercial life, including the aristocracy, had joined. "The unification of Italy ought to take place under the auspices of our kingdom. We are the greatest state in Italy and Naples is the sole metropolis on the Italian peninsula that can rival the other great cities of Europe." Tommaso was moody; when he was feeling pessimistic he complained about the inconsistency of the five leading European states: they encouraged the Greeks to seek their independence, but not the Poles. That wasn't all he complained about: the inequality of wealth in the industrial nations was only growing, bringing poverty, misery, and disease—for instance, cholera, which had spread throughout Europe—as well as discontentment. "The people are no longer willing to suffer," Tommaso would declaim, his voice growing louder. He felt no admiration whatsoever for the English; their policies were directed toward preserving the status quo and preventing French influence from being once again brought to bear on the Italian peninsula. The king, fearful and suspicious of both the English and the French, tended to cultivate a policy of isolationism, but this was no longer a practicable option: soon railroads, steamships, and the stunning new invention, the telegraph, would allow people and ideas to travel the world at incredible speed. The king did have the merit of having reinforced the kingdom's administration, industries, and economy, but nonetheless he was a despot; the police had unbridled power and the people were restless without liberty. Then Tommaso grew optimistic: the people's revolt would not be long in coming now, and then he would be able to devote himself to the unification of Italy, body, heart, and soul.

In the Aviello household, there were often dinner guests. The conversation turned not only to politics, but also to the arts and to literature; Sandra took part in the discussion on an equal basis. Agata realized that her sister was happy, even though there was no sign of children on the way, and she comforted herself with the thought that she too could have a life of her own, even if she was unable to marry. She believed that in time another world would come into being, where equality and respect reigned uncontested.

One afternoon Agata was on the small kitchen balcony, above the cornice of Palazzo Tozzi, watering the pots of rosemary and parsley. She lingered as usual, enjoying the panorama of the city viewed from above: the roofs of buildings, churches, and monasteries seemed to be glued to one another, so tall were they and so narrow were the streets. From far below the muddled noises of the city wafted up—voices, songs, neighing, shouts. That day, the breeze carried with it the perfume of the invisible gardens in the cloister and ruffled the surface of the turquoise sea in the distance, where foaming waves surged. Agata noticed across the street, and just a little to the left, beneath another roof, an open balcony: Giacomo appeared on it. She stood there, under a spell—the water from the watering can had flooded the vase and overflowed, dripping onto her feet. They couldn't hear one another's voices, they were too far apart. Resuming their old language made up of signals and gestures, he conveyed to her that he was studying at the university and that he would leave a note for her in the conciergerie.

The chief porter of the *palazzo* put on the airs of a very important man, and justifiably so. It was he who controlled the very movements of the building's tenants—summoning the rented carriages—and even the details of their lives; he was the building's mailman, and he accepted deliveries as well as packets of groceries. In Messina people did their shopping by lowering a wicker basket from the balcony, but in Naples that happened only in the poorer quarters. The *palazzi* were very tall indeed, and groceries were delivered to the concierge's office: he rummaged through the baskets, unwrapped grocery packets, and pilfered freely. Because he had taken a shine to Nora, he skimmed fruit, vegetables, and handfuls of spaghetti from other tenants' grocery deliveries and slipped the plunder to her, saying: "Take it, take it . . . eat, they'll never notice a thing."

Agata was afraid that if he ever took a dislike to Giacomo, he would stop delivering his letters, but no such thing happened. When she went out, he'd call out to her as she passed: "This is for you!" and then he'd wink at her.

From that day on, Agata began smiling for the slightest trifle and she became truly beautiful—her dark clothing highlighted her fair complexion and her happiness. Giacomo wrote her frequently and at length, but they still hadn't had an opportunity to meet in person. She was very much afraid of her mother's reaction and she spent her afternoons on the balcony, book in hand. He too, on his own balcony, read and studied. Then one of them would look up, the other would respond, and they'd smile at one another. When her mother found out about it, she didn't seem to be particularly annoyed. She asked her whether Giacomo had good and serious intentions and if there had been any changes, and little by little their interactions sweetened. One day he presented himself in the conciergerie to pay a surprise visit and Agata's mother allowed him to come upstairs. Agata had remained in her bedroom in fear, but

Gesuela came to get her, beaming: Giacomo had assured her that this time he would succeed in winning his parents' consent. She had given him until January to persuade his family, and in the meanwhile, she had invited him to visit them at home. Agata was overjoyed.

Despite her mother's permission, the young people were able to see one another only two more times before Giacomo returned to Messina, because from that day forward—no doubt, intentionally—Donna Gesuela constantly had chores and assignments for Agata to do and took her with her whenever she went out. He talked, talked, talked, and didn't seem to want to touch her; hopelessly in love, on the other hand, she was melting inside for the slightest caress—but Giacomo never again wanted to be close to her as he had on the Feast of the Assumption.

After Giacomo left, Agata no longer liked staying at home—everything reminded her of him—and so she would go to pay visits on Aunt Orsola. They tatted lace pillows together and chatted; other times Agata would sit reading by herself while her aunt tended to her business.

One afternoon her aunt was playing cards; Agata walked into the game room to bring her the pencil that Aunt Orsola thought she had lost—it was her lucky charm. The players were all male and female relations and two foreigners, an elderly gentleman and James Garson, who was sitting at her aunt's table. Agata hadn't expected to find so many people and she stopped at the threshold. Her aunt encouraged her to come over to her table. Play was interrupted for introductions: the mistress of the house explained that Garson's father and uncle, well-to-do shipowners and businessmen with close ties to the Rothschilds, had kept a home in Naples for two generations now; they were close family friends and great card players, and

James was no exception. "He does not disdain playing with elderly ladies like me," she concluded, coquettishly.

"Thanks very much for the book you sent through the admiral. I should have written to express my gratitude . . . " Agata was embarrassed.

"The admiral must certainly have told you that there was no need to write a reply, I was just leaving for London," he said. Then he asked: "Did you like it?" And he leveled his light colored eyes on her, with their straw-blond eyelashes.

"I read it all at one sitting, to tell you the truth." Agata stopped, embarrassed again.

"Do you have anything else to read?" James wouldn't let her go, and he listened to her attentively. He offered to send her more English novels. "There's no need to thank me, it's really no bother at all. I send them to my sister regularly. She's in boarding school. I'll just tell my bookseller to send a copy to you as well."

From then on, and as long as Agata stayed in Naples with her mother, books would arrive for her, wrapped in a handsome brown paper that she later cut into rectangles and pressed flat so she could paint watercolors. There was never a message from James; she knew who had sent them and she would write a note expressing her gratitude to the sender—Detken's bookstore—and describing her impressions of everything she had read. A few days later, she would receive another package.

6.
Winter 1840.
The last months of hope

The Christmas of 1839 was a sad one. Both mother and daughters missed the sisters back in Sicily. The letters from Messina were heartbreaking: furniture and other household objects had been sold off hand over fist; Carmela was pining for her mother, Amalia's oldest son was sick, and Anna Carolina's prospective marriage teetered in uncertainty because they had still been unable to scrape together the money for the dowry. With the excuse of the period of mourning, the Padellani relations had excluded "the Sicilian women"—as they referred to them—from the family Christmas celebrations. Even Aunt Orsola, normally so solicitous and affectionate, was avoiding them. Just as people had done when they first came to Messina, everyone asked the Padellani women when they were planning to leave Naples. The mother had been obliged to borrow money and she dreaded the days when creditors began demanding repayment; all the same, whenever visitors came, Nora, who had turned out to be a first-rate cook, managed to put together tasty meals with what little was on hand and the treats that the doorman skimmed off for her. In the presence of outsiders, Donna Gesuela put on a show of lavish generosity. She had ordered Anna Carolina and Agata never to accept invitations to any family receptions or celebrations, in the unlikely case that such invitations were extended, and not even to novenas at any of the more fashionable oratories, lest the Carnevales, sanctimonious nitpickers that they were, might find some pretext to find fault with Anna Carolina and refuse to honor their undertaking.

Throughout Advent and during Christmas, Naples celebrated. The scents and aromas of sweets and pastries—wafting ginger, cinnamon, cloves, sugar both caramelized and in the form of cotton candy, vanilla, anise—filled the air, emanating from pastry shops and from corner kiosks. Every day there were processions, religious feasts, displays of relics and novenas. These were sung everywhere, and not only before manger scenes—in churches and in oratories, on the street before shrines and holy niches, and even in the courtyards of aristocratic *palazzi*. At Father Cuoco's advice, Agata had attended the novena sung in Sicilian at the convent of Palma di Montechiaro by the Benedictines of Donnalbina, and she had found that she was deeply moved by the sound of her native language. There wasn't a church or patrician residence without its own manger scene of shepherds as tall as your arm, veritable sculptures, with outfits stitched in cotton, silk, or wool, depending on their rank, and bedecked with miniature jewelry, hats, shoes, and gloves, with animals of all kinds, and elaborate settings: grottoes, mountains, rivers, little lakes, and an enormous starry sky with a star of Bethlehem. The Neapolitan manger scenes was not limited to the Nativity and the visit of the Three Wise Men—it included the scene of the Annunciation and other secular scenes set in taverns, farmhouses, courtyards, where flocks of sheep blended seamlessly with sacred events in a distinctly Neapolitan atmosphere.

Agata also liked staying home and opening the drawing room's interior window to listen to the Christmas songs of the Poor Clares, or sit on the kitchen balcony, with a shawl over her shoulders and a blanket over her legs, reading a book with the background sounds of the street—shouts, the squealing of cartwheels, the music of bands, the novenas and songs of the women of Naples' *bassi*—faint and mingling as they wafted upward. At times like those, she thought of Giacomo.

By now, Agata was well acquainted with the Padellani relations, including the nuns: Sister Maria Giulia at the convent of Donnalbina and the two nuns at the convent of San Giorgio Stilita, Donna Maria Crocifissa, the abbess, and Donna Maria Brigida. The Padellanis, like all the other great aristocratic families, had "their own" favorite monasteries and convents where they sent their cadet sons and excess or unwanted daughters—as well as their bastards, as simple servants, friars, or lay sisters. Those monasteries looked like palaces. Of all the aunts who were nuns, Sister Maria Giulia was the most likable, because she had the same tone of voice as their father and she had confessed that, of all her relations, that brother was the one she missed most of all. Every time she mentioned him in the parlor, the aunt's voice changed, choking with emotion. Then she'd turn the wheel and out would come another pastry or biscotto for Agata, whom she treated like a little girl. But that aunt, even though she was more than sixty, behaved as if she'd never grown up past the tender age at which she'd been sent to the convent.

The other two aunts lived in the most prestigious convent in Naples, the convent of the high nobility, where the nuns who sang in the choir had the right to be addressed as "Donna"—My Lady—rather than "Suora"—Sister. Donna Maria Brigida was not in good health. Agata's mother told her that her aunt had had a stroke and that's why she mumbled and required constant assistance and care. Her aunt the abbess took a maternal attitude toward Agata and intimidated her with her questions. During the visits with her aunts, Agata caught a whiff of the mysteries of religion and the familiarity of blood relations. The monumental staircases and the sheer richness of the decorations in the parlors clashed with the devastating simplicity of the three iron grilles in a row behind which her aunt the nun was sitting. What little Agata could see through the iron bars—flashes of bright white veil and dark habit, patches of diaphanous flesh, the corner of a firmly closed mouth, the glitter of a curious eye—encouraged her to play the game of reconstructing eyes, mouth, nose, and a whole image of her aunt. Speaking through a grate reminded her of the grilles of the confessional: she responded with total sincerity to the forthright roughness of the nuns. Her aunts pelted her with questions about herself and her family and they wanted her to tell them about her father. Agata described him to his sisters as he had been: an old man with modern and not always conformist ideas, someone who read foreign books; a spendthrift, excessively generous and prone to piling up debt; a proponent of social justice; and a loving father. A man who enjoyed life. The field marshal and his wife had not been particularly religious, even though they complied like everyone else with the practices of Catholic devotion, and when they no longer had enough money to pay Miss Wainwright, they had sent their daughters to the less expensive Collegio di Maria— a product of the French Enlightenment, where their mother had been educated—intentionally ruling out the possibility of sending them to a convent boarding school.

Agata told Sister Maria Giulia that her father used to put on fanciful costumes every Carnival and that the year before he died he had told her about the time, when he was a gentleman of the chamber of His Majesty King Ferdinand I, that the two of them had dressed up as chefs. They cooked together in the royal kitchens, and amused themselves by selling what they'd cooked to the courtiers. At that point she thought she'd heard a stifled laugh and she seemed to glimpse a diaphanous hand covering the laughing mouth of the young Teresa Padellani.

At the end of January, good news arrived: back in Messina,

Donna Gesuela's sons-in-law had managed to secure a court ruling in her favor and they had secured a cash payment. It wasn't much, but it was enough to stave off the most persistent of her creditors. Donna Gesuela commented that this was a good sign and that it would help her to make the right decision in another matter that was very much in her mind, something that she preferred not to discuss. Admiral Pietraperciata, back in town from Lecce, where he had gone to spend the Christmas holidays, informed Donna Gesuela that he had managed to secure a loan for Anna Carolina's dowry, a loan secured by the future inheritance of a mutual Apulian relative—and so it was established that the wedding would take place within the year. Donna Gesuela then pointed her finger at Agata and in a sugar-sweet voice flutingly told the admiral: "With this daughter who resembles me so closely I'll need all your help as well." Agata blushed, contentedly—her mother was asking for assistance with her dowry too, she felt certain of it, because she'd just received a letter from Giacomo, who had stayed in Sicily after the Christmas holidays. He wrote that he would be back in Naples just as soon as his father had set a date for the trip up.

In February 1840 their mother decided to lighten her daughters' state of mourning. She therefore gave permission to Anna Carolina—who would soon be married—but not to Agata, to take part in receptions in the Tozzi household. Agata wasn't offended, confident as she was that her mother was doing everything within her power to make her own engagement to Giacomo become a reality. One day, while they were sitting down to a meal, Donna Gesuela announced that Anna Carolina's wedding would take place when six months had passed since their father's death, and that she would then go back to Messina. Agata's face lit up: her wedding would take place in Sicily. She was tempted to ask her mother if it was true, but she didn't dare: at that exact moment her mother had shot her a strange glance. Eager to celebrate her happy intuition, she asked if she could go downstairs, where her female cousins were holding an informal evening of dancing with friends—the last celebration before Lent. When her mother distractedly consented, she was certain she had guessed right and hurried to get dressed.

Agata's cousins talked excitedly about the Royal Academy of Music and Dance, founded a few years earlier by the king. At least once a week, the Academy held balls, concerts, and theatrical performances put on by amateurs or professionals. The king had set aside for their use the foyer of the San Carlo opera house; the president of the Academy was chosen from among the gentlemen of the king's chamber and took orders only and exclusively from the king and from the Minister of the Interior. Members of the Academy must belong to the families of the nobility who were allowed admittance to the great balls of the Royal Palace—families like the Padellanis. It was a way of satisfying the upper classes' demand for entertainment and culture and at the same time of keeping an eye on them, a way of reinforcing the government's isolationism, as well as keeping at arm's length from the kingdom the dangerously modern political and artistic ferment of mainland Europe. That evening the cousins had invited their friends from the Academy, to show their parents what they had learned, as if it were a recital.

Agata went downstairs to the *piano nobile* in the early afternoon to help out with preparations for the dance; she helped her cousins to dress, put on their makeup, select the right jewelry for their gowns, and make sure that the refreshments had been properly laid out and that everything was in order in the drawing rooms. She was thrilled and there wasn't a shade of envy in her excitement. She was ashamed of her own clothing and didn't expect to take part in the festivities; her dark dress clashed with the colorful costumes of the other girls, and she was afraid that she didn't know how to dance as well as they did. The guests arrived, beaming; she stayed in the background, out of the way, and before the dancing began she found a place in the venerable old musicians' loggia; the loggia, transformed into an alcove with curtains, was used every Christmas for a magnificent mechanical manger scene with streams and fountains with running water. She admired the guests contentedly. She loved the elegance of Neapolitan youth, so knowing and far more self-assured than the young people of Messina, and she was also happy to see how many foreigners there were: Swiss officers in the Royal Army and civilians of various nationalities. The young people from the Academy danced both the quadrille and modern dances with equal mastery, under the severe gazes of Aunt Clementina and her husband and of other married couples of parents who had little patience for modernity but, eager as they were to marry of their daughters, could ill afford to swim entirely against the current.

Transported by the music, Agata began to sketch out the steps of each dance while dreaming of her Giacomo. They were dancing a waltz. Agata lifted her arms as if they were wrapped around the shoulders of an invisible gallant escort, she arched her back and raised her head, chin held high, sliding back her left foot to make room for the right foot of her imaginary gentleman in the first movement of the waltz. She executed a pirouette, whirling and spinning, her back increasingly arched, then she stood erect and resumed the slower step, wreathed in smiles.

And so she was smiling when James Garson saw her. His curiosity aroused by the sound of tapping heels that came from the alcove, he had gone over to take a peep behind the curtain. Agata came to a sudden halt, in embarrassed confusion. He made his way carefully into the alcove and pulled the curtain shut behind him. Then he wrapped his arm around her waist, slipped his other hand between her fingers, and they resumed the dance that had been interrupted. Agata's foot, hesitantly, struck his longer foot. Just once. Then they danced slowly and in perfect time, managing even to pirouette in that cramped, confined space.

The music came to an end. "Thank you," he said to her. They were still standing, still in position for the dance.

"Go," she replied, without attempting to unravel their fingers. James lifted her hand and grazed her knuckles with a feathery kiss. Then he turned and left. The pianist had begun playing again and Agata went on dancing until the soirée ended. She was dancing with her Giacomo, with renewed transport.

That night, Agata had her first carnal dream, and she abandoned herself to it.

7.

Preparations for the wedding of Anna Carolina Padellani;
Agata instead receives a tray of pastries
from her aunt the abbess

Donna Gesuela had entered a phase of frantic activity.
With the help of Tommaso Aviello, she had completed
in record time the procedures involved in paying Anna
Carolina's dowry and she had set the date for the wedding on
the first day compatible with the liturgical calendar, immediately after Easter, in Naples. It was necessary to make sure that
there was no way for the Carnevale family to wriggle out of its
commitment, and with a view to nailing them down securely,
she decided to take the promised bride to Messina immediately and to stay there right up to the eve of the wedding. Agata
could go and stay with Aunt Orsola, who had generously asked
her stepson Michele to let them use the chapel and the drawing rooms of Palazzo Padellani to hold the religious function
and the wedding reception.

Agata wasn't thinking about anything other than her wedding, and she was happy to go stay with her aunt. Spring had
come early and in the mornings her aunt took her by carriage
down to the Marina, the Naples waterfront where she treated
Agata to pastries and ice cream. In the afternoons, she was permitted to sit at a corner of the table where her aunt unfailingly
played cards every day. The Princess of Opiri was under the
spell of cards: along with religion and opera, cards were her
guiding passion. Her Wednesdays were devoted to whist.

James Garson, who was likewise on the verge of being married, was a frequent visitor to the Princess's salons.

Agata listened to the conversations at the card tables and during refreshments and absorbed everything she heard like a sponge: through the assortment of gossip and the occasional anecdote, she was able to get glimpses of a larger political, commercial, and artistic world. She was burning with the desire to have her say, but she was ashamed to speak out. Once, Admiral Pietraperciata, noticing a gleam in her eye, asked her to express her view—they had been talking about the fact that Jane Austen published her entire body of work anonymously. Agata blushed, then looked around at the others sitting at the table: Aunt Orsola was studying her cards; Aunt Clementina, caught off guard, shot a glare at the admiral and then focused at her hand of cards; James Garson in contrast was waiting for her to speak, his eyes looking straight into hers. Once again, that gaze made Agata hesitant, but then she spoke with growing confidence.

That night Agata was euphoric when she went to bed, her cheeks burning and her heart pounding furiously. The conversation had been stimulating that evening, and for the first time she had savored the pleasure of meeting minds and comparing views with refined, educated people. After saying her prayers, her thoughts turned to Giacomo. She felt as if she could see his dark handsome face, his fleshy lips, and she realized that in Messina a conversation of that kind and on that level would have been unthinkable, especially in the Lepre household. With a faint sigh, she resolved that there was no alternative but to follow her beloved to Sicily, so that's what she would do. She fell asleep trying to guess who her aunt's partners at cards would be the next day.

Her aunt allowed her to visit with Sandra, even though her mother had fought with her again over money. Tommaso Aviello claimed that his mother-in-law had been more generous with Amalia and Giulia, when she'd dismantled the family home in Messina, because they were married to men of whom she approved, while he was merely useful to her in taking care of her business. Sandra took her husband's side in the argument.

At their home, Agata met young men who were quivering with passion for the Italian cause. She listened to them in admiration and did her best to understand what had lit that flame in their eyes, what made them willing to sacrifice themselves. Then, when she was alone, she knew that she had no desire to emulate them, she would be unwilling to sacrifice her life for anyone but Giacomo.

The months of February and March, which she spent in her aunt Orsola's home, were perhaps the most peaceful period in Agata's life.

Her mother and Anna Carolina had returned from Messina with Carmela and Annuzza at the beginning of April, three weeks before the wedding. They astonished Agata with their decision to stay at the Aviello apartment—Donna Gesuela had made peace with them now—leaving Agata with her aunt. Agata's feelings were hurt; she wished that she could stay with her sisters, especially with Carmela to whom she had been a sort of substitute mother in the past. Then she decided not to take it personally: after Anna Carolina's wedding, it would be her turn.

Her fond hopes however were soon cruelly dashed. Amalia sent her mother a letter to say that there had been a furious quarrel in the Lepre home, and that all Messina had known about it immediately because of the sheer volume of the shouting. Giacomo had been the loser in that fight: shortly after Easter he would be engaged to the heiress that the family had already chosen for him. Simultaneously, another letter arrived from Giacomo, addressed to Donna Gesuela, assuring her that he had no intention of giving up. He greatly preferred to live in poverty with Agata and he implored her to consent to their wedding, now that he had come of legal age.

Agata was crocheting, tatting a simple cotton lace for a hand towel. Her mother burst into the room and stood furiously in front of her, waving the two letters in her face: "Read them!"

Agata inserted the crochet hook into the ball of fine cotton yarn and took the letters. First she read the letter from her sister. Then she opened the letter from Giacomo. It was very short: not a word to her. She looked up at her mother, dry-eyed but aghast.

"Do you understand what that miserable scoundrel has done to you?!" her mother spat out.

"He wants to marry me." Agata's voice was trembling.

"Oh, certainly, he wants to marry you, but how does he expect to support you? Who'll pay for rent, groceries, and servants? What about your children, how would he feed them?" By asking Donna Gesuela for an impossible marriage, Giacomo had offended both her and her daughter. She inveighed against him: he was cunning, dimwitted, childish, and wrong-headed. Agata defended him and there ensued a scene that came close to deteriorating into an actual brawl. Agata's entire body was trembling as she sat in a pool of silent tears; her mother, leaning over her, continued to upbraid her, lifting Agata's chin so that she could spit the harsh truth into her face.

The next day, a package arrived for Agata. Inside it was a little gold box, inscribed on the inside with her and Giacomo's initials. Along with the box was a card made of glossy paper, its edges perforated like a piece of lace, and decorated with little red hearts, tiny colorful flowers, golden leaves, and a gleaming ribbon; at the center, a rosette with two robin redbreasts, their beaks joined in a kiss. Giacomo wrote exactly what he had written to her mother: they would be married, provided that Agata would wait for him and remain faithful to him. Agata believed him.

A few days before the wedding, Donna Gesuela was invited to lunch with her sister-in-law; she arrived early, and Orsola had not yet returned home. She was in a good mood, she seemed years younger, and she gathered Agata up in an impetuous hug. Shortly thereafter, the footman announced a visitor for Signorina Agata.

A woman in servant's clothing entered the room hesitantly with a large pastry tray in her hands: "Are you Signorina Agata?" When Agata nodded, she stood straight and recited, word for word, the message that she had memorized: "Madame Abbess, Donna Maria Crocifissa, your aunt, sends you her best wishes and wishes to inform you that the Chapter of the Benedictine convent of San Giorgio Stilita has voted unanimously in favor of your admission." At that point, she stopped, visibly satisfied, and then went on with the easier part of the message: "Please come, then, to say thanks to the nuns and to set the day for your entry."

This was Nina, the chambermaid of the other aunt who lived in that convent, Donna Maria Brigida. She extended the pastry tray with a broad smile. Agata accepted the tray uncertainly; she was about to venture a "you must be mistaken," when her mother burst in vehemently: "Please thank Madame Abbess on my part and on behalf of my daughter. Tell her that the young sister will be conveyed to the convent this very afternoon." She gestured with one arm for the woman to leave by the front door, and she shut that door firmly behind her with her own hands after she left, before the eyes of the astonished footman and a petrified Agata. Then, with a chilly hand, she seized her daughter's arm and dragged Agata, against her will, into her bedroom.

Sprawled across the sofa at the foot of the bed, Agata was wailing in despair, until her voice grew hoarse and raucous. The footmen buzzed around in the adjoining rooms and outside the door, unsure whether they should intervene. Agata begged not to be forced into the nunnery. Standing in front of her, Donna Gesuela was implacable. Then she glanced at the clock: it was almost time for lunch, her sister-in-law was about to return home. She wiped her daughter's eyes with her handkerchief and explained that the family's straitened finances and her behavior with Giacomo—she had learned of the gift of the little box with their initials—left her no alternative: Agata must become a nun. Admiral Pietraperciata would help her to find the money for her monastic dowry.

"Life is good in the convent, you'll be with the crème de la crème of the nobility, and you'll never go hungry. In the meanwhile, I want to entrust you to your aunts, while I hunt for other pensions. They'll coddle you, and the cloistered life will calm your heart." Between sobs, Agata continued to beg her to change her mind. Her mother grew tense. She told Agata that her father had left her without a dowry, without even a guardian, and that she was responsible for her fate and the fate of her sisters: "The laws of man and God demand obedience, and obey me you will." Agata fell silent. Gesuela seemed to grow gentler; she promised Agata that if she still didn't like the convent after two months, she'd take her back home to live with her. For the moment, she couldn't refuse to go, not after the vote of the full Chapter, which had been a great honor. Agata was aghast.

Her mother reached out and took one of her braids in her hand, stroking it, while she explained the benefits of the monastic life to her: it was an oasis of health, uncontaminated by the squalor of ordinary life, and every generation of Padellanis had given a number of nuns to San Giorgio Stilita. Agata would win honors, she would be revered, and without doubt in time they would elect her abbess. At these words, the girl only began sobbing harder. Her mother shook the braid as if it were a noose, then pulled Agata toward her, lifted her chin, and gazed into her eyes: they were bloodshot. She couldn't take her to the convent in that state.

Stung, she shoved her roughly away from her, warning her not to come down for meals or dare to sniff out another tear: "Look out! If I find you in the same state tomorrow, I'll take you anyway, and I'll introduce you to all the nuns as the little ingrate that you are."

Agata spent the rest of the day in her bedroom. She hoped that her aunt Orsola might pay a call on her, but not even she, in compliance with her mother's orders, dared to knock on her niece's door. She sent lunch and dinner up to her on a tray; Agata noticed that on a little dish on the side were her favorite almond biscotti. That's when she understood that there was nothing left to be done—no one would take up for her against her mother.

8

April 20, 1840.
Reluctantly, Agata goes to visit
the convent of San Giorgio Stilita

E arly the next morning, mother and daughter left Palazzo Padellani for the convent of San Giorgio Stilita. Aunt Orsola had ordered the most sumptuous carriage to be brought out, the one painted blue with the pure gold Padellani coat of arms on both doors and on the back. Donna Gesuela had ordered ice packs to be placed on Agata's eyes and cheeks; the swelling of her face had visibly diminished. "Just a short visit, then you can come home," she said encouragingly, "and remember to thank them for the pastries. Oh, you'll have plenty of pastries to eat in the convent." Then she repeated the promise to her once again: if she didn't like the monastic life, she could leave the convent two months after she entered it, which would be immediately after Anna Carolina's wedding.

The entrance to the convent was through a wooden door that stood at the bottom of a long staircase, designed to be accessible to sedan chairs. Agata took her time climbing the stairs. Every one of the thirty-three steps in volcanic piperno stone, broad and low though they were, seemed dauntingly high, and she had difficulty lifting her feet. Still, she had to go on, and go on she did, her mother's hand gripping her shoulder like a vise grip. She was already a prisoner. On her left stood the outer walls of the convent—high, double, and blank. On her right, the wall covered with delicate eighteenth-century frescoes of faux colonnades and coiling leaves, which she'd found so pleasing on previous visits, now instilled terror in her. She thought that she could detect amidst the fronds the pale and faded figures of Basilian nuns, flickering like ghosts, ready to cast a spell on her.

They reached the vestibule. There wasn't a living soul in sight. The nun at the door told them to wait. The bronze wheel right in front of Agata looked like a mouth bristling with teeth, ready to devour her. Slowly, the majestic carved walnut portal swung open and her aunt the abbess emerged to welcome her. Through the grilles in the convent parlor, Agata had been unable to form any idea of her face, and now she turned pale at the sight: her aunt had her father's exact features and even the same wart on the chin. The abbess embraced her and kissed her heartily, then she pushed her into the cloistered section of the convent through a little hidden door, camouflaged by other frescoes of leaves and columns. They walked into a spacious second vestibule with vast wall paintings, where thirty or so nuns were waiting for them, standing in a semicircle. Other nuns were assembling in the large room—all eyes were on Agata, motionless before them, at the center of the semicircle.

"Thank the sisters for the favor they have shown by voting for you to become their companion," the abbess spoke sternly to her.

Donna Gesuela thanked the sisters on Agata's behalf, explaining that her daughter was emotionally overwrought with gratitude. Agata could barely restrain her sobs. In the meanwhile, other nuns arrived in the hall and lined up in rows of two or three. They were quite different from the nuns of the Collegio di Maria where Agata had gone to school. Sumptuously dressed in black, with a pleated white wimple and two veils, a white one beneath a black one, impeccably ironed, they had an air of superiority that terrified Agata. The novices entered, the *monachelle* or little nuns: some of them stood on chairs to get a better look at her, and while her mother and the abbess were talking with the most important nuns, they did nothing but make comments on Agata, who had good hearing and understood everything they said—some thought she was short, some pretty, some ugly, and some unlikable. Until then, she had followed her mother like a puppet, looking straight ahead of her; when she heard those opinions, she lowered her eyes and felt as if she were going to faint. Her mother explained to all the new arrivals that her daughter was very sad because her father had died and she had been separated from her family. Then she turned to look at Agata with an imperious glare, ordering her to speak. But she couldn't.

At that moment, the other aunt, Donna Maria Brigida, arrived in the room; two lay sisters were supporting her. Younger than the abbess, she was afflicted with infirmities of body and mind. She raised her weary pupils and stared at Agata. "You're the daughter of Pippineddu," she mumbled, and reached out her arms to embrace her. The lay sisters carried her toward Agata and her mother pushed her toward her aunt; Donna Maria Brigida wrapped both arms around her neck, rasping her flesh with her hairy chin.

Agata trembled and felt a chill. She murmured words of gratitude. After coming to an agreement that she would enter the convent two days after Anna Carolina's wedding, mother and daughter left the cloistered section of the convent.

At Aunt Orsola's house, aunts and female cousins were waiting to congratulate her. When they saw her they were aghast.

Agata stayed in bed for a number of days, during which time she received visits from all the Padellani women, who were again interested in her—not in helping her, but in persuading her to accept her fate and then, later, to gossip viciously with the rest of the family about both mother and daughter.

Aunt Orsola, who had spent hours talking with her, was

worried about Agata's health, because she had stopped eating. Agata, certain that she was ready for marriage and motherhood, explained to Aunt Orsola the repulsion she felt at the thought of the cloistered life, and she recalled her father's firm determination not to force any of his daughters into a nunnery. Once she heard this, and seeing the depression into which her niece had sunk, the elderly princess decided that Agata would never be willing to take the habit; she then devised a plan to marry her off to a widowed duke, a relation of hers, who would have accepted her even without a dowry. She mentioned the plan to her sister-in-law. Donna Gesuela had watched her various female relations paying visits and she had listened to their comments—both those spoken openly and those muttered under their breaths. She had always managed to contain her fury; only now did she vent her wrath against Orsola, accusing her and all the Padellanis with her of miserliness, hypocrisy, and even lack of Christian charity toward her and her daughters. She threw it in Orsola's face that, when she had asked her for financial assistance in order to secure dowries for her daughters, the Padellanis had refused. Every last one of them. Now that she had been forced to send one of her daughters into a nunnery, they criticized her—and still no one offered her so much as a ducat.

Anna Carolina had kept her distance from Agata. A few days before the wedding she went to see her and, after treating her like a perfect stranger, told Agata that even in Messina everyone was talking about how selfish and ungrateful it was not to be overjoyed at having been accepted into the most illustrious convent in the kingdom, and that this would certainly undermine her relations with her husband's family. None of the married sisters, including Sandra, offered an opinion or said a comforting word: they didn't want to interfere with their mother's will.

One day, Nora managed to smuggle her a letter from Giacomo. He had given it to Annuzza, who was not allowed to go to Palazzo Padellani because she was dressed as a commoner and not as a maidservant. It was a saint card of Our Lady of the Assumption with his signature and nothing more. Agata, during all this time, believed that Giacomo had forgotten about her; the feeling that he'd remembered her with that special message was enormously upsetting to her. She felt ill and a doctor had to be called.

Agata remembered when she sang for her father his favorite Bellini, *Qual Cor Tradisti, Qual Cor Perdesti*, but now as in some delirium, it seemed as if she were hearing the reply of her Giacomo-Pollione:

> *Moriamo insieme, ah, sì, moriamo!*
> *L'estremo accento sarà ch'io t'amo.*[1]

She was visibly wasting away. Aunt Orsola sent for Father Cuoco, her confessor, and after he had a conversation with Agata, she decided to talk it over with her brother. The two of them came up with a plan. The admiral spoke to Agata alone and made a suggestion without having discussed it first with Donna Gesuela. Agata would go to the convent for the two months agreed upon; if at the end of that period she still didn't want to become a nun, he would give her a thousand ducats, half of her dowry. All she had to do was ask. Agata could use the money for any purpose, provided that she explain clearly to him what she intended to do. Agata accepted.

Aunt Orsola thought that Agata would recover more quickly if she were far away from her mother. She therefore suggested to her sister-in-law that she leave her daughter with her and go back to Messina immediately after the wedding;

---

[1] *Let us die together, Yes, let us die: / My last word will be that I love you.*

Donna Gesuela accepted the proposal willingly. It was what she would have preferred in any case. Still, the princess had another objective in mind: to break up the growing intimacy between her sister-in-law and her brother the admiral. She suspected that in the past he had facilitated certain of Gesuela's escapades and she was afraid that now he wanted his part and might run afoul of her. Gesuela wanted a husband: she wanted a husband at all costs. Orsola did not know that the one limitation her brother had placed on his generous gift—that he be informed as to the use of the money, but only by Agata, not by her mother, who was excluded from the transaction—had resulted in a violent argument between the admiral and Donna Gesuela, and that from then on their friendship had never been the same.

9.

The wedding of Anna Carolina Padellani and Fidenzio Carnevale

The week before Anna Carolina's wedding, Aunt Orsola had given Agata the use of a carriage to take Carmela and Annuzza on outings; she hoped that would brighten Agata's last days before being admitted into the convent. It wasn't hard: Agata was proud to show the two around her father's city, the only metropolis in the Italian peninsula.

She took them down to the waterfront, where they could watch seagoing vessels with foreign travelers, and every so often even an English yacht with mechanical propulsion touring the city and the excavations at Pompeii. She dreamed of setting sail on one of those luxury yachts to explore the world, while Carmela dreamed of winning the heart of the yacht's wealthy owner. Carmela loved those excursions. Annuzza, on the other hand, wasn't a bit happy to be in Naples. Agata would treat her to a cup of ice cream, and she would complain that they didn't serve it with a pastry the way they did in Messina. The carriages traveled too fast and the traffic was too chaotic. Even the Neapolitan vegetables, according to Annuzza, were inferior to the Swiss chard and the borage of Messina, so much fresher and more succulent.

One day, the carriage passed beneath the underpass of the bell tower of the convent of San Giorgio Stilita. Annuzza, finally impressed, asked who the owner of that fine building might be. Agata shuddered and changed the subject. Then she refused to say anything more. A short while later she ordered the coachman to stop at a candlemaker's shop so that she could buy Carmela a candle in the shape of an angel. Annuzza ogled, with a blend of curiosity and fear, the massive enclosure wall without windows or openings of any kind. Agata chose to ignore her: she had decided not to think about the coming two months. Comforted by Admiral Pietraperciata's promise and reassured as to Giacomo's love, she was convinced that she would leave the convent and be married immediately.

The wedding of Anna Carolina and Fidenzio Carnevale was necessarily intimate because of the period of mourning; it needed to be elegant in order to make a good impression on the Carnevales; and there were only a few very select guests, in order to facilitate the groom's family's foreign contacts, as the Carnevales were agents for a number of Sicilian sulfur mines. After the clash with the king in 1837, when British frigates had threatened to halt all the kingdom's maritime shipping, the English had become the uncontested arbiters of sulfur exports. For that reason, Aunt Orsola, with her brother's help, had invited a number of Englishmen, one of whom was James Garson.

Anna Carolina was the picture of happiness: she cut quite a figure in her taffeta wedding gown with bouquets of pink flowers, wearing her slippers with buckles glittering with paste diamonds. In order to appear more attractive, she had put drops of atropine in her eyes: through her dilated pupils in the center of her light chestnut irises, she could only make out a blurry field of sight, but she felt enchantingly beautiful, and that's how she looked to Fidenzio—a dark-haired young man with an impeccably groomed mustache—who only had eyes for his blushing bride. Their cousin the prince had outdone himself as the master of the house, and the nuptial banquet table surprised and delighted the Carnevales. The table was illuminated by six enormous Renaissance candelabra, each with eight arms, made of chased silver, set on mirrored trays that reflected their light upward onto an eighteenth-century chandelier in Murano glass, resembling a sailing ship with a thousand bellying sails. The banquet table's centerpiece was formed by a series of silver statuettes alternating with crystal fruit stands piled high with bonbons and candied almonds, made by the sisters of Santa Patrizia. Crystal dishes and goblets had a 24-karat gold rim with the Padellani coat of arms.

At their mother's orders, Agata and Carmela were dressed in mourning. The day before, Annuzza had brought Agata another letter from Giacomo in which he assured her that the next wedding to be celebrated would be theirs. The stubbornness of a fourteen-year-old girl in love, her natural optimism, her desire to enjoy life, inherited from her father, and the pigheaded determination she'd inherited from her mother all made Agata certain that she'd get what she wanted. That morning she had curled her hair into large soft ringlets and she had pinned three pink camellias she'd picked on her aunt's terrace, tied up with a tulle ribbon: she *felt* engaged. At the sight of her, her mother felt a wave of gloom; for her, sending her daughter to a nunnery was an admission of defeat, but she had no other options.

The wedding luncheon was almost over. The guests were still drinking and, their hunger satiated, they ate sweets and pastries and crunched the last candied almonds. Seated between her cousins Severina and Eleonora, Agata felt a stab of sadness: she thought of her father. Her gaze wandered somberly over the table and the guests; then it chanced to light on James Garson, sitting far down the table from her, among the guests who were not family members. With his golden beard and whiskers, and dressed in the uniform of the British navy, dark blue with gold braid, he was handsome; all the girls at the table were giving him sidelong glances of admiration. He was just lifting a forkful of cake to his mouth and he stopped, fork and cake suspended in midair, but Agata's eye had already glided along to the guest seated next to him.

It was the time for farewells. Moving adroitly and wending his way through the guests, James managed to find her standing by a window. Agata seemed happy to see him. Through their shared tastes in books, the two had established a semblance of intimate complicity.

"I'll be leaving in two weeks," he said. "My wedding is in June."

"You must be very happy," said Agata in a gentle voice.

His gaze seemed to harden. "I just hope that I'll enjoy as much happiness as I saw on the faces of bride and groom today," then he added: "I wish you all happiness, wherever you may be."

Agata turned pale: then he knew about the convent. At that moment, Carmela drew closer to her and slipped her hand in Agata's, trusting. Agata squeezed her hand and, looking down, murmured a meek thank you.

10.
May 11th, 1840.
Agata enters the convent of San Giorgio Stilita

I t was May 11, 1840. Agata got dressed for the last time in the bedroom that for nine weeks had been her home in the house of her Aunt Orsola. She looked disconsolately at the wrought-iron bed, the little round mahogany table with the single foot in the shape of a column, the boudoir vanity with the adjustable mirror and the chaise longue that had kept her company through good times and bad. She buttoned up her bodice and draped the peignoir over her shoulders so she could finish fixing her hair. She had curled it into the usual ringlets, but bigger than usual. Her mother had walked silently into the room and was watching her from the door.

"Have you gone mad? The idea of going into the convent with curls!" She was to be admitted to the convent with straight hair, her aunt the abbess had been quite specific. For once, Agata refused to obey; she pointed out to her that she would be going into the monastery for just two months, not as a convent schoolgirl and not even as a postulant. She intended to leave her hair the way it was. In response, her mother said nothing but grabbed the comb and brusquely straightened out her curls for her. Agata was about to try to stop her; then she glimpsed a tear on her mother's face and she lowered her hand. Her eyes riveted on the face she saw reflected in the mirror the whole time, Agata witnessed the destruction of her ringlets. She allowed her mother to twist her hair into a bun and pin it up to the nape of her neck, and as she watched her she struggled to hold back her tears. That was when her eyes began to become bloodshot. Her mother had brought a black veil, just as a precaution, and after carefully placing pins and clips, she placed it on Agata's head, covering her face in silence.

Admiral Pietraperciata, who had close ties with the Catholic curia, and Ortensia, the wife of their cousin the prince, accompanied the two women to the convent of San Giorgio Stilita. Agata had said goodbye to Aunt Orsola and the servants without even a shade of emotion. As soon as she got into the carriage, she opened the floodgates of sobs and that was how she arrived at the convent.

It was as if the abbess and the two nuns who were waiting for them had known in advance that Agata would arrive in tears. The nuns took her, removed her shawl and her veil before she had a chance to object and then pushed her, gripping her by the arms, through the Chapter Hall, the passageways, and a short flight of stairs, until they reached the choir. There they forced her to kneel before the gilt wooden railing that faced the nave of the church. Agata leaned her forehead against the wood and went on weeping.

"Don't cry, enjoy it: look at this marvel!" one nun told her. "Thank the Lord that he has brought you to this garden of salvation!" added another. "Ingrate!" muttered a third, seeing that Agata was reluctant.

The billowing scent of incense rose thick and pungent from the main altar. Looking down, the white and dark-blue tiles of the church's majolica floor glittered, as did the gold stucco of the walls and cornices. Agata prayed to God to give her the strength to stay in that place for the two months to which she had agreed, and she slowly regained her calm. She tried to stand up, and she found herself surrounded. Someone asked her if she liked the choir, someone else congratulated her on her sister's wedding, someone asked her how old she was, and many, many voices repeated the rhetorical question: "Don't you want to become a nun? Don't you want to become a nun?" Her two guardians dragged her away from the choir without giving her a chance to answer—the abbess was expecting her.

The abbess's drawing room, redecorated in the eighteenth century, was cluttered with furniture, paintings, and ornaments: in the long succession of abbesses, every one of them had tried to leave a tangible sign of their presence there. Agata recovered as she ate the biscotti and drank the lemonade that she had been given. She looked around her, curiously. "Come, then, say farewell to your mother," the abbess gently told her. "Now I'm going to call two novices, members of the Padellani family of Uttino, relations of yours, and they'll show you around. Then I'll join you and show you the rest of the convent."

The "little nuns" were first cousins, and they looked alike as two peas in a pod: close-lipped with olive complexions and aquiline noses. They had the same voice—low and shrill. They started their tour with the cloister, which was reached through the large carved wooden portal. The cloister was rectangular and split into two sections—one part a flower garden, the other an orchard and vegetable garden—by an exedra decorated with statues in stucco and clay. At that time of day it seemed deserted. Four symmetrical beds surrounded the monumental fountain—round and made of white marble, with mascarons, dolphins, and sea horses—that dominated the garden. Standing in front of the fountain and facing visitors were two statues: Christ and the Samaritan Woman—larger than life and leaning toward one another, the Christ ready to step forward and the Samaritan Woman coyly reserved, as if they were engaged in a gallant conversation. Those statues were completely devoid of any spiritual content, and would have been much better suited to an aristocratic *palazzo* or villa.

Everything was magnificent, ornate, and rich. The corridors, with piperno-stone arches and cross vaults, supported spacious majolica-tiled terraces, overlooked by the French doors of the luminous second-story cells. Those were the most desirable cells. The third-story cells had equally large French doors, but they only featured narrow balconies. In the orchard and vegetable garden, on the far side of the elegant exedra, orange, lemon, and other fruit trees grew; in the beds, greens, vegetables, aromatic and medicinal herbs were cultivated.

While they were showing Agata around, the two young girls chattered about altar boys and father confessors, using much the same language that Agata's cousins, the Tozzi girls, used when they talked about their beaus.

Suddenly the bells rang Terce. The young nuns fell silent. The cloister began to fill with black-clad figures; they scurried out of every staircase and door and walked rustling down the porticoed corridors, striding past her and hurrying into the little wooden door that led to the lower floor and to the *comunichino*, the little window through which the nuns took their communion. Agata wanted to be alone; she took advantage of the situation and offered to wait for her guides in the choir, so that they could attend Terce with the others. "Oh it doesn't matter, we can hear it from here," the two young girls reassured her, and they threw open one of the six arched doors that lined the south side of the cloister: on the other side was an alcove with a grated window and side seats, from which it was possible to see the nave and the main altar. The church of San Giorgio Stilita, seen from above, was a magnificent sight. The paintings in the chapels across the way, the stuccoes, the volutes, the putti, and the white-and-gold wreaths of flowers and fruit on the pillars and walls seemed stunningly close,

while the white marble altar, illuminated by eight silver candelabra, was like an island of light. Agata held her breath. From
the stone seats, the novices listened to the prayers with com-
punction.

When they returned, the nuns stopped to greet Agata. For
the most part, they were young and cheerful. "Don't you want
to become a nun?" was once again the question on everyone's
lips, and in response to Agata's repeated "no"—sometimes
immediate, at times terse, occasionally accompanied by a vigorous shake of the head, other times harsh and grim—they
laughed and added that Agata would soon change her mind.
When the throng of nuns had passed, Agata felt her cheeks
burning. The young sisters told her that the two of them had
entered the convent together, at the age of eight, and that they
were happy. They said nothing more, though, because now the
abbess was approaching. With a simple nod of the head she
intimated that they could go.

"Let's start with the kitchens," the abbess decreed, and she
leaned on Agata's arm. Agata extended her arm to the abbess
and instantly felt completely at ease with her father's sister. The
two were both the same height, one slender, the other stout,
but they soon fell into step.

Behind a pomegranate tree there were some workshops; in
one, various kinds of flour were being milled, in the other,
bread dough was being prepared. The first room in the
kitchens was a succession of wood-burning ovens, identical
and numbered. On the shorter wall were two ovens, both
much larger than the others. On a stone in the wall that had
been left uncovered, a phrase was carved in crude letters: "The
second week of December bread is not to be made: the large
and small ovens belong to Madame the Abbess." The abbess
pointed it out to Agata; it was an inscription from the previous
century. She added, with slight irony: "Even then they dis-

obeyed the abbess, if the poor thing had to carve it into stone!" Then she turned serious: "Work and prayer: that's the life of a Benedictine nun. Here our work is to make sweets and pastries, to be sold or given as gifts. It's hard work, if it's done right and conscientiously." Agata saw a gleam in her aunt's eyes: "When I was younger, I would commandeer all the ovens just to bake ricotta tarts for my relatives!"

They were walking through the Chapter Hall, on their way to the choir. The abbess was explaining to her that the nuns were self-governing and that in a certain sense that was their parliament: here they deliberated on admissions, such as Agata's, with votes that involved secret balloting. Then the abbess added with pride that in the old days, when male monasteries and female convents coexisted in the same building, it was the abbess who enjoyed seniority of command over the abbot, and not the other way around.

That second tour of the choir made quite an impression on Agata. It was a vast square room, with a majolica-tile floor, and it was built over the portico of the church. It communicated with the church through a gilded wooden grate with diagonal openings, embellished by tiny scrollwork that reproduced a floral motif. Like the grate in the parlor, this wooden grate made the nuns invisible to the congregation. It also fragmented their view of the church, preventing them from having a complete picture. The two levels of stalls were decorated with exquisite wooden intarsias and could seat two hundred nuns. At the center stood a podium for the abbess, who was thoroughly enjoying the sight of her niece's astonishment at such lavish grandeur. "I thank God for making me a nun," the abbess said. "Here we sing the entire Book of Psalms every week. Every day we praise the Lord, beginning with the Nocturnal Office and continuing with Matins, the prayers of Prime, Terce, Sext, and None, Vespers, and finally Compline."

Just then, the bell rang and the nuns—hands joined, eyes lowered, dressed in habits with flowing sleeves—were taking their places silently in the stalls. Pressed back against the wall next to the holy water fount, Agata observed. At a sign from the abbess, the nuns began singing a cappella in a single clear, pure, incorporeal voice. Faces that were wrinkled or fresh, hollowed out or pudgy, all diaphanous and impassive. Eyes focused on the glittering silver and gold of the altar, soft lips opening and closing in unison like the mouths of the living corals of a reef—it was wonderful singing. Agata was sorry when the nuns began filing out of the choir, as silently as they'd entered, two by two: they lowered their heads before the abbess and then they kneeled in the direction of the altar below them.

The abbess took Agata up onto the catwalks that ran from the choir, extending just below the roof along the entire perimeter of the church—these were narrow corridors, lit by double skylights set in the roof. On the wall overlooking the nave there were alcoves with grilles made of gilded wood. Through these, the nuns could watch the Mass and enjoy an uninterrupted view of the church. Along the outer walls, on the other hand, the abbesses belonging to the families of the sees of Capuana and Nido had built little altar shrines embellished with needlepoint, silverwork, enamels, statuettes, paintings, and crucifixes, all for their own personal use. They had thus vacuously emphasized the dynastic power and might of their families. Those luminous and airy parapets seemed more than anything else a place of regret, not of prayer: up there, alone, unseen by the congregation, a patrician nun would remember her family's love and be tormented by worldly concerns. Her aunt the abbess showed her the little altars of the other Padellani abbesses and went on at length with stories of the family's power and piety. Agata was sweating and her eyes were burning, as if from the grains of windblown sand tossed by the sirocco wind that was flowing down through the sky-lights on the roof, enveloping her and immobilizing her. At that moment, and for the first time, Agata perceived, as if it were corporeal, the haughty solitude of the cloistered life.

11.
The grueling two months of probation

More than once, during the long first day at the convent of San Giorgio Stilita, Agata had consoled herself with the thought that at least when night came she would finally be left alone. She was stunned when she was told that instead she would be sleeping with the abbess. In compliance with the Benedictine Rule, the abbess's living quarters consisted of a bare space, a bed without a headboard, and an enormous built-in armoire where the chorister nuns kept the silver of the monastic dowries; it opened out onto the spacious majolica-tiled terrace atop the arches of the cloister, where two rows of large terra cotta vases planted with orange trees, camellia plants, and jasmine trees created a private space. A bed had been brought in for Agata and placed at the foot of her aunt's bed, next to the pallet of one of her two lay sisters, Angiola Maria—a hulking middle-aged woman with sharply defined features—while the other lay sister, Sarina, a tall, skinny young woman with a gentle gaze, slept in the corner next to the bathroom.

The abbess was reciting aspirations at her kneeling-stool. Agata was already under the blankets. The flickering flame of the oil lamp burned faintly all night long and she was having trouble falling asleep. Every time she raised her eyelids she met the gleaming pupils of Angiola Maria, focused straight at her like a pair of charcoal embers. At last, Agata turned over and lay motionless, but still she could feel that unsettling glare on her back.

At dawn, she awoke with a start: bending over her was Angiola Maria, calling her for morning prayers and shoving her with both hands to get her out of bed. From that day forward the lay sister bestowed upon the niece of her beloved mistress all her uncouth solicitudes.

The first week went by quickly and not altogether agreeably. The abbess had given her a number of religious and monastic books to read. In the evening, after None and before Compline, she waited for Agata in the cloister. In the lengthening shadows of day's end, they strolled together in the garden, breathing the scents released by plants and watered earth, and they'd talk. Agata began to feel an intense love for her father's pious sister.

The convent of San Giorgio Stilita was more than a thousand years old and there was a time when it had as many as three hundred nuns, "every one of them with four quarters of nobility," her aunt told her, without any attempt to conceal her caste-pride. The spirit of the Enlightenment in the last century had reduced the number of vocations, and then the Napoleonic military occupation had put an end to admissions entirely for a decade. "But it was unable to destroy the quest for God through the cloistered life," the abbess added, wrinkling her nose slightly, and then she went on to tell Agata that after the Bourbon restoration, in 1815, there was a wave of new callings. The convent had another, secondary cloister, lined with cells not currently in use, and the abbess hoped that one day those cells might be filled with Benedictine nuns.

Many of the eighty professed nuns, the choristers, were young, and the same was true of the one hundred twenty lay sisters—religious who came to the convent from the less prosperous classes of society, many of them illiterate. Because they could not pay the monastic dowry, they had simply taken vows of chastity and poverty and they served a nun of high rank. The lay sisters were excluded from the Divine Office. When the bell rang the canonical hours for prayer, the nuns recited the psalms in the choir, while the lay sisters gathered in the hall outside the *comunichino* and recited together the *Pater*, the *Ave*, and the *Credo*. The humblest manual tasks were assigned to a hundred or so servingwomen—lower-ranking than the lay sisters, likewise dressed in the monastic habit but without the pleated wimple that was worn only by the chorists; these servingwomen did not take vows. Aside from taking care of various domestic chores, the servingwomen left the convent to carry out the orders of the nuns and to run errands. They and the helper nuns were the only residents of the convent who were allowed to go out into the world and have contact with others.

The convent's Chapter had resolved on an exceptional basis to admit Agata not as a *probanda*, that is, for a period of probation—as her mother had told her, and as procedure would normally have dictated—but instead directly as a postulant, the stage prior to that of a novice: just one of the many exceptions that were afforded to members of the leading families of the district. Her aunt the abbess wished to make it clear to her that, once she became a professed nun, she could obtain any status she liked, choosing among the offices of teacher of novices, cellaress, hebdomadary, herbalist, infirmarian, pharmacist, helper nun, and sacristan.

Now Agata had a cell all to herself on the third floor, in the hallway of the novices; she would be spending part of the day with them. Her first contact with those girls had been fraught and tense. Unwanted or burdensome daughters of the highest Neapolitan aristocracy, these young women were proud of their birth, station, and lineage and they were jealous of the privileges that Agata already enjoyed as the abbess's niece. The novices knew everything about her—while she knew nothing about any of them—and they were ill disposed toward "the Sicilian girl," as they called her, to begin with. There was no other Padellani di Opiri among them, and so Agata was sharply isolated; even worse, the two novices who were cousins of hers were actually members of the cadet branch of the Padellani family, the Counts of Uttino. That side of the family had been feuding for years with the Opiris over certain issues of inheritance, and so the two novices mocked and berated Agata. As if that were not enough, they managed to humiliate her in front of the other girls by alluding to the poverty into which Agata's mother had fallen, and ridiculing her with one insistent question: "Tell us whether the abbess is going to pay your dowry." Agata had reacted with haughty pride and from that day on a relationship of mutual dislike, if not outright hostility, was established. That unfriendliness extended to the other friends of the two Uttino girls, further worsening Agata's isolation.

Agata's aunt had encouraged her to make use of the archives room, which also served as the convent's library. The shelves lining the walls were made of mahogany, as were both the coffered ceiling and the little altar facing the entry door; on that altar an image of the Virgin Mary, set in a carved mahogany frame, was displayed. The most valuable books were protected behind glass doors: psalters, incunabula, and breviaries that had been illuminated by the Benedictines. Agata took refuge in the wooden stalls where she felt she was protected from prying eyes—if there were any eyes to pry: the room was seldom frequented—and spent her time there reading. It was also a way of escaping her companions. Next to the archives were the ovens and the kitchens. The mornings she spent reading were accompanied by the crunchy scent of biscotti, mingled with the musky aroma of freshly waxed mahogany, while in the afternoons—dedicated to Neapolitan ricotta tarts, or *pastiere,* and whatever other baked dishes might be ordered—the distinctive array of smells of cooking foods whetted her appetite. There Agata read happily.

The Benedictine Rule was the scaffolding that supported the larger structure of the Order. In the sixth century, Benedict of Nursia, disgusted by the corruption of the Church of Rome, set out to found an order that would put his followers on the path to God, supporting them along the way by a rigid division of each day and a healthy balance between prayer and physical activity. *Orare est laborare et laborare est orare—To pray is to work and to work is to pray.* Prayer was called *Opus Dei,* the divine office, and it traced the suffering and death of Christ, becoming the very reason for existence of the monastics. Silence was fundamental. During the day silence could be broken during the period of recreation after meals; after Compline, however, it was rigorous. Agata had been quite appreciative of Miss Wainwright's rigid routine and, after her initial dismay, she found the Benedictine structuring of the day into the canonical hours to be somehow reassuring; she was exhilarated by the reading of the Psalms and the *Regula.* And yet, as she looked around, she noticed to her horror that life as it was actually lived in the convent was quite different from the description. The rule of silence was roundly ignored by the nuns in the privacy of their cells and was often broken in the hallways and in the cloister, where there was a subdued hum of whispering; the rules of fasting and plain foods were broken on a daily basis by lavish meals, with multiple courses, sometimes as many as seven dishes on a weekday, and even more on feast days. As for the rule of *ora et labora*—it had become a farce: nuns and novices failed to show up at the hours of prayer, what with one excuse or another, and their chief form of manual labor, aside from embroidery—often making beautiful things in needlepoint for themselves—involved the manufacture of pastries, with the assistance of servants and lay sisters. Agata wondered why the abbess would tolerate all those infractions of the Rule, but she didn't dare to ask about it.

The garden was the responsibility of the kitchen servants and a few lay sisters. The choristers looked down upon gardening with disdain, while Agata loved it; the abbess had given her permission to help Angiola Maria, who was the chief gardener. Each morning, the lay sister gathered herbs and flowers, added a fistful of lavender, and filled a little muslin sachet that she presented to the abbess—and now she made one for Agata, too: from under her shirt, there wafted a fragrant scent all day long. Angiola Maria had truly taken a liking to Agata; she taught her the properties of the medicinal herbs and she never failed to give her gifts of whatever herbs she thought Agata might like: fresh green beans to be eaten uncooked from the garden, pods of tender baby peas, a butterfly imprisoned in a glass flytrap, ladybugs as good luck charms in a jar.

One morning, Agata was walking past the kitchen on her way to the archives room with her perfumed sachet in her hand; Brida, one of the servant cooks, gestured for her to come in. She was a servant who was respected by one and all for her good disposition and her mastery of the culinary arts. Petite in size, she would have looked like a little girl if it weren't for her wrinkled face, but she was a tireless worker: she carried the heaviest pots herself and worked into the small hours to make sure that bread would be baked for the morning meal, often a task that had to be put off to make room for the choristers' pastries. Agata, who had worked in the kitchens as part of the process of her induction, appreciated the woman's straight talk and the way that she worked with a smile on her lips; moreover Brida had a rich repertoire of aspirations for every situation. That day, however, the cook had a grim expression on her face. She said to Agata, without preamble: "I'd advise you to steer clear of Angiola Maria, it'd be better for you, and for everyone else." Agata's feelings were hurt. She remembered that her aunt had recommended that she be courteous with the serving-women but not to be too familiar with them. She gave Brida a scornful glance and continued on her way.

That same day, in the evening, Agata was in bed but she couldn't sleep—she was suffering from a maddening itch on her chest and shoulders. In the silence she heard a subdued sound of people talking. She stepped out into the corridor and followed the noise to the cell from which it was issuing. She looked through the keyhole. A dozen or so novices had removed their habits and were trying out awkward little dance steps in their heavy mannish black leather work boots, preening and posing in their fine linen undergarments adorned with lace, embroidery, and silk ribbons, pointing out details to the other girls. Two of them, perched barefoot on the bed, were talking about life at court and the gossip that they'd heard from their married sisters, and all the while they caressed arms, breasts, and necks; then, with smothered giggles, they lifted their skirts and hoisted their sleeves to show off their naked flesh to long and knowing gazes. Agata was appalled and began walking back to her cell, practically on tiptoe, when she heard a door creak, followed by more giggles. She flattened herself against the wall, her heart in her throat.

The next morning, in the garden, Angiola Maria offered her the usual scented sachet: Agata accepted it and looked up toward the open door of the kitchen with a challenging glare, but she didn't think there was anyone there to see her.

That evening, when she went back to her cell, she found three large cockroaches on the floor—the iridescent kind, black and green, with wings, deeply disgusting—and she shoved them out onto the balcony with tiny, fearful kicks. Then she wept with rage.

There were more and more cockroaches every day. Agata was suspicious of everyone. She had the impression that the novices were exchanging winks when she walked by them. She got into a bitter argument with an especially wealthy novice, who coveted the ambition to become abbess herself one day, and who saw Agata as a rival. She wanted the cell to which Agata had been assigned: she claimed that "the Sicilian girl" had no right to occupy that cell because her monastic dowry had been too scanty to cover the rent—at San Giorgio Stilita in fact the best cells were purchased and enjoyed by the nuns as a sort of annuity—and this novice had begun to incite other young women against her. One evening they ganged up on Agata in a corridor and shoved her into a broom closet. They forced her to kneel on the floor in front of them. They rubbed her cheeks with stalks of stinging nettle and heaped insults upon her. Agata started to feel persecuted. She walked timidly down the hallways and when she entered the archives room, she hurried past the kitchen: she felt as if they were looking daggers at her as she went by.

A short while later, an assistant cook fell sick and Donna Maria Clotilde, the prioress, transferred Agata back to the kitchens, where she had seemed to be reliable and hard-working. This time, Agata detected hostility from the other serving-women and no longer just from Brida. One day she had to lift a pot full of boiling custard; she was given a rag to keep from burning her hand when she grabbed the handle, but it wasn't thick enough. She asked Brida to give her another, and Brida tossed her an even thinner rag, shouting at her to hurry, otherwise the custard would stick to the bottom; in her haste, Agata scorched the palm of her hand and three fingers with the red-hot handle. They had to send her to the Sister Infirmarian, who treated the burn with tormentil root plasters.

That evening, Agata found a sheet of paper nailed to the

inside of her cell door; on it was a drawing of a cross, her name written in crude letters, and a red silk thread wrapped round the pin stuck into the cross in place of Christ. From that day forward, both the cockroaches and the letters stopped, but instead of being relieved, Agata was still more unsettled: she didn't know who had sent her the cockroaches and who had protected her with the exorcism or why.

She was troubled; she felt not the slightest vocation to become a nun and she couldn't wait to leave the convent. June was almost over and she thought more and more about Giacomo.

The heat was oppressive even under the arches of the cloister, which were generally quite cool. The two months were almost up. Her mother had given no sign of coming and the abbess had no idea where she might be. No one in her family had written Agata or come to visit her, as if they had all agreed to turn their backs on her. When July 11th, the last day of the trial period, came and went, Agata was plunged into grim despair. The anonymity of the monastic habit weighed on her. The worldly chatter of the novices repelled her. The rigid schedule of each day unsettled her. She considered herself to be the victim of two clashing outside wills: the family that wanted her to become a nun and the conspiracy of serving-women and novices who wanted her to leave the convent.

Now even the Feast of the Assumption had come and gone, and there was still no sign of her mother. When she remembered the party for the Vara the year before, her intolerance of the cloistered life reached a fever pitch and Agata decided that the time had come to force the abbess's hand. She had read a story about a female saint whose vocation had been strongly discouraged by her family; the young woman wore nun's clothing and prayed all day long, but her parents refused to consent to her wishes. And so she stopped eating, refused to speak, and would not wash. In the end, her father allowed her to take the veil. Agata would do the exact opposite of the saint in the story. She told everyone who would listen that she was going to leave the convent. She went downstairs into the cloister with her sash wrapped tightly around her waist, to show off her hips and breasts, and with her hair hanging free and curly, to emphasize the fact that she was worldly and not part of the cloistered life. She wandered around the convent and sang as she worked, the way she had done in Messina. During the period of silence, she walked around the cloister dragging her feet; she'd shake out her beautiful chestnut curls and stroke her hair. The teacher of the novices, Donna Maria Giovanna della Croce, with whom she got along very well, had to tell her to tie her hair up in a bun. Agata ignored her, more than once; in the end she was forced to obey an order from the abbess, who demanded an explanation. But she refused to talk even to the abbess, except to tell her that she wanted to go home to her mother.

Then, she started fasting.

12.

Two sisters-in-law discuss what to do
about their niece's unhappiness

The boiled potato vendor had set up his stall and his little stove against the wall, near the front portal of the convent of San Giorgio Stilita. In the middle of the stall was a pot of boiling water and to one side was a pyramid of raw potatoes: underneath the counter was a large pot, tightly covered, and wrapped in a filthy rag. It contained the potatoes that the vendor had already boiled, ready for sale. An aristocratic carriage stopped at the street door, just as the man was lifting the pot to stir the foamy boiling water. A cloud of steam reeking of potato starch wafted over the Princess of Opiri; the vendor went on stirring his potatoes in the most complete indifference, unconcerned at the annoyance he had inflicted on the noblewoman and the cry of "Cover them!" from the coachman. Orsola covered her face with her fan and hurried into the front door. The abbess had summoned her to talk about Agata—it was urgent—and she was baffled: as they had agreed, she hadn't set foot in the convent during the two-month trial period, and from the thank-you notes that Agata had sent her in response to her gifts—a saint-card bookmark and an article about St. Agatha that she'd found in a French magazine—she had supposed that her goddaughter was thriving.

The two sisters-in-law were sitting across from one another in the parlor, separated by the grate. They were distant relatives, and even though they didn't resemble one another, they had the same nervous tic: at times of tension, they both raised their right eyebrow and blinked spasmodically while wrinkling their nose. It had been that exact trait—and not the profound religious sensibility that both women shared—that had persuaded the prince, who was extremely fond of his sister the nun, to ask Orsola to become his second wife. The abbess came right to the point: she was worried about Agata's physical and spiritual well-being. She had hoped that after the first few days Agata would fit into the religious community and in fact that was what she thought was happening. After taking her into her own cell as a guest, she had given Agata a very nice cell of her own, all for herself. The abbess told her sister-in-law the various phases of Agata's induction, which she had thought was going perfectly well—the first time she went downstairs to the *comunichino*, the first psalms sung together, the pleasant walks in the cloister talking about the Rule—and she wondered where or what she had done wrong with her; as she listened, Orsola was reminded of her own youth, when she had been a happy convent girl and, later, a novice with the Poor Clares, until her desire to take the veil instead of being married had been vetoed by her parents. The princess regretted not having become a nun after she was first widowed, and she listened distractedly. "Agata seemed to be getting along nicely with the teacher of the novices, she read all the books that the teacher gave her and she discussed them—in short, she was beginning very well." The abbess paused. "Than all of a sudden, she changed, for no specific reason." And her eyebrow bounced up and down. Agata preferred the solitude of the archives room to the company of the other young girls, with whom she'd had a series of disagreements and minor spats, and when that happened their niece took on an arrogant and dismissive tone of voice. The abbess had hoped that this was merely a passing phase and so she had kept an eye on her, in the cloister. With her, Agata was always affectionate but reserved.

Ever since the beginning of July, every time that Agata saw her, she would ask the abbess whether her mother had come back from Messina yet. She hadn't displayed any emotions when the abbess told her that she had received no news either. But it soon became clear that Agata was deeply disappointed. She had begun to provoke the community by flaunting the more worldly aspects of her clothing, stirring up scandal. During the last week, she had veered to the opposite extreme: she neglected her grooming, becoming slovenly and even outright filthy. She stopped eating. She attended the divine office only reluctantly, she strode rapidly along beneath the porticoes, hands clenched behind her back, like a man. "These are symptoms of an imbalance, perhaps a mental illness, and something must be done," the abbess concluded. She chose not to say anything more, to keep from upsetting her sister-in-law whose breathing was starting to become labored.

They needed to decide whether to await Gesuela's return or intervene immediately and remove Agata from the convent. The two women decided to ask Michele, the prince, to convey a message through court personnel to their sister-in-law and to her brother, the Baron Aspidi, the only person Gesuela would listen to; they would reconsider the situation the following week. But Orsola seemed reluctant to leave. Weeping softly, she told her sister-in-law how deeply she desired the monastic life and how fond she had become in the last few months of her newly acquired niece, whom she had treated as a daughter. Orsola's heartbeat was beginning to race and drops of perspiration were pearling her brow. The abbess could hear her panting anxiously.

"Here, take this, it'll do you good," she said, and she turned the wheel.

Against the iron background there appeared a tray with a glass of cool lemonade and a crunchy warm puff pastry.

13.
End of August 1840.
The betrayal of Donna Gesuela Padellani

Agata waited hopefully for her mother. She had washed carefully and dressed painstakingly, her hair parted in the middle, covering both ears and then joined in the back into a bun on the nape of her neck. The evening before, the abbess had walked into her bedroom to inform her of the visit and to urge her to clean herself up. Agata's face had lit up and when the abbess left, she'd caressed Agata's cheek.

Donna Gesuela walked into the parlor with a bold gaze and a confident step—her handsome face was grim. Her brother had obliged her to cut short her stay with her relatives in Palermo because a court functionary had urged him to arrange for her to go immediately to Naples. She listened with annoyance to what her sister-in-law had to tell her.

The abbess conducted Agata out of the cloistered area and into the parlor; her mother coldly extended her hand for the ritual kiss. Agata covered her mother's hand with tiny kisses, and then she burst into subdued sobs. She told her about her misery at the hands of the novices, the hostility of the serving-women, her yearning for freedom.

"Now, now, calm down, the first few weeks went so well . . . " The abbess put her arm around her shoulders and comforted her: "Why don't you tell us what happened, just tell us and we can help you . . . " Agata stood up, dropping her mother's hand; her mother hadn't said a word. Agata asked, hesitantly, if she could be left alone with her mother; the abbess complied.

Standing before her mother, she begged her to take her away from the convent: she was certain that she didn't feel the calling. She'd given it her best effort, but she didn't have the vocation. She was born to live in the world; if she wasn't destined to be married, she could work as a governess or a schoolteacher and she wouldn't be a financial burden on her. She seized her mother's hand again and began kissing it. Her mother, saddened, stroked Agata's hair. Just then, Angiola Maria and Sarina entered the parlor with a tray of pastries and biscotti. Agata had been obliged to step aside, and she couldn't wait for the two of them to leave but, after the customary exchanges of compliments and greetings, they began pouring out praise of Agata's skill at recognizing medicinal plants and the diligence with which she studied. Instead of encouraging them to go away, Donna Gesuela was indulging them. At that point, the bell of Sext rang. Agata's mother leapt to her feet and said that she had to go to church; she promised to hurry back immediately after service and with a strained smile she left the room.

The lay sisters had conducted Agata back into the cloistered section and had then gone off to recite the *Aves* and the *Paters*. The nun concierge had followed them into the cloister. Agata stood at the door; she watched her mother until she vanished from sight. She returned to the vestibule and was about to go inside when she noticed a line of ants crossing the pavement of the portico. Instead of cutting straight across the floor, taking the shortest route to reach the wall up which they then climbed to follow the curve of the arch, the ants crossed the pavement diagonally, forming a sort of zigzag along the edges of the cobblestones and, in confusion, they wandered off along cracks that led them down blind alleys, only to retrace their steps. Agata was sort of half-hypnotized by that moving enigma. Then, all of a sudden, she understood. Like the ants, ever since her father's death, her mother had been pushing her along toward the cloistered life, without ever coming right out and stating it, but by making her life at home deeply unpleasant, by isolating her from her sisters and her relations, by planting seeds of fear in her of the future and of poverty, depriving her of the pleasures of music and singing, and by sabotaging her love with Giacomo—just like that mad zigzagging line of ants. She had oppressed her with predictions of imminent financial catastrophe; she had isolated her from the family in order to make her more willing to accept the cloistered way.

Now she understood why, whenever her mother went to lunch or just to visit with relations, she took Anna Carolina with her and left her, Agata, at home, with orders for Nora to serve her leftovers; why she was not allowed to go see her Aunt Orsola or even her cousins downstairs; why she had forbidden her to write to her sisters in Messina and to spend time with Sandra; why she had restricted the time Agata was allowed to play piano with the excuse that it bothered the neighbors, and why she had forbidden her sisters to write to her or to go see her in the convent. Agata would talk with her mother when she came back. She looked up at the sundial on the wall of the church. An hour had passed. Mass was over. The rustle of habits dragging on the floor told her that the nuns were returning, in silence, from the divine office, ready for lunch. Then, silence. Agata feared the worst. She shouted and went into her first convulsion.

She opened her eyes, her vision was blurred. Next to her, she saw Dr. Minutolo, kneeling, and a knot of whispering nuns. The doctor was administering a bitter beverage and, with the help of Angiola Maria, he lifted her off the ground and carried her toward a wicker armchair with poles running through the armrests like a low sedan chair. Agata tried to struggle free of their grip: she didn't want to leave the parlor. She was still clinging to the hope that her mother would come back that afternoon and she grew so agitated that it seemed as if she had gone into another fit. She wanted to be laid on her back on the ground and they complied with her wishes. Someone brought a pillow for her head, someone else brought her a glass of water, a third person gave her a tablet of sugar and mint.

Time passed and there was not even the shadow of her mother. Agata wept quietly. Two lay sisters entered at the abbess's order to take her to the choir. Agata resisted, she was sure her mother would come back any minute. She shouted at the women: "I have to wait for her here, that's what she told me!" They summoned the abbess. Agata heard her heavy footsteps and in order to forestall her, Agata dragged herself onto the prie-dieu in front of the image of the Madonna dell'Utria. She joined her hands in prayer.

"Let's leave her alone: she's praying. She's getting better," the abbess whispered to the two lay sisters, and they left together.

Agata had no other memories of that afternoon. She was told that after the divine office the abbess had found her lying face downwards on the pavement, breathing normally, before the miraculous image of the Madonna dell'Utria; the Madonna was smiling in the newly restored splendor of her jewels, surrounded by her glittering and traditional magnificence. That icon of the Virgin Mary, venerated with special devotion by the Benedictine nuns, had been gradually embellished over the centuries with golden ex-votos and precious gems—gleaming where they had been pinned to Her hair, Her neck, Her fingers, and the background of the painting, covering it entirely.

Two years earlier, the most beautiful jewels had been stolen and never recovered. The abbess had done everything she could think of to remedy that sacrilegious act; she had even promised to forgive the nuns who had stolen the gems, but it had done no good. That afternoon, through Agata's intercession, the Lord had persuaded the thieving nuns to return the jewels.

The nuns hurried from every corner of the convent to kneel by Agata where she still lay on the ground. Now however she'd been turned on her side and had a cushion under her head. The nuns were singing hosanna to the miracle, fruit of the prayer of the abbess's niece. Some of the older nuns were singing psalms in their lovely modulated voices. Angiola Maria was wandering around at the edge of the crowd without arousing notice. She was listening. She was observing. There was no one calling the miracle into doubt. At that point, Angiola Maria ran off, exultant, through the laundry room, and a short while later the bells in the campanile began to chime in staccato—announcing to all Naples that a miracle had taken place in the convent of San Giorgio Stilita.

The vocation of the daughter of the late field marshal Padellani was officially confirmed and the neighborhood gazette reported the news at length.

14.

After the miracle of the Madonna dell'Utria,
Agata denies her vocation, falls ill, offends the cardinal,
and finally leaves for her Aunt Orsola Padellani's house

It was shortly before Matins, and there wasn't a living soul
in sight. The bell announcing that outsiders were coming
rang down the hallways of the novices. Agata lay in a feverish delirium. She had lost consciousness more than once, and
the abbess had decided to summon Dr. Minutolo once again.
With the assistance of the sister pharmacist, Donna Maria
Immacolata, the doctor bled the young woman and obliged
her to drink decoctions that helped to lower her temperature.
Agata began to fall asleep, and the physician left her in the care
of Angiola Maria. He walked back through the maze of hallways, discussing with the sister pharmacist the potential causes
of her malaise. At the sound of the ringing bell, the novices
hurried to eavesdrop from behind their doors. Each novice
had prepared a story of her own, true or untrue though it
might be: Agata had had celestial visions, stigmata had
appeared on Agata's body, the Madonna dell'Utria was summoning Agata to Her side, in heaven. There wasn't a novice, or
a postulant, or an educand who wasn't eager to congratulate
her for the miracle and to verify in person her own version of
what had happened. The stream of visitors in Agata's bedroom
began just after Matins and never slowed throughout the day.

Agata had started raving again; in the days that followed she
refused both food and medicine, and as a result her fever
spiked again. This time the doctor diagnosed a diffuse weakness of both body and mind. He prescribed total rest, ordering
only very plain food and beef broth. To prevent visits, the

abbess sent Angiola Maria to act as Agata's custodian. In the meanwhile, news of the miracle had spread from the neighborhood to the entire city of Naples and had reached all the monasteries and convents. The *Gazzetta di Nido e di Capuana* reported it with sensational headlines and requests for meetings and audiences with the "miracle girl," as Agata was being called, poured in from all directions.

A prisoner of the convent, betrayed and abandoned by her mother, Agata had fallen prey to events. She was rude and resentful with Angiola Maria, who, at the abbess's orders, never left her alone for even a minute. Angiola Maria took it all patiently, murmuring, "My little miracle girl, my little miracle girl" in response to all Agata's imprecations. Agata answered her in grunts of one syllable and for the first few days refused to get out of bed. She refused to wash, comb her hair, even to change her sweat-soaked linen. When she opened her eyes, it was only to stare at the blank wall across from her bed. She hated her body, which was by now the one and only thing over which she had any power. She deprived her body of nourishment and she hurt it, digging her fingernails into her arms and slashing the flesh of her thighs with an old tonsure razor, in a series of parallel cuts. She was visibly wasting away.

Dr. Minutolo was walking, lost in thought, along the portico of the cloister, dragging his feet as he followed the servingwoman ringing the bell—another victim of that disease, this time a young lay sister eaten up by breast cancer. He couldn't resign himself to it. He slowed down in order to give two young nuns idling by the fountain a chance to hide from his sight. He passed in front of the abbess's drawing rooms, which were usually closed. That morning she was changing the arrangement of the paintings in the first reception room in order to hang a new one, a gift from the queen. Hammer in hand, Angiola Maria stood at the top of a ladder braced against the wall by two lay sisters, waiting for the order to drive the nail, while two other lay sisters, on tiptoes, held the painting up with both hands, moving it slowly along the wall under the abbess's sharp eye.

At the sight of the physician, Donna Maria Crocifissa left the lay sisters to go talk to him. Both of them had known nuns who had taken fasting to lethal extremes, and she was determined to avoid having that happen to Agata; they spoke in hushed voices about the best course of action and agreed that a change of air might be beneficial: Agata would go to stay with her Aunt Orsola as soon as she received permission from her mother. Otherwise, the abbess would be obliged to ask the cardinal's authorization.

Dr. Minutolo resumed his walk and the ringing of the bell echoed through the cloister. The abbess went back to her unfinished task. "Move it just an inch to the right, and then it's perfect!" she ordered, but the painting didn't move: both of the lay sisters were considering and elaborating what they'd managed to gather from the conversation that had just taken place, so they could repeat it to everyone else.

Agata remembered the cardinal's smooth jet-black hair and air of power from when he had officiated at her father's funeral. Sitting at the abbess's small round table, he seemed smaller to her. He extended his hand, adorned with rings, to her and, after she kissed it, he kept her standing in front of him; he watched her, uncertainly, with a scrutinizing gaze that shifted from benevolent to hostile. The abbess was sitting to one side and was reading some papers.

"I've heard that you won't eat. That's wrong, my daughter," he said, paternally. "Our Lord wants all the little nuns to be happy and healthy."

"Your Eminence, I'll try to eat."

"Did you hear that, Donna Maria Crocifissa?" the cardinal then said, speaking to the abbess. "Your niece has promised to behave and to eat." Then he turned back to Agata and repeated, aloud, in a threatening tone of voice: "You promised, didn't you?" He looked at her, and his eyes cast a spell on her. Agata began to tremble and once again she lost her voice; she nodded, lowering her head repeatedly, without losing eye contact. After a time that seemed interminable, the cardinal lifted his arm as if he were going to bless her. Agata lowered her gaze, in a sign of respect. A hand grazed her cheek and then caressed the line of her jaw. A fierce glance upward and then an immediate reflex—Agata slapped that hand away vehemently. Astonished at the enormity of what she had just done, fearful, she awaited the inevitable.

"Forgive me, Your Excellence . . . "

"Donna Maria Crocifissa, let's go to see the sisters, they're waiting for us. Agata has made a promise. She'll stay in the convent with you." The cardinal didn't take his eyes off Agata's emaciated, ashen face. Head bowed, she was staring at the cross on his purple-garbed chest, then up, up, to the Adam's apple and the bluish bulge of the swollen vein, the smooth chin, the tight lips, the slightly aquiline nose. Until she came level with his gaze.

"You may go."

Since then, Agata had persisted in her fasting. She wanted her mother and she asked for her every day. She denied her vocation and reiterated her determination to leave the convent. Her talk, after the miracle of the Madonna dell'Utria, was scandalous. Agata's words clearly showed that she couldn't tell fantasy from reality. For that reason, and also to accommodate her desire for solitude, the abbess allowed her to stay in her cell, while waiting to receive permission from her mother to send Agata to her Aunt Orsola's house. But Donna Gesuela had left for Palermo without a word as to if or when she would return.

When she found that out, Agata began to refuse water as well. She tore at her hair, she tugged handfuls of hair out of her scalp. At that point, Aunt Orsola decided to step in and take responsibility; she took Agata home with her to Palazzo Padellani.

15.

Agata discovers that her mother wants to marry her off
to another man and decides to go back to the convent

Agata had assumed that when she went back to Aunt Orsola's house, where she lived in the same room and had the same maid, she would resume the same life she'd been living, but it was not to be. The hairdresser, after grooming her aunt's hair, no longer came by to comb and tease her ringlets. Her aunt no longer invited Agata to come with her to the singing masses and to Vespers in the oratories, which she loved so much. Now Agata had to listen to Mass in the *palazzo*'s chapel, sitting with the help and with the young daughters of her cousin the prince. She sat at her aunt's table when there were just the two of them or when there were elderly guests. Otherwise she ate by herself in the small dining room. She wasn't allowed to enter the drawing room when her aunt was playing cards. Relatives and female cousins no longer wrote or came to see her; in other words, Agata was as isolated from the rest of the world as if she were already a nun.

All the same, her Aunt Orsola lavished her with attention and affection. Every morning she rode out with her in the enclosed carriage and treated her to ice cream and sweets, which were served to them without their having to descend from the carriage, however. She encouraged Agata to spend her afternoons reading on the terrace, while Orsola played cards. The terrace had been carved out of the attic. It was quite deep and was surrounded by rooms on three sides, to ensure that its interior was entirely concealed from prying eyes—just like a cloister. Her aunt also allowed her to play the pianoforte.

Little by little, Agata began to think of the future and even dared to hope; she was afraid to talk to her aunt about it—she knew that everything depended upon her mother, and she had written to her. She was awaiting her mother's reply, but it was slow in coming.

Once, out the window of the carriage, she thought she glimpsed Giacomo in the Via Toledo: he had his back to her and he was entering a men's clothing shop. From that day on, Agata fostered the belief that soon he would make himself known, and she let herself slip into a romantic daydream of her beloved. She secretly took books of poetry and tragedies by French and Italian authors from the shelves of the library; she lingered over the love scenes and the passages of great pathos, and she meditated over those verses as if they were versicles of the Psalms. She smeared onto her damaged skin her aunt's fragrant bergamot pomade and twisted her hair into ringlets; in a few days she had become beautiful again, if shockingly skinny.

The only family member that Agata was allowed to see was Sandra, but only in Palazzo Padellani, not at the Aviello residence. With the enthusiasm and recklessness of youth, Agata talked to Sandra about the books she was reading. Sandra, the best educated of her sisters, told her that some of her favorite books were the heroic tragedies of Corneille. *Horace*, in which the three sons of the Roman Publius Horatius challenge and defeat the three Curiatii brothers from the enemy town of Alba Longa, thrilled her: the sole survivor of the duel, Horace, is scolded by his sister Camille, the bride of one of the Curiatii brothers, for having failed to put family loyalty before love of country, whereupon he, in a fit of anger, kills her. The father defends his fratricidal son before king and populace, upholding the defense of love of country, and the Roman people decide to pardon their hero. "St. Paul is right, when he says that man was not created for woman, but woman for man," said Sandra, and she explained to her sister, exalting it, her role in supporting the work of her husband the Carbonaro: she, as a patriot, accepted without complaint his long absences, when he was away from Naples on secret missions, and the cost in terms of financial comfort. "But don't you miss him at night?" Agata asked. "No, it's so wonderful when I finally see him again, and I can feel that I'm worthy of him because I too am contributing to our cause."

Agata thought again about Horace's sister. But if a woman falls in love with a man who then becomes an enemy of her nation, how can she accept the need for her own brother to kill her beloved? she wondered. Then she said to her sister: "Shouldn't her brother be aware that he's killing his sister's husband? Couldn't he spare his life?" At that, Sandra exhorted Agata to abandon that attitude, so unworthy of a modern woman: "What you are saying would make it impossible for any woman to rise to become a true patriot. Tommaso always says so: a patriot's woman must remember that certain sacrifices are necessary in order to attain a given higher end: the unity of the nation and the good of the Italian people." And Sandra told her, stating first and last names, about mothers who encouraged their sons to take part in uprisings and expeditions of liberation in the sure knowledge that they were sending them to their deaths. "I don't understand. I'd prefer to go into war myself rather than send my sons," Agata replied. Sandra replied: "All the same, it happened, after the French Revolution, with the Société des citoyennes républicaines révolutionnaires, in Paris. But it didn't work. We women are different from men." Her sister decreed, with satisfaction: "St. Paul was right."

At long last, one morning the Princess of Opiri received the long-awaited letter from her sister-in-law. She insisted on reading it out loud to Agata in the presence of Sandra, who had in turn asked her husband to accompany her. The letter was brief;

Gesuela thanked Orsola for taking care of her daughter and ordered Agata to board the next mail boat for Messina and to bring all her summer clothing with her. She also commanded her to go with Sandra and buy whatever light muslin she liked for an elegant outfit. Agata rejoiced: her engagement! She regretted ever having thought ill of her mother, who had been far away, working to secure her happiness. She embraced her aunt and her sister, and broke into a slow pirouette on tiptoe, murmuring the words to the sweet melody of *La Barcata*, "the river runs down to the sea, flowing away like life, stretched out on the stern in a dream you think that the journey will never come to an end . . . " At every turn, she spun faster, her grey petticoat whirling outward and swelling as she expanded into a dazzling smile. Then, exhausted, she threw herself into an easy chair, arms thrown wide. Sandra's face was as puckered as a prune. "What's the matter? Don't you understand? I'm going to be engaged to Giacomo!" Agata shouted at her, and she turned to the other two for reassurance. She understood from their faces. At that point, her sister felt obliged to tell her the truth. Amalia had written to her in confidence, informing her that Giacomo had officially announced his engagement to the girl that his parents had chosen, and that their mother had arranged two marriages: one for Agata with the elderly Cavaliere d'Anna, without any dowry required, and her own with General Cecconi, who was stationed in Palermo, where she would go to live. Agata listened, and as she listened she tucked up her legs and curled into a ball in the armchair: with her back pressed against the armrest, she stuck her thumb in her mouth and sucked on it like a newborn. Her blank gaze was fixed on the flowered majolica tiles on the floor.

Agata had regained her composure and was now sitting in the armchair and speaking, coldly, calmly. She would not marry the man her mother had picked for her: she found him disgusting. She wanted to know whether, as a minor, she had the right to stay with her aunt and find work as a teacher or a governess without her mother's consent. She asked to be left alone to talk with her brother-in-law.

When can I be emancipated from my mother?" she asked Tommaso Aviello, as if she were a client.

"From fifteen years of age and up, but it's revocable, and in your case it wouldn't change a thing. It would give you the right to administer your own property, but you don't have any property. It wouldn't allow you to live on your own and work, without the prior consent of your guardian—your mother—who, unless you marry, will still have the obligation of providing for you and the right to make you live with her. A woman becomes an adult at twenty-one, though that does not change the obligation of her parents to provide for an unmarried daughter, nor the daughter's obligation to show them proper obedience. You can only leave your mother's house on your own free will when you are married, as stated in Title 9 of the first book of the Civil Code, *Delle persone.*"

"And what happens if I refuse to obey my mother?"

"She is your one and only testamentary guardian. It's stated in Article 502: if your mother has cause for grave concern over your conduct, she can ask the presiding judge of the tribunal to order your arrest for no more than a month, and he is obliged to do so, without stating the reason he's ordering the arrest. It's also stated in Article 290: the daughter cannot abandon her father's home during and beyond her minority, except once she is married."

"So that means I can't look for a job as a governess, without my mother's consent?"

"That's right. You can't find a respectable position without her consent, and even if you could, you'd have no assurance of holding on to that position."

Agata listened carefully, at times half-closing her eyelids as if she were trying to memorize what he had said. Tommaso added that her mother could file a report with the police against the Princess of Opiri, if she were to keep Agata as a guest in her home instead of sending her back to Messina as her mother had demanded. At that point, Agata implored him to find her a hiding place in his own home, or anywhere else in Naples, just to give her time enough to find employment, or even to leave the country if necessary, and she pointed out that many Neapolitan dissidents had taken refuge in Turin.

Agata's brother-in-law admired the courage of her reaction and her determination to analyze in a realistic manner the choices that she believed or hoped still remained open to her. Still, he was duty-bound to point out to her that the police and the spies of the Bourbon monarchy were exceedingly efficient and that General Cecconi was an influential man: they'd catch her wherever she might try to hide. At that point Tommaso revealed to her that he himself was being watched by the police and that he could not afford to risk his own freedom and that of Sandra in order to help her; in fact, he was afraid that his apartment was going to be searched any day now. He couldn't think of a secure hiding place for his books, let alone for Agata. "There is nothing to be done, you have to obey your guardian," he concluded. "You have no alternative."

When it was Agata's turn to speak, she corrected him—she definitely had an alternative: the convent. "My mother forced me to go to San Giorgio Stilita; she wants me to become a nun. I'm staying with my aunt because I was unwell; now I'm better and I can go back, even today." And she added that her mother would never dare to take her away from there against her will and the will of her aunt the abbess. Moreover, she was certain that, once she turned sixteen, her aunt would allow her to find some kind of work rather than forcing her to pay the monastic dowry, and she even had the steely nerve to offer her brother-in-law some practical help. She told him that her two steamer trunks, which had once belonged to her father, had a false bottom that was not being used; she would be very happy to conceal whatever "things" he might have in them and convey them to safety inside the convent.

The three of them agreed with Agata's decision and her aunt sent a letter to the abbess. The Aviellos promised to help her find a dignified position as a governess, if her mother would agree to it, but Aunt Orsola was displeased with the idea. She muttered under her breath that employment was hardly becoming to a woman, much less to a Padellani—a fine elderly widowed husband would certainly be preferable—and she vowed to speak with her niece about it again that afternoon, in the hope that this time Agata might take her advice.

16.

*Donna Gesuela Padellani arrives in Naples
to remove Agata from the convent
but she refuses to leave*

Agata was sitting with her Aunt Orsola, stitching needle-point while waiting for the abbess's consent to her return to the convent. It was slow in coming.

Between one needleful and the next, her aunt reminisced about her own past, trying to dissuade Agata from being over-hasty in her dismissal of an arranged marriage. Agata's hand jerked and the sharp needle, clamped between her trembling thumb and index finger, jabbed her other hand. A round drop of blood appeared on the linen. Aunt Orsola noticed and understood but still couldn't manage to keep her mouth shut, perhaps in part because she always found the memory of her virtuous sacrifices so particularly gratifying. Orsola was good-hearted through and through, but she was also insecure and just a tad conceited. She went on at length about her two mar-riages, neither of them love matches but both quite happy experiences, and her own desire to become a nun, set aside not once but twice out of filial obedience, and then a third time, because of two social pleasures she was unwilling to renounce

As a girl, Orsola Pietraperciata had been educated at the convent of Santa Chiara, in the order of the Poor Clares. She liked the cloistered life and she felt the calling very strongly. Then her older sister, who was already engaged to be married, died; her father took her out of the convent and married her off to her late sister's fiancé, an elderly duke, who loved her deeply; he was respectful of his young bride's religious calling, and allowed her to invite other devoted women—or *pin-*

zochere—to live with them and he did nothing to interfere with her pious pursuits. Orsola became pregnant but she lost the baby; a few months later, her husband died too.

Her first thought was to take her vows, but her father, who was also a widower, insisted that she come back and live in the family *palazzo* with him, and once again, Orsola obeyed. After her father's death, the prince of Opiri, a distant cousin, who was himself a widower and who had a very young son, Michele, asked her if she would be a mother to his boy. She wasn't particularly inclined to married life, and openly told him so. "I feel the same way," he replied, with great relief, and promised to respect her wishes, if she would only agree to care for him and his little boy. That too was a happy—if unconsummated—marriage.

Widowed for the second time, and now fully independent, Orsola was no longer willing to retire to a convent or a conservatory: she couldn't imagine giving up either cards or evenings at the opera—she enjoyed them both far too much. "Still," her aunt concluded, coyly plucking at a ringlet, "I'm quite certain that I would have lived much more happily as a nun. Think about it, Agata."

Her aunt had gone out to the San Carlo opera house and Agata was on the terrace. The gazebo, surrounded by huge potted jasmine plants and magnolia trees, and covered by flourishing and vigorously blooming carpet of morning glories, was a perfect retreat from the prying eyes of the help. Agata hadn't been crying, but still her eyes were swollen and reddened and she felt weak as a kitten. Her legs and arms ached as if she'd been hefting sacks of almonds all day long. The languishing rays of the setting sun were striking Mt. Vesuvius and the peaks of Castellammare. One of the many religious festivals of Naples was being celebrated that day, and she could hear the echoing sounds of the band and the jubilant crowd wafting

146 - SIMONETTA AGNELLO HORNBY

up to her like a distant, muffled crashing roar from the sea. From her chair, all that Agata could see was the red sky through the green of the foliage and the campanula blooms. Red. Green. Purple. Passion, hope, sorrow. A new wave of emotion swept through her. She was breathing in the free air; she felt alone, but no longer isolated. God would protect her, God loved her. And God was calling her. Not to the nunnery, but to Him. Agata responded to His love and sat there, talking to God, until nightfall, when the damp air rising from the sea enveloped her, making her shiver.

Aunt Orsola was home by now, waiting for Agata with a letter in her hand. The abbess had written to inform her that, after consulting with the cardinal, she'd decided it would be advisable to ask the Chapter of the Choristers if they were willing to accept Agata back into the Cenoby, or monastic community, for a second time. The response was unequivocal: Agata could come back to the convent of San Giorgio Stilita the following morning, after Terce, on the condition that she declare her irrevocable determination to become a nun and that she begin from the very first stage–the Educandate.

Agata had insisted that she be left alone at the moment of her entry into the convent of San Giorgio Stilita. To the sound of the doorkeeper's cry—"*Deo gratias*" ("God be praised," in Latin)—Sandra Aviello walked out of the vestibule and descended with a heavy heart the convent staircase. When she heard the creaking of the monumental door, she turned to look up, but the portal had already swallowed up her sister.

At that exact time of day, Donna Gesuela Padellani was on the wharf of Messina waiting to board a steamboat. She was furious. She had received a message through one of her future husband's secret informers: her daughter intended to enter the

convent of San Giorgio Stilita to undertake the path of nunhood—of her own free will and with a strong vocation.
Gesuela was trying to figure out who might have revealed to
her Neapolitan relations her matrimonial plans for Agata—she
had written an extremely circumspect letter to her sister-in-
law, precisely to avoid arousing suspicions about the Cavaliere
d'Anna, but Agata's precipitous return to the convent was
clearly prompted by that prospect.

Gesuela thought back to her own girlhood; she too had
been married off through deception. She was a thirteen-year-
old orphan. She was the acting mistress of the house for her
thirty-year-old step-brother and she was perfectly happy—the
two siblings got along perfectly and agreed on everything, and
the last thing she would have expected from him was an
arranged marriage at such an early age, much less with Don
Peppino Padellani, who was pushing forty. But her step-
brother had taken her to Naples, ostensibly for a holiday, and
before a month had passed he'd married her off to that old
man. In time, she and Peppino had come to love one another,
they'd worked out their compromises, and they'd found happiness; but their poverty, her husband's load of debt, and the
enormous effort to marry off her own daughters had worn her
down. Just when she thought she'd taken care of Agata's
future, and was herself on the verge of her second marriage,
she was going to have to take on new debt for the monastic
dowry for that rebellious daughter of hers; the rage she felt
toward Agata and her sister-in-law never subsided once during
the entire crossing, and it lasted long afterward.

The door swung shut behind Agata. Four serving women
were shoving her heavy trunks along the flagstone floor of the
corridor. In the cloister garden, concealed between the fountain and the Christ and the Samaritan Woman, both petrified
right in the middle of their pleasant conversation, the novices

were peering out at her, snickering. Well aware of the enormity
of the promise she had made, Agata hesitated, aghast; then she
followed Angiola Maria, who was taking her to see the abbess.
As she passed by the snickering novices she squared her shoulders, threw back her head, and twisted her lips into a challenging smile.

The abbess met with her in the formal reception room. She
did not embrace her; she extended her hand to be kissed.

"Do you understand what it means to take the veil?"

"Yes, I've thought it over."

"But before, you didn't want to." A pause. "I've been told
that you had an inamorato." And she gave her a stern look.

"He's taken himself a wealthy bride. I no longer want to be
married." Agata gave the abbess a grim look. She would have
preferred not to have to own up to Giacomo's betrayal.

"There are other nuns like you here, who would have preferred to marry a husband, but who were prevented from
doing so," said the abbess. Then she raised her voice: "Jesus
Christ does not deserve to be the second choice."

Agata's answer came to her easily and spontaneously: "But
I love God most of all, and He will help me!"

17.
The vestition of Agata the educand

The evening before the ceremony of Agata Padellani's vestition, the church, built thanks to the munificence of a sixteenth-century Abbess Padellani, had been closed to the congregation and to the clergy: it had once again briefly become the exclusive property of the convent and of that family. The nuns had decorated the altars with their silver and their candelabra and the church glittered.

Prior to Compline, Agata, with the abbess walking next to her, had marched the length of the nave holding a silver tray on which lay her educand habit. When they came even with the chapel dedicated to St. Benedict, founder of their order, they kneeled on the first step. At that moment the entire church was filled with the monodic chant of the nuns.

Intende voci orationis meae,
Rex meus et Deus meus.

Agata stood up and, alone, she walked up to place the tray on the altar. Then she descended and kneeled next to the abbess. She too was chanting:

Quoniam ad te orabo:
Domine mane exhaudies vocem meam.
Intende voci orationis meae,
Rex meus et Deus
Quoniam ad te orabo:

Domine mane exhaudies vocem meam.

In the morning, O Lord, you will hear my voice.

It was a soft late-September morning; beneath the shady arcades of the cloister, the air was still. The clickety-clack of shoes on the steps, the rustle of habits and a subdued murmur of conversation—the calm of the cloister had been shattered by the group of young people descending the staircase of the novices. Educand and postulants were accompanying Agata Padellani to the comunichino for her vestition; there were many of them, and they pushed her, touched her, caressed her. They were walking down the hallway that ran past the kitchens. Standing in the doors, serving women and lay sisters watched them pass with broad smiles. The elderly nuns had already occupied the lookout seats in the six alcoves the overlooked the nave of the church, and from up there they were waving hello.

The group of celebrants slipped through the small wooden doorway that led to the maze of staircases and corridors that led to the comunichino. They packed into the narrow hallway that ran along the wall of the church's transept, and then they descended a long unbroken flight of narrow steps; when they reached the tiny landing they made a sharp right turn onto another equally steep staircase. Shoved and squeezed by the other girls crowding around her, Agata stumbled and more than once was afraid that she was about to lose her balance and tumble headlong down the steps.

The hall of the comunichino, bare of any furniture, was filled with the smells of incense and the damp that soaked through from the outside wall. On the left, the Holy Staircase climbed up along the entire wall and stopped, in a dead end, in front of the enormous face of a blond Christ crowned with thorns; on the first Friday of every month, kneeling nuns seeking indulgence climbed up and down the carved wooden steps without ever touching the railing for support. An imposing seventeenth-century painting of Moses striking the rock to bring forth water occupied the wall across from the comunichino; in front of it was the armchair of the abbess. As soon as they entered the room, the girls, like a platoon of soldiers, spread out into compact rows, alongside and behind Agata, and moved slowly forward, taking small steps, until she, in the middle of the front row, had reached the exact center of the four-panel door that covered the grate of the comunichino. The two educands who had been assigned to open the door took their places, in front of Agata; then, in perfect unison, they folded back the panels on their well-oiled, silent hinges. The light of hundreds of candles burst into the hall while the music of the organ flooded the nave, followed by the voices of the choristers. All together, the altar boys, standing erect with their chests thrust out at their places on the steps of the main altar, turned to gaze at the comunichino, to the right of the altar. Seen from inside the church, it looked like the entrance to a particularly sumptuous chapel: a large radiant halo of iron and brass, flanked by two candelabra, masterpieces of the Neapolitan brass-worker's art, surmounted the three-sectioned grate behind which the nuns listened to the mass, receiving the Eucharist through the central aperture.

The congregation had turned out in great numbers: the people from the quarter had come en masse—both because they remembered the miracle of the Madonna dell'Utria, and out of respect for the Padellanis—but the only family members to attend were the prince, with his wife and stepmother, to distract attention from the absence of the educand's mother. The solemn benediction of the habit took place on the altar of St. Benedict, prior to the celebration of Mass. The canon and the altar boys began the singing, followed by the faithful. The censers held high by the four altar boys flanking the canon swung in unison. Each time they swung out to the apex of their parabola, they released clouds of incense and myrrh, mixed with ancient unguents—in keeping with the tradition of the Armenian nuns, who fled in the seventh century and founded the convent. The perfume saturated the whole church, wafting upward as high as the choir, which had begun singing Psalm 17 *a voci pari.*

The canon descended from the altar.

Exurge, Domine, praeveni eum et supplanta eum:
Eripe animam meam ab impio frameam tuam.

The canon handed the habit to Agata through the comunichino.

Ab inimicis manus tuae.

Agata wore the heavy shoes of the nuns and she had combed her hair into two flat bands that ran over her ears and were gathered and pinned to the nape of her neck with a comb. The educands undressed her and then re-dressed her in the black woolen habit, with narrow sleeves extending to the wrist and a small scapular hanging from her shoulders. Then they helped her put on the white muslin apron and tied a handkerchief made of the same material around her neck.

Ego autem in iustitia apparebo conspectu tuo:
Satiabor cum apparuerit gloria tua.

Once the vestition was complete, the new educand was the first to receive the divine host. Agata closed her eyes while the particle of holy wafer dissolved in her mouth. When she reopened them, she looked out at the congregation. In one of the first rows she thought she saw Giacomo with a woman sitting next to him, and she quickly shut her eyes again, very tight.

18.
The educandate of Agata

Agata's first week as an educand had gone well. The cardinal had confirmed that Father Cuoco would be her father confessor. The abbess, who until the vestition had almost seemed to be avoiding any opportunity to speak with her one-on-one, now behaved more affectionately toward her even than before, though also with greater restraint. The abbess also met with her every day, briefly, before Vespers, during the "time of the nuns," when they were allowed to read, pray, and meditate on their own as they chose.

Religious instruction was entrusted to the teachers of the educands and the novices, assisted by other novices who were approaching their solemn profession of vows; the young students were treated quite strictly. The school day was punctuated not by lessons but by the rigid schedules of prayer, with little time for recreation. Agata kept her distance from the other educands, who sought her out in order to hear from her lips the *true* story of her clash with her mother. She preferred to study from the books that they'd given her, but her thoughts kept returning to her mother, who she knew would soon be arriving from Messina, as she had been informed by the abbess.

Donna Gesuela did not go directly to the convent the minute she stepped off the steamer, as she had originally planned to do. At the advice of General Cecconi, she had first talked to relatives and friends in an attempt to understand what had happened with her daughter, so that she'd be able to take Agata back to Messina without necessarily undermining her relations with the Padellanis.

The day had arrived when she was scheduled to visit the convent of San Giorgio Stilita. The sister doorkeeper ushered her into the parlor, instead of into the abbess's private drawing room. Donna Gesuela, offended at being treated like any ordinary visitor instead of as a close relation, sat on the edge of the seat in front of the grate, without leaning against the backrest. As she waited, her resentment swelled to a slow boil.

Then, she heard a creaking sound behind her: her daughter and her sister-in-law were entering the parlor through the little door concealed behind the red and green volutes of the columns in the fresco. As she leaned forward to kiss her mother's hand, Agata displayed her hair, neatly combed and clipped into place, clearly revealing the bald patches where she had ripped locks of hair out of her scalp. That sight made Donna Gesuela forget all her best intentions: she upbraided Agata for having filled the convent with her protests against the cloistered life, declaring to the four winds that all she wanted to do was to be married—at this point Donna Gesuela began raising her voice, increasingly shrill—and then accused her of having concocted this diabolical plan in order to persuade everyone else that she had had the vocation, whereas in fact she was only motivated by disobedience: Agata merely wanted to avoid being married to the man that her mother had chosen for her.

"Gesuela, let's put an end to this. You can't always force other people to do as you wish. You're almost forty years old, you should have a little wisdom, now that you're a widow. Agata is staying here, that's what she wants . . . and it's what you wanted, the last time you and I talked." The abbess's words only made things more tense. Now Donna Gesuela lost her temper completely; she accused the Padellanis of conspiring against her, and the abbess in particular had betrayed her trust. She threatened to turn to the king's justice to get her daughter back. Without losing her composure, the abbess reminded her that the cardinal had been closely involved in the whole affair: "He has your daughter's best interests at heart, you know that." No, Gesuela hadn't thought of the cardinal at all, and she was thrown back on her heels at those words. "Then, allow me to assure you that I consulted with him personally," Donna Maria Crocifissa drove the point home, "when I received Agata's request. It was he who approved her return to the convent, provided that the professed nuns approve in a full session of the Chapter. He also knows that Agata wishes to become a nun of her own free will."

The mother glared straight into her daughter's eyes. Agata returned her gaze without flinching, until Donna Gesuela was forced to turn her eyes away, in defeat, in the face of such a bold challenge.

From that day until the day of her simple profession, Agata had no more contact with her mother.

19.

Agata thinks about love while kneading bread dough

The encounter with her mother had left a deep mark on Agata. She truly felt alone now, and she did nothing to try to change that: she avoided the company of the other young women and of the nuns. She worked, she studied, and she read. She was sad. In November, after the Day of the Dead, she was afraid that she was about to slip back into the slough of melancholy, from which song and the routines of the day saved her. She was orderly by nature and the alternation between work and prayer gave her a sense of satisfaction and comfort. Comfortably ensconced in the empty pews behind the choristers, she joined their chant and psalmodized, opening her heart and her throat to God and praying that He would save her from a world to which she did not belong.

The educand's day was regulated not only by the divine office and by the lessons, but also by menial tasks. The condition of entering the convent as an educand, which the Chapter had imposed upon Agata, was therefore a punishment that she gladly accepted. She liked getting her hands dirty working in the garden, kneading bread dough, cleaning silver, pleating the brilliant white wimples of the nuns, ironing and mending habits. She happily attended lessons and quickly learned everything that she was taught; then, on her own, she completed her education by reading whatever she laid her hands on in the archive, or the books that she had brought with her.

In Messina her mother had never allowed Agata to spend

time in the kitchen, which was down on the ground floor. Agata went there when her mother wasn't home, but she hadn't been able to learn much. In Naples, Nora had taught her to cook the peasant dishes that she knew on a bed of embers. Considering her lack of experience, the hebdomadary set Agata to make bread, but even that wasn't as easy as she had expected.

The kitchen was a big rectangular room with a platform in the center glittering with enameled tile. It culminated in a very tall hood supported by stout columns; the hearth, beneath the hood, with its fire blazoning in the subcellar, was a red-hot circular slab of iron, with holes of different sizes for cauldrons, pots, and pans. Along the short sides of the kitchen were, respectively, the room set aside for baking and roasting in the wood ovens and the anterefectory—both of those rooms had marble counters along the walls, supported on massive wooden beams that projected from the wall; these counters were used for leavening bread dough and for carving meat.

The cellars extended all the way out under the two refectories—the little refectory, for educands, lay sisters, and postulants, and the large refectory, reserved for the use of nuns and novices—and they were connected to the kitchen by a staircase. Air and light came down through two shafts protected by a railing. They were used as a storage area and as a wine cellar and they had their own well, with its own aquifer, and a large washing tub.

Sacks of flour and wheat arrived at the convent of San Giorgio Stilita from the convent's farmlands: the grinding was done by the serving women on old grindstones, in the garden. The pastry flour was stored in large metal barrels, while the kitchen flour was kept in grey sacks on which was written the type of flour and the date on which it was ground. Bread flour was yet another variety. It was Brida's job to teach Agata how to make bread. First off all, she decided to show her how to select the flour. She stuck her hand into the flour sack and then she plunged Agata's hand in too. "You must pay close attention to the color: the finest flour is a light yellow and it must be very soft to the touch," and so saying, she pulled her hand out of the sack. "You see? This is good flour because it sticks to your finger. Now take a handful of it and squeeze it." She pulled out a fistful herself and then opened her fingers one by one, showing Agata that the first class flour didn't powder immediately, but formed small clumps on her open palm—that was the flour that would be used to make communion wafers, fancy rolls, and bread for the dinner table. Out of that flour, a finer, more delicate flour would be sifted for the biscotti that were eaten in the convent. The third quality of flour, used to make bread for the serving women, for frying, to thicken sauces, to make pizza, was less white, almost dirty in color and, if compressed, it showed little grey spots. Agata was hypnotized by those operations and she felt alive, receptive: the skin on her hands became very sensitive.

Having shown her how to select the flour the first thing that Brida taught Agata was how to prepare the yeast. She took a handful of the dough that had already been prepared and then she started by punching it down. Then she kneaded it on the counter to refine the dough's consistency. Agata watched her with rapt interest. Brida gathered the scrapings of the kneading trough and all the bits of dough and the scraps that she found lying around and then she added a tiny amount of flour to give that ball of leftover dough the consistency of a very dense dough. She kneaded it with a very small amount of added water until it became a hard and compact little loaf, which she placed in a small pot covered with an old linen napkin. She covered that with a lid and then wrapped it in a clean rag, ready to be added to the bread dough they'd make in the coming days. Brida looked at it with satisfaction and said, "If

it's properly stored, this yeast dough can last for a long time."
Then she told her the story of how that yeast had come from
the mother dough that was brought from Aleppo hundreds of
years ago by the founders of the convent, the white-garbed
nuns on the walls of the main staircase. Forced to flee in a
panic by the advance of the Saracens, the nuns managed to
bring away with them nothing but the sacred relics and a ball
of yeast. During the grueling crossing of the Mediterranean,
they had suffered from terrible scorching heat. The mother
abbess flattened the ball and kept it between her breasts, soft-
ening it with warm sweat to keep the yeast from drying out and
dying.

Making bread became Agata's favorite job. She carved a
shallow crater into the heap of flour piled on the counter. She'd
mix it carefully with two fingers, slowly adding lukewarm water,
then she began to move faster, enlarging the hole with the handle of a broken ladle, adding more and more water and mixing
more flour to the fluid mixture until the original mountain of
flour had become a lake with high banks. At that point, she dissolved the yeast into hot water and stirred it into the fluid mixture to blend it thoroughly. It was work that required no particular concentration, and as Agata did it she would find herself
thinking: *Why did I wind up here? Is this my life?*

Agata added more water, or thickened the mixture with
flour if it was too liquid, folded over the edges of the flour into
the hollow and began feeding them into the white magma
without creating channels through which it could run out onto
the counter. Once all the flour had been worked into the mixture, it was time to knead it, which was crucial to the quality of
the bread. She kneaded the dough in small portions and with
great force. In order to obtain the desired elasticity she would
lift it—if it was very heavy, she'd arch her shoulders backwards
to keep from losing her balance—until it pulled away in a single piece from the counter, and then she'd punch it vigorously

with her fist. Last of all, she'd roll it out with the rolling pin to refine it and to eliminate any air pockets. *Is this the work that I wanted to do?* Once she'd attained the desired consistency, the dough, rolled into large balls, was set to rise in a warm place, in large covered bowls. *What does all this mean? Does it make any sense?*

Agata found answers to her questions only when she was kneading the risen dough, when she was shaping it, hefting it and giving it bulk, and decorating the bread. The bread became a living thing, then. The sharp, ripening senses of that fifteen-year-old girl were reawakening, to a quickening feeling of joy. Agata felt that she was part of a larger whole that had no beginning or end—life, growth—and she associated the mystery of bread-making with the mystery of communion, of the Eucharist. That an infinitesimal portion of the pellet of fermented dough that the abbess had carried all the way from Aleppo between her breasts, when mixed with water and flour from Naples, could still create fresh, flavorful, crunchy bread was a reprisal of the miracle of life and its growth. In those moments, Agata—her fingers sticky with dough—glorified God and was grateful and happy to have been selected to honor Him in that way.

The real difficulties began when it was time to control the embers in the oven and govern the baking times. However carefully she repeated in her mind the *Aves*, the *Paters*, and the *Credos* prescribed by the recipes, she never managed to produce creditable bread and biscotti. The oven wasn't something that suited her. She despaired over it, and one day Angiola Maria came to her rescue. She spoke to Brida, who agreed to take care of the baking if in exchange Agata agreed to see to the carving of the meat. Agata not only enjoyed cutting up the sides and quarters of slaughtered animals that arrived in the kitchen on feast days, as well as stripping out the gristle, but she was also happy to do the more tiresome tasks that demanded a special focus and effort, such as boning chickens, capons, and even quails and pigeons, while preserving the skin intact. That work, done while the bread was baking, increased Agata's profound sense of the sacrifice of Christ.

It was traditional for the nuns to make pastries to sell or give as gifts: all of them were required to know how to make the convent's specialty—the *pastiera napoletana*, a ricotta-filled Neapolitan tart—but each of them also had a specialty all their own. Agata dedicated herself to the Sicilian sweets—*dolcini*—that were prepared cold, made with almond paste (also called royal paste) and filled with pistachio preserves and *zuccata*, or candied pumpkin, and covered with a shiny white sugar frosting decorated with silver balls, leaves and rose petals made of communion wafer dough and adorned with floral designs in pastel hues. Her imagination ran wild when it came to decorating them. She had invented a method all her own: she used the plants from the garden as she had been taught by Angiola Maria and had devised a number of very beautiful natural dyes. Using brushes made from pigeon feathers she created fanciful compositions on the white glaze of the *cucchitelle*, which looked like jewel boxes made of French porcelain. Word of mouth ensured that these sold rapidly through the convent's wheel. Nuns and novices alike were jealous because the abbess had given her permission to paint them in her room, while everyone else was required to complete their pastries in the kitchen. To their eyes, Agata was afforded a dishonest advantage; this was a grave affront to their status and their personal dignity. It was through pastries and sweets that the cloistered nuns not only expressed their own manual creativity and taste, but also conveyed to the outer world their personality.

20.
April 1841.
Agata comes to know her father
through the stories told her by her aunt the abbess
and she develops a bond with her

Mirrors were forbidden in the convent, but there wasn't a single nun who hadn't hidden one away somewhere, not a lay sister who didn't use a specially polished metal plate or a piece of glass with a sheet of tinfoil. One afternoon the abbess and Agata were walking in the shade of the cloister's arcade talking about their favorite reading materials. Her aunt's sharp eye was surveying the double cloister. In the garden, beyond the exedra, and already shrouded in shadow, the serving women were taking dry cleaning rags down from the clothesline stretched between the pomegranate tree and the lemon tree. The sun was still beating down in the terraces and in the monumental cloister. A number of nuns were resting in chairs beneath the exedras, watching the water spray from the mouths of the seahorses on the fountain. Suddenly, a ray of sunshine shot at an angle onto the lush foliage of the camellia plant next to the fountain, illuminating it brightly. The light had struck a mirror carelessly left perched on the balustrade of the terrace, and it was darting noticeably. With astonishing rapidity, and stealthy silence, the abbess hurried into the garden to get a better look. The eyes of every woman and girl in the cloister were following the stout figure. The mirror fell and struck the abbess's leather shoe. In an instant, nuns and serving women had surrounded her and, in low voices, offered her comfort and aid. "No it's nothing, really, it's nothing," murmured the abbess, as she limped off.

Despite her heavy shoes, the abbess's big toe was suppurating and she was forced to stay in bed. Agata went to see her whenever she could. The birthdays of both her little sister Carmela and of her father fell in April. Agata was missing them both keenly, but she preferred not to talk about that to her aunt. Instead, the abbess, as if she could sense it, started to talk to her about her father. They were ten years apart in age, but they had been especially close; he could never get over the fact that she had accepted the family's decision to make her become a nun. "But let me tell you something," she pointed out, arching her eyebrows proudly, "he was wrong. I'm happy to be a nun. Now the Lord has sent you to me, and you're going to like it here just as I've liked it here. You will become abbess yourself, someday."

Agata asked her aunt why her father had taken that attitude. As a young man, Peppino read books that were on the Church's index of forbidden titles; he was a freemason, her aunt told her, crossing herself when she pronounced the dread word "freemason." "And then there was His Majesty . . . " She explained to her curious niece that, despite the fact that the king was fifteen years older than him, the two had become great friends. In fact, Peppino remained a gentleman of the privy chamber until he left for Messina. The king was lazy and capricious; he liked to hunt and he would play pranks on anyone. Peppino, himself a jokester, was always ready to go along with the king's antics. But there was an innovative and modernizing side to the king as well, and Peppino spoke of that aspect with admiration: the foundation of the Real Colonia di San Leucio. At the instigation of the leading minds of the Neapolitan Enlightenment, King Ferdinand had established a manufactory for the production of silk with a charter based on a concept of meritocracy. The families of the weavers lived in the "colony" in modern residences, with schools, hospitals, and everything that a prosperous community could need. "Like a monastery or convent in the olden days, and what's more they even had vaccination against smallpox!" exclaimed her aunt, and then pointed out that later, the king returned to his natural state of laziness and did no more than to approve his wife's reforms—she was in cahoots with an Englishman, the prime minister John Acton. "Before the terrible events of Paris," said the abbess, thus alluding to the storming of the Bastille, "the royals had done a great deal to modernize the university and encourage technology and the arts. But the king cared little or nothing about the monasteries: he and his queen wanted the Kingdom of Naples to be a bulwark of modernity and the leading state of the peninsula." She added, with a hint of satisfaction: "Of course, they failed."

Her aunt glided over the horrible years that followed in the wake of the beheading of the French royals, when Queen Maria Carolina, the sister of Marie Antoinette of France, reneging on her sympathetic attitude toward the Freemasons, had withdrawn all support for any and all progressive groups in the kingdom. The abbess was proud of the fact that her brother, who had witnessed the transformation of the king from a jovial prankster to a repressive monarch, still remained loyal to him. In the dark periods, he had even followed his king twice into Sicilian exile, while the other Padellanis drank to the health of the French usurper.

Then her aunt went on at some length about the reason for Agata's father's protracted bachelorhood: a womanizer, he married the thirteen-year-old Gesuela when he was on the verge of turning forty. In the family, everyone assumed that Carlo, the eldest brother, who had hitherto shown no interest in women, would not produce offspring. Peppino assumed that he would become the prince and at that point enter into an appropriate and "important" marriage. But Carlo surprised everyone when he was fifty, by marrying a widow from Lecce who bore him a son and then promptly died. "It all happened in less than a year, poor Carlo."

"Your father was happy that he married your mother," her aunt told her. "He loved her and he treated her like a little girl, and that was a mistake. She became capricious, even though she's a good woman." Donna Maria Crocifissa had criticized her sister-in-law; she regretted it immediately and promised herself to talk about it in confession. After that, she added, with a smile: "I can clearly remember the first time that he talked to me about her, I could tell that she'd made a good impression on him even when she was quite small, because she was well educated. He told me that, toward the end of the king's second exile, a new opera premiered in Palermo, *Così fan tutte*, in the new theater of the Baron Pisani, a friend of his whom I also knew. That evening, Gesuela sang him word for word a beautiful aria from that opera; evidently she was already familiar with it." She seemed to be trying to pursue her memory of the tune. "I wonder how it went," she murmured. Agata remembered it clearly, her mother still sang it now, with Agata accompanying her on the pianoforte, and in a low voice she sang Dorabella's aria, *È amore un ladroncello*. Her aunt, lowering her eyelids, listened raptly and beat out the time with her little finger. Transported by the sugary airiness of those verses, Agata had started singing it over again from the beginning, and her aunt followed along until she opened her eyes, fell silent, and for the second time was obliged to repent.

"After the king and queen returned," her aunt began reminiscing again, "the kingdom was crawling with spies and policemen." As he had done in the past, Peppino remonstrated with the king about the excesses of the police. "But that time, your father fell out of favor with the king and he was denied promotion in the army. Unwaveringly loyal, he put blame on the influence of the followers of the Duchess of Floridia; she had always pretended to be a great friend to him and to your mother when they had acted as her intermediaries and match-makers with the king, then, once she was married, she had betrayed their friendship, ingrate that she was. That's why they had to move to Messina just after you were born!" The abbess grimaced at the bitter recollection and then added, with a sigh, but with a faint smile as well, that every time he was in Naples, he unfailingly came to see her.

21.

October 1842.
Agata the postulant becomes an assistant pharmacist

Agata became a postulant at the age of sixteen, after two years of Educandate; none of the Padellanis attended the mass for the occasion. The abbess had asked her family members to reduce their contacts with her to a minimum, in order to allow Agata to immerse herself in the monastic life and preserve the precarious equilibrium that she had attained; her Neapolitan relations happily complied with the request, with a collective sigh of relief—the rebellious Sicilian girl was a source of much embarrassment—with the exception of Orsola and Sandra, the only ones who truly loved her. But for that very reason, they too had obeyed the abbess's request. Isolated from the rest of the world, the educands led a separate life from the postulants, the novices, and the choristers, and were protected from everyone. Agata liked studying and also had a new interest: the manufacture of *paperoles*—little temples and tiny altars containing miniature relics, or simply sacred images sat against a satin background and framed, created by the nuns in the eighteenth century using—instead of gold and silver thread, pearls and precious stones—strips of golden and colored paper, blades of straw, colored glass, sequins, and tiny mirrors. A French nun who had sought refuge in Naples had introduced them to the convent of San Giorgio Stilita; no longer fashionable and scorned by the choristers because of the inexpensive materials used, the art of *paperoles* had been preserved by the French nun's lay sisters, now quite old, and they had very few willing apprentices.

Agata depended upon the generosity of her aunt the abbess and on the money that she earned by selling *cucchitelle*. Now she had found a new way to earn money to pay for her modest needs. She created her *paperoles* with scrap materials that she found here and there or with odds and ends of silk given to her by the choristers. She specialized in little altar-shrines and floral decorations. She loved that work, which required patience and concentration. She felt enveloped in a cocoon woven by the loving care of her aunt the abbess and her other teachers, and she hoped that, just as a chrysalis is transformed into a butterfly, she too would receive the gift of a vocation when the time came for her simple profession, and that she would fly upward to God's side. Agata stubbornly refused to consider the alternative: becoming a nun against her will. She made every effort imaginable to *want* to become a nun, and she had even limited the time she spent reading the books that she had smuggled into the convent, incarnations of the temptation of civil society.

The nuns had once rotated through the various positions in the convent, from abbess to hebdomadary—the nun in charge of the kitchens—but it no longer worked that way. For more than fifteen years now the same helper nun had been in charge of relations with the outside world. The sister pharmacist, Donna Maria Immacolata, who also worked as the herbalist, had been attending to the sisters' health for many years and needed an assistant, but few of the sisters were interested in taking that job. Her Latin title was *monaca infirmaria*, inasmuch as it covered simultaneously the pharmacologist, the doctor, and the chemist.

When Agata became a postulant, in October 1842, she was assigned to assist her. Donna Maria Immacolata, austere and dark-eyed, had a lovely low soft voice, almost a whisper, a breath, a hush. With that voice, Donna Maria Immacolata carved into the silence the history of their order. She talked about how the medical arts had developed in Benedictine abbeys during the Middle Ages. Their medicine based the "hope of healing" on God's mercy and on the "action of simples," that is, the *medicamentum simplex*—a medicinal herb or a medicament made with officinal plants. This led, within the walls of their convents and monasteries, to the planting of gardens of simples for the cultivation of medicinal herbs and to the creation of the pharmacy, the *armarium pigmentariorum*, where they were stored and preserved over time. After the Cluniac Reforms, the Benedictines believed that meditation and prayer were preferable to the practices of the mortification of the flesh as an instrument of asceticism, "but you'll see that there are still sisters who use hair shirts and sackcloth and other ways of mortifying the body," she said, and she allowed her whisper to reverberate at a slightly higher tone. It was their duty to care for wounds and injuries without making comments or judgments; the pharmacist sister was there to help other nuns who were unwell or suffering from pain without asking questions or expressing her personal moral judgments. "In certain cases," and here Donna Maria Immacolata's voice grew faint again, "it is not advisable to call a physician. We take care of women's matters."

The garden of simples was divided between the two cloisters of the convent. Angiola Maria, assisted by Checchina, one of the lay sisters of Donna Maria Brigida, as well as by various servingwomen, was in charge of work in the garden of the main cloister. She was also involved in work in the cloister of the novices, dedicated exclusively to medicinal plants, under the jurisdiction of Donna Maria Immacolata. During the periods of harvest and preservation—drying, transformation into pills, tinctures, and essential oils—Angiola Maria supervised all the work, since she had taught herself the rudiments of reading in order to check the prescriptions and recipes.

The first time that Donna Maria Immacolata brought Agata

into the garden of simples she had asked Angiola Maria to accompany her; together they had helped her to identify every plant, and for each plant they had listed the medicinal characteristics and properties. Then they had moved on to the more practical suggestions concerning cultivation and care. There was an orderly chaos of individual plants, there were other plants in rows, bushes, shrubs, and potted plants. Donna Maria Immacolata stopped in front of the Cistus creticus, or pink rock-rose, a shrub with green leaves that was not particularly attractive: "We use this in herbal teas and infusions, it is a tonic and it strengthens the organism. Its resin was once burned to ward off illness. Now it is an ingredient in the incense for cardinals. When the cardinal is officiating, we use twice as much. Its scent is very sweet. I wonder whether our cardinal even notices, though. Sometimes, at services, he seems distracted . . . " The two women looked one another in the eye, prompting a sense of uneasiness in Agata that she was unable to decipher. She leaned over to admire a bunch of mauve-colored flowers growing in profusion at the foot of a shrub: each flower sprouted from a bulb. She thought she might pick one for the abbess.

"Stop!" the other two cried in unison. "Did you touch the stalk?"

Silence.

"She touched it!"

Donna Maria Immacolata grabbed her wrist and gripped it tightly; Angiola Maria, at the well, was frantically hauling up the bucket. They plunged her hand into the water and with their fingernails they scrubbed and scraped her fingers and the palm of her hand.

"It's called *Aconitum*, also known as wolfsbane or vegetable arsenic," Donna Maria Immacolata explained to her.

"Be careful! You'd best handle this plant cautiously. It's a deadly poison." That was not a suggestion, coming from Angiola Maria: it was a command.

22.
January 1844.
Agata is certain that she prefers nunhood to the marriage her mother wants for her

From inside the convent it was possible to keep up with what was happening in the outside world, just as it was possible to remain completely in the dark. According to the Rule, the nuns could write and receive letters only with permission from the abbess; Donna Maria Crocifissa readily gave that permission, just as she also authorized unsupervised visits in the parlor. Moreover, the nuns sent and received verbal messages through trusted servingwomen and they also kept up a constant traffic of packages and gifts with relatives, friends, and father confessors. Every day, dozens of trays of pastries went out from the convent, wrapped in tissue paper or oiled paper, depending on the type. They were wrapped in large sheets of heavy brown paper, skillfully tied with a stout twine; large boxes containing bedsheets and towels, custom-embroidered by the lay sisters, and baskets full of intimate linen sent to the nuns' family homes to be washed, including very fashionable and even coquettish articles of clothing, stitched between linings; less frequently, nuns sent gifts of *paperoles* to benefactors, prelates, and relatives. The same servingwomen made purchases for the nuns and brought back to the convent gifts from their families—books, both religious and otherwise, chocolate bonbons, pastries with cream toppings, candied almonds, and even sacred jewelry: crucifixes, chains, medallions, brooches, key rings.

The world entered and left through that remarkable subterranean traffic which mingled faith with pleasure, vanity and curiosity, news and gossip. Nothing was truly forbidden and no one could really claim to be impervious to what was happening outside the convent walls.

The time that Agata spent as a postulant was longer than usual because of her mother's lack of interest. Payment of the monastic dowry was supposed to be fully arranged before the postulant could be admitted to the preparatory course for the simple profession, but Donna Gesuela simply ignored all the letters that Agata wrote her. Agata's sisters in Messina did the same, evidently at their mother's orders. Aunt Orsola, the only one to have kept up relations with Agata, suffered from arthritis and when she came to the convent she was always accompanied by Sandra.

Agata knew little or nothing about what was happening with her family, and she knew still less about events in the kingdom, but she didn't mind a bit: she preferred to ignore the outside world—it was her way of surviving the cloistered life. She was frequently sad, but not entirely unhappy. She believed that she was pretty well along in the process of breaking her ties with the world. She still hoped that Giacomo hadn't forgotten her, and there were times when she thought that she recognized him as she looked down at the crowd of worshippers in the church. That hope was more of a comforting habit than it was a genuine hope. When she turned eighteen, the abbess told her that it was time for her to begin her studies for the examination of simple profession, and she asked Agata to urge her mother once again to present her proposal for the payment of the dowry. Agata wrote to the address that the abbess had given her, an address that had to do with the general's responsibilities: in fact, the general and his wife were often away from Palermo, where they had a house. In that period, they were in Catania. Like all Agata's other letters, however, this one too remained unanswered.

A few days later, a young nun who had just received visitors in the parlor breathlessly reported the news that Mt. Etna was erupting. A small knot of black veils clustered around her in the cloister—Agata was among them. Adding details of her own, the nun told them that all of eastern Sicily had been rocked by the earthquake and that there had been many victims. Catania was in danger: raising her pale hands skyward, the nun stated that the river of lava was about to engulf the Benedictine monastery of San Nicolò l'Arena, which had actually been rebuilt atop the solidified lava after the earthquake of 1693: she began a series of heartfelt supplications of St. Agatha, the city's—and Agata's—patron saint, as well as of St. Benedict. The other girls wanted to know more, but they hastily joined in the litanies, feeling the hawk-eyed glare of the prioress upon them. She had been watching them from her elevated vantage point on the terrace across the way.

Like a surging tide, her attachment to the outside world—places, people, things—was rising frantically, irrepressibly. How was her mother? And where was Carmela? Had people she knew been killed? Frustrated at her inability to find out, Agata smashed the bread dough down onto the countertop violently, making the little piles of flour in the corners leap into the air. She chopped the rump steak and yanked out the gristle with such force that it ripped the flesh. By nightfall she was gratified by her exhaustion and the aches in her muscles. At last, she implored the abbess to try to find out something from her married sisters in Messina. Amalia and Giulia replied promptly. It hadn't really been an "earthquake" so much as a series of minor shocks and tremors, and the eruption of Mt. Etna had posed absolutely no threat to the city of Catania. They both informed their aunt the abbess that their mother was angry with Agata for having refused to be married off to the Cavaliere d'Anna. She had intentionally failed to answer Agata's letters and she had ordered them not to write to their sister. The Cavaliere d'Anna still wanted to marry Agata and had announced that he would be willing to wait for her, well aware that Agata could legally leave the convent. Amalia wished to let Agata know that, after their mother's wedding, Carmela, who had stayed behind in Messina and now lived with Amalia, greatly wished to see Agata again.

The clash between mother and daughter was not a secret for long, in either Messina or Naples. The result was that it stirred the Padellanis from their torpor—one by one they came to pay Agata a visit—and it made Gesuela dig her heels in.

The first ones who came to see her were Aunt Orsola and Admiral Pietraperciata: both of them wanted to reassure Agata that they would renew their efforts to win her mother's consent to her becoming a nun; they conveyed greetings from her cousin Michele, the head of the larger family, who fully approved her decision to become a nun. Next came the prince's wife, Ortensia, a tall woman, insipidly beautiful, with whom Agata had spoken only very rarely. Ortensia too praised her decision and promised that she would speak to Donna Gesuela on Agata's behalf. The princess also shed light on the reason for the family's sudden renewal of interest in Agata; in fact, Agata had been baffled by it. The abbess, it turns out, had written directly to her sisters and to the prince, asking them to come out in support of Agata's vocation, and informing them as to Gesuela's impious intentions. The abbess had also made it clear, between the lines, that she would not look favorably on the candidacy of other girls from the Padellani di Opiri family at the convent of San Giorgio Stilita if Agata were to be torn from the oasis of salvation in which none other than her mother had first placed her. Ortensia, who had four young daughters, was keenly interested in placing at least one of them as a nun at San Giorgio Stilita.

Eleonora and Severina Tozzi also came to see her, now both married and still childless. Eleonora had had a series of miscarriages and seemed tense and exhausted. Severina, who was younger and a relative newlywed, asked Agata to pray for her to have a male child, telling her coyly: "My husband is really determined, he never gives me a rest . . . " The two cousins spoke as if they were in a confessional, about everything and everyone, without caution or care, even about intimate conjugal details.

While Eleonora stuffed herself on the puff pastries that Sarina offered her in the parlor, and between bites asked her to give her the recipe, Severina confided to Agata in a hushed voice that Eleonora had been threatened by her husband. He had told her that if she were unable to bring her next pregnancy to term, then he would "turn his back on her" and request an annulment. Agata remembered Eleonora as a vivacious young girl, an attractive and talented ballerina; now, at age twenty-two, she'd put on weight and had lost her lovely poise and confidence. As if she'd just read Agata's mind, Severina whispered: "If you could only see how badly she dances now, fat as she is!" Then, in a rush, she added: "Do you remember that time in the alcove when you danced a waltz with Captain capitano Garson?" Severina told her that she'd seen him again at a reception just the other evening. After his wedding, he'd stopped frequenting Neapolitan society: it was said that his wife had demanded that they go live in Menton, not far from Nice. When he came back to the kingdom, he took care of family business and only socialized within the populous local colony of English people. Suddenly, however, in the last few weeks, Garson was being seen everywhere. "I'll ask Admiral Pietraperciata, he'll surely know. I say they're no longer together. Or perhaps she's died. I've even heard that she's gone melancholic, and that she's been put in a madhouse." Agata had leaned her forehead against the grate; she could hear the notes of the waltz, but she couldn't see James's face; Giacomo was her gallant knight, and she was dancing in his arms, feeling his dark eyes upon her.

A sudden gust of warm, pastry-scented breath wafted over her; Agata was unable to recoil fast enough—Eleonora had thrust her face against the grate, in order to emphasize her request. "We all know that you have a special devotion for the Madonna dell'Utria, we know that through the power of your prayer you made the stolen jewels reappear," Eleonora said; she went on to beg her cousin to implore the Virgin to give her the grace of a son. "And pray for your sister Sandra, too, she has as much need as I do . . . "

After that visit, Agata fell into a different kind of melancholy. The conjugal miseries of her cousins unsettled her; they undercut her certainty that life with Giacomo would have been so greatly preferable to the cloistered life. She wished that she could simply stop the pendulum of time and stay as she was, a postulant at San Giorgio Stilita, with the option of leaving the convent when her mother finally accepted her refusal to be married off to the Cavaliere d'Anna. Once and for all.

Then she grew restless: she wanted to return to civilian life, read newspapers and novels, pay attention to politics, make friendships, get married. Right away.

One day, in a fit of agitation, she hastily emptied her trunk of linen and lifted the false bottom. At random, she pulled out a book, *Pride and Prejudice*, and then tossed the linen higgledy-piggledy back into the trunk and shut it, afraid of being caught. She read the novel in fits and starts, when she was able, but she couldn't wait to plunge back into it. She identified with the Bennet sisters and their beaus; the memory of Giacomo came back vividly, churning her emotions. She could no longer bring herself to become a nun. She wanted Giacomo. She yearned for him. She went so far as to prepare a decoction to placate her yearnings. But the next day they returned. She convinced herself that Giacomo was in Naples and, just as she was thinking about him, so he must be trying to find her. At the first opportunity that presented itself, she went to listen to Mass from the catwalk next to the choir, and she scrutinized the nave, looking for Giacomo from the grate facing the little altar of the Blessed Elisabetta Padellani, but she never saw him—never.

Agata tried to peer within, to understand her own behavior, but she was unsuccessful. She was baffled by herself, and she didn't want to talk about it with Father Cuoco—she didn't dare. She knew that she was too confused. She did her schoolwork and her chores, she studied and worked like the other postulants, but she felt like the brigantine that had brought her to Naples through the tempest with her father's coffin: storm-tossed and adrift, uncertain of everything and everyone.

February 5, 1844 was her eighteenth birthday, as well as the feast day of her patron saint, St. Agatha. She was watching Mass from the parapet. At last! But she had no time to enjoy the show: Giacomo was down there, next to a young woman dressed in green, who wore a hat trimmed with fur. Between them were two small children. He was clearly quite restless; he kept looking around him and he inevitably wound up with his head pointing in the direction of the comunichino. The little boy next to him reached up for his hand; Giacomo, arrogantly, yanked it away. The woman in the hat leaned down to say something to the little boy, then she resumed her stance. The little boy started whining and went on reaching up for his father's hand; the father made an impatient gesture to a serving girl in the pew behind them. Now the child was wailing in despair; he didn't want to be taken away, but the father shoved him rudely out of the pew. "Don't treat a little boy that way!" Agata exclaimed; then she watched what happened next, livid with indignation. The serving girl had left her pew and was standing next to Giacomo. He hoisted the child in the air and set him down hard, like a sack of potatoes, next to her; she dragged the child off up the nave of the church as he bawled his eyes out. The woman with the green hat didn't seem to have noticed a thing. The other child, smaller still, was holding his mother's overcoat, and now he tried to hold his father's hand. Giacomo pulled his hand away brutishly and held it high, out of reach. The little boy, gripping his father's sleeve, continued to try to seize the hand; unable to do so, he burst into tears. Giacomo ignored him.

"He's unworthy of me," Agata murmured, and turned to the image of the Blessed Elisabetta Padellani. Giacomo, in the meanwhile, had plunged his finger into his nostril, rooting intently, only to wipe it off on the skirt of his overcoat, while his wife soothed the toddler, still in tears.

That night, Agata finished reading *Pride and Prejudice*. She was head over heels in love with Darcy. The following morning, in a frenzy, she wrote a note to James Garson and sent it to Detken's bookshop with a servingwoman:

My Dear Mr. Garson,
I beg your pardon if I bother you after nearly four years. I'm not sure you'll remember me, but I've taken up the first novel you gave me again: I reread it with new eyes. It gave me hope. I wish you and your family the greatest happiness. From here I pray for you.

His only reply was to send her a new book.

23.
November 1844.
Agata, captivated by the novels that James sends her, wants something else, something more, doubts whether she has the vocation, and has a talk with the cardinal

At the end of November 1844, Donna Gesuela sent Sandra to inform the abbess, without any further explanation, that she would have no objection to her daughter becoming a nun: she couldn't guarantee payment of the monastic dowry, but she would do her level best. The abbess decided that the following year, once she'd turned nineteen, Agata would study for the admission examinations for simple profession. Then, after her year of novitiate, at the age of twenty-one, Agata could study for her solemn profession.

Agata did not welcome her mother's decision with anything resembling relief. Since turning eighteen, she had felt like an adult, a different person. She was no longer happy to remain in the safety of the convent; now she was restless and curious. She wanted to return to ordinary life and work. She had persuaded herself that sooner or later her mother would let her do so. After all, she had the qualifications to do the same work that Miss Wainwright did. But now Agata wanted something different, something more. In response to every note that she sent thanking him for a book and expressing her observations, Garson would send her another book—poetry and novels, at first in English and then in Italian and even French, some modern, others not, romantic, adventuresome, and melodramatic—these books only increased her restlessness. She dreamed of emulating the heroines of the novels and she desired the love of a man. Very much. Oh, so very much. Then reality swept over her: she was penniless and unwanted by her family, with her back to the wall. So she set about trying to "want" her vocation, but all too soon she succumbed again to the siren call of the world outside. She asked Sandra to hide something for her to read in the basket of personal linen that she sent home to wash, and she avidly listened to everything the other nuns reported after visits from their relations. From Sandra's newspapers she received a hodgepodge of information about current world events, but she couldn't seem to put it into any order: in Germany there had been an uprising among the weavers against the owners of the spinning mills in a bid to improve salaries and working conditions; in the Antilles, there was the insurrection of the people of Santo Domingo against the Republic of Haiti, which had in turn won its independence by rebelling against French colonization; in English, labor organizations were demanding more inclusive electoral reforms and universal suffrage; in the Holy Land, the Ottoman Empire, in response to internal and external pressure, had allowed the return of the Jews; in Calabria the royal army had drowned in blood the revolt instigated by the Bandiera brothers, two adherents of the Giovine Italia, a revolutionary sect that was calling for the creation of an Italian republic instead of a unified Kingdom of Italy. She had also learned, both through Sandra and from other nuns, that a book written by Vincenzo Gioberti, a Piedmontese priest living in exile in Brussels, *Del primato morale e civile degli italiani—The Moral and Political Primacy of the Italians*, called for the unity of Italy in a confederation under the leadership of the pope.

Agata understood that, beneath the apparent calm of the kingdom and of the rest of the world, social tensions were rumbling like the magma under Mt. Etna, ready to erupt. No longer certain she'd always enjoy the protection of the convent, she was afraid of an uncertain future.

She turned to the teacher of the novices, Donna Maria Giovanna della Croce, who became for her an example and an informal spiritual guide. With her help, she came to appreciate silence as one of the paths that lead to God, and she attained the level of self-awareness whereby every action becomes prayer, and prayer becomes contemplation, in turn transcending reality and leading to the vastness of the Divine. Agata told her that she felt isolated in her cloistered life. "Our life is stable, but it is neither repetitive nor monotonous: we operate on liturgical time, our working day is not punctuated only by our praise of God and the personal dimension of solitude. There is not a single day that is identical to another day. We are not isolated," she replied. Agata told her that she wanted to do good and alleviate the sufferings of others, of children, of the sick. "Prayer joins us with the outside world and, like a thurible full of incense, it purifies that which surrounds us as it burns." The suffering and the calvary of Christ, upon which the monastic day was modeled, was nothing other than a way of growing. They talked about the renunciations implicit in the condition of nunhood. "It's normal for there to be critical moments, they form part of our process of spiritual growth and they help us to ripen our decision to choose the cloistered life. You must not be afraid of change; you must accept with docility the surprises that life holds in store for us, and savor them to the fullest." Agata revealed to her the secret of her intense desire to fall in love, be fecund, bear children. Donna Maria Giovanna della Croce encouraged her with her usual sweet smile. "Renouncing children is not necessarily the same as renouncing fecundity. We must remain virgins in order to be fecund and to live every second of our lives with Love for the universe. I am in love with silence, through love of God and God alone. Like Mary the sister of Martha, I want to sit at Jesus's feet and listen to His words. You should do the same."

Agata tried.

But, in her conversations with God, Agata revealed to Him the indestructible certainty—which she was forced to smother during the day—that she wasn't suited to seclusion. Every night the truth revealed itself forcefully, and she, by candlelight, immersed herself in books of poetry and the tragic, heartbreaking love stories of the novels concealed under the false bottom of her trunk, all the while yearning for those things to happen to her. By day, she once again believed the persuasive words of Donna Maria Giovanna della Croce. "Wait. You love God. Knowing how to wait teaches you how to enjoy," she told Agata. "The calling will come. Trust me and do your best to see things through my eyes."

Before being admitted to the simple profession of vows and formally becoming a novice, the postulant was required to pass a colloquium with her spiritual father and with the abbess.

Agata did not lie; she told both her spiritual father and the abbess that while she was happy to take the vows of chastity and poverty, she did not feel the calling; she would do her best to find it. She believed that she had passed her colloquia. Instead the cardinal in person wished to speak with her.

They were in the abbess's drawing room, alone and standing face to face.

They looked at one another in silence. Agata was the first to turn her gaze away: from the round window above the door, the light that came filtering through from the cloister fell on the floor in an oval that reminded her of the shape of the *pastenove* that she carved out of the puff pastry dough. "I've heard that you believe that you lack the calling, and that you're worried about it," the cardinal began. Agata lowered her head in assent. "I don't see why you should be worried," he went on, with a hint of annoyance in his voice. "St. Teresa of Ávila was obliged to wait many years for her vocation. You are committing the sin of pride, if you try to hasten the process. The calling will come, your spiritual father is certain of it. You have completed fine periods of work in the infirmary and your pastries are selling like hotcakes. But why don't you tell me what you like best about the cloistered life." And he stepped toward her.

Agata looked up—she hadn't forgotten that many years before he had touched her face—and answered in a rush, to put an end to the conversation: "Listening to the choir and singing.".

"Explain why."

"It brings me closer to God."

At that moment, the bells rang None. A gentle, insistent chiming. He stood looking at her. Then he moved, and strode past her in a rustle of purple fabric, without coming near her. He threw open both panels of the door that led into the hall where the abbess and her secretary were waiting.

"Let's go to the choir together. All of us. From this day forth, Agata Padellani, our future novice, will sing with the choristers."

The nuns were moving through the Chapter Hall and walking down the corridors toward the choir with downcast gazes, occasionally casting sidelong glances at the fluttering hems of the cardinal's cassock; followed by his altar boys, the cardinal was leading the way, walking briskly, erect and proud, by Agata's side.

Agata slipped into the choir and made for the seats in the back. Decisively, the cardinal seized her arm: "I want to see you. Here, next to the mother abbess." And beneath the astonished eyes of the choristers, the aspiring novice was forced to go over to the abbess and remain there, in full view, blushing from head to foot. When the abbess gave the signal, Agata

began the Lauds. It was Psalm 119, the longest in the entire
Book of Psalms.

Alone in the sight of God, Agata sang. Like David. And a
great feeling of calm spread through her.

O that my ways were directed to keep thy statutes!
Then shall I not be ashamed, when I have respect unto all thy
commandments.
I will praise thee with uprightness of heart, when I shall have
learned thy righteous judgments.
I will keep thy statutes: O forsake me not utterly.

Every so often, the abbess looked sidelong at the cardinal.
He was on the threshold of the choir, lips compressed, with
eyes only for Agata.

24.
April 1845.
On the verge of her simple profession,
Agata withdraws but then gives in

Her mother had not replied to the letter the abbess sent her to inform her that Agata, after a conversation with the cardinal, had been accepted for her simple profession and, at the same time, to urge her to bring to conclusion the negotiations for the payment of the monastic dowry.

But when Aunt Orsola heard the good news, she went to the convent to congratulate Agata, accompanied by her brother the admiral. Not only did he renew his offer of a thousand ducats towards Agata's monastic dowry, he declared that he was willing to contribute seven hundred ducats more for the reception. Agata's aunt told her that her mother had not only set aside money for the dowry, but now she fully approved her decision to become a nun—once again, and without providing explanations, on one condition. Agata's simple profession was no longer in doubt.

In the long years of cloistered life, Agata had regressed to the world of her childhood—preordained by adults, in which obedience is an absolute requirement—and she had gained access to a spiritual world in which prayer was a step leading upward toward peace. She had diligently read everything available to her, from medical science to theology, and she had been scrupulous in her sacred readings. Outside of that scrupulous devotion, Agata wavered between the hope that she would be visited by her calling—and in that hope she was greatly aided by *The Imitation of Christ*, four slim books by a medieval monk, Thomas à Kempis—and the certainty that she wanted to live in the outside world and find love, like the Bennet sisters.

It was in fact over love that Agata was tormenting herself. She loved God. But she also wanted the love of a man, she wanted to have children, she wanted a love made up of the kisses, caresses, and thrills that culminated in the union of two bodies. The closer the moment of her simple profession drew, the more it broke her heart to say farewell to her hope for a love that might lead to motherhood. The ineluctable nature of her monastic fate was, however, softened by her fondness for her aunt the abbess. It was for her that Agata was agreeing to become a nun. She darkened at the thought of what would become of her after her aunt's death.

Agata was walking in the cloister. Regular steps, head bowed, hands crossed in front of her—apparently untroubled; but inside, tangled in the throes of turmoil over her mother's unexpected demand: after ignoring her for all these years, now she wanted Agata to spent the last two weeks before her simple profession with her.

She was terrified at the thought of leaving the convent to go to stay at Sandra's house, meet her relatives, see her mother and sisters again—things she'd yearned for over the years. She was afraid of the streets, the carriages, the crowds, the horses, the dogs, the cats, the ungrated windows, the sounds of the city. She thought about all she'd lose during those two weeks. She would be disoriented by days not punctuated by the canonical hours, she'd miss singing in the choir. As she had gradually reduced her expectations, she'd become accustomed to the tiny yet great pleasures of the cloistered life— waiting in expectation: would the eggs in the swallow's nest in the rain gutter hatch? would the clusters of oleander flowers bloom? at dinner, would they serve the soup blended with tomatoes or plain? would the white butterfly fluttering over the castor-oil plant land on the back of her right hand or in the palm of her left hand? She'd learned to love the small things. She'd become accustomed to solitude. She trembled at the thought of chatty women and the idea that she would be forced to answer the inevitable questions. And the thought of being once again tempted by what she had so painfully learned to renounce—when she thought of that, Agata truly desired to be a nun, in full.

And so it happened. Agata began thinking of Sandra's comfortable home, full of books and prints of Pompeii. And the pianoforte, which she'd missed so much and would probably no longer know how to play. And music. The harp, the violin, the oboe. The mandolin. And then dance. Now she slipped into her memory of the waltz, unforgettable. There she was again, in the alcove off the drawing room in the home of the Tozzis, dancing with James Garson; together they were pirouetting, beating time, following the rhythm as if they were a single body. She was ready for life. Just as during a lesson, when with a few vigorous strokes of the sponge she erased all the writing on the chalkboard, so too, with just a few sharp blows, Agata had wiped out all the years she'd spent at San Giorgio Stilita. And that wasn't all. Giacomo Lepre no longer existed for her. It was James she desired now, excruciatingly.

In the pharmacy, Agata had just finished preserving a batch of white willow bark. An entire cartload had just come in from some of the convent's farmland. It was a very painstaking operation. Once the bark had been rinsed and dried, she had to chop and dry it a second time to prevent mold. Then she put it into little sacks, carefully noting the dosage on each one: the sacks were sent to other convents and monasteries, in exchange for other medicinal herbs. The willow bark decoction was given to nuns with fevers or for the pain of rheumatism, but it was also given to young nuns suffering from carnal desires, as a sedative.

One evening Agata was so taken with her thoughts of James that she had to run back to the pharmacy to make herself a decoction of white willow bark. The sacks of bark had already been sent out and for the first time in her life, Agata found herself stealing. She took chasteberry to calm her nerves, a remedy that had been handed down by Armenian nuns. Then, curled up in her bed, she broke into sobs of shame and relief.

The peace of the cloister, so hard-won, became more of a burden day by day. Then, a yoke to bear. She avoided Donna Maria Giovanna della Croce. She psalmodized in the choir—and was burning to be somewhere else. She was in the middle of doing needlepoint, and she set it aside without even finishing the needleful. They gave her silver paper for her *paperoles*, and she rumpled it in her pocket. Everything that she'd always liked about the cloistered life she suddenly couldn't stand. Agata only wanted to love and be loved by a man.

She spent her nights reading by candlelight, like a madwoman: first, the love story by Madame de Staël, the story of Corinne and an Englishman, in which the heroine was admired and feared by men, and therefore destined to a life of solitude. The novel explained Italy and the essence of Italians, and not just to foreigners. Then she read the books of Giuseppe Mazzini, which Tommaso had concealed in her clean laundry, for fear of police searches. The visionary thinking of this man opened a new world to her, a world that gradually became attainable and real; the world she'd always known receded before these unfamiliar images.

By day, Agata was the dutiful future novice, ready for the

solemn moment in which she would pledge herself as a bride of Christ, but by night she was a clandestine reader of books outlawed by the king and placed on the Index by the Church. Every morning, she woke up with the taste of forbidden dreams. She was fixated with James Garson and the books he sent her. Agata felt a strange affinity with certain nuns that she'd always avoided till then or had chosen to ignore: each of them had found their own form of forbidden love, there, in seclusion. But she didn't want to wind up like them.

Her simple profession was drawing closer. This lie she was living had become an intolerable burden. Agata couldn't become a nun, she could no longer ignore it. She had to tell her aunt the abbess.

Donna Maria Crocifissa was indisposed. She sent for Agata as soon as Angiola Maria told her that her niece wished to speak to her. She was sitting on the terrace, which had been transformed into a veritable little hanging garden, filled as it was with the round and rectangular terracotta pots in which Angiola Maria was capable of getting anything to grow. In that period, both oregano—which was particularly difficult to cultivate in a pot—and mint were flowering, in great profusion. A potted Japanese camellia, the *Oki no Nami*, "waves of the sea," was at the height of its blooms. Against the background of the blistery foliage—a periwig of glistening green hair—there stood out, as if they'd been pinned in place, the full-bodied flowers with their pink petals, with white striations and edges; from the center of each projected, erect, a dense topknot of yellow pistils. Hypnotized by the opulence and the perfume of the *Oki no Namis*, Agata stood speechless. The abbess coughed to attract her attention. Agata hesitated, then spat out the words, brutally: "I don't have the vocation, I don't want to become a nun." And she waited, in fear.

Her aunt covered her face with her emaciated hands and sat

there, her chest heaving with sobs, her shoulders hunched forward, her head bowed. Her hands resembled the small, feminine hands of Agata's father.

She would become a nun. And that was that.

25.

Agata spends the last two weeks with her family
before beginning her cloistered life
and she encounters James

It had been decided well in advance that Agata would leave the convent to go to the Aviello home on exactly June 3, 1845.

Ever since it had become clear to the people closest to Donna Maria Crocifissa that the abbess did not have long to live, Angiola Maria had paid closer attention to the gossip of the cloister and, through trusted servingwomen, had maintained contacts and exchanges with the outside world. Among the novices, a wide array of rumors were circulating—that Agata's mother had been given a sharp discount on her dowry as well as favorable terms on the payment of the installments, that her simple profession had been moved up for the convenience of a very important visitor, that a foreign power was interested in her, and even that the cardinal had paid the monastic dowry for his young relative in full. Angiola Maria warned Agata of what she was hearing, and encouraged her not to let the backbiters and gossips embitter her; she stayed especially close to Agata, when she could, and she had made Agata promise to report to her anything odd that might happen.

The evening before she was scheduled to leave the convent, Agata worked late in the pharmacy to make sure that she left everything in order. Angiola Maria had urged her to go, assuring her that she would make sure everything was taken care of and that she would bring her an infusion of herbal tea to help her sleep.

Agata said goodbye to the abbess and the nuns she loved the

best. She still had to fill her trunks with all her possessions: she was afraid that someone might rummage through her things if she left them in her cell. Suddenly, she remembered that she had forgotten to say goodbye to Donna Maria Brigida, her now demented aunt. She found her curled up in the arms of her favorite servingwoman, Nina, a small pile of bones in a nightshirt, like a little naked baby bird, slumbering as she sucked her thumb. When Agata went back to her cell, she noticed on the night table, next to little boxes of herbal teas, packets of officinal herbs, and jars of tinctures to take as gifts for her sisters, a glass with a warm amber beverage. She felt sure that this was a kind thought on the part of Angiola Maria; deeply moved, she decided to write her a thank you note immediately. It was a time-consuming task, and it absorbed her attention—she had to use very clear handwriting and simple words for the functionally illiterate lay sister: she didn't hear the knock on the door, nor did she hear the door being opened.

Agata was trying to come up with just the right word. Perhaps the best thing to do would be to take a break and sip some of that herbal tea. She reached out and picked up the glass. Like a vise grip, a powerful hand grabbed her arm and another hand yanked the glass out of her fingers; she resisted the unseen aggressor and the glass slipped out of her grip, shattering on the floor. Now Angiola Maria, down on all fours, was gathering up the shards of glass and crying. Agata was completely bewildered. Then she noticed a tray on the bed, a tray that Angiola Maria had been carrying: on it was another glass of herbal tea, almost the same color as the one she'd been about to drink, and then she understood. There was someone who wanted to hurt her. Angiola Maria tasted a bit of the liquid that had spilled on the ground. "That's poison. I have more than just an idea of who it might have been." She assured Agata that nothing like this would ever happen again, she would put a stop to it. She stayed to help Agata close and fasten her trunks and she watched as she drank the herbal tea. It had a wonderful effect. Agata fell asleep immediately.

Agata and Sandra were heading for the Aviello home, riding in the enclosed carriage that Aunt Orsola had once again put at their service. Agata looked out the window without pushing the curtain aside; the world appeared opaque. She was curious, but she was anxious, too. Naples had changed, and it was prettier now. The gaslights along the streets, a system that the French had put in, had been inaugurated six years earlier; now all the main streets had their own handsome lamp posts. People were dressed in a fashion she'd never seen; everyone looked a little better off. Gleaming and sumptuous new carriages rolled through the streets, there were more shops, fewer beggars; many of the façades of the *palazzi* had been rebuilt and new buildings were under construction. Sandra gripped her hand tightly; she told her that her mother and Carmela were waiting for her at home, while General Cecconi would arrive next week from Palermo, aboard the steamboat *Rubattino*. Then she fell silent. Agata turned to look at her; her sister's eyes looked dead.

The concierge of the *palazzo* in which the Aviellos lived opened the carriage door with a sweeping bow. Dazzled by the light glancing off the white stone façade, and intimidated by the sight of men loitering on the sidewalk and inside in the courtyard, Agata hesitated. Then Sandra took her by the arm and they started upstairs. Her mother gave her a hug as if she'd just left an hour ago; her only comment was on how tall Agata had become—and she really had grown—with no reference to the past or the future. Carmela, now quite the young woman, latched onto her sister and followed her around like her shadow all day. Agata saw the signs of the passage of time on the faces of all three women: her mother's lovely body had filled out almost to stoutness; sumptuously dressed, the Generalessà—as she was now called—still cut a very fine figure, but every so often a shadow passed over her eyes, and she clutched her bejeweled fingers together as if she were trying to hurt herself. Sandra had lost weight. Sloppily dressed and tense, she seemed pensive; but when the two sisters' eyes met, Sandra still had a ready smile. Carmela had become a blooming thirteen-year-old girl with distinctively provincial manners, distinctly similar to her mother's.

Those two weeks were supposed to be the final test of a postulant's rejection of the worldly life, but actually for the first week Agata lived a semi-cloistered existence. She wasn't allowed to go out into the city, or take walks or carriage rides. She received a few visits from relatives curious about her dowry—she was thought of as Messinese and therefore different—but no one was really interested in her.

When no visitors were scheduled to come, her mother and sisters went out, leaving Agata alone in the apartment. She was glad of it, because she already missed her solitude. She hesitantly approached the piano, and played somewhat gingerly; little by little she gained confidence and familiarity, but she was still far from the fluency she had once possessed. She read everything that came within reach and, when they were alone, she talked with her brother-in-law. At the age of forty, Tommaso Aviello was a handsome man with salt-and-pepper hair. Agata remembered him as someone who believed passionately in the pillars of Carboneria—the equality and dignity of all Italians, united in a state governed by a constitutional monarchy—and who was proud that in 1820 the Kingdom of the Two Sicilies was the first nation on earth to hold an election with universal suffrage, even for illiterates. She considered him a dreamer with his feet on the ground who managed to keep his sense of humor as well as a perceptive lawyer who was able to analyze and solve even the most complicated situations.

But now, Tommaso was discouraged. He had hoped that the king might understand that he had a chance to unify the peninsula by expanding his kingdom northward. But instead the king had retreated behind a wall of surly isolationism and, unsure of the loyalty of the royal armies, he had humiliated his soldiers and officers by hiring mercenaries and running up debts with the Rothschild banking house. He had gradually undermined the liberties that had been won by his people, while his police and secret services increased their ranks and their power with their successes: Mazzini's popularity was plummeting, the Giovine Italia, the movement that he had founded, had been unsuccessful in not one but three attempted insurrectional coups, and Naples was no longer the headquarters of the Carboneria. Tommaso was afraid that the movement to which he had dedicated his life was about to be stamped out throughout Italy.

Then Tommaso screwed up his courage and began talking about Gioberti's *Primato degli italiani*, the possibility of a customs union and federation between the Italian states with the Papal State at its head—but the pope was a reactionary. "Something is going to have to happen, the people are suffering and nationalism can no longer be suffocated. Naples is still teeming with secret societies. The king, humiliated by the English who rule the seas and control all commerce, behaves like their underling—he must shake off their rule; he will do it!" Tommaso seemed hopeful. After a while, though, he plunged back into his dark pessimism. "The internal situation is precarious. Like so many others, I'm going to have to consider exile. I may go to Tuscany. I've lost nearly all my clients, and I have a family to feed." More than once he told Agata that he mistrusted General Cecconi, who had once been a reactionary, and was now making gestures of interest in the Carboneria. He was certainly a police spy.

Despite his bitter outbursts, Tommaso often went out alone, and when he did there was a bounce to his step; when he returned he was always in a good mood. Agata thought that it would be hard to rely on a man who went from depressed to exalted like that; she was worried about Sandra.

The arrival of General Cecconi, an older man with a handsome appearance, a snowy white beard and whiskers and bushy black eyebrows, brought about a change in her mother—Gesuela was wreathed in smiles, her voice was contented, and she hurried to satisfy all her husband's slightest whims. She stayed at home and received visits from relatives and friends, where Agata was expected to look on. The general was utterly indifferent to Agata and Carmela, while he never missed an opportunity to talk to Tommaso and express gallant compliments to Sandra.

Agata happened to catch Sandra sobbing. She was sitting in an armchair, almost indifferent to Agata's presence. Sandra seemed to be seeking some form of liberation. Agata didn't ask, but Carmela later confided that Sandra was unhappy because her husband no longer loved her—she had heard her mother say it.

Agata found social conversations intolerable, along with affected manners and even the company of her family. She even began to miss the quiet of the cloister. And she began to yearn for it, desperately, when, during a visit to her Aunt Orsola, her mother informed her of the plans that her cousin the prince had made.

"Michele and Ortensia are going to hold a grand reception for an English duke of royal blood, who has come expressly to attend the ceremony for your simple profession," her mother told her as they were eating ice cream.

"And just how did this Englishman find out about my simple profession?" Agata asked, suspiciously.

"Come, come, don't put on such a face! The princes of Opiri have many connections with foreign royals, lots of them come to Naples. Michele must have spoken to them about you." Gesuela looked to her sister-in-law for assistance, but none was forthcoming. Then, seeing that her daughter was anxious, she added: "It's an honor, for all of us. I expect you to make me very proud of you." Now General Cecconi weighed in; with his massive voice he explained to Agata that the recent resumption of diplomatic contacts with England and other European nations had increased the number and quality of foreign travelers to Naples and even to Palermo—royal yachts were frequent guests in the ports of the kingdom and many prestigious visitors came to winter in the new grand hotels or were invited to stay as guests in the *palazzi* of the nobility or else of wealthy businessmen and entrepreneurs. The general looked around haughtily and pretended not to notice Tommaso's behavior: the minute he had begun speaking, Tommaso had turned his head to look out the window and seemed to be staring at the roof of the *palazzo* across the way.

Aunt Orsola, who until then had been off to one side, broke the silence: she offered to give Agata a chaste evening dress for the reception, and also said that she'd like to lend her a parure of amethyst and gold filigree. She asked if her niece could sleep at her house, the night of the reception.

Agata was not allowed to wear jewelry, and she was required to wear the dark outfit of the postulant, a short veil on her hair and on her feet the black leather monastic shoes, Gesuela replied, in a resentful tone of voice. Her husband intervened again, and persuaded her to grant at least her sister-in-law's last request. That night, Agata could sleep at her aunt's house.

The reception held by the princes of Opiri was magnificent. The enfilade of drawing rooms on the *piano nobile* of Palazzo Padellani, all opened for the occasion, reiterated infinitely in the large plate glass mirrors at the two extremities of the rooms, increased the luminosity of the bronze and crystal chandeliers in the style of the Emperor Napoleon—a gift from Murat to the prince of Opiri. Agata walked through the throng of guests flanked by the master and mistress of the house; after her, they were only waiting for the arrival of His Britannic Royal Highness. Dazzled by everything and deafened by the music of the quartet that was playing in the main ballroom, by the buzz of distant conversations, by the voices and the laughter of the groups near her, Agata could sense that she was about to swoon; but then she resolved to be strong and continued on. She moved mechanically and obeyed anyone who was near her—her cousins, her aunt Orsola, or anyone else. The sumptuousness of the *palazzo* decorated for gala festivities and the elegance of the guests made no particular impression on her, nor did the abundance of food. She exchanged kisses and hugs with strange women bedecked with jewels; she greeted with a grimace that was meant as a smile men who came close to look at her, and then in embarrassment extended their hands. Like a trained monkey, she bestowed a *buona sera* here, another *buona sera* there, a *grazie, prego*, and an *arrivederci*, and she responded to the compliments and best wishes of people she'd never seen in her life.

When the prince came to get Agata so she could be introduced to the English duke, she obediently followed her handsome cousin, who was tall and blond like an Austrian and very different from the Padellani. The guests made way for them and Michele nodded greetings to them as they passed, while telling her the story of how he had first made the acquaintance of their illustrious guest. Admiral Pietraperciata, who had attended boarding school with the cardinal and had remained on very close terms with him, had informally asked Michele whether he would have any objection to allowing the English royal to attend his young cousin's simple profession. Then the cardinal had forwarded the royal's formal request, adding that he himself had chosen Agata. "It's a great honor for us Padellanis, and it may have significant repercussions." And her cousin whispered in her ear that the cardinal—of whom it was rumored that he was a future candidate to the throne of St. Peter—was hoping to establish ties with the Catholic clergy of England, just then experiencing a great revival in the wake of the passage of the Catholic Emancipation Act by the British Parliament, abolishing almost all civil restrictions. The cardinal was also a close acquaintance of the famous Anglican cleric John Newman, who had now converted to Roman Catholicism, and who had also come to Naples a few years before. By agreeing to be present at the reception, Agata had helped Michele to establish a direct contact with the English monarchy, and he was grateful to her for it. "I realize that this has been very unpleasant for you," her cousin added, and he squeezed her arm.

His Royal Highness was corpulent. Agata made a reverence, bowing in her tight black gown. When she looked up, she realized that James Garson was standing next to the duke—he was part of his entourage. She blushed, in embarrassment. In the thank-you notes for the books that he sent her, at times she had ventured to talk about herself and to criticize the convent, confident that she would never run into him.

"Are you happy to become a nun?" the duke inquired.

"Yes," Agata blushed.

"The love of Christ must be very powerful, to persuade one to abandon the world, don't you find?" he insisted.

Agata thought it over before answering: "Any love, if it is a true love, is equally powerful. I have read about English ladies who fell in love with foreign men in Arabia and India, and who abandoned their own world for the much poorer and more primitive world of their beloved."

"Our guest is interested in knowing about the cloistered life," the prince broke in.

"To live in a magnificent cloister full of trees and flowering plants, with a gurgling fountain, and adoring Jesus Christ is the height of happiness for someone who has the calling. What might appear to be a prison is transformed into a palace. Our abbess, who is also a Padellani, tells me that at the convent of San Giorgio Stilita she has been happy since the day she entered. I believe her. I would like to emulate her."

The duke nodded with satisfaction. He thanked her and made a bow; then he turned to Ortensia who was standing nearby. Stunningly elegant in her green satin dress, resplendent in the famous parure of Padellani emeralds that highlighted the blonde curls cascading over her ears, she was inviting him to come tour the armory. The little crowd that had formed around them, all eyes and ears on the conversation between the foreign nobleman and the princess, immediately forgetful of Agata, trailed after them; after a moment's hesitation, the prince followed in their wake.

James Garson still had not moved. They were left alone, facing one another. He leaned toward Agata and whispered: "And do you have the calling?"

For the rest of the evening he never lost sight of her, but she was so overwhelmed that she never noticed. When it came time to say for the guests to say goodnight, Agata was placed next to the master and mistress of the house, heightening her discomfort with the sharp contrast between her own dark dress and the splendid outfits of her cousins. The first to leave, of course, was the guest of honor. As the prince and princess chatted with the duke, James spoke to Agata: "May I send you books, after your simple profession?"

Agata lit up: "Please do, by all means!" and then she turned serious again. "But I won't be able to write you and say how much I liked them, unless the abbess gives me permission."

"All right." And with a sparkle in his eye, he added: "We'll talk about it later. I'm sure that we'll meet again."

It was wonderful to go back to Aunt Orsola's. Agata noticed that nothing had been changed in the room that had once been hers, and that the servants were the same as before—older now, just like the house. In her aunt's drawing room, the sunlight had faded the wallpaper to such a degree that the copper plate designs were almost invisible; the hems of the green damask curtains, brought upstairs from the *piano nobile* and never properly shortened, dragged on the majolica tiles and were tattered; the lacing of the central springs in the upholstery of the chairs had begun to loosen and each spring pressed against the red satin of the seats, creating the appearance of tiny craters in eruption. But the plants and bushes and trees had grown splendidly; the terrace looked more like a hanging garden than ever. The aunt and her niece drank hot chocolate together in the gazebo before leaving for the Aviellos. The footservant announced a visitor: Captain Garson. Agata felt herself blush, and she looked down at the tray of biscotti, pretending to look for one with pinoli.

"I've come to see how the camellias are doing, and I've brought you two new species; one comes from the Mile End Nursery, and is an early bloomer; the flowers are a most extraordinary color, bright red," James explained, as the footmen walked slowly forward, two by two, carrying heavy vases in their arms. He looked at Agata and went on, "They contrast wonderfully with the fertile, golden yellow stamens. The other one is Belgian, the camellia Mont Blanc, just on the verge of blooming into double floors, peoniform and very rich in petals." He looked straight into Agata's eyes. "Pure white." She blushed again.

Her aunt and the captain began conversing about the hibiscus, exchanging information concerning the Syrian variety.

Agata only knew about the plants in the garden of the simples—Angiola Maria was very jealous of "her" plants in the
main cloister—and she asked what this hibiscus was that they
were talking about. "They're over here, in the vases along the
railing," James explained, and offered to accompany her to see
them; her aunt didn't want to stand and suggested that the two
of them go look at the hibiscus.

James pointed out to Agata the delicate funnel-shaped
petals. The pale pink hue turned darker at the base and formed
a blood-red ring around the long pistils; he told her that the
Romans ate them as salad—Cicero binged on them—and that
it was also a medicinal plant. "The flower wilts the day after it
blooms," he said, "and perhaps that is why it is used by young
people in the mute language of flowers. In Polynesia the girls
wear one in their hair to announce that they are unattached,
while the young man in search of a fiancée wears one behind
his right ear . . . " James was bending over, looking for something; then he picked a bud about to open in its ephemeral,
fleeting glory. "This is the *Hibiscus syriacus*," he said, as he
handed it to her. Agata spun it between her fingers and looked
at it: the leaves were folded one atop the other like the fabric
of a parasol and like the pleats of a wimple folded in a drawer.
James added, with determination: "In Syria, offering one to a
woman is tantamount to telling her how beautiful she is."

They were walking toward her aunt; suddenly, he asked her,
in English: "Are you happy?"

She looked down and said nothing. "Are you happy?" he
asked again, insistently.

A seagull overhead called. It sounded as if it were crying.

The next day, Agata was cheerful, almost giddy with everyone in a way that even she couldn't understand.

26.
June 18th, 1845.
The simple profession

After her cousin's reception, a hail of invitations arrived for Agata; her mother asked her at least to accept a few, but Agata dug her heels in: she wanted to stay in her bedroom at home. That increased the widespread belief in the strength of her vocation. In reality, Agata had other business to take care of: she wanted to read the books of ecclesiastical law and the legal codes concerning monastic seclusion that Tommaso had procured for her, with the page numbers of the significant sections concerning procedures on dismissal from a monastic order.

Carmela had confided to her that the Cavaliere d'Anna, who continued to consider himself engaged to Agata, had openly declared that after Agata's simple profession he would feel free to be engaged to another woman, and he was certainly willing to marry Carmela. Agata was forced into the realization that her baby sister was quite contented with that unholy marriage, in which—leaving aside the issue of the sheer distastefulness of the man himself—the age difference between groom and bride was more than fifty years. The marriage contract, originally drawn up for Agata, entailed the groom's donation to the bride of two landed estates of a thousand hectares each. "So I'll be a rich widow while I'm still young, and I can marry whoever I want," her baby sister told her, gleefully. Moreover, she whispered to Agata that she had learned from the concierge that Tommaso, disappointed at Sandra's failure to give him an heir, had fathered an illegitimate son with a Tuscan woman and that every day, instead of going to court, he went to visit his other family; Tommaso made sure the mother and son had everything they needed, lavishing money on them while pinching the pennies he gave Sandra for household expenses. Carmela noticed it because the general and their mother had given Sandra money for groceries and even gave her a gift of fifty ducats. Not only was Agata heartbroken over the situation with the Aviellos, whom she had always considered to be an exemplary and modern couple, but she also felt responsible not only for her own misfortunes but for Carmela's fate. It was in this state of mind that she was preparing to enter nunhood.

The morning of Agata's simple profession a crowd of relatives and friends thronged into the Aviellos' apartment. When there was no more room in the apartment, the men conversed out on the staircase. The women chattered away loudly, waiting for Agata to emerge from her bedroom. A few young women were sitting down at the pianoforte and banging away at love songs.

The hairdresser left the bedroom with an air of satisfaction. Agata was wearing a white moire dress, gauzy and gathered at the waist, with bouquets of white flowers embroidered on the bodice and on the skirt; her hair had been combed out into loose cascading ringlets, covering her breast and shoulders, with jasmine flowers pinned here and there and everywhere. A garland of snowy white camellias, a gift from her Aunt Orsola, would secure the veil to her hair. Two of the four "godmothers" of the prospective nun—noblewomen chosen by her mother, practically strangers to Agata—helped her to place the white, floor-length tulle veil on her head.

The interior windows of the *palazzo* were crowded with damp eyes and smiling faces. Every voice called out best wishes and compliments for the young nun. Agata was beautiful to behold: her deep emotion and excitement had colored her cheeks with red and the tears she was choking back gave her eyes a glistening luminosity. Her two godmothers helped her into an open carriage and, when the coachman cracked his whip, the team of horses trotted out into the street through the *palazzo*'s street door, flanked by two cheering lines of people, who burst into a deafening wave of applause.

Agata obeyed and did exactly as she was told. She felt detached from her own body and incapable of feeling any emotion. It was traditional for a prospective nun to pay visits to various other convents in order to allow other nuns to get to know and admire her. At the convent of Donnalbina, the last visit scheduled, Sister Maria Giulia, her father's sister, burst into tears at the sight of her; those tears alone were sufficient to shatter Agata's emotional armor. She swayed and staggered, and was on the verge of fainting. The nuns beat two egg yolks in a bowl with sugar and Marsala for her, and urged her to swallow the mixture in a single gulp.

The carriage was rattling through the neighborhood of San Lorenzo and was now drawing close to the convent. The populace—which had learned about the details by reading the local newspaper, the *Gazzetta del Seggio*, by word of mouth, and from the pealing church bells—filled streets and balconies. Some tried to touch the carriage, others called out to Agata to remember sick children and parents in her prayers. Ashen, she leaned back against the upholstery of her seat. Every so often, the bang of an exploding firecracker filled the air. Along the Via San Giorgio Stilita, a Swiss band was playing music to the crowd.

Her two other godmothers were waiting for her in the portico. At the portal of the church, she was greeted by a procession guided by a priest holding a cross high in the air; he was followed by twelve other priests with candles in their hands; they were all garbed in paraments embroidered with gold thread on a light blue background, just like the Padellani coat of arms. The church, divided down the middle by a white and red partition, was a jubilant spectacle of lights and colors. The ladies sat on the right side, where they were greeted and ushered in by Donna Gesuela, while the gentlemen sat on the left, welcomed by the prince of Opiri.

Led by the priest carrying the cross, with her godmothers walking on either side, and followed by the other priests, formed into two lines, Agata entered the church. The minute she set the toe of her slipper on the first white-and-blue majolica floor tile, the thronging congregation leapt to its feet; simultaneously, a wave of organ music swept over the crowd, followed by the voice of a mezzo-soprano.

The procession reached the middle of the church. The canon emerged from the presbytery and came to meet them. He gave Agata a silver cross to hold in her left hand, which she held against her breast, and a candle to hold in her right hand. The procession resumed.

Agata walked slowly past the pews where her closest relatives were seated. Carmela had an aisle seat. When she saw her sister go by, she burst into tears: "Don't do it!" Carmela sobbed, her shoulders quivering. Agata slowed her steps. She looked down at her sister and then looked up and straight ahead at the altar, which looked like a flaming sun. Then she went on walking.

She came to a halt at the foot of the main altar. The cardinal was waiting for her, seated on the left side of the altar, next to the Epistle. The priests that had accompanied her to the altar now moved off in another direction.

Agata and her four godmothers were kneeling. Swelling music filled the church. Then all five women walked forward to the cardinal. The godmothers remained standing, while Agata kneeled before him. At that moment, both music and song ceased. Silence. A priest wearing a magnificently embroidered surplice presented the cardinal with a silver basin containing a small pair of scissors, which the cardinal used to snip a lock of Agata's hair. At that, the choristers resumed singing a cappella—high, pure, sublime voices.

Agata stood up; at that moment, the voices of all the other chorists suddenly fell away and only the voice of Donna Maria Giovanna della Croce continued, accompanied by the organ. Then the voices of the choir burst in, for the last time, while Agata—together with her godmothers and preceded by the same procession that had greeted her at the front portal—left the church beneath the eyes of the guests and all the other eyes, furtive and glistening, behind the grate. When they reached the portico, the procession turned to the left while Agata, followed by the Swiss band and surrounded by the delirious crowd, walked down the street that led to the front door of the convent.

Flanked by her four godmothers, she climbed the steps of the monumental entrance to San Giorgio Stilita; the memory of her visit to the convent as a convent girl, brought a lump to her throat. The massive wooden portal swung open and she walked into the cloister, leaving her godmothers behind her in the vestibule. As soon as she saw the sister concierge, Agata burst into subdued weeping. The choristers were waiting for her, ready to accompany her to the hall of the *comunichino*. No one spoke.

Agata was standing. There was no music, no singing. Behind her, the hall was packed. All eighty choristers were there. Behind them were all the other nuns, novices, lay sisters, postulants, and educands.

Across from her in the church, standing before the brass gate, was the cardinal. Behind him was a throng of canons, priests, guests, and relatives—the English duke in the first row next to her cousin the prince. Agata kept her eyes locked on the cardinal's eyes.

The sister teacher of the novices took her by the hand and led her to a corner, where she and the prioress stripped her of her magnificent garments, beginning with the veil and the flowers in her hair and ending with her shoes and stockings, and as the two women undressed her, other women re-dressed her in the homespun woolens of the novitiate.

With her curls disheveled, barefoot and dressed in black, Agata returned to the *comunichino*. The cardinal blessed the scapular and passed it to her through the brass bars. It struck Agata that his fingers had sought contact with hers and she felt a wave of revulsion. She put on the scapular without stepping away from the *comunichino*. Then she turned and went straight to the far end of the room, where the abbess was waiting for her, seated on the throne of gilt wood, against the wall, beneath the canvas depicting Moses bringing water forth from the rock. On the left was the monumental blind staircase. On the right, the sister choristers, in order of seniority. The English duke had knelt down and, with the cardinal's permission, he was watching the intimate ceremony through the aperture of the *comunichino*.

Agata prostrated herself before the abbess, the soles of her bare feet projecting from her habit. The nuns gathered her long hair into a single tress. The abbess seized the large scissors and prepared to cut the hair.

The silence was absolute.

A powerful voice arose from the congregation: "Barbarians! Don't cut her hair at least!"

Everyone turned to look. There were loud whispers about a madman. The priests imposed silence. The cardinal remained impassive; he knew who had shouted.

The nuns were in turmoil. The abbess held the scissors in one hand, suspended in midair. Then came the confident voice of a deaconess: "Cut! He is a heretic!"

The tresses fell onto the stone flagstone. And Agata took the veil.

27.
June 18th, 1846.
The solemn profession

During the year of her novitiate, time rushed by for Agata: study, work, prayer, conversations with Father Cuoco and with the abbess. Her aunt's health was steadily declining; she was in constant pain, and after Nones, she remained in her bedroom. Agata went to see her. The medicaments that Dr. Minutolo and the sister pharmacist prescribed for her were of little if any benefit. Still, she remained untroubled. She tried to follow the rhythm of a prayer and was mortified when she was unable to do so. "To rise in the middle of the night to praise the Lord purifies the soul and helps me to love life, as well as God, and it makes me feel better." Prayer, punctuating the course of the liturgical week with distinctly Benedictine precision, gave a certain meaning to life; it also confirmed to Agata, however sure she might already have been, that the direction for which she was most naturally suited was that of conjugal love and the love of her children.

Ever since Agata became a novice, she had been accorded privileges and even the occasional liberty. She was treated by the choristers as one of their own, or close to it; some of them had imparted knowledge to her that was not to be repeated outside the doors of the Chapter Hall—gossip of all kinds, to start with, concerning financial matters and dynastic resentments. Still, they scrupulously avoided mentioning the scabrous situations and ferment within the Church that she, acute observer that she was, had already intuited. Agata was even better informed than many of them. Sandra continued to send her pamphlets and newspapers concealed in the baskets of clean linen and one of the deaconesses, the sister of an aristocratic Carbonaro who relied upon her prayers, occasionally allowed Agata to read the letters that he sent her concerning political developments throughout the peninsula.

She was permitted to climb up to the belvedere in her free time, in the afternoon. There she filled her lungs with fresh air, breathing in freedom, and her gaze ranged from the open sky—so different from the sky that hung over the cloister like an awning—to the dark blue waters of the bay. The noise of the traffic and the voices of the Neapolitans rose faintly from below, melded into a general buzzing, just enough to make her feel at one with the people—as when she followed the Mass from behind the grate—and a little more. Agata felt a need to be with other people and to work on their behalf: at times like that, she believed that she could even do it from within the cloister, through the power of prayer. But it wasn't always like that, and her novitiate was marked by a seesawing oscillation between an acceptance of the values of nunhood and an irrepressible desire to live in the world along with the certainty that, with God's help, this would come to pass. The previous day they had celebrated with a solemn mass the election of the new pontiff, Pope Pius IX, a liberal cardinal. The royal family and the cardinal were devastated: they had waged a ferocious campaign against him, in emulation of the example set by Austria. Loyal to the sentiments of the cardinal, the abbess had arranged for an excellent dinner but, according to the deaconesses, not quite as excellent as the dinner prepared to celebrate the election of the previous pope, a detail that had prompted plentiful and speculative gossip. Agata did not feel like a nun and she felt justified disenchantment toward the cloistered life and toward her own family, who had simply ignored her after her simple profession. Even Sandra came only rarely, and only with Aunt Orsola. From the high vantage point of the belvedere, that disenchantment merged with the good of the people: she quivered with yearning, like the heroines of the novels she read, for the advent of a better world in which justice and brotherhood supplanted privilege and selfishness. At those moments, Agata, certain as she was that she would eventually return to civil society, felt great spiritual freedom and experienced her life in the cloister with serenity. The rhythm of prayer and meditation, rather than isolating her, helped her to stay in contact with the outside world through God, and to love that world.

Agata liked to recite the rosary, sitting on the rim of the fountain in the cloister, where she looked up at the statues of Christ and the Samaritan Woman in arcane conversation. The bubbling jet of water and the rhythm of her words conveyed her to the heart of the very meaning of meditation. *Ora pro nobis peccatoribus nunc et in hora mortis nostrae.* "Why *nunc*? Does that mean that *now* is when I must find happiness? It's life that matters, not death. And what is life without love?"

Light footsteps, the rustling of grey aprons: a novice had experienced a vision of Christ while cooking, and the nuns who'd been with her were running for the stairs leading up to the bell tower. At first Agata didn't want to run with them, but then she changed her mind. She encountered them as they were returning: they told her to make sure she closed the door tightly and to take the key back to the prioress.

Built atop the arcade that in the Middle Ages had joined the convent of San Giorgio Stilita with the male monastery, and long since replaced by the church's Baroque campanile, the tall bell tower was now used only to announce miracles and the election of the abbess. Agata had never climbed so high. Frightened into flight by the pealing bells, the doves were flying spread-winged around the tower in a circling carousel of flight; occasionally a few would swoop through the high loggia, grazing her veil. Like them, Agata circled around the double bells and looked out from each of the four twin-light windows of the loggia, captivated by the view. Far below, in the portico, the faithful were awaiting the news—they looked like ants. Agata was suddenly swept by a powerful feeling of love for them, and she leaned out over the broad sill. For an instant, she thought she had experienced vertigo, but that wasn't it at all. She had turned into air and now she was whirling around the tower in a spiraling flight that widened and rose higher and higher with every revolution until she was high in the heavens. The earth and the sea below her had vanished. And so had the clouds. She climbed and climbed, in ever-widening circles. With every loop, her love for the whole world grew vaster. So did her love for her creator. Agata was bursting with happiness. She fell to the floor in ecstasy.

Before she could be admitted to the solemn profession, Agata would have to pass the examination of the vicar general and, after that, undergo two weeks of spiritual exercises. She was anxious: the purpose of the examination was an investigation of her free will, of her determination to abandon the world for God and her ability of live the cloistered life.

Agata feared the fateful question: "If you were to fall in love with a man, would you leave the life of seclusion?" But she wasn't alone in fearing that question: the vicar general was even more anxious than she was. Both of them knew that if it emerged from that examination that the novice lacked a calling, she would be obliged to leave the convent within twenty-four hours. Where? She had no idea where she would go. In the cloister, Agata had heard horrifying stories: once it was determined that she was unfit for the cloistered life, the prospective nun was left to the tender mercies of the other nuns who, in a crescendo of rage, ripped the scapular off her back, dressed her hastily and roughly in her civilian clothing, and expelled her from the cloistered area immediately, leaving her alone in the vestibule to wait for her indignant family to come get her.

The vicar general steered clear of the more dangerous reefs and asked her only the blandest of questions, to which Agata gave him the answers that were expected.

"What would you do if His Majesty the King proposed that you go live in the royal palace?"

"The splendor of court life is of no interest to me."

"What would you do if someone offered you a vast sum of ducats in exchange for leaving the cloistered life?"

"My life is not for sale."

"What would you do if one of your sisters were sick and entreated you to go live with her in order to nurse her?"

"I would explain to her that I have other duties and that I will pray for her."

The spiritual exercises were administered by the canon. Agata was uncomfortable with him just as she was with all the other canons of the church: at the moment of communion, fingers had grazed her face more than once. The other novices said that those caresses were normal and they didn't mind them at all.

Agata passed the tests, thanks to her unquestioned, stubborn determination to become a chorister: she owed it to her aunt the abbess. She was well aware that over the long term her sacrifice would be pointless, because her aunt hadn't long to live. But there was nothing she could do about it. She'd promised.

In the meanwhile, interminable negotiations over the amount of her dowry and the terms of payment proceeded feverishly. General Cecconi was willing to underwrite the dowry only to a minimal degree. Her mother was therefore forced to turn to lenders. In the end, the Chapter agreed to accept a smaller dowry than was customary and to take payment in installments. No secret remained a secret for long in the convent of San Giorgio Stilita: when the conditions attached to Agata's dowry became public, the resentment that the nuns and novices already felt toward her—the favorite of an abbess drawing close to the end of her life—erupted, and so did the passion with which they actively tried to thwart her. Compressed inside the prison of the cloister, those feelings defied any attempt at mediation and were bound to break out into violence in time: Agata awaited that moment with fear.

It was the day set for her solemn profession, exactly one year after her simple profession.

Agata was finishing her lengthy confession, while the church filled up with guests—there were a vast number of them, and they poured out onto the portico. They were dressed for a gala occasion, with medals and decorations, and once again there were distinguished foreign visitors among them. Then she watched the service from the hall of the *comunichino*, together with only the choristers.

The cardinal, dressed in magnificent paraments embroidered with gold filigree, intoned the pontifical blessing; then, silence. The organ fell silent, and so did the hundreds of guests. The cardinal slowly approached the *comunichino*. The guests watched him without a sound. Agata advanced toward him, flanked by four nuns, each of whom carried a candle in her hand. She stopped when she was face to face with him.

It was the moment of the oath. They had given her the parchment, written in Latin. Agata began to read; her voice failed her. "Louder," one of the nuns hissed at her, the one that had brought her the parchment. With an effort, she raised her voice and pronounced the four vows: chastity, poverty, obedience, and perpetual seclusion. She kept stumbling over her words and at times she had to stop entirely. During a pause, the candle slipped from the fingers of one of the nuns and fell to the floor.

She had signed her oath; the abbess and cardinal underwrote it. She turned: there, behind her, a dark carpet had been laid out on the floor, and four candelabra with large candles burned at the corners of the carpet. She lay upon it facedown. The four nuns covered her with a black blanket, in the middle of which a large needlepoint emblem in silver thread glittered: a skull. From the campanile there rang out the doleful tolling of the death bell, slowly pealing, and between one peal and the next the laments of the women rose from the far end of the church; with each peal of the bell, another row of pews joined in the moaning in a tightly controlled crescendo. Just as a wedding is for a bride, so for a nun the solemn profession meant the end of a previous life. Through this death, Agata was becoming the bride of Christ.

"*Surge, quae dormis, et exurge a mortuis, et illuminabit te Christus!*" The cardinal pronounced the exhortation three times in Latin, speaking to the skull.

"Awake thou that sleepest . . . " The nuns pulled the blanket off her.

"And arise from the dead!" Agata, still lying facedown on the carpet, now looked up and arose partway.

"Christ shall give thee light!"

Donna Maria Ninfa, professed nun, leapt to her feet.

"*Ut vivant mortui, et moriantur viventes.*" The cardinal blessed the habit and extended it to her. She donned it and then she received communion. Behind her a long line had formed. The abbess first, followed by all the other nuns in hierarchical order, came to kiss her while the nave and the hall of the *comunichino* were filled with the voices of the choristers of the congregation and by the solemn music of the pipe organ.

The altar boys swung their censers with renewed emphasis, and the perfume that they released was so powerful that it made the throat itch. After a sermon of which Agata did not hear a single word, the service was at an end.

The parlor, decorated with the silver of the Padellani choristers past and present, looked like the drawing room of an aristocratic palace. The buffet tables loaded with pastries and sweets and refreshments remained intact: the guests were waiting for Donna Maria Ninfa before serving themselves, but Agata required some time before she was able to calm down. Then the door opened, the abbess gently pushed her out and the two women, side by side, joined the guests. The foreign visitors insisted on admiring her habit: it was made of black wool with a very long train and loose draping sleeves—the last relic, maintained over the centuries, of the nunhood of Madame Maintenon. In the meanwhile, the other guests launched themselves upon the delicacies made possible through the generosity of Admiral Pietraperciata.

That night, Agata slept peacefully. Her aunt's joy had been enormously rewarding. As for her, from this day forth she would be Donna Maria Ninfa. Her mother had chosen the name together with the abbess, in memory of the Palermitan origins of the Aspidi family: Santa Ninfa was one of the four patron saints of Palermo, along with Agata, Oliva, and Cristina. But this wasn't destined to last forever. Deep in her soul, Agata knew that God was with her. And that her duty was to be at the service of others, in the seclusion of the cloister and then out in the world at large. Each night the words of Thomas à Kempis lulled her in her sleep: "If you would persevere in seeking perfection, you must consider yourself a pilgrim, an exile on earth. If you would become a religious, you must be content to seem a fool for the sake of Christ."

28.
The daily life of Donna Maria Ninfa, new chorister nun

In the sixth century, when the Benedictine Rule was formulated, the convents were an exquisitely democratic organization; amidst the Neapolitan obscurantism of the second quarter of the nineteenth century, the convent of San Giorgio Stilita, under the prudent governance of the abbess, Donna Maria Crocifissa, could still make that claim. The Chapter, in which all chorister sisters sat by right, met to make decisions concerning the convent's administration, the admission of educands and novices, whether or not to accept nuns from other convents, and the expulsion of nuns from the Cenoby. All votes were individual and secret, and a decision required only a simple majority—though in the case of particularly important matters, that margin rose to two-thirds. For minor issues, the abbess made decisions in consultation with the deaconesses—wise older nuns, who were frequently former abbesses. Agata, with her aunt's encouragement, had from the very beginning contributed to discussions in the Chapter.

Donna Maria Crocifissa was not a modern abbess. She was tolerant, with one exception: she discouraged requests for *brevi*, leaves that allowed a nun to spend a few weeks with her family. Aside from that aspect, under her rule as abbess the more austere edges of the cloistered life had been rounded off, in particular the practices of the mortification of the flesh: at San Giorgio Stilita the use of hair shirts was frowned upon while the wearing of wrought-iron bodices was forbidden entirely. Within the confines of the Rule and in the context of prayer in the Cenoby, the choristers were largely free to do as they pleased. They could receive packages, they could give the pastries and sweets that they made to whomever they wished, and they could see more than one visitor a month. The abbess tended to allow correspondence with the outside world. There were those who abused their privileges. For instance, at the first sign of a headache or a cold, certain choristers stayed in their cells and had meals brought to them on a tray, rather than go to the refectory, and the many choristers who had their own servingwoman and one or two lay sisters, depending on their financial resources, had these servants assist them in some of the heavier offices, so that they could freely devote themselves to their religious devotions or else, simply, to idle leisure.

Most of the nuns had been admitted to the convent when they were children, and on the whole they were happy and lived in the Cenoby—the only place they could call home—for many years. Those who had been adolescents when they were admitted, like Agata, often had trouble adjusting, unless they already had the vocation—which was uncommon. Often, they "found" a vocation, induced by their families and by the atmosphere of the Cenoby. They too, on the whole, led a good life in monastic seclusion.

Each chorister had a father confessor, chosen by the vicar general from the secular clergy and not from the monastic orders; nuns had the option of changing their confessor. The confessionals were occupied all day long, and it was necessary to make a special effort to secure one of the larger ones, which practically offered the privacy of a bedroom. The wealthier nuns had special confessionals built to order—spacious and comfortable—and refused to share them with other nuns. Given the length of the confessions, the nuns did not kneel, but instead sat upright in a comfortable chair, and were even allowed to offer their confessor coffee, hot chocolate, and lemonade with biscotti, to refresh and reinvigorate him. Many nuns were possessive of their confessors and heaped them with gifts and attention; some even spoke of them as if they were their lovers. Agata continued to be satisfied with hers, Father Cuoco, a native of Nardo, good natured and quite intelligent, and felt none of that obsessive attention to father confessors and altar boys; even the cardinal irritated her.

Agata was different and she felt different. She didn't like to chatter with the other choristers, nor did she enjoy attending the little receptions that they liked to give on the slightest pretext—for the feast day of their patron saint, for an anniversary, for a visit—taking turns showing off the porcelain and silver that they kept in their closets. When she was in company, she spoke very little about her family or herself.

She was also different because she was poor. Her mother hadn't fully paid her monastic dowry and therefore her stipend was so tiny as to be meaningless. She rarely received gifts from her aunt the abbess. She had no lay sister or servingwoman to allow her to save money, she sent her clothing to Sandra's house to be washed, and she supported herself by selling her *cucchitelle*; this was humiliating.

She read. James Garson kept his word, and the first novel, *Nicholas Nickleby*, by Charles Dickens, reached her just a few days after her simple profession. The abbess gave her permission to send him a *paperole* as thanks, and Agata inserted within the door of the little embroidered temple or in the cover of the central oval a tab that, when pulled, would disclose the small note that conveyed her thoughts about what she had read. She never received any reply other than a book, and from then on, all her thank-you notes, laboriously conceived though brief, were ignored. Agata came to believe that not only did James not receive them at all, but that the choice of books had been delegated to an impersonal third party. She continued to write back to the return address—the usual bookseller—and her notes became increasingly intimate; at times she even recorded her thoughts on the back of the paper petals and leaves of the *paperoles*, as if they were the pages of a secret diary that no one would ever read.

Singing and music, which she taught to the novices, were her one great comfort. Sometimes she joined the choristers with pleasure, for instance, when they went to church on the eve of an especially important religious occurrence. Belonging as they did to the great families of the episcopal sees of Porta Capuana and Nido, all the nuns brought with them, aside from their trousseaux, sacred furnishings and silverwork. In order to preserve the humility of the order, those objects were kept under lock and key in their cells and used only for religious occasions. The sacristan, on the order of the sister sacrist, would clear the building and lock the doors and the choristers then entered the church carrying their treasures to be displayed on the altars.

It was deeply moving to walk on that white and blue floor, which Agata watched seven times a day from high above, in the choir, and stand there, motionless, before the main altar, swollen with gold and silver, as if a tiny nun garbed in black were challenging the massive structure of marble and precious metals. When the entire church flickered with thousands of candles, the nuns, as if dazzled by so much light, wandered through the empty nave and the side aisles, stopping before images that from high above they could only see foreshortened, marveling at their beauty. The younger nuns ran, drunk with light, and stopped before the huge outer doors, locked tight, and then turned to run back to the main altar. Other nuns stopped to pray before the convent's precious relics: the heads of St. George Stilites, St. Blaise, and St.

Stephen, covered with silver; a bit of wood from the Holy
Cross; two arms, one belonging to St. Julian and the other to
St. Lawrence; the chain of St. George Stilites—which bound
him to the column atop which he lived for twenty-seven years;
and the blood of St. Stephen and St. Pantaleon, which, when
liquefied, changed into three different colors.

Donna Maria Giovanna della Croce had remained Agata's
great and only friend. Like the abbess, she considered herself
fortunate to have received her calling. "We constantly receive
instructions from God, but we are unable to understand them.
It will come to you as well. That is why it is so fundamental to
listen, to the Holy Spirit and to other people, and to create
silence within ourselves." She encouraged Agata to make room
for silence in order to allow the voice of God to summon her
to Him. "Don't be afraid of death: it is only the completion of
a cycle," she said to her, and Agata tried her best to find her
vocation. When she thought she had succeeded, the sullen
reality of the convent and the magnetic pull of the instinct to
procreate made the cloistered life intolerable to her.

Agata regularly went to visit her father's other sister, Donna
Maria Brigida. The Padellani cousins, long-time nuns, had told
her that, unlike her aunt the abbess, Donna Maria Brigida had
never adapted to the monastic life and as a young woman had
become mentally disturbed. One afternoon, just before Nones,
Agata went to visit her demented aunt, who by now never left
her cell. The lay sisters who were supposed to provide for her
had left her to the care of the servingwomen, who were mocking her cruelly. She would rave about children and newborns
and she called all the other women "*mamma*." They had
stitched little rag dolls for her and when she was upset they'd
give her two of them. "Here, why don't you feed your daughters," they'd say, and she would hold them to her breast, laugh-

ing and covering them with kisses. Other times they told her
that if she was good, the father confessor, with whom it was
said she had once been head-over-heels in love, and who had
died years ago, would come to hear her confession.

That day, her aunt refused to take her tranquilizer and had
spit it out, staining her snowy-white wimple. She twisted on
the chair to which she had been tied and tried to snap her middle finger against her thumb to imitate the rhythm of the cas-
tanets and, winking at Agata, she intoned in a faint, out-of-tune
voice:

Me faje fa' vicchiarelle,
Me faje jire a l'acito:
Gue' Ma', voglio o marito,
Non pozzo sola sta'.[2]

Agata listened and thought to herself. The rhythm of the
Neapolitan song reminded her of the English nursery rhyme,
"Oranges and Lemons." It brought back her faded memories
of Messina, of Giacomo, fiery, possessive, irascible; of his sweat
and his magnificent charcoal eyes fringed with long eyelashes.
Immature. Cowardly. Agata thought of the glaring contrast
with James Garson, delicate, cultivated, detached. And chilly.
Both married, one dragged wife and sons to the church in
search of the thrills of a youthful love long dead, while the
other behaved gallantly toward a woman who was destined for
a life of seclusion. Agata felt deeply offended. Her gaze
returned to her aunt the nun. From somewhere deep within
her memory, from her afternoons with her father, she remembered an aria by Cimarosa and began to sing: "*Ma con un marito via meglio si sta, via meglio meglio si sta.*"

---

[2] You make me old / You make me bitter / Oh, but I want a husband /
Alone I cannot stay.

Full of love for the world, Agata firmly believed that, under this new pope, Italy was on the threshold of a better, free world, in which she would be liberated from the yoke of nunhood, she'd find fulfilling employment, and she would live happily on her own.

29.
September 1846.
Agata believes she can overcome the murkiest aspects
of the cloistered life by taking on the office
of sister infirmarian

The choristers held a variety of offices; they were required to change them every year or every three years, but the Chapter of each convent could also reconfirm them in their offices and that is what frequently happened. Agata could choose whether to assist the sister cellarer, the sister hebdomadary, the sister herbalist, the sister infirmarian, the sister pharmacist, the sister who worked the convent wheel, or the sister sacrist. She could not hold the office assistant helper nun, who was in charge of external relations and was allowed to leave the cloister and go out into the world. That position was reserved to choristers with a certain seniority. She chose the office of assistant infirmarian, which wasn't particularly sought after, and which allowed her to be close to the abbess. She worked in close collaboration with Donna Maria Immacolata, the sister pharmacist. Donna Maria Assunta, who was quite old, soon entrusted her with a number of responsibilities.

The sister infirmarian saw to the health of body and soul. Agata was surprised to discover the quantity of medicines and natural products that were dispensed to the nuns to treat their "nervous disturbances." Agata discovered that the convent was a veritable wasp's nest of groups and factions, riven by jealousy, resentment, and vicious campaigns of hatred that crushed the losers underfoot, driving them to brink of madness. Beneath a still surface, San Giorgio Stilita was a churning whirlpool of unholy passions.

One chorister, Donna Maria Celeste, clearly wished to

become one of Agata's friends. Agata was wary, because as a postulant she had suffered from her bullying cruelty. At that time, Maria Celeste had just become a nun and she had suggested switching father confessors with Agata. "Father Cutolo is young, conscientious, and well disposed toward you," she had told her, but Agata chose not to take her advice.

Both postulants and novices came to speak with her; they too recommended Father Cutolo, some of them with a notable degree of insistence. At that point, Maria Celeste stopped being a friend and turned into Agata's enemy. She was peevish and angry with her, and regularly humiliated her. Agata was an object of contention between two bitterly opposed rival parties, and they both wanted the same thing from her—for her to select Father Cutolo as her confessor—but each wanted to boast the honor of having persuaded her to make the change. One day, Father Cutolo sent her a note. He felt that he'd been insulted and unfairly rejected and he suggested they make an appointment to get to know one another so that he could persuade her to change her mind. Agata, curious now, went to the place that he had suggested, the cloister of the novices, where the pharmacy was located. The priest was sitting in a corner, on a low interior wall, next to a slender column. He was young, fit, and fair-skinned. His eyes were dark and smoldering. He paid her a number of compliments and asked her about the books she'd read. Agata answered his questions, but she had the impression that he hadn't heard a word she said: he was looking at her hungrily and she felt as if he was undressing her with his eyes. Agata blushed; she looked down and fell silent. The priest pulled one hand out of his pocket and ran it over her lips, poking at them with his finger. Agata bit his finger hard and ran away, without noticing that the sister pharmacist and her lay sister had been watching the two of them for a while.

From then on, there were mutterings against Agata. One by one, the other young nuns came to act as emissaries: some

226 · SIMONETTA AGNELLO HORNBY

scolded her for having behaved rudely to Father Cutolo, others explained that the father confessor belonged to Maria Celeste and that she should never have accepted the meeting without asking her permission, and there were those who urged her to see Father Cutolo again because he was desperately in love with her and he was wasting away before their eyes. That horrible chapter finally came to an end when the cardinal came to visit the convent, accompanied by Father Cuoco, and suggested that Agata say confession that same day. For a while, there was a diet of gossip about the favoritism that the abbess and the cardinal had shown for the "Sicilian girl," until that topic was discarded for other, newer matters. But every time that Agata encountered Father Cutolo, he undressed her hungrily with his eyes.

Maria Celeste had matured; now she seemed to genuinely desire the company of Agata, now a chorister herself. Maria Celeste taught her how to make the biscotti di San Martino and gave her lessons on baking in a wood-fired oven. They had discovered that they both read novels; they exchanged books and discussed them together. Agata never mentioned their youthful quarrels or Father Cutolo, who was said to have since fallen in love with another novice. Maria Celeste was frequently sad, and she had recently grown very pale in the face; she had dark circles under her eyes and was puffy-faced. Agata gave her reconstituent syrups and Maria Celeste took them. Only once did she ask Agata for a medicament against nausea and after that she stopped appearing in public: it was whispered that she was indisposed, but she never asked for help. Agata, as sister infirmarian, would go to pay calls on her; they would have pleasant conversations, but Maria Celeste never told her anything about herself and never asked for anything.

30.
January 1847.
The death of her aunt the abbess, the death
of Donna Maria Celeste, and the death of the cook Brida

S ix months had passed since Agata's solemn profession. Neither her mother nor her sisters wrote to her, and the short notes that Sandra sent her were infrequent and steeped in pessimism. Agata was afraid that the Aviellos were about to choose to go into exile, and if they did she would lose all contact with her brother-in-law and everything that he represented: modern thought and the future. Agata was afflicted by melancholy. She didn't feel like a nun and she had not cut her hair again. Donna Maria Giovanna della Croce suggested that she request a *brevi*: a stay at home often helped a young nun to break ties once and for all with her family. The abbess wasn't happy about it, but she forwarded the request to the cardinal, who refused permission. Agata didn't really mind, because in that period the abbess's health had deteriorated quite noticeably. Dr. Minutolo was keeping an eye on her; he seemed worried, but he wasn't prescribing any medicine for her. Angiola Maria, on the other hand, made the abbess infusions against pain and cared for her with extraordinary devotion. Agata studied herbs that relieved pain and changed the dosages of her potions; she would go to see her during the day whenever she could and unfailingly every evening, after Compline—the period of rigorous silence. They looked at one another in the candlelight and sat, hand in hand, whispering together the prayers begun by the abbess. Her aunt would start them out, "*Ave Maria . . .* " and Angiola Maria and Agata would follow up, "*gratia plena, Dominus Tecum . . .* "

That was when Agata fully came to appreciate the consoling power of group prayer.

One afternoon Agata was in the infirmary, taking care of a sick nun. Angiola Maria came to summon her, urgently.

Already in her aunt's bedroom when Agata got there were Donna Maria Clotilde, the prioress, and Donna Maria Giovanna della Croce. The brazier was incandescent and the heat in the room was intolerable. The air was motionless. The winter sunlight was illuminating the linen cloth hung over the French doors as a sort of curtain, making it luminescent. Her aunt was already wearing her night veil; she was in pain, suffering as she struggled to catch her breath, trembling, and soon she sank into a wheezing gasp that was barely audible. She raised her hand to her throat, in irritation. Her blouse, with its linen collar and buttons running up the back, was squeezing her neck and chest like a high corset. Her aunt was feverish.

"Loosen her blouse," Agata ordered the lay sister.

Angiola Maria glared at her. Snorting impatiently she leaned over the sick woman and wrapped her arms around her to lift her so she could undo the top buttons. The abbess opened her eyes in fear; at the sight of her niece, she calmed down. Her breathing returned to normal. Then, with a gesture of the hand, she summoned Agata closer. The prioress moved out of her way. Before sitting down, Agata leaned over to kiss her aunt: she inhaled a stench of rot mixed with lavender; it vanished as soon as she straightened up. It was emanating from her aunt. Agata took her hand and began stroking it. Angiola Maria had keenly scrutinized every motion and she had noticed Agata's flaring nostrils. "Madame Abbess is tired, she needs sleep," she ordered. The other nuns crossed themselves and left, but Agata remained behind.

"You too must leave." Angiola Maria urged her to go a second time, glowering at her.

The abbess was listening; she clutched Agata's hand and

once again her breathing collapsed into death rattles; the abbess reached her hand up to her neck, doing her best to loosen the collar of her nightshirt. She was sweating and panting. Her fingers danced frantically. Helplessly.

"Unbutton her blouse, can't you see that she's suffering?" Agata shouted. Angiola Maria ignored her. She wanted Agata to go away, immediately. It was a battle of wills. Agata lifted her aunt, hastily unbuttoned her entire bodice, assisted by the fluttering panicky fingers of the sick woman. The milk-white skin of the abbess's neck and shoulders was still completely free of lines or wrinkles. The stench that Agata had smelled before came from the bandaged breast. She was impatient, she wanted to be naked. She yanked her bodice down, unsuccessfully because of the narrow sleeves. Staring at Angiola Maria, she asked with her eyes for help.

Angiola Maria brusquely shoved Agata aside and leaned over to loosen the bandages that were tightly bound around the suffering woman's breasts. The stench of rot filled the room: her right breast was split by a purulent tumor that had been compressed under bandages and lavender sachets.

Donna Maria Crocifissa died a short while later. While she was dying, Agata, instead of praying, remembered what her father had told her about Violante, how he kept insisting on referring to her as his beloved sister. He regretted having gone so rarely to visit her in the convent: he was a coward, but it just caused him too much pain. He had begun going to see his sister again thirty years later, when he was married. "Your mother loved to eat the piping hot puff pastries at San Giorgio Stilita and she always made sure there were plenty when we would come." During one visit, her mother left them alone in the parlor—Donna Gesuela and the two chaperone nuns had gone together into the cloister. Embarrassed, he was unable to make out her features through the grille and he was struggling to reconstruct the features of his sister's face. "Do you want to see me?" she had asked him. A moment later, the door leading to the secluded area opened and his sister appeared on the threshold, as if in a painting. He didn't recognize her. She realized it and beat a hasty retreat; then from behind the grate she said to him: "That was a mistake. I truly am dead." And brother and sister had waited in silence for the others to return.

The interment of nuns was something that was done differently in every convent. There was a time when they dressed them in their finest garments, seated them in stalls, and placed them in cool, well-ventilated crypts to mummify in an eternal choir. After the suppression of the monasteries and convents by the French in 1808, the Neapolitan convents had modernized. In San Giorgio Stilita the procedure—exceedingly simple—remained unchanged. The prioress verified that the nun was deceased, then it was the duty of four lay sisters to bury the corpse in the dormitory of the novices, which had a beaten earth floor. The burial took place immediately, without anyone else being present, and without any ceremony. The corpse—fully dressed in the habit and wrapped in a white sheet—was placed on a special canvas sheet with four handles: it was carried down into the cellar along a staircase that ran from a corner of the cloister and was closed off by a door with a chain lock. The life of the Cenoby suffered no interruption. The same thing happened when a nun learned of the death of relatives: once the news was delivered, she returned to the duties of her office.

Angiola Maria was evidently grief-stricken at the death of Donna Maria Crocifissa, and she was incapable of containing her sorrow. She had wept at length with Agata and she continued to feel the need to talk to her about the abbess. Agata had learned to accept death as a fact of nature but she felt duty-bound to help the faithful lay sister. "Whosoever is born is already on the road to death," she would tell her. They met furtively in Agata's bedroom, after Compline, and, resuming the ritual conversations between aunt and niece, they'd talk in whispers about the life of Donna Maria Crocifissa. Angiola Maria had a wealth of knowledge about the family nuns and she was comforted by the thought that Agata too would bring honor to the name of Padellani, there in San Giorgio Stilita.

During one of these vespertine meetings, it happened that three cockroaches emerged from under the door, dazed and disoriented, as if they'd just been released from captivity. Agata clearly remembered a similar episode, when she was a new arrival at the convent. She shuddered—cockroaches disgusted her—and gathered up the hem of her habit. One of them shuttled rapidly toward the wall, the second followed it, waving its antennae, and the last one moved forward, stopped, changed direction, and stopped again. The first two together headed straight for the bed, vanishing rapidly under the fringework of the bed cover. At that point, the third one rushed after them and slipped under the cover as well. Angiola Maria leapt to her feet and, with the eyes of a madwoman, opened and shut her fists, wordlessly. Then, as if nothing had happened, she went on talking—same tone of voice, different subject—but addressing Agata with the informal "tu" for the first time.

"You should know that your aunt left you a sizable purse of ducats. Don Vincenzo, the prince's secretary, knows all about it, and he'll give you the money, but you have to go there, to the Palazzo Padellani."

"What did she leave you?" Agata was curious, but the lay sister had no intention of answering that question.

"She gave me enough, while she was alive, out of her stipend. I had the keys to the money box. Remember that Donna Maria Crocifissa asked me to serve as your guardian angel. Wherever I might be." And the lay sister lowered her eyelids, as smooth as the eyelids of Donna Maria Crocifissa.

From the cloister came a rush of feet. Then subdued, excited voices. Confusion and noise.

Donna Maria Immacolata, the sister pharmacist, was knocking at the door of Agata's cell: "Hurry, a servingwoman has fallen down the well!"

Two nuns, secretly conversing on the terrace, had seen Brida descend into the cloister, down the stairs across from them. She had gone straight to the fountain, she'd immersed her hand in the water and, kneeling before the statue of Christ, she'd crossed herself. Then she had calmly walked over to the well and lifted the iron cover.

A thud and nothing more.

31.

*Angiola Maria and Checchina, lay sisters of the Padellani
nuns, run away from the convent of San Giorgio Stilita
and there are murmurings against Agata*

The choristers presented themselves at nocturnal prayers
just a few hours after the suicide of the cook, as if nothing had happened. That was the power of the cloistered
life, thought Agata: any death was treated as normal; she liked
that.

During the Lauds at Matins, Donna Maria Giovanna della
Croce gave her a warning: "I'd better tell you now so that you
can get used to the idea. Angiola Maria and Checchina, Donna
Maria Brigida's lay sister who often works with the sister
herbalist, have vanished. The others are likely to blame you."

Agata had no time to digest the news before the Padellani
cousins, who already knew about it, showed up, gossiping away,
and told her the secret story of Angiola Maria. They did it with
a fury and a zest that Agata would have even found funny, if she
hadn't been so horrified. It was as if they wanted to liberate
themselves and liberate Agata too. "She was your aunt!"
Angiola Maria actually was the illegitimate daughter of Agata's
grandfather, and that was why the abbess, God bless her, had
protected her and kept her close in the convent—she was her
half-sister. "She's a bad person, half woman and half man!" The
abbess by rights should have tossed her out of the convent from
the beginning, because Angiola Maria was a hermaphrodite and
she had trysts with servingwomen, lay sisters, and even nuns.
After the affairs were over, they always remained in love, as if
Angiola Maria had cast a spell on them. "That's the way it is
with hermaphrodites, once you fall in love with them, you never

get over it!" Everyone knew that Brida, the cook, had been dropped for many other women, including Checchina, with whom Angiola Maria had been having an affair for years. But Brida, crazed with jealousy and convinced that her true rival was Agata, had viewed the meetings between the two women in Agata's cell to mourn together over the death of the abbess as unmistakable proof of Angiola Maria's betrayal. "That's why Brida killed herself." Agata started to think it over: Could Brida have been the one who sent her cockroaches and threatening notes? Who tried to poison her? Who tried to put the evil eye on her? Gradually these thoughts became a certainty.

"Don't you worry about Angiola Maria, she'll be better off than any of us. She's bought a house and she has money. She stole from the abbess, and she got away with a lot," said one of the cousins, and then added, knowingly: "They say it was her who took the ex-votos from the Madonna dell'Utria, and then put them back on the sacred image the night that you were unwell." The other one redoubled the accusation: "I've heard that the emerald earrings and 24-carat gold chain are both gone, she took them back from our Madonna!" Then they explained to her that Angiola Maria, who was cunning as a fox, wanted Agata to stay at the convent and had orchestrated the false miracle to strengthen her vocation: Agata could be useful to her when her mistress was no longer alive.

"She was the devil among us and it's just as well that she's gone," the two cousins concluded in unison.

"What does Checchina have to do with any of this? She's nothing but a poor fool who wouldn't hurt a fly," Agata asked.

"She has plenty to do with it, plenty!" said the cousins. Then they changed the topic.

The next night, Agata was summoned by Donna Maria Celeste's lay sister: she wanted the sister infirmarian to go to her bedside; her mistress was delirious. Maria Celeste had a high fever and didn't recognize her; she was calling for Father Cutolo, and claimed she was on her deathbed. Agata gave her a small dose of *Colchicum autumnale*, or autumn crocus, to alleviate her pain and lower her fever. She stayed with her for a long time, placing cold compresses on her forehead. From time to time, she put a few more drops into the glass and tipped it up to the nun's lips. Before Matins, Maria Celeste regained lucidity but spoke very little. She was waiting for Father Cutolo.

There was a stale smell in the air. Agata was breathing the scent of death—bitter, faint.

"Father Cutolo is coming!" Heralded by the shuffling clatter of footsteps, a lay sister had appeared in the doorway.

Donna Maria Celeste wanted Agata to stay in the cell: she had no intention of saying confession. When she saw Father Cutolo, she fell back into a sort of delirium, her hands trembling, outheld toward him, eagerly grasping for love—a physical love made of arms, kisses, caresses, embraces. She implored him to take her away with him. "*Avanti, ramm' nu vas', nu vas'*! Come here, give me a kiss!"

The priest, standing above her with a crucifix in his hands, looked down at her ashen-faced. Every so often, he looked rapidly at Agata, who had not dignified him with so much as a glance.

"*Ramm' nu vas'*, just one kiss, put your arms around me, embrace me," Donna Maria Celeste implored him again, louder this time.

Father Cutolo held out a trembling arm toward the nun, showing her the crucifix. "Embrace it, embrace your divine spouse." And he held it high.

"No! You, you embrace me!"

"Christ is your husband!"

"*'Nu vas' solo*, my love, just one kiss!" she pleaded.

"Christ is your husband. Embrace Him!" the priest ordered her, raising his voice, his eyes hard with fear. "Embrace Him!" The nun looked, now at the crucifix, now at him. Then she fell back onto her pillow.

The following night Agata was awakened by Donna Maria Celeste's lay sister: her mistress was on her deathbed, and was calling for her. Agata ran and in the corridor where the nun's cell was located she encountered two servingwomen who were running too, one carrying a bucket and the other carrying a bundle of rags. When they got there she was emitting a death rattle. "What happened to her?" she asked. The lay sister looked at her and then, silently, lifted the covers. The nun had her nightshirt wrapped around her waist. Below her waist she was naked: between her legs, clots of blood.

They wrapped the corpse in oilcloth. The lay sister placed a bundle wrapped in the same oilcloth on her belly. "Then she hemorrhaged and died," she said. Agata and the lay sister covered the corpse with a snow-white sheet, to prevent the prioress, whose job it was to ascertain her death, from becoming suspicious. Only then did they summon the lay sisters of the burial detail.

32.

The new abbess is opposed to Agata;
the cardinal denies her brevi

A gata's sense of justice demanded that Father Cutolo be punished for having seduced Donna Maria Celeste and caused her death, albeit indirectly. And also that he be deprived of the opportunity to destroy other lives. Agata had a clear, practical mission: to inform the mother abbess, the cardinal, and the vicar general, in order to make sure that the priest was expelled from San Giorgio Stilita and deprived of the right to serve as father confessor to any female religious. For good. She expected intense pressure to cover up what had happened and to prevent any scandal.

Agata knew that she was the subject of much gossip and whispering but she was unaware of the specific content. In the convent, the conversation returned incessantly to the escape of the two lay sisters and the death of the cook and serving-woman; Agata was accused of having provoked that tragedy. Some of the nuns said that Agata painted scenes of putti and little birds kissing one another on the beak on the milky frosting of her *cucchitelle* in order to make Brida fall in love. The poor thing did fall in love with Agata, but then she was abandoned for Angiola Maria. The evening of her suicide, Brida had gone to see if her suspicions were justified: she'd glimpsed their shadows in Agata's cell and then she killed herself. Others said that Agata had demanded that Angiola Maria break up with Checchina, who everyone agreed had always been Angiola Maria's true love. Still others claimed that Angiola

Maria, having stolen the jewels of the Madonna dell'Utria, had run away with Checchina, who did not share her inclinations and had been forced to go with Angiola Maria.

Agata requested an interview with Donna Maria del Rosario, the new abbess, who summoned her to meet in her drawing room, along with the prioress, Donna Maria Clotilde. She extended her hand for Agata to kiss and then invited her to sit down.

"The flight of Donna Maria Crocifissa's lay sister must have come as a surprise to you." The abbess had seized the initiative. She was a noblewoman belonging to a family that was hostile to the Padellanis; she was a staunch traditionalist.

Agata had another subject in mind, and she prepared to lay out the story: "I am here to talk to you about a very grave matter, something that has nothing to do with Angiola Maria," she began; whereupon she launched into the dark story of Donna Maria Celeste. The abbess listened with a growing sense of unease and, before Agata had reached the details of the abortion, interrupted her, in an icy voice: "You are telling me that a highly respected chorister, a distant relative of mine, fell ill and began to rave in a delirium. You yourself, as sister infirmarian, took excellent care of her and, from what you are telling me, your treatment restored her to lucidity, until the sickness proved fatal. Clearly you misunderstood the words that the poor sick woman addressed to her father confessor."

"No, abbess. She was speaking of carnal love, of kisses. She wanted kisses! She wanted them from him!"

"That's enough! I forgive you because you are a young nun; you do not know ecstasy, which can be misunderstood by those with sin in their hearts."

Donna Maria del Rosario waited for Agata to leave. But she wasn't finished.

"Mother abbess, I was there when Donna Maria Celeste died. Her lay sister lifted the covers, and I saw!"

The abbess stood up abruptly. Just as a peasant woman repeats "shoo, shoo," and scolds the hens to chase them out of a courtyard, so she accompanied her "Go away! Away! Away!" with the very same gestures, and like a chicken, Agata backed across the abbess's drawing room, propelled by those frantic waving arms. "I forbid you to repeat this lie to anyone else." The abbess had opened the door leading out onto the cloister. Agata hurried away, but not before she caught a parting "Miserable liar!" She turned around and looked back: the face of the abbess was a mask of appalled fury.

Donna Maria Clotilde had followed Agata, and she was walking at her side, as if to ensure that she said nothing inappropriate to the other sisters.

"My daughter, I swear that I had no suspicion at all about what you say concerning the death of the unfortunate Donna Maria Celeste," she said to her.

"Well, of course not, the lay sister and I took great care to make sure that you had no suspicions. I already explained that to you." Agata was impatient.

"Then why did you bring it up now?"

"Because it's the truth, and to protect other nuns from that priest. Do you remember how her body was wrapped in sheets up to her neck? It was to conceal the oilcloth. We can ask the lay sister, she knows everything."

"We would have to disinter the corpse. In the history of our convent that has never happened!" She went on emphatically: "And what good would it do? Just to create a scandal? To ruin our reputation and the reputation of a poor nun?"

"To ensure that Father Cutolo is never again allowed to be the confessor of another nun, here or anywhere else! If it wasn't for him, Donna Maria Celeste would still be alive!" Agata had raised her voice in exasperation.

"Why do you say this about a priest?"

"Because he seduced her!"

"Seduced?" And the prioress took on the tone of voice of a schoolteacher. "Let's think this over. He might very well say the reverse. He is poor, and Donna Maria Celeste enjoyed a very substantial stipend. She gave him gifts. Think of how delighted they would be, the enemies of Holy Mother Church, if they learned about these accusations!" Then she took a deep breath and put her hand on Àgata's arm, with a protective gesture. "Trust me, let this be. The new abbess is very strict and she will keep all aspects of monastic life under close control, nothing will escape her notice, I assure you! Go, and don't think about it again."

Agata went to see Maria Celeste's lay sister. She couldn't find her. Then she was told that the lay sister had been transferred that same afternoon to work directly under the mother abbess.

From that time on, Agata was treated dismissively by the abbess and the prioress. She had to obey the seal of silence imposed upon her by the abbess, but not in confession. And so she spoke to Father Cuoco about it. He listened. "What do you want to obtain?" he asked her, and added: "Vendetta?" When she said nothing in reply, he raised his voice: "In that case, go away from here, those aren't things to discuss in a confessional."

"Father, I want justice," said Agata.

"Justice? In that case, too, I am unable to help you: it is God Almighty who administers justice, after death."

Agata wasn't going to give up. "And yet we must try to protect the innocent souls of the sister nuns!"

"Remember that you are all noblewomen and much wealthier than us priests, and just as man can tempt woman, so woman is quite capable of leading man into temptation; indeed, all the more, since she is descended from Eve. In time, that father confessor will leave the convent. He must have suffered from the scene that you described to me, and deeply so, especially if he's innocent, as I believe him to be."

"Father, you forget that I saw the miscarriage."

"My daughter, forgive me if I doubt what you in good faith believe you have seen. First of all, it was nighttime, and candlelight can play tricks on your eyes. Second, you've never seen what you claim to have seen and which you call a miscarriage: there are other illnesses and misfortunes, perfectly innocent, that can cause discharges of that substance even in virgins, I know this very well from the confessions that I hear. Third, we do not know whether the lay sister exaggerated, perhaps she too in perfectly good faith, like you, or out of mischief. Let us never forget that someone could have intentionally placed there the innards of a chicken, to give you a mistaken impression and cause trouble for Father Cutolo." Father Cuoco stopped to take a breath, with weariness in his voice: "We don't know. Let's leave well enough alone." And he gave her absolution and the usual penance of *Aves* and *Paters*.

Agata, indignant, prayed with desperate passion for God to help her. In a law book belonging to her aunt the abbess, she found a reference to the Concordat of 1822, which sanctioned the primacy of ecclesiastical law over the monasteries and convents of the kingdom. She could not simply leave with impunity: the cardinal had the right to demand that she be arrested and imprisoned in a religious institution.

All the same, she could still forward a request to the pope for a *brevi* for a limited or lengthy period, for considerations of health. In any case, she would have to request the cardinal's approval, and he would be required to verify the request and issue an opinion. A nun could also file a demand to dissolve her monastic vows, something that in her case would certainly be difficult, but not impossible. That demand had to be sent within the first five years of her profession of vows and it required proof that there had been moral violence in the process of becoming a nun. The case would be examined first by the Curia of Naples and then by the Curia of Rome.

Suspicious of everything and everyone and a target of hostility from many of her sisters, Agata was a bundle of nerves. She was losing weight. She performed her duties and then retreated to solitude. She devoured the books that she received from James Garson. Often she took one up with her to the belvedere and read as she walked back and forth.

One day, Agata received an unexpected visit from her mother. Donna Gesuela was in Naples while her husband got a medical checkup; seeing her in that state, she suggested that her daughter request the *brevi*. She could come back to Sicily with them. A few days later the cardinal, visiting the convent, asked to see her. Agata walked across the cloister, followed by glances of envy from the other nuns: they considered her to be fortunate and privileged for the favor that he was bestowing upon her.

"I don't understand the reason for this request of *brevi*, so soon after your solemn profession," the cardinal began.

"It's already been eight months, Your Eminence. I would like to spend some time with my mother, her husband is unwell."

The cardinal's gaze hardened: "You haven't seen one another for six years."

"She's my mother." And her eyes glistened as she thought of her father, as his voice rang inside her: *Deep down, your mamma is a good mother.* "If my father were still alive . . . " she mumbled dolefully.

"Donna Maria Ninfa, you were reborn with your solemn

profession, you no longer have either a father or a mother. I'm here now, for you."

She was crying.

"Come, come, get a hold of yourself! I'm going to Rome and when I come back I'll come to see you. You'll feel better." And the cardinal brushed her cheek with two slender fingers.

Agata sent a note to her mother, giving her the bad news that she would not be allowed to leave the convent. The note was returned to her: General Cecconi and the Generalessa had left for Palermo.

And it was them that Agata decided to file a demand to dissolve her monastic vows and to withdraw from the Cenoby.

33

April 1847.
Agata is not well loved at the convent and does
everything within her power to leave the cloistered life

From then on, Agata lived in the convent as an outsider and a rebel. She continued to sing in the choir assiduously, but she skipped Mass, though she still said confession regularly. She performed her duties as infirmarian, which she considered to be her civic duty, and then she spent her time reading, making her *cucchitelle*, upon which she now painted hibiscuses and camellias, and creating wonderful *paperoles* with bird feathers, scraps of paper, threads teased out of rags, dried leaves, and pressed flowers. She walked frequently and at length, in her seclusion; she followed a route that she had created for herself, passing in front of the staircase that led down to the underground cemetery, into the cloister of the novices, and then upstairs into the uninhabited dormitories, walking through abandoned halls, taking stairs and passageways, opening doors that had never been open, concealed behind curtains weighed down by dust, and making her way onto tiny secret terraces tucked away on the convent's roofs. From up there, she could see Naples and she felt at one with the outside world. And she prayed for the others. How many times had she sought out the city from high above? How many times had she felt it calling to her, like a hope, like a natural destination? Hers was a prayer that called for fullness, space, action. She couldn't bring herself to feel shame for such a swelling wave of feeling. But she was confused. She let her hair grow, and she was vague and distracted. She prepared the request, but she didn't send it. Aunt Orsola, with whom she had spoken of her desire to leave San Giorgio Stilita, suggested another, less controversial way: seek an appointment as a canoness of Bavaria, an ancient knightly and religious order; the practical effect of that move would be to preserve her vows of chastity and poverty, but not the other two; the canonesses of Bavaria had the right to live independently, far from the cloister. Admiral Pietraperciata had offered to sound out his contacts with certain German noblemen of his acquaintance and to pay the 390 ducats for the honorific.

The abbess's lay sister had come to convey the message that Donna Maria Ninfa was wanted by the cardinal. It was a formal meeting, in the abbess's drawing room and in her presence. "It is my pleasure to approve this new honorific for Donna Maria Ninfa," he said and then, looking her straight in the eye: "But, for the moment, I don't want to deprive the new chorister of the joy of life in the cloister. I will therefore permit you to wear the insignia of the Order of Bavaria on your habit." Then he furrowed his brow and said that she could go. Agata died inside: she realized that the demand to dissolve her monastic vows would likewise be rejected by the Curia of Naples.

In the convent, the atmosphere had become intolerable. Veiled accusations and allusions to Brida's suicide came up continually. From that evening on, there was also gossip to the effect that Agata had caused the death of Donna Maria Celeste by administering the wrong medications, and that that was why she had asked to leave the convent, first with a request for *brevi* and then with the stratagem of her appointment as a canoness of Bavaria. Agata felt that she was under suspicion. Donna Maria Giovanna della Croce encouraged her to confide in her, but Agata was forced to remain silent by the obligation of obedience to the abbess.

They were sitting outdoors, embroidering a chasuble.

"Something new is tormenting you."

"There is a dark night in my soul," Agata burst out in reply.

Donna Maria Giovanna della Croce pinned the needle trailing purple silk thread into the damask and let her eye wander around the cloister beneath them; then she murmured, keeping her gaze directed away from Agata: "Just when it seems that everything is going wrong, when you are experiencing the 'dark night' of the soul, that is when the process of purification is beginning. The seclusion of the cloister is not pointless, the vocation is to live every second full of love for the universe."

But Agata's dark night showed no sign of ending. To avoid the murmurs and the open hostility of the other nuns, she refrained from eating meals in the refectory with the excuse that she was indisposed; in time she became accustomed to not eating. She was visibly wasting away, but she didn't care. Instead, she longed to learn things, to find out what was going on outside of the convent, from reading the *Gazzetta del Seggio*, which unfailingly found its way into the cloister, and through accounts of the conversations that other nuns had in the parlor. Agata began to frequent the more "worldly" and social choristers, despite their shallowness, just so that she could learn from them what was happening outside and the gossip from within their own families. Every time that she sent her linen out to be washed, she sent Sandra little notes requesting help in small tinfoil tubes baked into the *cucchitelle*. What came back was invariably clean laundry and nothing else. And yet she was determined to leave the cloister, God was with her.

Agata's behavior and her emaciation were impossible to overlook, and the abbess wrote about it to the princess of Opiri; she in turn informed Donna Gesuela, who reacted this time with motherly concern: not only did she make a special trip to Naples, but she seemed to regret her neglect of her daughter and she suggested to Agata that they go together to see the cardinal and ask him for the *brevi*. The request for an interview was granted immediately, and mother and daughter together went to the Abbey of San Martino, where the cardinal, on a spiritual retreat, had agreed to see them.

The veiled carriage clattered up from Via Mezzocannone and had reached the intersection with Via della Certosa. During the trip, Agata avoided looking out the window—it made her head spin. She pulled back the curtain only to peer out at the distant view of the Castle Sant'Elmo; it loomed, massive, against a gleaming, intensely blue sky, like something painted on glass. She remembered her carriage ride with Carmela and Annuzza before Anna Carolina's wedding, and her pride as she had showed them *her* Naples—memories from another life. At the age of twenty-one, she felt hollowed out, stripped of all vitality and hope for the future.

The team of horses was struggling as it pulled through the last few hairpin turns. The Abbey of San Martino was in plain view, high atop the hill. Agata began to feel uneasy; she couldn't understand the cardinal's attitude—he'd swung from benevolent to punitive for no apparent reason. He imposed his will upon her with a harshness that verged on the sadistic, as if he were her master, and yet she seemed to detect some genuine fondness for her, as if he just wished that she would bend spontaneously to his will. Likewise, Agata couldn't understand her own reaction to the cardinal's behavior. She, who was not rebellious by nature, almost instinctively became rebellious toward him.

They were walking through the abbot's apartment, accompanied by the cardinal's secretary. Agata, her face veiled, was walking with her head bowed, close by her mother's side. It was not only the vast space of sky and earth, but even unfamiliar interiors that disoriented her; she paid close attention to the white-and-green diagonal tiles of the majolica floor. The secretary left them in the Cloister of the Procuratori, which offered a magnificent view of the Gulf of Naples; he would come back later, to give them a tour of the Charter House. The air was fragrant with the airy perfume of linden blossoms. The grey piperno-stone arches stood out against the *pietra serena*, a grey sandstone, and the plaster of the walls. Agata lifted her eyes and immediately lowered them again, overwhelmed.

The cardinal came toward them from the opposite door. He seemed annoyed by the ritual kissing of the ring and he gestured for them to rise. "What new problems do we have with our young chorister?" he said in a cutting tone of voice. The narrow tip of his right slipper was tapping the floor.

Her mother lifted Agata's veil with a gesture of ownership. "My daughter is wasting away, just take a look at her! Send her home with me for a while, the next time I come." Donna Gesuela had drawn herself erect, back straight, chest thrust out; beneath the hem of her dress, lifted slightly off the floor, the light-green leather tips of her shoes could be seen.

Agata stubbornly kept her eyes glued to the floor. She had once loved those fetching little shoes. Her mother's shoes, with silver buckles and knife-sharp heels, next to her own shoes, black and clumsy, made her feel incongruous and out of place, as did the soft morocco leather slippers worn by the cardinal, directly across from her.

"If it's so urgent, shouldn't you want her with you immediately?"

"I have a husband to take care of. I came in a hurry because Orsola was so worried about my Agatuzza that . . . "

"About Donna Maria Ninfa!" he corrected her.

Donna Gesuela leaned back against a column and crossed her ankles, one small shoe with the heel raised and the tip dug in against the floor. "Whatever her name might be, she's still a daughter of mine . . . Will you let me have her, then?" And she stamped her heel.

"I see no reason to do so. Your request for *brevi* is for health reasons. Either your daughter truly needs fresh air, and if so she will have it immediately, or else she does not, in which case she will not be given leave at all. Are you ready to take her away tomorrow?" His purple slipper was tapping time.

"How can I do that? You tell me! My husband isn't well . . . " And her voice cracked.

"We all make our own choices and we all take on certain obligations, and we must meet those obligations. Donna Maria Ninfa took the monastic vows of her own free will, after passing the appropriate examinations. Her physical and spiritual health is very dear to me." A pause, and then, "As is that of all the servants of God in the diocese." Then he pushed forward his right foot, practically toe-tip to toe-tip with Donna Gesuela. Agata lifted her eyes but she did not dare to look him in the face. The two were practically chest to chest.

"Well, then?"

"'Well, then,' what? You, Generalessa, should go home to your husband. Our young nun will return to San Giorgio Stilita, where her fellow sisters will cook her delicacies and delights of all sorts to tempt her to eat." The cardinal had turned toward Agata and he whispered: "You will try to eat, won't you?"

Agata didn't answer.

"The poor girl doesn't have the strength to answer! Are you trying to kill her?" Donna Gesuela was quivering with indignation. "You need to give us this *brevi*!"

Her back flat against the column, Donna Gesuela was twisting the silk bow that dangled from her hat, draping over her breasts, murmuring all the while. He responded by fiddling with the cross on his chest.

There was an unspoken discussion in the air between them, and Agata was its designated victim, caught like a hare with its leg in a trap.

"I'd like to hear what Donna Maria Ninfa has to say." And

he stiffened back into his initial position, feet flat and parallel on the ground in a wide stance.

"I too would like to speak with Your Eminence, alone." Agata had screwed up her nerve. The cardinal sketched out a hint of a bow to the Generalessa and stepped aside with Agata onto the portico overlooking the Bay of Naples.

"Tell me, my daughter."

Agata started laying out the details of the story of Father Cutolo, but she was immediately interrupted. "I've already heard it, from others," he said, quite dismissively. Then, in a silky, almost caressing tone of voice: "I ask you to show compassion. We aren't executioners, nor are we judges; those are prerogatives of the Lord." And he said, again: "Compassion, I beg of you." He looked her straight in the eyes, the glittering black of his pupils shining beneath his half-lowered eyelids.

Agata accepted the challenge.

"You've never shown any compassion for me. Never. And you should have, you of all people. I would like to be better than you . . . " Agata had spoken all in a rush. She stopped to catch her breath. Then she went on: "But, like you, I have no compassion for a priest who seduces a woman, whether she is a nun, an old maid, or a wife." She lowered her eyes to the parapet. The rocky escarpment beneath her made her head spin.

After what seemed to both of them like an interminable interval, the cardinal laid a hand on her shoulder. "Come now, let's go, your mother is waiting for us," and he gave her his arm as they walked back.

In the narthex of the Charter House, the cardinal's secretary was showing them a painting of the destruction of charterhouses by the English during the Reformation. The bodies of the monks in white habits being murdered occupied the foreground. Agata and her mother listened distractedly. The cardinal was in the background, silent. At that point he spoke:

"Remember, it was the English who did this, treacherous they were and treacherous they remain." She took this as a personal criticism, but she only needed to take a look at him before deciding not to dignify it with a response: he was pathetic.

In the carriage, Agata was relaxed. Her mother snorted in annoyance at how late they would be returning home. "You seem very pleased with yourself, as if you didn't care a fig whether you leave the convent or not," she said, "but for me this has been nothing but a waste of a day!"

Three days later, Dr. Minutolo was summoned to the convent in the middle of the night: Agata was twisting in agony. The sister pharmacist had no idea of what to do. They did their best to identify her last meal: it was a bowl of salad, which still sat on its tray, in her cell. They discovered that the oil had been dusted with verdigris. Agata had ordered the salad from the kitchens and the tray had been left outside her door: anyone could have added the poisoned oil.

The abbess appointed one of Donna Maria Brigida's servingwomen and Sarina, Donna Maria Crocifissa's lay sister, to keep an eye on Agata. No one else had access to her cell and nothing could be sent to her from the outside world, including the linen that Sandra washed for her. Once again, someone wanted to do her harm.

34.
May 1847.
The cardinal learns that someone tried to hurt Agata and he removes her from the convent of San Giorgio Stilita

Agata truly was afraid now; she had no idea who would want to poison her or why, and the fact that Angiola Maria had disappeared meant that now there was no one to watch over her. The abbess had shown herself to be prompt and thoughtful, for the first time, suggesting that Agata keep to the safety of her cell; the abbess's lay sisters would bring Agata her meals. Her suspicions aroused by this sudden turnabout, Agata thought it over at length and concluded that Donna Maria Celeste's lay sister, now working for the abbess, was the only one who might have a reason to want her dead, out of fear that she might reveal the abortion that she had helped her mistress procure in that ugly situation. So she refused to eat. On the third day, the abbess came to her cell and with a half smile informed her that the cardinal had authorized *brevi* at her mother's home in Palermo. Agata was free to leave the convent as soon as her health improved; while waiting for her mother to come and fetch her, she could stay at the conservatory of Smirne. She neglected to tell Agata that her already modest stipend would be cut in half—the convent would keep the other half—as well as that she and the deaconesses had decided to suggest to the choristers that they vote against her readmission to the Cenoby, should Donna Maria Ninfa ever ask to come back to San Giorgio Stilita.

But Agata had already understood. Anxious about her transfer to the conservatory, which the other nuns spoke of with unconcealed disdain, and uncertain about the welcome she would be likely to receive in Palermo, she felt alone and destined for a vagabond life, shuttling between various religious institutions and relatives who were unlikely to welcome her. Even before she'd lost them for good, she missed her life of religious seclusion at San Giorgio Stilita and the friendships she would be leaving behind. She felt ready to receive the vocation, but now it was too late. That evening, while the others were all at Vespers, she managed to send Nina and Sarina away with a subterfuge and slipped stealthily out of her cell, making her way to her favorite refuge: a little terrace off the uninhabited dormitory of the novices, enclosed by very high walls, from which it was only possible to see a square patch of sky, the inviolate territory of pigeons. The birds' deafening cooing drowned out the noises of the city. After the first frantic burst of wings, though, they accepted her, focusing their pinhead eyes upon her, waiting to regain mastery of the place. Agata, at the center of the little terrace, watched the sky change from light blue to blinding white and then to the red of a hidden sunset, and she prayed for her fellow nuns, certain that God was listening to her. That was her farewell to San Giorgio Stilita.

The following morning she was ready to leave. Donna Maria Giovanna della Croce had brought her a saint card of her namesake, St. John of the Cross. They knew they'd never see one another again but that their affection would endure.

"True love knows no measures and is untroubled by the thought of being repaid; it is free. I give myself to you, in our friendship, without expecting anything in return, just as I did with God," she said to Agata.

"But love between a man and a woman is different, it demands something in return," Agata observed.

"It's a complex love, because there are children involved. But there, too, if it seeks a *quid pro quo*, it is not true love," Donna Maria Giovanna della Croce repeated. "My first and only love was Jesus, ever since I was a little girl. They wanted to marry me off, because my older sister went lame and . . . "—the nun blushed—" . . . wasn't as pretty as me, according to my parents. I had to beg and plead before they'd send me to become an educand, and I never regretted it. I live happily, in this imperfect convent, for God."

When the time came to say farewell, Donna Maria Giovanna della Croce embraced her. "You were made to serve the Lord in the world. If you have a daughter, pray that she has the calling, and don't dissuade her. Remember that."

Aunt Orsola's carriage conveyed Agata, alone, to the conservatory, not very far from San Giorgio Stilita. She had put all her books in the false bottom of her trunks: it had been some time since she'd received any new ones and she wondered whether her last note, in which she had made no secret of her sense of helplessness and despair, might have annoyed the Englishman. Perhaps that was why he'd decided not to send her any more books. She felt as if she'd been abandoned by everyone.

35

June 1847.
At the conservatory of Smirne. Agata can leave
and walk around Naples; she receives a letter from James

The conservatory of Smirne was built in the center of a populous quarter of Naples, around the nucleus of a chapel in which the image of the Madonna of Smirne, thought to have saved Naples from the plague of 1526 and again from the plague in 1603, was venerated. Following the French occupation, it had been given back to the Curia in very poor condition and never thereafter restored. With four cloisters built to gridiron plan and a monumental entrance, it was a collection of bare corridors with very high vaulted ceilings, overlooked by a series of dank cells. It housed women of different religious orders and categories, who lived in the dormitories adjoining each cloister. Occupying one cloister were oblates and widows belonging to the petty bourgeoisie who had embraced vows of poverty and chastity, although they were members of no monastic order, occupied one cloister; the adjoining cloister housed nuns who were either invalids or mentally ill, sent there from a variety of Neapolitan convents, in order to free the other nuns from the burden of caring for them, or else to give them a change of surroundings; the third cloister was occupied by repentant women who had dishonored themselves with one violation or another, fallen women and problem girls who sold, through the turnstile, their needlepoint embroideries and whatever they could cook or bake. Agata would be housed in the fourth cloister, together with a group of oblate sisters and other nuns who, for one reason or another, were no longer accepted at their convent and had nowhere else to go: rebellious, penniless, or on the brink of madness.

Accustomed to the Baroque elegance and the sheer opulence of San Giorgio Stilita, Agata's first impression of the conservatory was not good. The coachman had unloaded her trunks and left them in the front hall. The doorkeeper, a coarse and uncomely lay sister who waved filthy hands and fingernails edged with black in the air as she spoke, told Agata to haul her trunks up to the third floor, where she would be staying.

"I can't do that myself. They're too heavy," Agata complained. "Send me two strong people to carry the trunks upstairs."

"I'll send nobody. You have to go find two servingwomen who'll carry the trunks on their backs, and you'll have to pay them! Otherwise the trunks stay here, at your own risk," she replied, and she smirked at her.

The cell was furnished with a folding bed covered by a filthy, grimy mattress, a table and a chair, and a chamber pot. The ceiling was stained by a patch of dampness and the flaking plaster sifted onto the terra cotta floor tiles next to the bed. Spurts of light came in through a window six feet off the floor, dwindling into the shadow of the facing wall, where the gobs of sunshine only accentuated the contrast with the penumbra. The other nuns, many of them demented, stayed holed up in their cells; their shouts echoed down the corridors, and on the rare occasions that Agata encountered one, she was invariably filthy, obscene, and frightening. The sole refectory was used in rotation by the occupants of the various cloisters; the food was awful and the nuns who read the divine lesson shortened and modified the texts as it pleased them.

The abbess of the conservatory had been obliged by the Curia to take her in, and she was annoyed by the terms given her under her *brevi*—she was allowed to go out every day for no more than three hours, between dawn and nightfall, and the abbess found that to be grossly excessive. She warned Agata that life in the conservatory was Spartan and discipline very strict: latecomers returning after the deadline would not be admitted until the following morning.

Agata was not allowed to go visit relatives or receive visits from them without special permission from her confessor, and Father Cuoco had not yet come to see her. She had nothing to do, except for going to the chapel to pray, alone, and taking care of herself: cleaning the cell, washing her clothing, and cooking, unless she wanted to go eat in the refectory, where she would have to pay. Along with her books, Agata had brought her nursing supplies—bandages, alcohol, medicinal herbs, unguents, and tinctures—but few if any of the things that she had assumed would be provided for every nun at the conservatory. And so she was obliged to purchase all the little things that she needed: a pitcher and a basin with which to wash herself, soft soap, a broom and a rag to clean the floor, and everything necessary to cook and eat. Now she understood why she was allowed to go out every day: she had to do her grocery shopping.

Unaccustomed to the din of the crowd and the city's deafening racket of wheels and voices, at first Agata was afraid of the streets and the surging and receding flow of pedestrians; she'd make short excursions into some of the less packed parts of the neighborhood, stopping in churches and oratories for prayer at the appropriate times of day in accordance with the Benedictine Rule, then go back to the conservatory and out again after taking a moment to recover. She was also afraid of being recognized by relatives or friends and she wore the turquoise cape of the Order of Canonesses of Bavaria: thus attired, she went out into the marketplaces and, after comparing prices and thinking it over several times—her savings were almost entirely exhausted—she would buy fruit, greens, bread, and sometimes fried fish.

One day, as she emerged from a church, she caught an irresistible whiff of the scent of bread; with the few coins left to her she purchased a piping hot flatbread from a street vendor with a tray slung around his neck who had emerged from an alley. Agata was yearning to eat it immediately, and in order to avoid being seen doing so she quickly dodged into the alley. She sat down on a boulder at the foot of a blank wall, in a wide spot in the alley, which seemed to be uninhabited. She chewed the crunchy dough, lost in thought. Filthy half-naked children, boys and girls, emerged seemingly from nowhere and she was soon obliged to share the flatbread out with them, laboriously distributing chunks that were roughly equal. The bigger children gobbled their pieces down immediately and then turned to snatch the smaller children's chunk of flatbread out of their fingers, occasionally out of their very mouths. Agata shouted at the children to stop, but it was all over in the blink of an eye—the children had vanished back into their dark holes. She sat weeping quietly. She felt something damp on her hand, like a dog's tongue, and she swung around quickly. There, a toddler no older than two, completely naked—arms, legs, and shoulders less flesh than bones and a belly swollen like a wineskin, the belly button looking like it was about to pop off—was licking the palm of her hand in search of any crumbs that might still be stuck to it. The child looked up in fright. Its dirty blond hair was clumped stickily to face and neck, and the bleary eyes were blank, expressionless. The toddler grabbed her hand and began licking, first the back of the hand and then one finger at a time.

After that, Agata never dared to stop again. She walked incessantly through the city, pushing further and further everyday, in a vain search for places to be alone in the heart of Naples. This, she thought, is what they're talking about when they say they want a more equitable society. This is what they've seen, this is what they continue to see.

When she perceived the life of the city from on high, from a distance, she knew that underneath, in the shadows, there was a poverty that was apparently irredeemable. She had read, and reading had sharpened her senses; it was through her senses that she now absorbed the unmistakable evidence of injustice.

Agata had sent a note to Don Vincenzo, her cousin's administrator, to ask if he could send her whatever the abbess had left her, because she was truly in need: the conservatory demanded advance payment for food and board, her meager savings would soon run out, and she had no idea when she would receive her half-stipend from the convent. Her cousin the prince replied in person: Don Vincenzo knew nothing about any supposed inheritance, but he regretted to inform her that her Aunt Orsola had died suddenly, without suffering, the week before, after playing a game of cards; she had left her three ducats, which he had sent to the abbess of San Giorgio Stilita, whom Agata should contact.

Agata wrote immediately to the abbess, explaining that that tiny bequest was urgently needed because the conservatory demanded payment in advance for the rent. The following morning, Nina, the servingwoman and shopper of Donna Maria Brigida, came to see her; she had brought the abbess's reply. The parlor was occupied; overcoming her shame and her pride, Agata decided to receive her in her cell. It was a deeply moving moment: Agata had always kept the servingwomen at arm's length, but the two of them knew each other very well, because the lay sisters who ought to have seen to her aunt's every need and requirement usually left the more disagreeable tasks for Nina to do. For the first time, the two women embraced and wept together. Nina gave her the letter from the abbess, and then, warily, looking around as if the little black stains of dampness on the ceiling were so many eyes watching her, she rummaged in her basket and pulled out a package from Detken's bookstore. She had found it weeks ago, in a pile of things to be burnt; the servingwomen went through those piles item by item, inspecting them to see if there was anything that could be reused.

Once Nina had left, Agata dissolved into a stream of tears: now she really was alone and friendless in the world. She anxiously opened the letter. The abbess was sending her just fifty ducats; she explained that the cardinal had issued the *brevi* to her on the understanding that any inheritance, as well as her stipend, would be split equally between the convent of San Giorgio Stilita and the Benedictine convent that took her in; just this once, on an entirely exceptional basis, and with the cardinal's consent, she was sending her that money. Agata looked around her, devastated—another brutal blow inflicted by the cardinal—and she met the glazed eye of a *tignuseddu*— a gecko—clinging to the wall with the suction cups on its feet, lying in ambush just inches from her head.

She opened the package—it was another novel, *The Monk*. The title made her smile. She wondered who might have chosen it. She leafed through it, as she always did. Every book has its own identity and characteristics, and Agata had a ritual that she followed in order to get to know and love a book. First she looked at it, observing the inscriptions on the spine, the color and patterns on the paper endsheets glued to the inside of the cover, the typographical characters and the intensity of blackness of the ink. She felt the uncut pages, with delicacy, respectfully, to sense the finish and the thickness on the surface of her own skin. Last of all, she hefted the volume, passing it from one hand to the other, to become accustomed to its weight, and only then did she pick up the paper knife. She put the little uneven tabs of paper that ripped off as she cut the pages into her mouth, as if they were communion wafers.

As she sliced the pages with her paper knife, her gaze chanced upon words and phrases of dialogue, and she wondered just what kind of book this was. She'd made her way more or less halfway through when an envelope addressed to her slid out from between two pages and into her lap. The handwriting was different from the lettering of the address on the package, which was very familiar to Agata. She opened it, absent-mindedly, thinking it might contain an odd, personalized sheet of *errata corrige*.

My dear Agata,
I beg your forgiveness if I dare to write to you in this fashion; if what I am about to say to you should offend you, please rest assured that this is certainly not my intention. Let me come straight to the point; I certainly understand that you might well prefer to let your silence convey to me the answer that I so fear.
The first time that I met you, ten years ago, I was the exact age that you are now, twenty-two years old; I had already traveled around the world and I was accustomed to fighting to achieve the objectives that I had set for myself. You already know that I come from a family of shipowners and that we are responsible for the sulfur trade in the Kingdom of the Two Sicilies. We own a house in Naples, but our roots were and remain in Devon, where my Norman forefathers settled long ago. I mention these details to make it clear to you that I belong to a family of glorious lineage, that I possess considerable personal wealth, and that when I give my word of honor it is the honor of my entire ancestry that is at stake.
In September 1839 I left Messina for Naples, where I was to meet my fiancée Georgina, a gentle girl whose family has

more than once intermarried with my family, a girl I loved and who loved me. I chose to challenge a furious gale rather than miss my appointment, and I took your family aboard my ship as my guests and as passengers. It was dawn, and the storm had subsided. I heard you sing a song from my childhood; then I saw you leaning against the door of the cabin. Storm-tossed, wind-beaten, and exhausted, we were able to carry on a polite drawing-room conversation, until you looked me straight in the eye and bared your soul, speaking openly about yourself, of your dearest affections, and of your family. The wind had pinned you against the cabin door and it revealed your body to me—legs, hips, belly, breasts; you were looking into the east and the low rays of the rising sun were caressing your face. I desired you. When you spoke to me about your inamorato, *I was stabbed by a bolt of jealousy so powerful that it made me stagger. That was when I realized that I loved you, more than any other woman on earth, and that that would always be true.*

While you were following your father's casket, I was revealing to Georgina that I loved another woman; I offered her the opportunity to break our engagement. She refused to give me back my freedom; she said that it was merely a passing infatuation. I begged her to reconsider and pointed out that I felt no physical attraction for her and that our marriage would be in name only.

It wasn't very difficult for me to arrange to see you again; it was enough to make a point of spending more time socializing with your extended family. Every brief meeting we had only confirmed my love. I kept track of your fate through contacts and—let me admit it—spies. Even before the birth of our only son, our conjugal relationship had flickered, and so it remains. Georgina does not enjoy good health, and I feel that I am responsible for that: she has certainly paid a high price for refusing to believe me. She lives in France and I go to see her four times a year. Our child is at boarding school. I have no intention of failing to maintain her, nor would I ever want to humiliate her.

I love you. More than before, if that's possible. I can't stand this life of waiting and celibacy any longer. We are made for one another. We think alike—you like Pamela more than you do Clarissa—we believe in a constitutional monarchy more than we do in a republic, we laugh at the same things, we have the same tastes, we brood over the same thoughts. I have learned all this from your comments on the books that I send you and from the notes that you've written me recently.

I offer you and I give you my word of honor that you will always have my love, ample economic independence, and the life that you want to live, where and as you wish. I am willing to move to Sicily, to remain in Naples, or to go to any other country you care to choose. I want your happiness and my own. And I want children with you, children who would feel no lack or disadvantage with respect to their older brother.

I cannot offer you marriage.

I wonder, however, just what "marriage" could mean, in your eyes and mine, if not a promise between two people to love and respect one another to the exclusion of others, and to raise a family together. I never made such a promise to Georgina. I am more than willing to do so with you. You too have made a marriage that you regret, with Christ; you took the veil to satisfy your family and to avoid much worse. You lack a vocation. A "marriage" between the two of us would be acceptable in God's sight, as it would be the only marriage desired and intended.

I have no doubt that my feelings might indeed be shared by you, and perhaps they really are. In order to be able to be closer to you, I have accepted a diplomatic role between our respective governments; at times I am summoned to London or I am sent to Sicily. In the future my interests will take me to England, unless I receive an answer from you, and I urge you to give me your answer as soon as you are able, but not before reading the novel that I enclose.

It is full-blooded and carnal. Like the relationship that I desire with you.

Yours always,

James

Agata was weeping. She had so missed the English books that he sent her, and now she understood why he had stopped. He had taken her silence as a refusal. It had never occurred to her that she might love him and now, as in a mosaic, she reconstructed his personality through his literary choices. She felt a stirring within her. Exhausted, she fell asleep with the letter in her hand.

36.
July 1847.
The doorkeeper of the conservatory of Smirne
refuses to admit Agata, who has returned late

Agata missed the choir—the musky aroma of freshly waxed wood, the dense cool air that poured in through the open windows, the wafting gusts of incense, the rituals, the chants and songs, the silences. Chanting the Psalter had become part of her very being. Those were moments when she actually found herself desiring the seclusion of the cloister, though afterwards she revised her views, blushing with no one to see how deeply she depended on her senses. One afternoon, eaten alive by her yearning for *her* choir, she went to the church of San Giorgio Stilita; she took a seat in the back pew, in the shadows, to keep from being noticed. From there she would rejoin her sister nuns. She waited for the hour of the Vespers in the silence of the empty church. Then she heard a scraping of feet. Three tall well dressed men were taking a tour of the church, beginning with the side chapels. The youngest man was acting as their guide. The young man had turned and with a sweep of his arm was showing them the choir above the portal. Agata recognized the blond beard: it was James Garson. It seemed to her that their eyes had locked. He continued the tour, as if he hadn't recognized her. She covered her face with her hands and went on praying.

She peeked out at him from between her fingers. James had returned to the transept and was looking at the *comunichino*. In that instant Agata felt something like an electric shock: she knew he thought of her with an almost animal intensity, and although she failed to understand it, she instinctively felt it in return. Then James caught up with the other two and together they headed slowly for the exit, admiring the rich decorations as they went. Just then he recognized her. Their eyes met for an instant; Agata felt her cheeks burn and she ducked her head suddenly: she prayed to God to help her understand her feelings for James.

Vespers was beginning.

Agata had sharp hearing and she heard the rustling footsteps of the nuns preparing for prayer in the choir. The few worshippers were mostly seated in the front pews.

"Make haste, O God, to deliver me; make haste to help me, O Lord," intoned Donna Maria Assunta, and Agata, from her hiding place, beneath the choir, like the other choristers, remained seated as she intoned the psalm; then she stood up at the *Gloria* and like them lowered her head at the word "father." At the end of the *Gloria* they began to sing the hymn of that day, the *Magnificat*:

Magnificat anima mea Dominum,
et exultavit spiritus meus in Deo salutari meo;
quia respexit humilitatem ancillae suae,
ecce enim ex hoc beatam me dicent omnes generationes.

As if she were with her sister nuns in the Choir, Agata saw one of the Padellani cousins go to the lectern for the reading. She recognized her voice. Then, the Silence, followed by the responsory, antiphon to the song of Mary, intercessions, and the *Pater noster*. Agata nourished her soul in the choral prayer and asked God to show her the right path. She prayed with such intensity that she failed to notice that the Vespers were over and the church was now empty. The shuffling feet of the sacristan brought her back to reality, and she scurried out of the church before he recognized her.

*

She was already late getting back. Looking for a shortcut, she'd taken the wrong turning and now she was lost in a maze of alleys.

The hour when workers returned home had already passed. Poorly lit by the lamps that burned before the shrines of the saints, the narrow lanes of the *bassi*, the poorest part of Naples, were crowded with the many paupers who had no home to return to: a populace of faceless men, women, and children—vagabonds, mendicants, lepers, musicians. They stumbled along aimlessly, slowly because they had no idea where they were going, nor what would become of them by the time day dawned and they opened their eyes from sleep. Agata had lowered her hood over her face. There was no need: none of them were thinking of her.

She walked into a sort of funnel, a cul-de-sac that had been colonized by a cluster of paupers. Squatting on the ground in a circle, they were slurping soup and gnawing on something dry that was left over or had been wheedled from some rich person's table. Old men with children clutching their legs and invalids were sitting on chairs or reclining on pallets. A couple of them looked at her without asking a thing. In a few adjoining hovels, women had finished their meal and were sweeping the filth out of their houses and directly onto the stone slabs of the street. Every so often the quiet muttering was interrupted by the sound of a patrol, the sound of booted feet, either the police or the army.

In the back alleys night was not all that different from daytime. Carts towering with loads of vegetables swayed as they creaked through crowds of walkers, threatening to sweep away the chairs set out in front of street doors, to drag down laundry hanging out to dry. The balconies were cluttered with pots and pans and oddly shaped receptacles, crates, splintered chairs, with sleepy old men perched on them, half-naked children wandering in and out of the hovels, and shopping baskets waiting to be let down—but in the *bassi*, people never went shopping, they stole what they needed.

Agata's eyes saw nothing but James, his golden beard, handsome as the Christ of the Holy Staircase in the hall of the *comunichino*. Beneath a wall shrine housing an effigy of the Virgin Mary—eyes raised heavenward, diaphanous smile—what had from a distance seemed like two children actually turned out to be two adolescent lovers. The young woman had her back to the edicule and her skirt hoisted around her hips: a beggar boy, panting, was mounting her. Agata lowered her eyes; as she went past she glanced at their bare feet: the girl's feet were light and curling as if she were levitating, his feet, braced and thrusting. She envied them.

She'd made her way through the maze of narrow lanes to a thoroughfare. The main façade of the conservatory of Smirne occupied an entire block—three rows of black windows with double grilles and the vast Renaissance portal. It looked like the backdrop for a stage play.

Agata knocked at the heavy portal: no answer. The infrequent passersby glanced at her, uncertain whether they should offer to help. She knocked again and again. From high above came the voice of the sister doorkeeper: "Madame abbess says that you know perfectly well: those who fail to return by the appointed hour can come back tomorrow morning." Seized by panic, Agata pleaded; then with all the arrogance of the Padellanis, she commanded the doorkeeper to open the door immediately, threatening to report her to the cardinal; when silence was the only response, she went back to pleading. In the end, she was forced to face up to it: she would have to wait there until morning. She was afraid. The shadows of night were growing thicker and darker; the desperadoes were emerging from the *bassi* and the carriages of the nobility began to pick up their pace. Shoulders wedged into the corner between

the portal and the massive stone doorjamb, Agata glanced warily around her and mechanically repeated the *Aves* and the
Paters in order to invoke divine protection.

The clattering sound of horses' hooves, the screech of iron
wheels on the cobbled street. The abbess's voice, calling down
from high above: "What excuse do you want to palm off on me
this time?" was drowned out.

Flattened against the conservatory's heavy wooden doors,
Agata was panting. The darkness was beginning to be broken
by the light of dawn. The meowing of cats, the creaking of
carts, the crowing of caged roosters. In the hundreds of times
that she attempted to relive that night, Agata was never fully
able to reconstruct the sequence of emotions and events.

She couldn't remember whether in the carriage James had
taken her hand to place it against his cheek or to kiss it; she
couldn't remember whether she had first laid her veiled head
against his shoulder, or whether instead he had wrapped his
arm around her shoulders, drawing her toward him.

She couldn't remember when she realized that the carriage
was heading down toward the harbor, when she had first
glimpsed the yacht moored along the wharf, or even when the
carriage rolled up a planked gangway on board the vast yacht,
threading its way carefully up a ramp no broader than a cattle
path through a field.

She couldn't remember when and where, aboard the yacht,
they had eaten salted biscuits and olives, or even whether they
had eaten bread and cheese instead.

She couldn't remember which of the two of them had first
started talking about the books that he sent her and that she
read. She couldn't remember when they'd started talking
about themselves—the more one talked, the more the other
drank in the other's words, and the more they felt a swelling
sense of urgency to know one another completely.

She couldn't remember which of the two of them had

removed the pin that held up her veil, pulling away the veil itself, who had untied the knot on the string that held her wimple snug around her face, who had tugged free the hairnet that imprisoned her short curls.

She couldn't remember whether it had been she who removed his jacket and one by one undid his mother-of-pearl shirt buttons.

And she remembered little or nothing of what came afterwards, when they lay as if they were glued together, like dogs, she remembered only that it seemed completely normal, right, and in accordance with God's will, that the two of them should love each other carnally, in the simple and joyful way in which they acknowledged one another as lovers and glorified their love.

The only thing that Agata recalled clearly was the exchange of words, before dawn, when the time had come to take leave of one another.

She'd said to him, with a feeling of death in her heart, that it was too late for them to have a life together; he had replied, decisively: "It could never be too late for the two of us," and slipped into her hands his little book of poems by Keats, with his penciled notations.

37

August-October 1847.
The terrible punishment for Agata in love: isolation

"M adame abbess wishes to see you." The lay sister swung open the door. It was as if the abbess had been waiting in ambush in the conciergerie; she appeared before her as she was climbing the first flight of stairs, and she climbed alongside her, declaiming in a thunderous, unclear voice: "I'm going to speak to the vicar general this very day. You aren't leaving here again, and if you do, you'll never come back." After which, she hurried up the last ramp two steps at a time; once they reached the third floor, she vanished.

Agata was a prisoner, and no one had told her how long she would have to remain there. They brought her meals in the cell—bread, soup, sometimes fruit—in silence, and they gave her enough water to drink and wash herself with a damp washcloth. She was obliged to wear the same clothes every day. When she swept and dusted her cell, the dirt remained in a pile in the corner. There was a stale stench in the room. A serving-woman was in charge of changing the chamber pot once a day; but as for any other cleaning—nothing. By day, flies and ants took away whatever they found, at night, cockroaches emerged from their dens and fed on the filth, watched by mice that, from high atop the window sill, tipped their snouts down curiously before shuttling along to the next cell along the window ledge.

She had become accustomed to the squalor, but she suffered from the lack of daylight, which meant that she could only read during the hours when the sunshine streamed directly onto the wall. She had decided to reread, in the order in which she had received them, all the books that James had sent her, and she tried to puzzle out how and why he had selected them. Sometimes she managed to find a common thread, and when she did she felt close to him and loved him even more. During the rest of the time, she prayed intensely for herself and for James and often she dozed off. Since she wasn't doing any physical exercise, and eating as little as she was, she slid into a consoling state of lethargy. Then she'd close her eyes and listen to the noises of the city. Gradually, she remembered the words of a poem that James had recited to her:

> *O soft embalmer of the still midnight!*
> *Shutting with careful fingers and benign*
> *Our gloom-pleased eyes, embower'd from the light,*
> *Enshaded in forgetfulness divine;*
> *O soothest Sleep! if so it please thee, close,*
> *In midst of this thine hymn, my willing eyes.*

She had learned that city life too has its own punctuation of time. In the morning, there was the traffic of the farmers, fishermen, and market gardeners who brought food to feed the city: she heard the clucking of cartloads of hens, the anxious cooing of pigeons in cages, and the tingling bells of nanny goats, their udders swollen with milk. Then there were the voices of strolling vendors and craftsmen—knife sharpeners, cobblers—and those who set up shop with a rag on the pavement or on a folding table, to sell anything imaginable: fruit, vegetables, needles, thread, buttons, scissors, candles, playing cards, each and every one calling and praising their merchandise. More or less at the same time, the guards and the soldiers passed by; the rhythmic pounding of their feet on the cobblestones echoed in her cell. The sound of the shoes of horses pulling aristocratic carriages threw her into a frenzy: each time she imagined that it was James and dreamed that he was leaning out in hopes of catching a glimpse of her; he didn't know that she was a prisoner. At times like that, Agata was seized with an overwhelming need to look out the window. She would climb up on the bed: from there, through the window grates, she could see the convent across the way and a patch of sky between two buildings. Sometimes, a dove or even a seagull would cross the sky.

Three weeks later, the abbess came into her cell. She sniffed the fetid air and then told Agata that the cardinal would have to prolong his stay in Rome; Agata would have to wait, and in the meanwhile, there could be no further contact with the outside world.

She was afraid that she would never see James again, and her revulsion for food returned. She scorned herself for making use of the weapons of weakness—misdirected violence, because it was turned on herself—but there was nothing that she could do about it: whenever she ate, she threw up. She lay in bed and dreamed she was talking to James. He had told her that the conversation between them had begun during the crossing from Messina to Naples, even though at the time she had not realized it; it wouldn't be interrupted again until they finally saw one another, and then they'd never be parted. Agata believed it. Intensely.

38.
October 1847.
Agata heals the abbess and obtains privileges;
suddenly, the cardinal sends her to Sicily

Agata wasn't about to give up. The *brevi* stated that Father Cuoco had the right to approve visits from her relatives, but there had been no sign of her confessor. In response to her repeated requests, the abbess had insisted that he was in the Salento with his sick mother; then, seeing that she looked anxious and wan, she had promptly "brought him home again."

Agata knew that the cardinal had appointed him as her confessor because he was under the cardinal's control. She avoided all mention of her encounter with James, even though the questions he asked made her think that he must know something, and she told him that she wished to visit with her sister Sandra. Father Cuoco was forced to inform her that the cardinal had taken it solely upon himself to decide whether or not she could receive or make any visits—once again, Agata had her back to the wall.

In the meanwhile, the cardinal had returned to Naples but there had been no sign of him. Then, without warning, she was ordered to go to the episcopal palace; Agata refused, giving her uncertain health as an excuse. She had remained steadfast on that point, even when the abbess intervened and made it clear to her that by insisting on that point she would make the cardinal furious. Which is what happened: the cardinal stopped payment of her stipend entirely. Agata had no money: this was war.

At that point, she shook herself out of the lethargy into which she had fallen: she began to do the calisthenics that Miss

Wainwright had taught her, to restore vigor to her weakened muscles; she sang psalms, she repeated this admonition to herself: "*First keep peace with yourself; then you will be able to bring peace to others. A peaceful man does more good than a learned man.*"

The abbess had been given orders to keep an eye on her, and she came to visit her every day. She watched her eat her meal and sometimes she brought her extra bread and butter or cheese. Agata had been stung by a horsefly, and the bite had suppurated. She had treated the bite with a plaster of herbs that she had brought with her from San Giorgio Stilita. The abbess noticed the box with *Infirmary* written on it, and she asked what it continued. One day the abbess asked Agata to help her: she had a very painful abscess on her groin. Agata offered to heal it for her, but only on the condition that she be allowed to send and receive letters. At first, she flew into a rage and refused, then, as the pain worsened, she gave in. Agata lanced the boil and medicated it properly. In her gratitude, the abbess became more tractable and gave her permission to receive packages as well. Sandra immediately sent her biscotti and a book. From James, nothing.

After that, the abbess began to ask Agata for help with sick nuns and oblates. An orphan girl was in great pain in the aftermath of a badly managed abortion and the abbess insisted that Agata treat her; for the first time, she showed that she had feelings. "They're pitiable. They don't do it on purpose: they're tricked into it or they're forced into it." Agata considered abortion to be a form of murder and, tortured by the memories of her experience with Donna Maria Celeste, she didn't want to have anything to do with the girl. But the abbess insisted and insisted until Agata reluctantly agreed. In exchange, she was allowed to go secretly up onto the belvedere of the cloister during the rigorous silence, when the other nuns were in their cells for the night. The abbess also procured medical textbooks for her and a copy of an old edition of Matthaeus Silvaticus' *Pandectae Medicinae,* which she'd found in a crate—it was a medieval lexicon on simples.

Soon Agata had many patients. Some of the women gave her gifts and others paid her what they were able; little as it was, that money helped to alleviate her financial straits: she certainly had no other way of meeting her obligations. From one of the women she learned that there had been an uprising in Messina in early September, and that it had been put down with great bloodshed. Agata was afraid that her brother-in-law and her sister had been involved in it, but she had no way of finding out for sure.

She was intensely anxious. She was waiting for James to answer the note that she had sent him, as in the past, care of the Detken bookstore in the Piazza del Plebiscito; she thanked him for the poems by Keats and wrote her comments, as she had always done in the past. Moreover, she informed him that she could also now receive newspapers. A slim volume by Leopardi arrived, without the note from him that Agata had so hoped for. She leafed through the book with trepidation, thinking to herself that James's white hands had caressed the pages before giving it to the bookseller:

Vive quel foco ancor, vive l'affetto,
Spira nel pensier mio la bella imago,
Da cui, se non celeste, altro diletto

Giammai non ebbi, e sol di lei m'appago.[3]

---

[3] That flame still lives, and that affection pure; / Still in my thought that lovely image breathes, / From which, save heavenly, I no other joy, / Have ever known; my only comfort, now! [trans. Frederick Townsend]

Next to it was a very faint *J*; the same *J* was repeated elsewhere. And so, from then on, James began to communicate with Agata through faint *J*'s on the outer margin of the page, but never a single line of writing.

So many books, from James, in those days of late autumn. And so very many *J*'s.

Her mother and the cardinal, on the other hand, had begun a busy and not entirely friendly correspondence, that concluded with a concession of *brevi* for a one-month visit to Palermo for Agata, beginning on December 12. When Agata found out about it, she was devastated: she would be forced to break off her exchange of books and letters with James. She hurled herself face down on her bed and burst into sobs, weeping until she had no more tears. Late at night, she stealthily made her way upstairs to the belvedere: she felt as if he were close to her there and she hoped that they could see each other; up there the sluts and fallen women who were her patients sent and received messages by gestures. It was a dark night. It had rained and the sky was covered with clouds. The moisture bathed her hair and weighed down the wool of her habit. Agata leaned out in the hopes of seeing him. But there was no sign of James, or of anyone else—the neighborhood, which at that time of night was sleepy but still awake, seemed deserted. The roar of distant thunder. A flash of lightning illuminated the silhouette of the volcano against the blackness— then it all went dark.

The gas streetlamps illuminated the pale facades of the *palazzi*, covered by a grey patina, a mysterious slush blended of dust and rain. She was tired of waiting, of hiding, tired of the constant fear that by now had become a part of her life. Agata looked at the steeple in the center of a small square upon which three streets converged. Dizzyingly tall and pointed, it looked like a dagger whose handle had swollen into scrollwork, garlands, festoons, fish, dolphins, fruit, and flowers, wrapping the long blade until only the razor-sharp tip plunged into the sky was left bare. It began raining again in powerful noisy gusts. Agata kept her ears alert, in case by chance James called her, but instead she heard the calls of animals: a few dogs, the braying of a donkey. She squinted to see better through the rain: black, empty forms—she couldn't tell if they were creatures of her imagination or living things—walked along, brushing close to the walls. She jumped with a start: something was rubbing against her legs. A rain-drenched cat had wriggled under her habit and now was squeezing against her to rid itself of the detested water. They looked at one another. The animal, as unfortunate as she was, emitted an arid meow and looked up at her with blank eyes, filled with unspoken supplication. She felt as if she were losing her mind.

39

In Palermo at her mother's house

The brigantine sailed placidly into the gulf. Agata, with her servingwoman-jailor standing next to her, looked out from the bridge. Palermo looked out upon its half-moon bay, at the foot of Mt. Pellegrino, at the westernmost edge. Dark blue and pink, dotted with a maquis of maritime pines nestled between boulders, rooted in tiny patches of earth, the promontory thrust up, then plunged down and surrendered to the arms of the sea. The day of the departure she had fainted, which she interpreted as a sign from the Lord that she should stay in Naples. In vain: two lay sisters had helped her to get up and get dressed and they had carried her aboard the ship on a stretcher. The servingwoman wouldn't even let her look out the porthole as the steamer chugged out of the harbor. During the crossing she never left her side. Agata felt hope dying: the cardinal knew all about James and was sending her away from Naples.

Palermo, built on a water-rich plain and enclosed by a semicircle of hills, overlooked the Tyrrhenian Sea just as Naples did, and just as regally. Just as proudly. The city lay spread out before Agata's eyes in a cascading succession of terra-cotta tile roofs of noble *palazzi*, cupolas of convents, monasteries, churches, and oratories, creating a phantasmagoria of colors— many of those domes were covered in majolica tiles, green and white, dark blue and white, yellow and green; some of them, red as a faded cherry, were rounded and clearly of Islamic influence; others were Baroque, made of golden stone and set atop colonnades. Here and there stood the rare medieval tower, incorporated into Baroque *palazzi* and thus saved from the ravaging wave of eighteenth-century modernization.

The ship entered Palermo's harbor and anchored across from Castellammare, at the southernmost tip of the bay: a forest of mainmasts with furled sails and trawlers, small and large, boats with lateen rigs, polacres, feluccas, sardine boats, and fishing dinghies, pitching and yawing at anchor alongside tartans and xebecs. To the north, the waterfront was a rampart of paved ashlars interrupted here and there by terraced half-moons. Then there was a clearing of pounded earth along the walls of the city, incorporated in the *palazzi* of the aristocracy. It was sunset, time for the evening outing. Shiny and black, the carriages rolled along at walking speed, lined up like so many lazy ants. They passed one another, halting to exchange greetings, and lingering outside cafés.

The Cecconis lived in an eighteenth-century *palazzo* that had been burned during the revolt of 1820. The façade was pockmarked by hurled stones and bullets, like a face ravaged by smallpox. Inside, however, the apartment was beautifully restored. Her mother had furnished it with inlaid furniture and bronze decorations, which clashed with her husband's Neoclassical furniture, simplicity in comparison.

Agata was hoping to see Nora and Annuzza, and she was disappointed when she was told that they had remained in Messina, in service to Carmela, now the wife of the Cavaliere d'Anna. General Cecconi concealed beneath rigid courtesy his annoyance at having his wife's daughter, a nun, as a houseguest; nor was there any joy in her mother's welcome. Agata had the sensation that she was a guest unwanted by both her host and hostess, even when her mother presented her with a bowl of her favorite dessert, chocolate rice, similar to the *cuc-*

cìa that is made in Sicily in December, for the feast day of St. Lucy. The rice is boiled in cinnamon- and clove-scented milk with a pat of butter, a spoonful of semolina and another heaping spoonful of sugar, then covered with chocolate cream and garnished with peeled, finely chopped pistachios: it was a treat to be eaten warm, in tiny scoops on the tip of the spoon, slowly, varying the proportions between the white cream and the chocolate cream. But Agata wasn't allowed to savor the dish the way she liked it. Donna Gesuela wanted her to gobble down spoonful after spoonful and then hurry off to change into a clean, neatly ironed habit for a visit from her uncle, the Baron Aspidi. "Behave nicely with him, my brother is the only one who has helped us out with money when things were bad," she told her. And that's how it always was in Palermo. The *brevi* put Agata under her mother's control, and Donna Gesuela wanted her at home, available at all times to see relatives, without any advance warning.

Agata soon became accustomed to the routine of the Cecconi household. Every morning, while the house was still asleep, she went to the first mass at the Oratorio del Santissimo Salvatore, around the corner, with Rosalia, her mother's housekeeper. When the priest said *ite . . .*, even before he could get out the words *missa est*, Rosalia was already pushing her out of the pew and down the aisle toward the door, so that she could get home to make coffee and take it, with two biscottini, to the Generalessa, in bed. The general was leisurely in his morning ablutions and he spent time chatting with his barber; then he would go out and come home loaded down with papers and a jar of colorful candy. He retreated into his study and received visitors until lunchtime. Her mother tended to her own affairs and Agata followed her lead, performing the office according to the Rule and reading. In the afternoon, on the other hand, she joined them in the drawing

282 · SIMONETTA AGNELLO HORNBY

room, in order to save on candles and coal: the general was extremely stingy when it came to daily household expenses. After leaving the army he had been given a few assignments by the king, but they were not at all well remunerated—at least that's what her mother told her, adding that he hoped to be given a position in the new financial institution, the Cassa di Sconto del Banco delle Due Sicilie. The women did their household chores and mostly read. Every so often he would offer them one of his candies, and for a while the silence was broken by the sound of sucking on the solid sugar surrounding the cinnamon center.

In Palermo, too, Agata was a prisoner. She could neither send nor receive letters. Her mother only took her out to pay calls on relatives who were nuns. After one or two visits to the convent of Sant'Anna, Donna Gesuela decided that she had had enough. "We have nothing to say to one another and these misers charge us for the pastries they serve us!" Agata felt that she was being watched by her mother, and soon enough she understood the reason why: the general, who was left a widower quite young, had been the administrator of his wife's estate, held in trust for his only son. When his son came of age, he had brought a lawsuit against his father, accusing him of having profited from the estate. Agata's mother told her that the case had dragged on for years, costing the general a vast sum, and that recently it had been decided in the son's favor. Gesuela was yet again in a precarious financial situation. Agata understood: her mother was counting on her, once she left the nunhood, to take care of her in her old age.

Mother and daughter were putting linen into the armoire with the help of Rosalia. "Did you know that Carmela is pregnant? Annuzza is overjoyed and every morning she makes her an egg yolk whipped with sugar!" her mother told her, smoothing out an embroidered sheet. Agata froze—a son by the Cavaliere d'Anna! "She seems happy, to judge from her letters. And to think that I expected this youngest daughter to remain a spinster so she could take care of me!" she commented. She ran her hand over the knotted fringework of the towels, shiny and stiff with starch, and added, pensively: "This one here's all I have left . . . if he lets me have her." And she went back to counting the Flanders flax linen towels.

It was the beginning of January 1848. Agata was looking at the crack-ridden plaster of the façade across the way, a book open on her lap. She was meditating on the word "blemish," noticing new aspects and dimensions of the word. Then she came back to reality: she felt estranged from her mother and couldn't wait to get back to the conservatory of Smirne, certain as she was that James would succeed in helping her win her dismissal from the monastic order.

The maid came to call her: the general and the Generalessa were waiting for her in the study.

"The cardinal has ordered you to enter the convent of Montereale di Chiana," her mother said in a flat voice. She was clearly upset.

"What's happened? Where is it?"

The general broke in. "There is no time to waste. The cardinal, who is your relative, has received intelligence that there is going to be a revolt in Palermo, and I am in agreement. It's imminent. Tomorrow morning at dawn a lateen-rigged tartan will pass by the main harbor of Palermo, the Cala, carrying nuns directed toward a convent in Trapani. You will board the ship at the landing place of Sferracavallo; we'll have to set out at dawn in order to be there in time. The tartan will not stand in to tie up at the dock." He added, imperiously: "You'll have to beat out to the ship in open water, aboard a fishing boat, and you won't whine about it!" Then he informed her that the Benedictine convent of Chiana, an old feudal village set on a salubrious hilltop in the ancient *comarca* of Naro, would be nothing but a first stage of her journey; the cardinal would decide when and in what convent she would ultimately be placed.

"Why can't I go back to Naples?"

"You are to obey." Her mother's voice was harsh.

"Chiana is closer. You could even come back to stay with us, when things calm down. I've already told you that we're expecting a revolt, and so it is quite likely that there will be no ships leaving for Naples," the general explained, barely able to contain his impatience.

"Not even an English ship?"

"What a question!" her mother promptly replied, beating her husband to the same exclamation.

"Like when my father died." Agata gave her mother a cold, hard glare.

"Ah, of course, Captain Garson was there . . . "

The general calmed down; he pricked up his ears and murmured under his breath: "An influential man . . . "

Agata had heard. "Does he have influence with the cardinal?" she asked.

"The cardinal is keen to establish close ties with the highest ranks of the English Catholic community, and those contacts necessarily pass through the hands of Garson."

And the general picked up the day's newspaper.

40.
January 1848.
Agata leaves Palermo on the cardinal's orders

The entire island of Sicily had almost no passable roads. Goods and foodstuffs traveled along the island's coastline in small coasting vessels that traveled from dawn to dusk, because there were few lighthouses or maritime signals. The network of sixteenth-century signal towers built at the orders of Emperor Charles V and long neglected had fallen into a state of decay. In practice, every boat captain had his own set of landmarks, generally silhouettes of mountains and promontories with conspicuous points. Only a particularly skillful commander would set sail in the afternoon, even in the winter, with predictions of good weather, and expect to reach port at the first light of day.

Xebecs and tartans circumnavigated the island, making short hops from one port to the next, embarking and discharging goods at each landing place. Tartans, single-masted with a lateen rig, and smaller than the broad-beamed xebec, were chiefly cargo vessels, and they had many uses: for fishing, to haul freight, but also to transport passengers in rudimentary cabins.

The tartan captained by Master Cirincione, nicknamed Scopetta, had set sail the night before from Cefalù for Palermo, where at dawn it would moor and embark a load of ferrous materials and cordage for agricultural use; then it was bound for the island of Pantelleria, after docking at Trapani to load salt to be used for preserving capers. An emissary from the Curia was awaiting the vessel at the Cala, Palermo's harbor: he carried a request for the master and commander, asking him to convey a number of important female passengers, nuns who were being taken to convents in "more tranquil" locations. It was the cardinal's wish that one of these nuns, a young Benedictine sister, not be "seen" in Palermo, and the tartan should therefore weigh in to take her aboard at the landing place of Sferracavallo, and even there do its best to remain inconspicuous. The nuns would disembark at Trapani, except for the Benedictine sister. There, Master Scopetta would find the Benedictine sister passage aboard a "trusted" ship, bound for the wharves of Licata on the island's southern coast. As the word "trusted" was uttered, a pouch of gold coins changed hands.

Agata had borne up with considerable fortitude during the brief but exceedingly choppy journey from the dock of Sferracavallo out to the tartan; since Agata would be the sole passenger, her mother had decided to send Rosalia out with her on the small sardine boat that awaited her. There were high seas and a chilly north wind. Rosalia, terrified, had wrapped her arms around the fishing lantern that had been left in the small watercraft, and at a certain point, in her agitation, she had tipped it overboard into the waves. Intimidated by the rough voices of the sailors, she had turned to Agata for consolation and, as she clutched at her, had torn the veil from her face. Upbraided, the poor thing had burst into tears and never stopped sobbing until she was back on dry land.

Agata had clambered aboard with high hopes, certain that James was somehow behind the cardinal's order. She had a feeling that she would see him soon, perhaps in Trapani. She put a good face on the hardships of the primitive cabin, the abysmal food—bread and a questionable fish-and-potato soup—and her traveling companions. The young Capuchin nuns glared at the Benedictine sister in a decidedly unfriendly fashion, but she ignored them and looked out to sea. It was chilly and the mountains above Palermo's fertile plain, the Conca d'Oro, were snow-covered. After roughly an hour's sailing, the tartan was veering into the gulf of Castellammare. Low cumuliform clouds were shrouding the mountains in the interior. Agata caught her breath: mountains, sky, and sea were all unified by an extraordinary harmony of colors. The air was still and Agata sensed a great bated tension in the atmosphere. In the meanwhile, Master Scopetta was cursing his bad luck and furiously maneuvering his ship into the lee of San Vito lo Capo, before the dangerous libeccio wind springing up from the southwest could unleash high and choppy seas.

For two nights and a day, the tartan was hammered by powerful gusts of libeccio wind and intermittent downpours of rain. Shut up with the other nuns in the dank confined space of the cabin, Agata could smell her own stench: there was no water to wash with, nor was there any private space for the basic hygienic necessities. All the same, she was happy—soon she'd see James.

At five in the morning on the second day she was awakened by the steady rolling of the vessel: they were scudding along, sails bellying, before a light breeze out of the east. Pepi, Master Scopetta's son, brought them a porridge of dried broad beans and chickpeas and laconically announced that they'd reach Trapani in five hours of navigation, if everything went as expected. Agata decided to head up onto deck; the sunshine was warm, but she kept her short turquoise cape of the order of the canonesses of Bavaria on so that James would be sure to recognize her immediately. She kept her eyes glued to landward; instead of reciting the Psalter, she magnified the Lord for the beauty of His island. Winter on the northern coast had been rainless and dry. The low hills inland were barren and sere. The land along the coastline, beyond the black line of cliffs, jagged and broken here and there by crescents of golden beach, was all scrub and stubble, streaked with charred sections. Mt. Cofano, stout and dark, was completely barren. The rain of the last two days had drained into the bowels of the earth through the cracks in the sun-scorched soil; solitary peasants were whipping their mules in desperate attempts to break with iron plowshares the crust of sunbaked topsoil, harder than ever before.

The tartan had entered the Mar d'Africa. Mt. Erice loomed massively over sea and land; it too had sere, sunbaked slopes, but not the summit: verdant and tree-topped, it was surrounded by a bright white little cloud, like a halo. Master Scopetta sailed clear of the dangerous rocks of the Asinelli and the Formiche, where breakers crashed. Then he came about and brought his ship straight into the port of Trapani.

The Capuchin sisters flocked chattering down the gangway to where the prelate stood waiting for them on the dock. There was no sign of James at all. Agata stood veiled on the deck and wept. Salt tears wet her lip; she wiped them away with the tip of her tongue and soon her mouth was intolerably bitter. Still, she remained on the deck, wrapped in her turquoise mantle, until Pepi ushered her back into the wheelhouse. Master Scopetta was very pleased with himself: he had found a fellow commander, Master Livestri, about to set sail with his tartan, bound for Siracusa. On that vessel, the Benedictine sister could have a cabin all to herself. Faithful to the orders he'd received, he offered to pay his fellow commander lavishly to convey the nun to the wharves of Licata and ensure that, once disembarked, she reached the convent of Chiana safe and sound. Then he went on to explain to Agata that she could also land at Marsala, where the fleets of the Ingham, Woodhouse, and Florio companies loaded wine and oil to carry to Malta, making port in Licata to take on additional loads of wheat and sulfur. Their vessels would surely be more comfortable than Master Livestri's tartan, and the journey would also be shorter. But he couldn't assure her of finding a cabin. There were many English people leaving Sicily for Malta, out of fear of the expected uprisings.

Agata would have preferred an English ship—she could send a message to James, or perhaps he was in Marsala—and for an instant she was swept by panic. She was alone, penniless, ignorant of everything, in unfamiliar places. Master Scopetta did his best to guess what was passing through the eyes that he could barely glimpse behind the black veil, and he remembered his own daughters, Santina and Annunziata: at home, they were a constant earthquake—for every piece of mischief they committed, they thought up a hundred more—but they became timorous creatures, frightened of their own shadows, once they set foot outdoors. A heartfelt impulse drove him to say that he would send Pepi with her on the tartan, to make sure that everything went as planned. Agata accepted.

She regretted it the instant the commander turned and left. But now there was nothing she could do.

Master Livestri's tartan was small and was painted red and dark blue; the cotton sails were amaranth, from the hue of the goop smeared onto the canvas to make them waterproof. Referred to as *"u capu"*—"the chief" in Sicilian—by his mariners, Master Livestri was a hulking, blue-eyed man, with thinning blond hair and massive hands, swollen and cracked from exposure to salt water. He gave a respectful welcome to his important passenger and introduced his son Totò, who served as his bosun. They set sail with a north wind, bound for Marsala.

To the west the brilliant blue sky was suddenly transmuted into a blazing mass so dazzling that the sun was almost entirely drowned out; little by little it merged into parallel strips in every variation on pink, orange, flame red, vivid carmine, and amaranth. The strip that marked the horizon line settled over the sea, a luminous intense green, and then darkened to pitch black. Suddenly an orange globe appeared in the center, bright and menacing. And then it sank behind the horizon. Agata thought to herself that this journey around her island was a way of saying farewell to Sicily, but she wasn't sad. She was destined to go with James, wherever he might take her. Pepi had told her that in Marsala there was a British consul, and in Licata, a vice consul: that was enough to convince her that James was already at sea aboard a fast ship, waiting for her arrival in one of the two ports, enough to settle her nerves. She tucked hungrily into the fresh-fish chowders, the dried fruit, and the candied quince that she was served in bowls of glazed earthenware; she avoided her cabin and spent hours on deck, looking out to sea and back to land. She also enjoyed her newly reacquired solitude. The breeze had turned soft and the sky was diaphanous. Both landscape and climate had changed. The coastline as far as Marsala was white, flat, and sandy, in a succession of salt marshes and basins of seawater enclosed by sandbanks, islands that weren't islands, all part of what was known as the Laguna dello Stagnone—the Big Pond Lagoon. A profusion of single-masted shallow-draft vessels, perfectly suited to the lagoon waters, were plying its surface, carrying cargoes of salt and tufa stone. The coastline, flat along the waterfront and sloping gently downhill as it ran inland, was spangled with the windmills of the salt marshes and little cone-shaped greyish mountains of salt. The bottom was shallow and treacherous, and for that very reason superlatively beautiful. The transparent water changed from green to sky blue, to light blue and to black, depending on the depth of the sandbanks, the configuration of the buried reefs—the long parallel crests of the rocky ridges that here and there broke the surface—and the varieties of marine vegetation—underwater meadows of seagrass, expanses of bottle green sugar kelp, acres of gulfweed—which gave different colors and hues. Only the morphology of the settlements—little villages perched high in the hills out of fear of Barbary raiders—and of the Baroque churches with onion-dome bell towers remained unvaried. After Selinunte the sea was a succession of shallows and shoals extending into the distance—glistening submerged ribbons of water; from the coast, the white marlstone cliffs glowed in the sunlight reflected off the surface of the sea.

Agata held her breath when she glimpsed in the distance, perched on a ridge covered with pale yellow ruins, an outpost of Girgenti, as Agrigento was then known, a Greek temple, intact, saved from devastation because it had been transformed into a Christian house of worship. Solitary amidst the ruins. That temple of a dead religion reminded her of her mother. Agata remembered the silhouette of the couple at Sferracavallo, while she was setting out to sea aboard the sardine trawler. Leaning one against the other, the general had placed his arm around her shoulders. She hadn't realized, until then, that they loved one another. One thing the general did had been vividly impressed in her mind—he gently pushed a lock of hair tossing in the breeze away from his wife's lovely face and tucked it under her hat, tenderly. Agata gripped the little book of poems by Keats more tightly in her hand, a token of her night of love with James. She preferred not to think about James's wife, but from then on the faceless image of the unfortunate woman remained in her mind.

It was dawn. At the Licata wharf, there was a vast silence. Tied up along the waterfront were polacres, small watercraft, and sardine trawlers in the coasting trade. Two men, standing next to a pyramid of golden-hued sulfur, were waiting for the string of mules loaded with sacks full of sulfur to make their indolent way along the hill. The town seemed to be fast asleep.

The morning breeze teased Agata's disappointed, trembling hands, crossed over her chest. Not a sign of James.

Totò proudly informed her that Master Livestri had managed to get a servingwoman and a lay sister to come down from the convent of the Benedictine nuns of Licata to accompany her to Chiana, in a genuine carriage, not some farm cart. Before stepping up and into the carriage, Agata thanked him, but her voice was lifeless. The boy pulled a bag of dried yellow peaches out of his rucksack, the kind she had liked during the voyage, and clumsily proffered them. That courteous gesture melted the ice in her heart just a little, but she had given up hoping for James.

The carriage was more of a covered cart than a genuine carriage. The side windows, crazed with cracks and covered with glued paper, were black with filth. The wooden benches had folded blankets instead of proper cushions. The journey to Chiana seemed endless, jerking and jolting along the rocky cart track, with two silent women for company. Part of the way they had to walk because a section of road was in such poor repair that it became necessary to push the carriage along by main force. Agata rejected the offer of a ride in a litter and walked up the narrow lane alongside the two women. She tried more than once to engage them in conversation, but their lips were sealed.

41.
In Chiana, in the Benedictine convent
of the Santissimo Sacramento

The abbess of the convent of the Santissimo Sacramento of Chiana considered the arrival of the Neapolitan nun to be an unreasonable imposition on the part of the clergy: the cardinal of Naples had written a letter to the archbishop of Palermo, who spoke to the abbot of San Martino delle Scale and with the provincial mother superior of the Benedictine order; then all three men had written to the bishop of Girgenti and directly to her: neither the abbess nor the bishop could hope to withstand such high-placed pressure.

In the seventeenth century the pious founder of the convent had settled the first group of nuns in his own *palazzo* in order to comply with the vocation of his favorite daughter; the central wing of the convent still preserved that original structure: drawing rooms divided into cells, the inner courtyard become a cloister, and windows blinded by wood timbering painted black. Inside, everything had been whitewashed and left simple and bare. The convent of the Santissimo Sacramento was well known throughout the *comarca* for the devout adherence to the old ways of the choristers who, in the previous century, loyal to the intentions of the founder, had refused to give in to the deterioration of mores of the period, which had infected most other convents. There was no shortage of vocations, and the convent was packed. The level of frugality was in sharp contrast with the richness of the building and the decorations and furnishings of the church, which was built in the eighteenth century. The walls and the chapels were decked with white-and-gold festoons, angels, and cherubs, contrasting sharply with the rich dark brown of the magnificent wooden coffered ceiling. The acoustics were perfect.

Agata stepped out of the carriage and hesitated: the staircase leading to the front entrance was not indoors; instead it opened out like an outspread fan and descended down to the square before it. The two women on either side of her urged her to climb the steps. Midway up the steps was a platform from which two other sets of stairs ascended; these steps too were semicircular and cone-shaped. One led to the convent and the other to the portico in front of the church. The three women climbed up to the oaken front door of the convent, which swung open before they could knock. The Chapter Hall was filled with choristers—there were a great many of them, all waiting for the new arrival. They made much show of the honorific title of "Donna," but they struck Agata as so many bumpkins unaware of outside events. They knew nothing of the uprising in Palermo—Agata had referred it in order to explain her presence among them—or of anything not directly connected to life in Chiana, where nearly all of them had been born. They spoke a different variety of Sicilian from Agata's Messinese dialect and, like her fellow sisters in Naples, they immediately and roundly mocked her accent.

During her stay in Chiana, Agata was treated by the monastic community with ill-concealed suspicion. For her part, she did little to win them over; she expressed lavish thanks for the infrequent courtesies she received and she diligently obeyed both the prioress and the abbess. During her leisure time, she retired to her cell or climbed up the campanile: the convent was lightless, and she felt a pressing need of open sky and sunlight. And yet, if it weren't for her anguish at having completely lost contact with James and being unable to do anything to find out where he was, Agata would have gladly preferred the convent to her mother's house.

*

In contrast with the convent of San Giorgio Stilita, at the convent of the Santissimo Sacramento the nuns followed Chapter 39 of the Benedictine Rule—which forbids eating the flesh of quadrupeds—and scrupulously respected all the requirements of abstinence and fasting. It was not just devotion that imposed their dietary regimen; it was poverty. The Santissimo Sacramento was a poor convent. During meals, there were always the canonical "three things," and, on the days when it was allowed, a "fourth thing" as well. The dishes, however, were by no means lavish: the "first thing" was a watery soup, the "second thing" was a varied array of casseroles made with stale bread soaked in water and vegetables, sometimes with eggs, or with tiny scraps of chicken or fish; these dishes were cleverly inspired by the dishes of the high cuisine found in the wealthier Bendictine abbeys. A spoonful of pasta cooked in grape juice might constitute the "third thing," while a slice of apple or orange might be the "fourth." That cuisine, which was primarily composed of bread, vegetables, legumes, pasta, and eggs, was very tasty indeed; with the addition of the gifts brought by the faithful—milk, cheese, ricotta—and spices, which were plentiful in that cuisine, the nuns transformed the most humble ingredients until they were mouthwatering. Just before Lent, Agata tasted the best dried codfish she'd ever had in her life: baked with a filling of almonds scented with cloves and oregano from the Madonie mountains. The nuns provided for themselves with the help of their families, through charitable donations, and by selling biscotti that were famous throughout the district: the *biscotti ricci*, or curly cookies. All the nuns made the biscotti together. No one had a specialty of their own, the way they had at San Giorgio Stilita. The aroma of freshly made almond flour, mixed with vanilla—work that had to be done every day by hand, with mortar and pestle, in order to make sure that the baking released the scents of the essential oils—filled the corridors lined with cells and every room in the convent, finally wafting forth to blend with the acrid scent of the incense that invaded the convent through the grated windows.

It was time for Agata to choose a job. She thought of the pharmacy, but the sister pharmacist seemed to be nothing more than a habited sorceress—she cast spells to ward off evil and dripped oil into a basin of water to "read the oil" of the sick woman, rather than offering any treatment. In the small dark cloister, there was no garden in which to cultivate simples. Sometimes families brought unguents and medicines to sick nuns, but that was rare: faith was expected to heal all ills. And so Agata chose to make bread, as she had when she was a postulant.

Every day that passed only confirmed Agata's initial impression: that the convent had remained anchored and faithful to the stern severity of the Counter Reformation. At the convent of the Santissimo Sacramento, the routine that punctuated the day was an integral part of the nun's very being; there was not a single nun who tried to avoid common prayer, and they all sang in the choir with true passion. The mortification of the flesh, fasting, and ecstatic prayer were all practiced by many of the nuns and were considered by those who didn't to be simple and straightforward forms of religious devotion. Agata had never encountered such a welter of spirituality as she found at the convent in Chiana. It became clear to her that there was really no difference between sacred love and profane love. This only encouraged her to abandon herself to her desire for James. Like her sisters in Christ, she trusted in James and his promise: soon they would be together—soon, and for the rest of their lives.

The nuns were passionately in love with their spouse, a beautiful and carnal Jesus. Scuffles and fights broke out over where to place the small icon of that Jesus during the recitation of the rosary when the nuns were working outdoors, over whose turn it was to dust the large crucifix on the steps and, in the Chapter Hall, over who was allowed to sit closest to the glass casket that contained a wonderful papier-mâché Christ, life-sized, with dreamy eyes, His head languidly resting on one arm, virtually naked, with only a thin cloth draped over His groin. In the chapel, they meditated upon a blond depiction of Jesus, with a trim little goatee and straw-yellow eyelashes, just like James'. And Agata let herself slip into desire, while making bread, without the slightest sense of guilt or restraint. She punched and kneaded the dough after the first and second risings, using first one fist, then the other to crush out the yeasty air; then she rolled the dough up into long cylindrical loaves, smooth, swollen, and glistening. She caught her breath, wiped the sweat from her brow with her sleeve, and went back to work. She lifted one loaf at a time and ran her flour-dusted hands over it to keep it from sticking to the wooden kneading board. Then she worked them all into a single lump of dough, without haste. She caressed them, squeezed them, folded them, and braided them together. When they were well amalgamated, Agata went back to her kneading—one fist inside, the other outside—and then rolled out the dough, only to repeat the process and work out the last air pockets. She kneaded the bread dough, thinking of only one thing: James, the way she knew him.

At the convent of the Santissimo Sacramento, the nuns were neither isolated from the village nor buried alive, the way they were at San Giorgio Stilita. The stream of gifts and notes exchanged between the nuns and their families was intense and entirely free of censorship, provided the nuns only spoke about it during recreation after their midday meal. They owned small plots of farmland outside the town of Chiana—

part of their monastic dowry—and they went there to work and for their health: the convent was overcrowded, cramped, and sunless. In January, they took turns spending entire days on the land, harvesting oranges. Their faces covered with veils, they would leave the town by cart and then finish their journey on foot: like most Sicilian towns, Chiana had no passable roads. The garden, as Sicilians call their citrus groves, was surrounded by dry-laid stone walls, and stood not far from the white marlstone cliffs that reared up from sea. The sky was dazzling and bright from the excessive sunlight. From there, it was possible to look back at the hill and the town—a cluster of churches and monasteries huddled around two aristocratic *palazzi* built with yellow limestone, porous and wind-worn—and the ruins of the Norman castle, high atop the hill, looking as if it were melting back into the earth. Agata, like the other nuns, loved the garden; there had been plenty of rain on that coast of Sicily in December and the land was green. Agata gathered tiny meadow flowers, caressed leaves and buds, sucked on the tender stalks of wood sorrel; she drank in the tastes and aromas of Sicily—the scent of wild oregano, bald-money, and pungent whiffs of rosemary. In February the nuns went on country outings to their almond grove, a large plot of land—part of the monastic dowry brought to the convent by a *"burgisi,"* the daughter of a large landowner—on the terraced ridge of a rocky hill, to celebrate the blossoming of the almond trees. There, on the south side of the island, the almond trees bloomed early. Indigenous to the Mediterranean basin, and considered since antiquity to be particularly healthful, the almond trees grew straight and erect on the fertile soil, and the plentiful pink blossoms completely concealed the grey bark of the branches. Other almond trees grew stunted among the rocks; they were short and angular, but they too, covered with dense clusters of pink blooms, were beautiful to behold. The nuns wandered from one tree to the next, exclaiming in wonder, touching the tiny white and pink blossoms, careful not to bruise them. Then, equipped with basket and knife, they tucked their habit and scapular between their legs, like peasant women, and went in search of the vegetables that grew wild: borage and Swiss chard.

During those outings the nuns had no contact with the secular world, except for the carters, who knew that they were expected to look straight ahead. But from the windows of the distant town, those black-clad figures were caressed by the loving eyes of mothers and sisters.

Visits to nuns in the parlor were practically a daily occurrence and the supervision of the deaconesses became three- and four-way conversations—everyone knew everyone else, in Chiana, and everyone was related. The townspeople considered the convent to be part of civil society: every sort of litigation—even those involving prelates and prominent citizens— was submitted for meditation or arbitration to the abbess, and everyone accepted her judgment. Sick children were brought to the convent to be given a healing prayer. Aside from people who came to the parlor to tell tales of woe, young newlywed couples would present themselves in order to receive the congratulations and best wishes of their relatives who were nuns, as did students who had successfully passed an examination or anyone who had had a piece of good luck. Newborns were brought here immediately after their baptism and when they were toddlers, ushered into the seclusion of the cloister to receive a loving hug from their aunt the nun. People came to talk, to laugh, to joke.

And yet the same nuns who enjoyed their country outings and participated in the lives of their families through the grate in the parlor, also employed sackcloth, self-flagellation, and fasting to attain ecstasy. One nun, during Lent, wore a painful rasped iron bodice that had been handed down in her family from one generation of nuns to the next. It was unusual but not unheard of for one or more nuns to immolate themselves by fasting for a serious and sacred purpose, such as the recovery of the Holy Father or perhaps a bishop.

Agata did her work, listened to the prayers of the choir, and then curled up in her cell to await James' call. It struck her that, in spite of all their differences, the convent of the Santissimo Sacramento was simply an extension of the convent of San Giorgio Stilita: she felt as if she'd lived there for years. She wasn't alone, she'd learned the habits of the solitary *tignuseddu*, the gecko that every day, around Sext, penetrated from outside and perched in the well of the little window of her cell, head down, watching her. Then, when the sun struck the facing wall, the *tignuseddu* quietly moved away, only to appear on the facing wall. From there, the *tignuseddu* continued to watch her, or at least that's what she believed. Agata wondered how the lizard managed to reach the opposite wall: did it climb down and cross the narrow lane? or did it leap the five-foot gap? Or perhaps it sprouted wings like a bat, so that it could fly towards the sunlight.

As many had predicted, the uprising of Messina in September 1847 was not the only one. Still, no one could have ever imagined the strength and the popular support of the revolt in Palermo on January 12, 1848—the first uprising in the year of the revolutions that swept Europe—nor the sheer violence of the king's reaction. From shouts for the restoration of the 1812 Constitution it was only a short step to angry demands for the independence of Sicily, and from there to the immediate, cruel, and disproportionate repression visited upon Palermo by the fleet of the kingdom, bombarding the city from the sea, killing and destroying, and stiffening the spines of the Sicilian revolutionaries, hardening a resistance that lasted sixteen months in conditions of partial independence.

In his haste to get Agata safely away from Naples, and not

only because of his fear of political unrest in the capital, the cardinal had committed a gross error of political analysis. After the failure of the bombardment of Palermo, the king acceded with indecorous swiftness to the demands of the riotous Neapolitans by promising them a new constitution on January 26, thus restoring a provisional calm. The Sicilian uprising, in contrast, proved to be much more violent and stubborn, a genuine revolution. Communications between Naples and Sicily were interrupted, and the Sanctuary of Chiana was no longer safe.

The sole intermediaries between the illegal Sicilian government and the Bourbon administration were the British diplomats. James Garson assisted Lord Pinto, the British consul in Naples, and both of them shuttled between Naples and Palermo. Garson's ships were among the very few vessels that set sail from Malta and passed through the Strait of Messina, undisturbed by either the rebels or the royal garrison that subjected the city to daily bombardments from the Messina presidio, which overlooked the Strait.

James was able to learn that Agata had gone to stay with her mother in Sicily, but the trail went cold after her stay with the Cecconis. One of his informers had said "too much" to a man who was close to the cardinal. Worried that he risked becoming *persona non grata*, James temporarily suspended his investigations of Agata's whereabouts. The strategy of doing nothing had borne fruit: at the end of February the cardinal turned to him and asked him to help bring Agata back to Naples. James plunged into the work of preparing for the trip.

One evening after Compline, Agata found a Bible on her chair. Pressed between the pages of the Pslams was a dried camellia petal. She glimpsed a faint, small J alongside the words of Psalm 119: "I am thy servant; give me understanding, that I may know thy testimonies." And she waited, trusting.

42

The long journey to reach her beloved

The carriage conveying Agata to the loading docks of Licata rattled through the almond groves. It was a day of sirocco wind, murderous for the blossoming trees. With every gust of hot wind, the petals tumbled from the branches, fluttering and then falling to earth or lodging in the low stone walls. A wave of wind rushed through the open carriage window. A coat of pink and white petals covered her habit and veil: a promise of a wedding, soon.

It had happened all at once. The week previous, the abbess had received a visit from "important" people. She had cleared the parlor especially for this meeting, a place where two or three visits were normally going on at any one time. Then she had summoned Agata to her little drawing room. "They tell me that you speak English, is that true?" she asked her, torn between disgust for the language of the heretics and admiration. Agata confirmed that she did. Then the abbess wished to know if she would be willing to talk with the British consul at Girgenti, in English, in her presence, and Agata said that she would. Then the abbess told her that Cardinal Padellani had summoned her to return to Naples, but the English captain who would convey her there had requested proof of her identity and free will: the abbess's word was not enough for him. "He wants to have this talk in English," she muttered, the corners of her mouth downturned in indignation at such shamelessness. The convent of the Santissimo Sacramento was all abuzz; they wanted to knew where, when, and why Agata had learned English and all the rest. She explained the honest truth. Familiarity eliminated their mutual distrust and the few days that remained went by in an atmosphere of affectionate support. Exceptionally, the English consul, Mr. Stephenson, had been received in the parlor. The abbess sat behind the grate to monitor the conversation; next to her, an employee from the consulate was acting as her interpreter. Agata walked into the parlor, uncertainly, her face covered by her veil. "I would like to ask you two questions," the consul began, in some embarrassment. "The first is this: do you own a volume of John Keats?" Keats was a forbidden author. Agata hesitated; she'd have to think quickly. Was this a trap? The silence was intolerable. Then she raised her head and, looking him in the eye through her veil, declaimed, in a clear voice: "*Dry your eyes, o dry your eyes, For I was taught in Paradise To ease my breast of melodies.*"

"What did she say?" the abbess asked her interpreter.

"Nothing, nonsense. True Christians don't engage in chitchat, because they have been taught that Paradise is in the sacred music."

"*Brava*, Maria Ninfa, *bravissima*. You teach this heretic what it means to be a servant to God!"

The second question was in Italian: "Are you ready to leave?"

"Yes, if that is my Lord's will."

"Good girl, this young nun!" exclaimed the abbess, stroking the crucifix on her breast. Now that she had passed the test, the consul explained that Donna Maria Ninfa would board a sailing ship and depart Licata for Siracusa, where she could catch the steamship that was en route from Malta to Naples.

At the loading dock in Licata, Agata was entrusted to two sister nuns from home, who like her were departing for Naples to go stay with their brother, an official of the kingdom. Together they boarded a tartan that was smaller than the one

she had arrived in, and which alternated fishing with the coasting trade between Licata and Siracusa, with a stop at Pozzillo.
The voyage lasted six days. The tartan was packed with passengers who, like them, were leaving Sicily because of the revolution. Agata and the two women were forced to share a
cabin, which was nothing more than a cramped little closet
with some pallets and a chamber pot. Her travelling companions were intolerable; they didn't get along and each of them
tried to draw Agata over to her side. When she could, Agata
went up on deck, alone. On the fifth day, the tartan rounded
Cape Passero, then passed Marzamemi and finally Pachino.
After sailing around Cape Murro di Porco the ship slowed
down to swing around into the grand harbor of Siracusa at
seven the following morning. The English ship, in contrast,
was immense. It was brand new and gleaming with brass fit-
tings. It had twenty cabins. The crew wore new, crisply ironed
uniforms. When the two nuns learned that a cabin had been
reserved only for Agata, and that the two of them were
expected to bunk down in a women's dormitory down below,
they clung to Agata and wore her out with their lamentations
and exclamations until she finally agreed to take them into her
cabin. Agata had no idea of what had been happening in
Naples, nor what the outcome had been of the revolt in Sicily,
and she lunged at the pile of old newspapers, English and from
the kingdom, pamphlets and scraps of local gazettes that she
knew had been put there for her by the express orders of
James himself. As she pored over the news, the two nuns,
exhausted by the voyage, recited their rosaries. Only then did
she realize that the revolution had swept through the entire
kingdom and all of Europe as well: after the insurrection in
Palermo and the city's staunch resistance to both the army and
the shelling from the sea by the royal navy of Naples and Sicily,
all Sicily had revolted against the sovereign, leaving only a presidio in Messina. In the meanwhile, in Naples the king had

promised a constitution. She was reading eagerly and as she read she grew to understand that the change Tommaso spoke of had become a possibility. Perhaps a reality. Then she thought about James and searched for faint J's in those newspapers, but there were none. The two women tiptoed over to her. They wanted to know what she was reading and why: Agata explained, but the two of them, intrusively, refused to go away. "A game of cards?" and the younger of the two pulled out a deck. Agata had no interest in playing cards. Offended, the woman swept all the newspapers off the little table, shouting that she'd suffered through the voyage in the stinking tartan and now she had a right to a distraction. Agata gathered the newspapers up off the floor and smoothed them out, one by one. Then she laid them on the table. The nun snatched them up and clutched them to her chest. "Now we're going to play cards!" she cried, with a smirk on her hairy face. Agata offered to let the two of them use the table to play cards. No, they had to play cards together, all three of them. Agata wanted her newspapers. The woman snickered and refused to hand them over. Agata made a grab for them and the nun jumped out of the way. A page was torn. That was when Agata yanked the bell pull and ordered the stewards to remove the unwanted guests from her cabin. The staff complied with her request immediately—a clear sign that James was behind all this.

The sea was glittering and the sun had almost vanished below the horizon; the afternoon clamor of voices had subsided. The few passengers on deck were knots of foreign travelers who looked like refugees. They had crates and suitcases heaped around them, and the frightened gaze of people with no idea of what lies in store for them. Agata lifted her gaze, eyes weary from reading, and looked out the window.

In the silence, she heard a voice singing:

Oranges and lemons, say the bells of St. Clement's.
You owe me five farthings, say the bells of St. Martin's.

The song was repeated; it was a man's voice:

Oranges and lemons, say the bells of St. Clement's.
You owe me five farthings, say the bells of St. Martin's.

Her heart was racing: could that be James? It seemed a natural thing to sing her response:

When will you pay me? say the bells of Old Bailey.
When I grow rich, say the bells of Shoreditch.

A broad-shouldered man with a dark mustache turned to look, but behind the glass he saw only Agata's dark, disappointed eyes.

Agata spent the rest of the voyage alone in her cabin; she prayed and worked on a *paperole* that was meant to have a gleaming white consecrated host at its center. She thought about James, and the words of Donna Maria Giovanna della Croce: "You were made to serve the Lord in the world." Each time she tried to embroider the consecrated host, it transformed itself into a camellia; on the outer petals she wrote with tiny chain stitches verses taken from love poems; in the center, which she was supposed to cover with tiny round balls done with fill stitch, the needle seemed to have a will of its own, ruching the shiny silk into a mass of striated petal-shapes done in outline stitch with blood-red thread. In the middle, a chaotic profusion of stamens.

43.

The ship docks at Naples
and Agata is abducted by an unknown woman

Seagulls flew low, skimming over the choppy swells. The breakwater of the Angevin Fortress stood out against the sleeping city in the morning darkness. The steamship slid over the water and came to a halt alongside another steamship flying the British flag.

Dressed in her finest habit, Agata was waiting. She was repeating her paternosters, serenely. A peasant woman carrying a basket and a broad sack burst into her cabin. She commanded Agata to undress and put on the clothing that she had brought with her, and then to put only her bare necessities into the sack. They'd leave the rest, along with her habit, in the cabin.

"Tell me who sent you." Agata had raised her voice. The woman looked out the window and answered her in a whisper: "Be quiet and be quick."

Agata found herself removing her habit in front of that woman. Embarrassed, she dressed uncertainly in the kind of rough homespun, narrow-waisted clothing that she hadn't worn since she was fourteen. She insisted on carrying the basket full of books and, arm in arm with the other woman, they walked down the gangplank amidst all the other passengers. Before stepping into the carriage, Agata turned and thought she glimpsed James's golden beard in an enclosed carriage not far away. She brightened and waved. The woman grabbed her hand. She reddened in shame: that reckless gesture could have spoiled everything.

James climbed the gangplank. The captain and his steward were waiting for him, and together they went to knock at the door of Agata's cabin. There was no answer. They knocked again; then the steward pulled out his skeleton key and unlocked the door. There on the bunk, neatly folded, lay Agata's habit, tunic, and scapular. The white, finely pleated wimple contrasted with the black of the habit like a round meringue.

James sent the others away. Sitting on the bunk next to the habit, his fingers teased at the pleats of the wimple, and he thought. In early January he had been informed that in Palermo a Carbonaro was walking the streets of the city, announcing a revolt to take place on January 12, and that squads of field guards under the command of the pro-independence baronry and armed bands would join with the liberal bourgeoisie. The minute he learned that Agata was no longer at the Cecconi home, the vision of her torn from the house and subjected to the violence of the mob had tortured him, until the cardinal asked James to bring his niece back to Naples. Excited at the prospect of seeing her again soon, James was soon tormented by the fear that her mother had persuaded Agata to stay with her. He had to find out what Agata's feelings toward him were now. After the visit from the British consul at Girgenti to the convent, he had arranged to embark her on one of his steamships as soon as she set foot in Naples; he would send her to England, while he took the necessary steps with the Curia and the Pope to have her vows dissolved—an easy enough task, if conducted diplomatically. But now Agata's inexplicable disappearance from her cabin had thrown him into a coil of black despair.

The cardinal had sent Father Cuoco and two lay sisters down to the Naples waterfront, in an enclosed carriage, to convey Agata to Gaeta, and from there into a convent in the Papal

State. The three of them waited for the last passengers to leave the boat before they went aboard. They were shocked when they found the cabin door blocked by the captain and crew: the nun had vanished; access to the cabin was forbidden.

James Garson's coach and six had just entered the courtyard of the cardinal's residence. The minute the cardinal received the note in which James informed him that he had information about Donna Maria Ninfa, he had agreed to see him.

The sweet scent of early-blooming jasmine filled the air—the odor of power, thought James, with irritation.

"I am distraught over what happened, and I hold myself personally responsible," he began.

"Tell me." And the cardinal listened with close attention to the details of Agata's voyage, beginning with the trip aboard the tartan from the loading docks in Licata. James drew out the little or nothing that he had to recount in the hope that the cardinal might inadvertently let slip his plans for Agata. He told the cardinal that the captain of the steamer had questioned the crew; it seemed certain that Agata had been in contact with no one, besides the two nuns that James had arranged to have sent aboard to care for her, and that she had asked to be given a cabin all to herself, a request that had been granted. "This morning, Donna Maria Ninfa ate a hearty breakfast and waited in her cabin to be taken away. She seemed very contented, and she even sang to herself."

"She has a lovely voice," the cardinal had sighed. Nodding agreement, James had betrayed himself. "You know her, don't you?" The cardinal's gaze was cutting.

"Certainly. It was I who offered passage to the Marescialla and her daughters, when the field marshal died, and I also met her at Palazzo Padellani before her simple profession."

"I was forgetting." A new thought filtered into the cardinal's mind: that it might all have been organized by Donna

Gesuela, to keep from losing her daughter. "What about Palermo?"

The Sicilians were like so many drunks, James said, they did not seem to realize that governing is a difficult task. They talked about waging war, but they had no army—neither troops, nor officers, nor generals, munitions, or provisions. No money. No administrators. Neither roads nor fleets. The illustrious exiles who had returned to their homeland had been given offices for which they were ill suited. Take the case of Amari, who had been put in charge of the Ministry of Finance: he was personally penniless, and had lived off the kindness of his Sicilian friends during his years in exile in France: he knew less than nothing about finance. "These is no education, there is no tradition of political involvement."

"I must agree with you. And how could it be any different: out of a hundred Sicilians, only eleven know how to read and write!" said the cardinal. "Perhaps you don't know that when the Jesuits came down here after the Council of Trent, they were speechless at the conditions in which the denizens of the two kingdoms lived—poor, uncouth, ignorant, and superstitious. In order to instill even a modicum of Christian conscience they were forced to employ instruments of persuasion that ranged from the gentle to the intrusive, striking fear, encouraging violent acts of penitence. In the late sixteenth century, the metaphor of the *indios de por açá* had become a commonplace."

"Now you're going too far, Eminence. A remedy can be found. You are certainly on a par with the other peoples of Europe."

"Leopardi was right: the Italians are the equals of more advanced nations save in two fundamental aspects: literacy, and a complete confusion of ideas." He paused, and then spoke freely, as if he were alone: "People forget and become weary of the good and the evil done by others, of other people's lies and dishonesty, and treat both the good and the wicked with indifference, ignoring all moral and ethical values. Italians have empty lives, lives lived entirely in the present. But, being a social animal, the Italian cannot do without the esteem of his fellow man. And he obtains it, by working with what he possesses, that is vanity, of which however he has a complete understanding and utter scorn.

"The Italians laugh at life: they laugh at life far more heartily and with greater truth and intimate persuasion of their chilly scorn than any other nation on earth. Other nations laugh at things, not at individuals, as the Italian does. A society cannot remain unified if its people are busy mocking one another and continually expressing their utter contempt for their fellow man. In Italy, people take turns persecuting one another, they sting each other until the blood runs. If you do not respect your fellow man, you cannot in turn hope to be respected," and here he paused. Then he resumed, slowly but inexorably, as if he were savoring James's impatience.

"The chief foundation of an individual's morality and of a people's morality is a constant and profound sense of self-respect and the effort taken to preserve that sense of self-respect, a sensitivity concerning one's honor. A man without self-respect can be neither just, nor honest, nor virtuous. Mazzini, an intelligent thinker—God and Fatherland, republican unity, equality of all citizens—is bound to fail. His vision will run aground as soon as it hits the *los indios de por açá*—the Indians on this side. An illiterate will not know what to make of his thoughts."

"Why do you say that? It's a defeatist attitude." James couldn't take any more. He wanted to know about Agata and nothing else.

"So that you, Captain Garson, will understand that the fewer the dealings you have with Italians, and with Donna Maria Ninfa in particular, the better it will be for everyone.

Donna Maria Ninfa is safe and sound, wherever she may be. She has Padellani blood in her veins. And I'm here, worrying about her." At that, the cardinal tugged his bell pull.

"So am I, Eminence."

And James followed the cardinal's secretary, who was holding the door open for him.

44.

In the Garden of Minerva, in Salerno

In the carriage, the woman had kept her eyes focused on Agata, studying her. The coachman let them out on the outskirts of Naples, alongside a road leading into a fishing village. Agata stretched her legs and looked around, expecting to see James at any minute. The seagulls skimmed low over the water; then they veered away, soaring up and turning toward the coast, arcing through the sky in broad loops before turning down to the sea again. Moving quickly, the woman stepped over the ditch that ran alongside the road and walked into a cultivated field. She walked a short distance, stooped down, and grabbed a handful of mud. She went back to where Agata was standing and without a word smeared mud on her shoes and the hem of her skirt. Then she seized both of Agata's hands with her own filthy hands and massaged them, making sure that dirt got under her fingernails. Agata's lovely delicate hands had now been transformed into the hands of a peasant woman.

They ate bread and onion while they waited, speaking no more than was necessary. Not a word was said about James. Then the cart arrived, with other passengers and baskets full of hens. The two women climbed aboard after haggling over the price, and only then did Agata learn that they were going to Salerno. That night they slept in a roadside inn, sharing a cot crawling with lice, and in the morning they boarded another cart. Even then, the woman spoke as little as possible. Agata assumed that this was all necessary and was done according to James's instructions, and was calm.

Since the thirteenth century, there had been a garden in Salerno, built atop the city's Longobard walls, with six terraces, a seventeenth-century staircase running up the side of the massive walls, and a handsome portico protecting the staircase from the blazing sun. Famous for its anise and simple herbs, the Garden of Minerva had belonged to a single family for many centuries, the same family that, in the fourteenth century, had created there the forerunner of all the botanical gardens in Europe. The two women had struggled up the steps of Salerno: Agata had insisted on carrying the heavy bundle of books, letting the other woman carry the lighter bag with her linen and a few possessions of sentimental value. She felt as if she were climbing the stairs of heaven, and that at the top she would find James. She began to have some doubts when, finally arriving in the garden, she saw not a trace of a house or a habitation of any kind.

Meanwhile, two women clumsily dressed in dark-colored secular clothing were coming down the steps; on their heads they wore the veils of the pious old bigot. Angiola Maria came bounding down the last flight, taking the stairs two-by-two. With a "How pretty you are!" she wrapped Agata in her arms, and she was immediately followed by Checchina. Agata couldn't understand. James had told her about his contacts in the Curia, but she had no idea that he knew Angiola Maria. Agata immediately asked for an explanation of what had happened, but Angiola Maria refused to tell her, at least not until Agata satisfied her curiosity: where had she been? how was the conservatory? what did she think of the abbess? why had she gone to Sicily? how had she managed to get back?

The two women showed her the garden before offering her bread and water. On the first, lowest, and broadest terrace, there was a fishpond. The water ran down from the hill, and every one of the other terraces had its own pond and its own little fountain. The shed roof over the steps was covered with grapevines, and on the uppermost terrace there was a pillared loggia from which it was possible to look out over the sea and the surrounding mountains, to the accompaniment of the burbling sound of a fountain that ran constantly, fed by water springing from the wall. There were two fig trees and two bitter orange trees; it was said that this bitter orange tree was a descendant of the original bitter orange that stood in the garden when it was first planted, during the time of Longobard occupation. Behind the loggia were two small cabins in which the two women lived.

Angiola Maria liked to tell the story of her succession of triumphs. She had redeemed the garden from the descendants of the original owners with money that her mother had left her and the money she had earned in the convent. She and Checchina were the owners and in the time since they left the convent they'd both worked hard to fix the place up. Now they sold herbs and herbal teas, and they had a number of loyal customers. Angiola Maria explained to Agata that at San Giorgio Stilita she had at first worked with the sister pharmacist. The pharmacist was a young chorister whose sisters, back home waiting to be married, were dying like flies. When the last of her sisters passed away, the sister pharmacist's father and mother forced her to quit the veil and take a husband. Her brother the canon took care of the details; he also bought the potions that the two of them made in the pharmacy, even those that were slightly dangerous. The sister pharmacist married and had children. She and Angiola Maria had remained friends and she came from time to visit Angiola Maria in the parlor. Through her and her brother the canon, Angiola Maria had kept track of the cardinal's schemes and plans—here she cocked an eyebrow, placed a finger on her lip, and rolled her eyes, making it clear that she would never say a word.

"They told me that the cardinal wanted to bring you back

316 · SIMONETTA AGNELLO HORNBY

from Sicily by convincing you and everyone else that he'd send you to the conservatory of Smirne, which is apparently a place you liked. In fact, however, he meant to send you to the Refuge in Capua, where the most shameless hussies of the entire kingdom are sent, genuine sluts who receive clients inside the walls of the Refuge. Just a pandemonium. Why it is I couldn't say, but the cardinal clearly has it in for you. So I had you abducted and brought here by a good friend of mine. You must remain hidden, the cardinal is sure to report your abduction to the police. This is serious business."

Agata was speechless: so James had had nothing to do with it. Her turmoil was soon over; she felt certain that James would find her soon; in any case, she would send a note to Detken's bookstore as soon as possible. In the meanwhile, she would stay with Angiola Maria and Checchina and work with them, which was something she didn't mind at all.

The two lay sisters lived in two one-room cabins, joined by a shed-roof, up on the seventh level, the highest terrace in the garden, which offered a view of the gulf below. Angiola Maria had whitewashed the exterior, and she showed Agata where she would be sleeping: on the dirt floor, in the room that served as their herbal laboratory and workshop. Then she took her into the other room, where they cooked and ate—in one corner was the cot that she shared with Checchina. Agata looked at the cot, pensively. Angiola Maria noticed and took her aside: "Listen, everything they've told you about me and other women is true, it's just the way I am. The friend that brought you here is one of them, she's trusted. But my own flesh and blood, no one can touch that. That pig of a father of mine came here to buy an aloe pomade that had the effect of keeping men young; he took advantage of my mother, and she had two daughters by him. Here, you are the mistress, and you will be protected. We'll just tell them the truth, that you're my niece. You have to behave like a peasant woman and speak the local dialect. Until you learn it, it would be better for you to stay here in the garden. Be careful: don't set foot in the convents, and do your best to stay away from the churches: the king's spies are everywhere, and so are the cardinal's." With that, she put an end to Agata's hopes of getting in touch with James.

Once again a prisoner and bitterly disappointed, Agata threw herself into her work: cataloguing the dried herbs and packaging them for sale, each with its own handwritten label, and preparing sachets of seeds for plasters and poultices. Angiola Maria taught her to make beauty creams and ointments, according to ancient recipes. Aside from the workshop, Agata was in charge of the garden and the stall where they displayed their products for sale. People came to smell and buy the things that the women grew and produced, as well as the things that Angiola Maria simply purchased and then palmed off as her own production. Angiola Maria went out every day; she made the rounds of the markets and had created a network of contacts; she found books and recipes of all kinds; Agata leafed through them, looking for finds. Checchina never left the garden; she did the housework and was the assistant gardener.

Different from one another though they were, the two sisters got along well and loved each other. Checchina followed, in her manner, and with a simple religious spirit, the order of prayers from the convent; in her case, that was limited to the rosary and the *Credo*. Angiola Maria, on the other hand, said the rosary with them every evening, impatiently, eager to plunge into her nightly reading of the *Gazzetta*. Since she'd left the convent, Angiola Maria had learned to read from a schoolteacher in Salerno, and now she followed with keen interest the political developments of the kingdom, the French, and the

Papal State—the rest of the world was of no interest to her. Besides the *Gazzetta*, she read the *Amicus Veritatis* and the *Arlecchino*, satirical newspapers that had sprung up in the wake of the recent conquest of freedom of the press; she struggled to sound out the hard words or the words in Latin; when she managed to get a joke or a witticism, she burst into a belly laugh that shook her whole body, as well as the chair she was sitting on, until her hilarity died out in a gurgle. Checchina watched her out of the corner of her eye, perplexed, then looked up at the small icon of Christ with the crown of thorns glued to the wall and went on stitching the sachets for the lavender.

Agata had just turned twenty-two; she was a person who "felt" more than she "reasoned." For that reason, her mood, her inclinations, and her thoughts were constantly swinging between her vocation and the outside world, between the marriage forced upon her by her mother and the chastity of the cloistered life, between prayer for the good of others and a concrete demonstration of her commitment to the humble and the needy, between the comfort of the cloistered life and the challenges faced by a poor girl in living and making her way in world created by and for men. Now Agata knew that she belonged to the world. She had loved. She felt grown up and she had finally learned to how break away from the two people who had given her life. She felt no sense of guilt, no resentment. It was clear to her by now that each of the two wanted to force her into a life designed not for her good, but in order to purge her of her sins. *Ora et labora. Ora et labora.* Work had redeemed her. Agata no longer vacillated between two opposites. Checchina's simple hard work and religious spirit did not contrast with the worldly nature and carnal desires of Angiola Maria. The faith and love that God had lavished upon her gave Agata the certainty that she was right to love James. But if James were to suddenly vanish from her life, she would go on working and do her best to preserve her own tranquil contentment. Perhaps, like Mazzini, Agata would educate the children of the poor, help them to grow up straight and deep-rooted, the way she did with seedlings. Her wild seesawing between states of mind, from the source of her torment, had gently subsided into a mild back and forth.

45.
April 1848.
Checchina is left alone

Spring had already arrived; Agata had received no word from either James or anyone in her family. She was heartbroken for Sandra and Tommaso; she was worried about her sisters in Messina, under bombardment, and for her mother. Moreover, Agata had a hard time putting up with Checchina: when she wasn't reciting intentions, aspirations, and prayers, she chattered constantly and heaped Agata with affection when she would rather have spent time alone, in silence. Even reciting the rosary together was difficult because she had to keep up the other woman's pace.

Angiola Maria had felt duty-bound to take on the same protective role toward Agata as Donna Maria Crocifissa, and Agata liked it. But Angiola Maria was not up to the job because of her lack of culture, wisdom, and sensitivity. The two women were genuinely fond of one another, but Agata didn't confide in her—she never had before. Moreover, they saw very little of one another. Angiola Maria returned from her marketing in the early afternoon and ate whatever Checchina had cooked; then she remained seated at the table and read the day's newspapers before going out to do the heaviest work: plowing, hoeing, repairing the stone walls, pruning trees, chopping firewood. At night, she went to sleep before the others, who cleaned up after dinner.

Agata followed the divine office on her own; she put the ring of her solemn profession on the finger of her right hand—

it was a ritual that she found comforting. Whenever Angiola Maria was present, Agata noticed her gaze of bafflement and almost of reproof.

"Why don't you get rid of it?" she asked Agata one day.

"I find it comforting."

"If you want to know," and here Angiola Maria's gaze turned stony, "I've seen a world of filthy tricks played in the name of Jesus Christ, and anyway I don't believe in all that. This garden is named after Minerva, who was the goddess of science and who, in my opinion, is much better than the Virgin Mary."

Agata felt she'd been upbraided and was about to reply, but stopped herself. Seeing that her niece was on the verge of tears, Angiola Maria put a hand on her shoulder and apologized.

From then on, Angiola Maria looked after Agata attentively: she made sure that she got plenty to eat, but she didn't know how to distract her and how to chase the sadness from her niece's beautiful eyes. She bought her newspapers that she thought Agata would like to read. She started taking her with her when she went out, to show her the places where she could safely go on her own.

Meanwhile, James continued assisting Lord Pinto in his negotiations with the Sicilian rebels and maintained contacts with the Bourbons; it was crucial to be on the winning side if he wished to secure Agata's liberty; he believed that she had been taken to a convent outside of Naples. His spies in the Curia, however, were unable to discover the exact location. The cardinal was expecting news from Sicily and enjoined complete silence concerning the failure of Father Cuoco's mission: he even suspected that James might have taken her hostage, and had come to see him in order to ward off his suspicions.

The Sicilian rebels had halted the mails and Sicily was isolated from the mainland; it was not until late March that the cardinal managed to obtain confirmation that Agata had obeyed his order to take a steamship for Naples. At that point, he informed the intelligence services and the police that Agata had been kidnapped by unknown malefactors. James was told about this development by his own informers but he was unable to abandon the negotiations, which were interrupted on April 13, when the Sicilians declared an end to the Bourbon dynasty of Naples and offered the crown of the Kingdom of Sicily to Ferdinand of Savoy.

Now James set out to track down Agata. There was no time to waste. The cardinal was now his enemy; he had listed her among the missing, but he was ready to pounce like a hawk at the first clue. In the meanwhile, James had discovered that Angiola Maria was a blood relation of Agata's, family ties that the cardinal would have preferred to keep shrouded in silence. He was convinced that Agata had taken refuge with her, he could feel it.

In order to shake the secret police and the spies of the Curia off his tail, he took a party of English visitors for a sail down the Amalfi Coast. He moored his yacht at Salerno and decided to try his luck: he would go in person to the Garden of Minerva.

It was time to put the potted seedlings into the earth and the women went out to buy, barter, or beg little plants to put into pots or in the tiny patch of land in front of the house. Angiola Maria had put the plants that were to be sold next to the wall, near the entrance. Checchina was in charge of selling them to customers. The first customer knocked at the door: Checchina was expecting a woman and was disconcerted at the sight of the blond foreigner who spoke Neapolitan; she called Angiola Maria, who was just about to leave. It took Angiola Maria no more than a glance to understand that this one hadn't come looking for plants. She let him speak, then she explained one by one the properties and traits of each plant, luring him out along the wall, where he couldn't see their house.

"I must confess that I didn't come here to buy plants. I'm searching for Agata Padellani, Donna Maria Ninfa, whom you know. I know her too, and I care only about her well-being. I know that she lives here, with you. I have an important message to give her, in person."

"If you know her as well as you say," and at this point, Angiola Maria gestured with her hand and frowned, dubiously, "you should know that a lady of Donna Maria Ninfa's standing would never set foot in a place like this: a lovely garden, no doubt, but with nothing but a shack, a hovel that I share with my sister. After spending a night here, at best she would simply ask me to find her a place to stay that would be more befitting of her."

She looked him right in the eye: "If you care about Donna Maria Ninfa's well-being, leave her in peace. She's not here, in any case. A nun as fine as her deserves a much better oasis of health than this!" Then, seeing that he was just wasting her time, she added: "If you want to buy plants, I'll send my sister down to see you. I have to go out."

The minute he left the garden, James kicked himself for having turned down the offer.

Angiola Maria shot the bolt home behind the departing visitor and waited for his footsteps—and those of the two litter-bearers who had accompanied him with an empty litter, with drawn curtains—had faded away down the steps. Then she climbed up to the workshop and called Agata.

"We have to take care; the cardinal isn't satisfied with summoning me to the Curia. Now he's sending the English to look for you." And she described James and his visit. Agata felt herself die inside. Angiola Maria understood that there was something special with the Englishman; she had to find a way of preventing her niece from winding up like her mother— seduced and, in this case, taken somewhere abroad and then abandoned—just when she had hopes that the three of them could create a full fledged manufactory and become rich. Her affection for Agata and her dynastic ambition, deeply intertwined, led her to refrain from pressing the young woman with questions and instead to head for cover.

Agata had learned enough of the dialect of Salerno to get by, and she liked going out, accompanied by Angiola Maria and, rarely, on her own. Promptly, Angiola Maria persuaded Agata to wash her hair with an herb that turned it light red; that dye would fool anyone who came looking for her. Now she sent Agata out on a series of errands. Agata, upset, had a hollow feeling in her stomach; she didn't know what she could do to get in touch with James. She went down to the harbor, but his steamship, the very same one that she'd come in on, was setting out to sea, the English flag barely visible in the distance. She swallowed her tears and went on walking. She had finished her errands, but she still couldn't return home: Angiola Maria had told her to stay out until lunchtime.

She wandered sadly through the center of Salerno, and suddenly found herself in front of the large Baroque portal of a hospice. It was an old convent that had been transformed into a hospital by the French and left the way it was after the Restoration. She managed to slip in under the concierge's nose and started wandering aimlessly, though with a confident step, to keep from being noticed. She emerged into a cloister; it wasn't beautiful, like the one in San Giorgio Stilita, but it was airy and spacious and did have a piperno-stone arcade; a burning wave of nostalgia for the monastic life swept over her. She wandered through the corridors on the second floor, above the arches of the cloister; crammed one next to the other, on chairs, cots, straw pallets, even piles of rags on the floor, were men, women, old people, young people, and infants, voiceless, slowly consuming themselves, like white butterflies with broken wings. Agata fled.

That night Angiola Maria asked Agata where she had gone. She listened carefully. "Excellent," she praised her, "go out often, from now on. If they do come, it's better if they don't find you here. I've been told that the cardinal wants to come to Salerno." She shot her a glance. "If he asks to see you, what should I tell him?"

"That I don't want to see him!" Agata blurted out. Angiola Maria took her hand and squeezed it.

"That's what I did too, when I was younger. They aren't worthy of us."

James got in touch with his informers: Agata's trail had gone cold in Salerno. That's where she must be. He decided to make one more attempt and went back to Salerno. He took rooms in a hotel overlooking the main square, supposedly in order to gather information about the medical school of Salerno. One day he happened to spot Angiola Maria in the street, and he followed her: he saw her negotiate a fee and then board a cart heading out of town; he immediately took that opportunity to go to the Garden of Minerva. Checchina greeted him. James purchased two small rosemary plants, and then asked if he could see the bitter orange tree, which he had heard was quite ancient. "Wait, let me ask my niece, she knows more about these things than I do," the woman replied, and then shouted to Agata: "There's someone here who wants to see the bitter orange tree, I'm sending him up to you!" Then she told James to climb up to the topmost terrace; the tree he wanted to see was there, right in front of the workshop.

James waited, impatiently. He peered into the workshop. Agata was praying in a corner, but the dazzling sunlight prevented him from seeing anything in the dim shadows; it looked as if the room were empty. He turned to observe the bitter orange tree.

Agata appeared at the door, her white smock knotted at the

waist. She recognized him, even though his back was turned: it was him. She couldn't move. James didn't turn around; he was looking at the tree's graying bark. Then he heard the rustle of cloth behind him and asked, in a loud voice: "So is this the historic bitter orange tree?"

"James," she whispered, slipping the ring off her finger, and this time it was he who lost his voice.

Checchina was weeding around the fishpond and every so often she looked up, keeping an eye on the two of them.

"I'm here," she said, in English.

"Are you ready?" he asked her.

Together they walked down the stairs. As they went past the fishpond, Checchina asked Agata: "What are you doing?"

"I'm accompanying him."

"Where?"

And James answered: "To the harbor."

"All right," said Checchina, and resumed her hoeing.

ACKNOWLEDGMENTS

T he inspiration for the story I told in this novel came to me four years ago.
    In those days, my knowledge of the monastic world was limited to the infrequent purchase, through the wheel of the cloister, of the *biscotti ricci* of the Benedictine convent of Palma di Montechiaro and the family stories of a female forebear, Aunt Gesuela. An unusual stay-at-home nun, she had underwritten the convent of the Boccone del Povero in Favara but she also never denied herself, every other year, a nice trip to Paris.

Shortly thereafter, I was invited by Francesca Medioli to talk to her students at the University of Reading, and I wish to thank her first, because on that occasion she gave me a gift of a fascinating piece she had written about a Venetian nun; in a note she referred to *I misteri del chiostro napoletano*, published in 1864, the autobiography of a former nun, Enrichetta Caracciolo. My second thank-you goes to her; I am indebted to her in particular for her descriptions of the ceremonials.

Let me also thank Alfredo De Dominicis for helping me to know and love his city of Naples in the only way possible: by talking and strolling through the city, as long as our feet held out. The memory of our walks together is indelible.

I would like to thank Gianbattista Bertolazzi and Piero Hildebrand for introducing me to the world of heirloom camellias.

My thanks go to Gaetano Basile for introducing me to the cloisters of Palermo with the evocative power of his stories.

I've read extensively about monasticism, and not only the monasticism of Southern Italy. I'd like to thank Father Anselmo Lipari—prior of the Abbey of San Martino delle Scale, respected university professor, and author—for our conversations and for what I learned from his books while I was gathering documentation on the various monastic rules; I would also like to thank in the same connection Luca Domeniconi and his team of Feltrinelli booksellers for suggesting so many interesting readings and David Bidussa, director of the library of the Feltrinelli Foundation, for his patient and unfailingly intelligent assistance in the selection of material about the Neapolitan and Sicilian Risorgimento.

Let me thank Uberto De Luca, my "long lost" cousin and connoisseur of the sea and of the history—naval and otherwise—of our island, for having meticulously corrected—and in part inspired—the descriptions of the crossings on which I sent my heroine.

My deepest and most heartfelt thanks to the abbesses and nuns of the convents I visited throughout Italy, from Sicily to Lombardy, some of them more than once. They allowed me to glimpse a life made up of work and prayer in which little and few become much and many, in which solitude becomes a communion with the outside world and the spirit rises above material things: there, love reigns supreme.

I thank Piero Guccione: meeting an artist of his quality was a gift. The beauty of his paintings has honored the covers of my books twice.

As always, last of all, a heartfelt thank-you to Alberto Rollo, Giovanna Salvia, and Annalisa Agrati. Not just for their unmatched professional dedication, but also because when I was tempted, the way that nuns are tempted, to go back to my old life, each of them silently made me understand that there is no longer a way back from the writing life.

Europa Editions publishes in the US and in the UK. Not all titles are available in both countries. Availability of individual titles is indicated in the following list.

Carmine Abate
Between Two Seas
"A moving portrayal of generational continuity."
—*Kirkus Reviews*
224 pp • $14.95 • 978-1-933372-40-2 • Territories: World

The Homecoming Party
"A sincere novel that examines the bond between individual human feelings and age-old local traditions."
—*Famiglia Cristiana*
192 pp • $15.00 • 978-1-933372-83-9 • Territories: World

Milena Agus
From the Land of the Moon
"A jewel of a novel, it shines like a precious, exquisite gemstone."—*Libération*
120 pp • $15.00 • 978-1-60945-001-4 • Territories: World except Australia & NZ

Salwa Al Neimi
The Proof of the Honey
"Al Neimi announces the end of a taboo in the Arab world: that of sex!"—*Reuters*
144 pp • $15.00 • 978-1-933372-68-6 • Territories: World except UK

Alberto Angela
A Day in the Life of Ancient Rome
"Fascinating and accessible."—*Il Giornale*
392 pp • $16.00 • 978-1-933372-71-6 • Territories: World

Jenn Ashworth
A Kind of Intimacy
"Evokes a damaged mind with the empathy and confidence of Ruth Rendell."—*The Times*
416 pp • $15.00 • 978-1-933372-86-0 • Territories: USA & Canada

Beryl Bainbridge
The Girl in the Polka Dot Dress
"Very gripping, very funny and deeply mysterious."
—*The Spectator*
176 pp • $15.00 • 978-1-60945-056-4 • Territories: USA

Muriel Barbery
The Elegance of the Hedgehog
"Gently satirical, exceptionally winning and inevitably bittersweet."—*The Washington Post*
336 pp • $15.00 • 978-1-933372-60-0 • Territories: World except UK & EU

Gourmet Rhapsody
"In the pages of this book, Barbery shows off her finest gift: lightness."—*La Repubblica*
176 pp • $15.00 • 978-1-933372-95-2 • Territories: World except UK & EU

Stefano Benni
Margherita Dolce Vita
"A modern fable...hilarious social commentary."—*People*
240 pp • $14.95 • 978-1-933372-20-4 • Territories: World

Timeskipper
"Benni again unveils his Italian brand of magical realism."
—*Library Journal*
400 pp • $16.95 • 978-1-933372-44-0 • Territories: World

Romano Bilenchi
The Chill
"Accomplishes what books three times its length seek to do."
—*Boston Pheonix*
120 pp • $15.00 • 978-1-933372-90-7 • Territories: World

Kazimierz Brandys
Rondo
"[Brandy's has] quickened the conscience and enriched
the writing of the twentieth century."—*Time*
400 pp • $16.00 • 978-1-60945-004-5 • Territories: World

Alina Bronsky
Broken Glass Park
"Bronsky writes with a gritty authenticity and unputdownable
propulsion."—*Vogue*
336 pp • $15.00 • 978-1-933372-96-9 • Territories: World

The Hottest Dishes of the Tartar Cuisine
"Utterly entertaining. Rosa is an unreliable narrator par
excellence."—*FAZ*
304 pp • $15.00 • 978-1-60945-006-9 • Territories: World

Massimo Carlotto
The Goodbye Kiss
"A masterpiece of Italian noir."—*Globe and Mail*
160 pp • $14.95 • 978-1-933372-05-1 • Territories: World

Death's Dark Abyss
"A remarkable study of corruption and redemption."
—*Kirkus* (starred review)
160 pp • $14.95 • 978-1-933372-18-1 • Territories: World

The Fugitive
"[Carlotto is] the reigning king of Mediterranean noir."
—*The Boston Phoenix*
176 pp • $14.95 • 978-1-933372-25-9 • Territories: World

Bandit Love
"*Bandit Love* is a gripping novel that can be read on different levels." —*Il Manifesto*
208 pp • $15.00 • 978-1-933372-80-8 • Territories: World

(with **Marco Videtta**)
Poisonville
"The business world as described by Carlotto and Videtta in *Poisonville* is frightening as hell."
—*La Repubblica*
224 pp • $15.00 • 978-1-933372-91-4 • Territories: World

Francisco Coloane
Tierra del Fuego
"Coloane is the Jack London of our times."—*Alvaro Mutis*
192 pp • $14.95 • 978-1-933372-63-1 • Territories: World

Rebecca Connell
The Art of Losing
"This confident debut is both a thriller and an emotional portrait of the long-term repercussions of infidelity."
—*Financial Times*
240 pp • $15.00 • 978-1-933372-78-5 • Territories: USA

Laurence Cossé
A Novel Bookstore
"An Agatha Christie-style mystery bolstered by a love story worthy of Madame de la Fayette . . ."—*Madame Figaro*
424 pp • $15.00 • 978-1-933372-82-2 • Territories: World

An Accident in August
"Cossé is a master of fine storytelling."—*La Repubblica*
208 pp • $15.00 • 978-1-60945-049-6 • Territories: World but not UK

Giancarlo De Cataldo
The Father and the Foreigner
"A slim but touching noir novel from one of Italy's best writers in the genre."—*Quaderni Noir*
144 pp • $15.00 • 978-1-933372-72-3 • Territories: World

Shashi Deshpande
The Dark Holds No Terrors
"[Deshpande is] an extremely talented storyteller."
—*Hindustan Times*
272 pp • $15.00 • 978-1-933372-67-9 • Territories: USA

Helmut Dubiel
Deep in the Brain: Living with Parkinson's Disease
"A book that begs reflection."—*Die Zeit*
144 pp • $15.00 • 978-1-933372-70-9 • Territories: World

Steve Erickson
Zeroville
"A funny, disturbing, daring and demanding novel—Erickson's best."—*The New York Times Book Review*
352 pp • $14.95 • 978-1-933372-39-6 • Territories: USA & Canada

Caryl Férey
Zulu
"Powerful and unflinching in its portrayal of evil both mindless and calculating."—*Publishers Weekly*
416 pp • $15.00 • 978-1-933372-88-4 • Territories: World except UK & EU

Elena Ferrante
The Days of Abandonment
"The raging, torrential voice of [this] author is something rare."—*The New York Times*
192 pp • $14.95 • 978-1-933372-00-6 • Territories: World

Troubling Love
"Ferrante's polished language belies the rawness of her imagery."—*The New Yorker*
144 pp • $14.95 • 978-1-933372-16-7 • Territories: World

The Lost Daughter
"So refined, almost translucent."—*The Boston Globe*
144 pp • $14.95 • 978-1-933372-42-6 • Territories: World

Linda Ferri
Cecilia
"A passionate and meticulous account of a young woman's search for her spiritual identity."—*La Repubblica*
288 pp • $15.00 • 978-1-933372-87-7 • Territories: World

Damon Galgut
In a Strange Room
"A taut, mesmerizing novel."—*New York Times*
224 pp • $15.00 • 978-1-60945-011-3 • Territories: USA